THE HEREDITY
OF MAGIC

A Haunted Law Firm Novel

Robert L. Arrington

*This is a work of fiction. Any resemblance to any persons,
living or dead, is a matter of coincidence only and not intentional.*

BOOKS BY ROBERT L. ARRINGTON

The Ethics of Magic

The Pathways of Magic

A Snowstorm of Magic

A Cascade of Magic

The Heredity of Magic

DEDICATION

To the memory of Bryan Arrington, who was for years my favorite (and only) nephew.

CONTENTS

Chapter One
WEST VIRGINIA - 2005

"He looks like…a baby," Lara Martin said, her voice almost too soft to be heard, even in the crèche-viewing area of the hospital wing, where the only noise was the soft hiss of the ventilation system.

But the doctor standing next to her and her husband, a tall, thin man with a receding hair line and round wire-rimmed glasses, whose name-tag on his white lab coat said, "Dr. Valenski," heard her.

"He *is* a baby," the doctor said. "A human baby, perfectly formed in every way. No one can see his DNA signature."

Lara smiled and took her husband's hand. "Of course he is. I don't know why I was expecting anything else."

"Probably because we've seen so many crude re-creations of Neanderthals," said Darren Martin, giving Lara's hand a gentle squeeze. This was the infant they had signed adoption papers to receive weeks ago, in a judge's chambers at a courthouse only a few miles away. It had all been quietly arranged by the federal government and a compliant local attorney who had signed a non-disclosure agreement. The required waiting period had expired. Now they were here to take their new child home.

"Here" was a secret installation buried in a mountainside in southern West Virginia, of which the hospital was only a small part. They didn't know what went on in the rest of the facility, but apparently there were laboratories. They had driven here, accompanied by an escort in an Air Force uniform, immediately after the leaving the courthouse, through mountains splashed with autumn reds, yellows, oranges and golds, down to a narrow road between ridges where the sun didn't reach unless directly overhead, making the drive gloomy despite the window of blue sky above.

"But what will he look like when he grows up?" Darren asked.

"We're not completely sure," Valenski said. "But we don't think he'll attract too much attention. Your baby was cloned from DNA taken from a body found in western Ukraine, almost perfectly preserved by natural mummification. We think he was drowned in a bog about 50,000 years ago. There is some reason to think it was a sacrifice. The DNA we recovered indicates a first-generation hybrid of Neanderthal and modern human. The body had a modern-shaped skull, which we think was typical.

"He'll mature fast, so you may have to rein him in a little when he starts playing competitive sports. He won't be very tall, we think perhaps five-eight or five-nine, maybe a little more; but he'll be broad shouldered and incredibly strong.

"But it's unlikely anyone will think you're not related to him."

Darren nodded. The story would be that the birth mother was one of Lara's cousins, even though the birth mother was actually a host mother who had been well-paid by the United States to carry the baby to term. He glanced from his wife's flaming red hair to the red fuzz on the infant's head.

"So," Lara asked, "he won't be stooped and bow-legged?"

Valenski chuckled and rubbed his bald spot. "No," the doctor said. "Stooped and bow-legged Neanderthal skeletons are from people who suffered from rickets and arthritis. Your son, with a good, warm home and modern nutrition, will have neither."

Lara Martin, who was a pediatric nurse (one of the reasons the Martins had been selected to foster the infant) had been doing some reading. "Will he be able to talk?" she asked.

Valenski nodded. "We're confident he will," he said. "Our research here is pretty advanced, and we've changed our minds on the theory that Neanderthals couldn't talk well. Anyway, he'll have pretty much a modern human skull and voice box. If he does have any issues, speech therapists will be made available.

"You're just going to have a short, strong, normal kid."

The Martins looked down at the infant, whose crèche was the only one of the four in the room beyond the plate glass that was occupied, and saw his bright blue eyes looking back at them. They smiled down, and their son smiled back, showing gums.

"Well, Mr. and Mrs. Martin," the doctor said, "now I need to turn you over to Captain Hutton. He will have some other papers for you to sign, and then you can leave with your kid. We have some baby clothes and formula to get you started. Good luck!"

He offered his hand and they took it in turn. Valenski had referred to the fourth person standing with them, a solidly built African American who had been introduced as Captain Fred Hutton. Captain Hutton, who was with Air Force Intelligence but was being transferred to the Defense Intelligence Agency, was going to be their contact from here on out.

"Just come with me, folks," Hutton said, extending an arm, palm open to a door opposite from the one they'd entered. He led them down the hallway to a sparsely furnished office, decorated only by a photo of Hutton with a smiling woman and two small children. Clearly, it was a family photo.

As they walked, Lara smiled up at her square-jawed, robust husband. They knew they had been selected with care. Darren had begun his military career as a Combat Controller in Air Force Special Operations, but after injuries in un-named places had left him with a plate in his skull and pins in an arm and a leg, had transferred to IT and worked with Intelligence. Lara had been an Air Force nurse before studying pediatrics, and they'd met while she was nursing the man who'd later become her husband. Now, Darren was retiring from the Air Force and had accepted a position with Simmons IT and Security in Martintown, North Carolina. They both had security clearances. They were childless, and would remain so unless they adopted. They fit the government's profile for foster parents for this child perfectly.

Signing did not take long. The Martins had already read drafts. A JAG Corps officer had been made available to them to answer any legal questions they had, but they hadn't had many.

"We don't want to be intrusive," Hutton said. "We want your kid to grow up as normal as possible. We'll check up on him from time to time. He'll have tests he'll believe are just standard medical examinations, and that's largely what they'll be.

"We're also available if you need anything. Your kid – have you decided on a name, by the way?"

"James Douglas Martin," Darren said. He smiled and continued, "After Jimmy Doolittle and Douglas MacArthur. We'll call him 'Doug.'"

"Well, your Doug will have free medical care and a college scholarship," Hutton said. "That's in the paperwork, as you know. And…" Hutton hesitated, and continued, "If we get an Academy man or a Spec Ops soldier out of him, so much the better. If not…well, we want him to have choices like any American."

"We wouldn't have agreed if it were any other way," Lara said. "We won't raise a slave for you."

"No one is asking you to," Hutton said.

"Good," Lara said, standing. Darren stood with her. They shook hands with Hutton and left to collect their new son.

Chapter Two
MARTINTOWN, NORTH CAROLINA, AUGUST 2022

WNCB RADIO

Crowder: Good afternoon, high school sports fans. This is Bill Crowder of WNCB – your station for high school sports here in the mountains and foothills – with this season's first edition of "Inside High School Football." Today we are privileged to have with us Danny Jarvis. Danny is a freelance writer who has written for the Charlotte *Observer*, the Raleigh *News & Observer*, *Sports Illustrated*, and the Associated Press. That's just to name a few. Welcome, Danny.

Jarvis: Thanks, Bill. It's great to be here.

Crowder: Danny, it's no secret you are here to cover the big game tonight between Brainerd Central and West Brainerd. Folks here in Brainerd County have been excited about that ever since it was announced last winter. But just what is getting attention from all over the state? Why, I understand there's no room in the press box for every reporter.

Jarvis (laughing): Well, there was barely room for me, Bill. I'm just glad they're letting me in the stadium. But it's no secret why we are here. It's a rare thing for two schools so close together, especially here in Western North Carolina, to have so much high school talent in the same year. And these two are in different classifications. They don't play each other very much. That's what's attracted all the media – and attracted a lot of college coaches. That's news in itself.

Crowder: We're going to talk about all that talent in a minute, Danny. But let's talk about those coaches first. Who do you understand are coming?

Jarvis: Bill, most of this is unconfirmed, but let's see…I have information that all of the big schools here in North Carolina are sending someone. That's North Carolina, N.C. State, Duke, Wake Forest, East Carolina, Charlotte, and Appalachian State. Some are sending more than one. I'm told North Carolina is sending its offensive coordinator, its running back coach, and its linebacker coach. N.C. State is sending two, probably running backs and linebackers. And that's not all.

Crowder: What about out-of-state schools?

Jarvis: My information on those isn't as good, but let's see…Virginia Tech for sure. I'm pretty confident Tennessee and Clemson will have someone here. I'm told South Carolina, Georgia and Georgia Tech are sending people. I've confirmed Wisconsin is sending a coach. And there's a rumor – I haven't been able to confirm this – that Alabama and Ohio State are both sending someone. That's not counting a bunch of smaller schools. Remember, the college season doesn't start for another week, so they have some time to recruit.

Crowder: Wow. I don't know how Central's stadium is going hold all the press and the scouts, not to mention the fans…So, now let's talk about what is bringing them here.

Jarvis: Bill, you start with two words: Jeremiah Billups.

Crowder: Yeah. The Central tailback. People are saying he's the best running back prospect from this part of the state since Leon Johnson played for Morganton Freedom way back in 1991. And Johnson went on to star at North Carolina and then in the NFL.

Jarvis: He did. But I think Billups is better. He has it all: speed, power, change of direction, pass catching. You name it. Now he hasn't had to block much. But he'll learn that in college. Unless – God forbid – he's injured, he's "can't miss." Can't. Miss. He's already announced he's committed to North Carolina, but you can bet any number of schools are trying to change his mind.

Crowder: Everybody knows about JB. But let's talk about some others the college scouts are watching. Who comes to mind? Start with the Central team.

Jarvis: Central has several guys who are going to play college ball, if they want to, somewhere. Not all of them are Bowl Championship Series level prospects. The biggest names after Billups are Markus Caldwell and Dimitri Jones.

Crowder: Talk about Caldwell first, then Jones.

Jarvis: Markus Caldwell is a huge man already, six-five and 280 pounds, and he's going to get bigger. He plays both ways but will probably play defensive line in college. He's a junior but already has been offered by Appalachian and Wake Forest, among others. He'll get more offers. Incidentally, the whole offensive line is good. They have another tackle named George McCurry who isn't as big as Caldwell. He's a senior. I think he's headed to Charlotte, but could get a look by some bigger schools.

Getting back to Jones, he's a 6-3 guy, fast, who plays safety and wide receiver. I hear Carolina wants him as a safety, but State is likely to offer at wide-out, which he prefers.

Crowder: What about the quarterback, Len Benfield?

Jarvis: He's an excellent high school quarterback, but he's a little small. Under six feet and maybe – maybe – 170 pounds. But I bet he gets a scholly somewhere. Maybe Western Carolina or East Tennessee State.

Crowder: Before we run out of time, let's go on to West Brainerd.

Jarvis: West Brainerd is really an interesting story. It's really incredible the number of good players they have. They're just an AAA school. Coach Steve Watkins has really done a good job developing their talent. Counting Southern Conference and even smaller schools like Lenoir-Rhyne, they also have a number of guys who can play at the next level.

But you have to start with Doug Martin.

Crowder: "Stump."

Jarvis: Yes. One of the opposing coaches last year said that blocking Martin was like trying to move a tree stump, and tackling him was about the same.

Crowder: What position is he going to play in college?

Jarvis: That's a good question. Some people say he's too short for linebacker – he's only a little over five-nine – and too slow for running back. But that's bull-s -- I mean, nonsense, in my opinion. I watched him in the play-offs last year. On defense, he's like a heat seeking missile. Really has a nose for the ball. On offense – and he doesn't play offense all the time

– he's much, much faster than people think. He's super-strong and he's evasive, too. If the bigger schools back off because of his height, he could go somewhere like App State and get drafted by the pros. But I don't think they will…There is a little concern about his endurance, especially in hot weather.

Crowder: What about their other players?

Jarvis: They have two pretty big senior linemen, Abernathy and Simpson, not as big as Caldwell, and probably mid-major prospects. Abernathy is a little slow. They have a tall but a little skinny tight end named Herman Dale, who has really good hands. He's a senior, too.

They have two good backs in Henry Warren and Tommy Mason. They're juniors, and if they grow a little they'll get some attention next year. Warren is the tailback. Mason plays fullback but goes to the slot when Stump is in on offense. Their offense is actually pretty similar to Central's, but they run more plays from the shotgun than Central.

I want to mention two more guys. Les Bronson is just a sophomore, but started late last year as freshman. He's a tall raw-boned kid that, if he develops, is going to attract attention at quarterback. Has an arm. And here's a real story: The little wide-out, Javon Shade, can't be bigger than 5-6 and 145 pounds, but he can fly. Somebody will offer him; he's another senior.

Crowder: We're about out of time. Who's going to win?

Jarvis: Well…Okay, I think West Brainerd will stay with Central for three quarters. But Central is bigger and deeper, and they have Billups. They win in the fourth quarter.

Crowder: It should be quite a game. Thank you, Danny.

Jarvis: My pleasure.

Chapter Three
BRAINERD CENTRAL STADIUM, AUGUST 2022

THE VISITORS' LOCKER ROOM

Doug Martin sat on a bench in the visitors' locker room at Brainerd Central Stadium, waiting for the team to go back on the field to start the game. He mopped sweat from his brow with a towel provided by a team manager, and ran a hand through bright red hair that was curling in the hot, damp, late August air. The team had returned to the locker room from warm-ups just a few minutes ago.

That was the problem with ball games played before Labor Day, and really up to about the middle of September, even later in the eastern part of the state. Summer weather still persisted. It was a particular problem for Doug, who was prone to heat exhaustion unless he took care to remain hydrated, and took breaks. And that was the reason Coach Watkins had told him he would mostly play defense only, especially in the first half.

"The second half will be cooler," Coach had said. "We may need you on offense at any time. So be ready."

No one was sure why Doug was so prone to suffer from high temperatures and humidity. The team physician had joked that he "must be a throwback to some Viking ancestor." His father had allowed that might be true. His mother was Boston Irish, and his dad, who grew up in Brainerd County, was supposed to be Scots-Irish. But how could you tell after several centuries on this side of the Atlantic?

Tommy Mason, his replacement at fullback, sat next to him, and Jack Abernathy, his best friend on the team, sat beyond Tommy. Both were sweating, but not as much as Doug. Tommy slapped him on the shoulder.

"Are you ready, Stump?" he asked.

"You know it," Doug answered. "Are you?"

"I'm ready to be out of here where I can get some room," Mason said. "You take up the whole bench." He was referring to the width of Doug's shoulders, which had required a special order for his practice and game jerseys.

Doug was five feet, nine and one-half inches tall, and weighed 217 pounds, most of it in his shoulders, chest and thighs, brought on by his natural build and by years of training and physical activity, not only football but baseball, track, and his father's lessons in martial arts. He didn't look like he could, but he could stay even with Henry Warren over forty yards, even though Henry could beat him over a hundred.

The whole team was tense, more so than for most games, even playoff games. This one was for bragging rights in Brainerd County. The whole West Brainerd team had a chip on their shoulders over being the smaller, poorer school. And everyone knew that they would be watched by college coaches. There was even a rumor that Dabo Swiney was coming in person.

Doug wasn't sure where he was going to college. He'd had dozens of letters, visits at school by a bunch of coaches. Appalachian State was just up the road, and he'd been to several games there. His mother wanted him to think hard about Carolina. His dad just told him to choose carefully. Coach Watkins stayed neutral.

He knew Tommy was wanting to attract attention from App, and Jack was hoping to go to Western Carolina. Henry had hopes of going "somewhere big." Other teammates were having similar thoughts. It added to the pressure.

But they had to win first. Just win, baby.

Coach stood and cleared his throat. His pre-game message was coming next. Then they would go out on the field and it would begin.

INSIDE THE STADIUM

Rob and Samantha Ashworth, and Marc and Tiffany Washington found their seats at about half way up on the thirty yard line on the Central side of the stadium. They were early, but the stadium was already almost full. The grassy bank beyond the end zone on the end opposite the field house was covered with general admission spectators, some of whom had brought lawn chairs or blankets, neither of which were going to be practical on the steep slope, with people standing in front of them.

They were sitting on the Central side because Sam and Tiff were alumna. Bob, who was from McDowell County, and Marc, who had grown up in Orangeburg, South Carolina, only wanted to see a good game. Samantha's parents, Jack and Libby Melton, were on the Central side somewhere, sitting with Bill and Darlene Norville. Mitch and Diana McCaffrey and their kids were on the West Brainerd side, because Diana had gone to West and had an axe to grind with Central. Ben and Alyssa Callahan were still on their honeymoon at Alyssa's condo on Grand Cayman. Rick Barton and Aleksandra Tatarkiewicz (who went by Alexandra Tabarant here in the United States) were in Boone, and weren't coming.

Sam and Rob were feeling grumpy. They had stopped at a concession stand for soft drinks, and someone in the crowd pressing about had bumped into Rob, making him spill about a third of his drink on his sneakers. Sam had a sweater in case it got cooler later, but right now was wearing a sleeveless blouse, as was Tiffany. There was still some sunlight, thankfully in the eyes of the West Brainerd fans across the field, and the weather remained hot and humid, making Samantha's blouse stick to her and causing her hair to frizz, which she hated.

Samantha, despite the heat, felt a chill at the back of her neck, and turned her head to look at the seats behind them. Sure enough, about four rows back, sat Monica Gilbert with a sharp-faced, slender man Samantha didn't know. Monica was looking daggers at the four of them. As well she might, Samantha thought. Monica had a history with all of them, and it was not a good history. She nudged Rob with an elbow.

"Don't look," she said into his ear, not trying to whisper because it was useless with all the noise from the crowd and the bands around them. "But Monica Gilbert is behind us. About four rows back."

But of course Rob turned and looked. He turned and leaned toward the Washingtons, and when he'd passed on the news, they looked, too.

"This is good," Tiffany said.

"How is seeing Monica ever good?" Sam asked.

"Because hopefully, seeing us ruined her day."

Samantha laughed. "There is that. I...I hope she doesn't try anything."

"With Mitch and Diana in the stadium?" Tiffany sniffed. "I doubt it. She knows better by now."

"Maybe," Samantha said, her tone implying doubt.

By now both bands were on the field, and the public address announcer asked everyone to stand for the national anthem. They all stood and sang. Sam refused to look to see if Monica was standing. She supposed so, but nothing bad was past the woman.

The bands filed off the field and the West Brainerd stands stood and erupted as their Redwings ran onto the field. Seconds later, the Central Cougars ran onto the field, and their side of the field stood and cheered. Both bands were playing competing fight songs, and the stadium noise was almost deafening. The game hadn't even started.

But it was about to. They watched the team captains go to center field for the coin toss.

In the standing room only press box above them, Danny Jarvis took a note pad from his pocket, and prepared to take notes.

ON THE SIDELINE

Eva Martinez and the other cheerleaders, all wearing white with russet trim and letters, ran onto the field ahead of the Redwings, and then trotted to the sideline, where they stood, bouncing on the balls of their feet and waving pom-poms. She tried to catch Doug's eye, but he was in the middle of a bunch of players who were shoving and pounding one another in their pre-game frenzy.

Eva and Doug had been dating regularly for about a year, and had been "talking" (as young people were now calling dating casually) for a few months prior to that. Years ago, teenagers would have said they were "going steady"; but no one used such outmoded terms anymore. But they were as committed as any young couple, both of whom had big plans for life after high school, could be.

Eva liked Doug. He was smart and funny, good looking in a rugged, outdoorsy way; and he wasn't too tall for her. She was only about five-five and could look up at Doug without having to crane her neck too far. He could talk about books and animals and music, and not just sports. Not that sports were bad. Eva was pretty athletic herself. In addition to cheerleading, she played on the girls' volleyball team, and took gymnastics lessons.

Eva was an "it girl." She was well aware that she was, but tried not to show she was aware. Her mother always said that a girl with too much ego about her looks was just vain, and she wanted her daughter to be more than that. Eva tried to take it to heart.

Her mom was a local girl, a graduate of West Brainerd and Appalachian State University, who was a loan originator at Western Piedmont Bank. She had surprised everyone by marrying Joe Martinez, Cubano by descent, who now owned his own landscaping business in Martintown, but who was working for someone else's company when they had met at Appalachian, where she studied finance and he took landscape architecture.

The Martinez' had produced only one child, this athletic beauty with her father's dark hair and her mother's hazel eyes. They were proud of her, but they were strict. She went to mass every Sunday. They imposed curfews. Eva did not rebel. Her one beef with her folks was that they had named her "Evangeline" because her mother loved the Longfellow poem. Eva had shortened it and outright rejected "Vangie," which her dad had suggested.

She saw that Central had won the coin toss and would receive. She and her teammates jumped up and down and shook their pom-poms in the air. Doug would take the field in a minute.

Eva was excited but apprehensive. She wanted her Redwings to win. She wanted Doug to star. And she didn't want him the way he always was after a loss when they went out after the game.

BACK IN THE STANDS

Lara Martin squeezed her husband's hand. They were seated with other parents on the West Brainerd side of the field. They were about to watch their son go into the stylized combat that was football. She always feared for him when he did.

Doug had always escaped injury, despite taking some fearful hits. Their family doctor said their son's bone density was really extraordinary. It was almost, he said, that Doug was an atavism, having the bones of an early ancestor. If only the man knew.

She and Darren stood and cheered when the teams took the field. She squeezed her husband's hand again. He leaned toward and spoke into her ear, loud enough that she could hear over the crowd noise.

"Don't worry," he said. "Doug will be fine. He's always been able to take care of himself."

Chapter Four

BRAINERD COUNTY, SEPTEMBER 2017

Lara O'Malley Martin sat across the kitchen table from her son. She had arrived home early from her shift at the ER to find an assistant principal, Glenn Murphy, waiting in a black Ford Explorer in the driveway with Doug beside him in the passenger's seat. She had had to call in a favor to leave work early because Darren was working on a project for a customer all the way down in Valdese; and the principal's secretary who had called the hospital, and waited on hold for Lara to be summoned, had not been particularly nice about telling her that her son was being sent home, and suspended for the rest of the week, for fighting at recess.

Murphy, in contrast, had been almost apologetic. He was a young guy, big, sandy-haired and a little paunchy, who helped over at the high school coaching football in addition to his duties at the Middle School.

"Doug just got caught in a situation," Murphy said. "We know the other kid's a bully, and he's two years older than your boy. I don't think there would have been any suspension if Doug hadn't broken the kid's nose. But Principal Denton has these 'zero tolerance' policies, and fighting is one of them."

Murphy had paused and allowed a smile, which he quickly wiped from his face. "Doug's a good kid," he said. "A good athlete, too. I can't wait to have him in football. He's *strong*."

Now the good kid was sitting across from her rubbing sore knuckles with his left hand. Probably should get some ice on that hand in a minute, she thought.

But first, she'd get her son's story. "Tell me what happened," she said.

It turned out there were several classes from grades six through eight, at recess at the same time, while teachers watched. Doug's group was playing softball, while next to them, an eighth grade class was playing touch football. One of Doug's friends, a skinny kid named Herman Dale was playing in the outfield. When Herman backed up to catch a pop fly, he backed into a kid from the football game, causing him to drop a pass.

The eighth grader was a big kid named Ralph Beck, big because he had already repeated grades twice. He shoved Herman to the ground a kicked him twice. And then Doug was in his face, not much shorter than Beck and much broader. Beck had shoved Doug, too. And then Doug had hit him.

At least their son hadn't used any of the martial arts techniques his father had taught him, Lara thought. That was good. Doug had been lectured sternly about not doing that. Evidently, he had paid attention. But a simple punch in the nose had been enough to put Beck on his back, his nose streaming blood.

So now here he was. Doubtless there would be a meeting with the principal at school, probably involving both sets of parents. Lara didn't look forward to that. Janet Denton was convinced she knew all of the latest pedagogy, most of which involved rote obedience to the latest clichés of the day. Well, that would wait.

For now, she sighed and said, "All right, son. Let's get some ice on your hand. Go to your room for now. Do your homework, or read, or whatever. We'll tell your father later."

She had just given Doug and ice-pack and sent him on his way when the doorbell rang. What now? She thought.

Lara opened the door to find a short, pudgy woman in too-tight shorts and a tank top, peroxided hair showing dark roots and piled into a loose something atop her head, scowling at her.

"Is this the Martin residence?" she asked, her voice already accusing.

Lara said that it was.

"Are you Doug Martin's mother?"

"Yes, I am." Lara had been dealing with hostile patients at the Emergency Room for years, and she knew to keep her voice low and level.

"Well, you and your husband are going to pay my son's medical bills. And damages. We don't know how bad he's hurt. We'll take you to court if we have to. Just look at him." The woman threw an arm, flesh quivering, at a rusty and mud-spattered brown Subaru in the driveway. Through the dirty windshield, Lara could – barely – make out a figure in the passenger's seat, whose face was swathed in bandages and some type of plastic shield.

"You better pay up quick," the woman continued. "Unless you want your boy expelled. We can get that done, too. I already told that woman principal we will."

Lara had had enough. She knew Doug hadn't lied to her. But she wasn't about to yell back at the woman.

"I'm very sorry your son was injured, Mrs. Beck," she said, making the effort to control her inflection. "We certainly don't approve of Doug fighting, and we will deal with him. But you might want to talk with your son about picking on younger boys. That can get him in trouble."

She paused and added with malice aforethought, "Or hurt, like it did today."

The woman's face, already pale, turned paper white, and then bright red. "We'll see you in court!" she screamed, and then marched to her car, pausing to shake a fist back at Lara.

"Good-bye," Lara said. She noticed that two of their neighbors, who had been out walking their dogs, had stopped to watch the drama. She turned back inside without giving them a chance to ask questions.

Lara went to the kitchen to begin preparing dinner. She though Doug might come out to ask her about who was at the door, but he didn't. We were told he'd mature fast, she thought. He was already 5-7 at eleven years old, and broad in the shoulders; but if the government doctors were right, he probably wasn't going to get a great deal taller.

But he's going to get broader, she thought. And stronger. We're going to have to double down on teaching self-control, she mused as she took chicken from the refrigerator. She sighed again. Poor kid. He really does try. Maybe it will be good for him to play football. As long as he plays clean, that could be a good outlet for him.

The Becks didn't sue. Both Doug and Ralph were suspended for a week, and everyone, parents included, had to sit through Janet Denton's pious lecture. Doug was required to review some online materials that his father said were bullshit. The Becks moved out of the district.

Years later, Lara noticed from newspaper stories that Ralph Beck was playing football for Brainerd Central, and had a waiver to stay on the team at age 19. But he had graduated by the time of the big match-up.

Chapter Five
BRAINERD CENTRAL STADIUM, 2022

THE FIRST HALF (FIRST SERIES)

Doug was the "wedge-buster" on the kickoff team. It was his job to disrupt the blockers, who usually tried to form a wedge for the returner to follow up the field. West's kicker was a sophomore named Johnny Long, who had practiced and practiced on his own and under supervision. Coach Watkins and his assistants had high hopes for kicking this season.

Long's job was complicated by needing to kick away from Jeremiah Billups, so that he had to angle the kick as well as smack the ball hard, and had to see on which side of the field Billups lined up before kicking. That was important because sometimes Central moved him around.

Long's kick was high, end over end, and tumbled into the arms of one of Central's wide receivers, who was deep to Long's right when he kicked. Doug tried to do his job, bouncing off more than one blocker as the coverage team charged down the field. He must have done okay, he thought as the whistle blew, because little Javon Shade had squirted downfield and dropped the returner at the 23 yard line. That was a "win" for the coverage team, because a fair catch would have placed the ball at the 25.

Doug was the defensive captain, and called for base defense in the huddle. That meant that Abernathy would be at nose tackle over center, flanked by the defensive tackles and defensive ends, including Herman Dale on the left. At linebacker, Doug would react to the play, while Tommy Mason was to "spy" on Billups and shadow him on every play, unless the call was for a linebacker blitz or for Doug to take the spy.

Brainerd Central's offense was usually pretty "vanilla". A lot of it was Billups right, Billups left, and Billups up the middle. But why wouldn't it be, with Jeremiah Billups at tailback? Central's base formation was a slot-T with a wingback or slot back to the right and a tight end on the left. The slot back and tight end did a lot of blocking with some receiving mixed in. The lone wide receiver, Jones, was a good ball player, usually a decoy; but you couldn't count on that.

Their first play was almost always Billups off the right side, with the wingback blocking down on the linebackers and the fullback leading, right over the butt of big Markus Caldwell. As Doug lined up, he didn't sense anything different. Sometimes he did, and would shout a warning to his teammates. But not this time.

And here it came. The quarterback handed the ball to Billups, who was running right, and continued rolling to the left, his arm faking a throw in the hopes of "freezing" the West Brainerd safeties. Doug was in motion hard to his left almost before the handoff. He knew without knowing how that the slot back would dive at his knees and cut slightly left to make him miss.

In the meantime, Harry Simpson, West's best tackle, was trying to fend off Markus Caldwell. The scouting report said Caldwell played a little "high," and Sammy's coach had preached all week about not letting the big man get under his pads. Simpson hit low. That took him out of the play, but clogged things up. Herman Dale did his job, too, and stood up the fullback, keeping him off Doug.

Billups was going to cut right, off the fullback's block of Dale. Instinctively, Doug cut with him, tackling low and in good form, arms locking and driving with his legs. He heard and felt the collision, then heard the whistle ending the play. He was vaguely aware of cheering from the West Brainerd side of the field, and rose to see where the ball was spotted.

Jeremiah Billups, widely thought to be the best high school halfback in North Carolina, and one of the best in the country, had gained a yard, But it was only the first play of the game.

The next play was a straight dive handoff, also to Billups but off the left side, that is, to the defense's right. The good Central line power blocked straight ahead, driving the West defenders back. Doug and Tommy flew to the ball, and the play was stopped after a gain of four yards, bringing up third down and five to go.

Doug so far hadn't received a signal from the sidelines to go out of base defense, but this time Coach Murphy (the same guy who had driven him home after he'd punched out Ralph Beck years ago) signaled a blitz, with Doug as the blitzer. That was risky, because with Mason spying Billups, there was no one to drop over the middle to defend a quick pass. The strong safety would have to cover that on his own. There was also the chance Central would run Billups again. The hope there was for him to run into the blitz.

And that's how it turned out. Central tried to trap block Abernathy, but the big nose tackle wasn't moving. Doug charged hard off Abernathy's right, and hit Billups just as he took the handoff. Loss of one, bringing up fourth and six.

Central would have to punt.

WEST BRAINERD'S BALL

The Central punter didn't get off a good punt. The ball shanked off the left side of his foot. It hit the ground at about the West Brainerd 40 yard line, took a bounce in the Central's favor, and finally rolled out of bounds at the West Brainerd thirty-three. Doug supposed the guy was trying not to kick to Javon. In that respect, the kick succeeded.

But West had pretty good field position, if they could do anything with it.

As Doug came off the field, he heard whistles. The officials had called a time out because there was something wrong with the clock.

Coach Watkins called out to Doug. "Martin, get over here."

After Doug trotted over, Coach asked, "How do you feel?"

"Good," he said. "I'm doing fine."

And he had done better this year in not draining out in hot weather, all through fall practice. Coach had noticed it. Doug's father had said he suppose Doug was becoming acclimated.

"How is that possible?" Doug had asked. "I've never lived anywhere else."

"Just a figure of speech, son," his dad had said, and didn't elaborate. But Doug thought it had been a funny thing to say.

"All right," Coach Watkins said. The offense was already gathered around. "Stump, you're in at fullback. Tommy, you go to wing. Herman, I want you over at wide-out. Javon, you and Freddie" – the regular wingback – "be ready. We'll need you."

"But right now, we're going to run the same first play they ran at us. Henry will sweep right. Herman has the linebacker. Harry, hit Caldwell low. He tends to stand straight up. Doug, if you need to, chip Caldwell on your way to help Harry, then go hunting for people to block. Henry, this is your time."

Coach Murphy took Doug by the arm. "If you get the chance," he whispered, "I want you to lay that son-of-a-bitch Beck out. Maybe not this play, but sometime."

Doug grinned. The Brainerd Central left linebacker was Billy "Buster" Beck, Ralph Beck's younger brother. He already had a reputation as a dirty player.

"With pleasure, Coach," he said.

The timeout ended and they took the field. As Coach had said, the play was almost identical to the one Central had used to begin the game. As Doug charged to his right, he felt, and then saw Harry begin to lose his block on Caldwell. But Markus was a little off-balance, and Doug put his left shoulder into the big tackle hard. He stumbled a little with the impact, but kept going, Henry Warren right behind him.

Herman Dale's block on Buster Beck had not been completely success-ful, and Beck, a little off balance, was still in the way, until Doug hit him, causing him to hit the ground and roll. When Beck rose, the play was past him.

Doug staggered a little but kept his feet. Now he was looking for targets of opportunity. He sensed, rather than saw, a blue jersey coming hard from his left. Jeremiah Billups, who played safety on defense, had an angle on Henry. Doug found another gear somewhere and ran his pads into Billups' side, a clean block that took him out of the play.

And then Henry Warren was past them all, and in the end zone. The West Brainerd fans were jumping up and down. The band was playing. The extra point kick was good.

West Brainerd, the Class AAA upstart playing AAAAA Brainerd Cen-tral, led 7-0. The Redwings had run only one offensive play.

IN THE PRESS BOX

Danny Jarvis stood at the back of the Press Box. He had no choice. There were no seats. A reporter for the Asheville paper stood next to him. He didn't know the guy.

The crowd noise had still not subsided from the touchdown run. The reporter from Asheville had to yell.

"Did you see that?" he asked.

"Good run," Jarvis yelled back.

The noise had lessened, now, and the reporter was able to speak more normally. "Yeah, it was; but what I meant was did you see what Stump Martin did? He helped block the tackle, finished off the linebacker, and wiped out the safety – all without slowing up. That's amazing."

Jarvis nodded, and listened as the other man continued to enthuse. "I'm telling you, this kid's a real throwback. A Neanderthal fullback. A real Neanderthal."

Jarvis nodded, but the man's choice of words made him think. He remembered a TV special he'd seen recently about Neanderthals and how they hunted big game animals.

Nah, it couldn't be. But…it might be interesting to do something in depth about this kid. He'd have to stick around and do some research.

THE HALF ENDS

The rest of the half was the Jeremiah Billups show. Central took the kickoff and marched down the field. Four yards. Five yards. Then four again. Another sweep, this time blocked better, for fourteen yards. A surprise trap play to the fullback for twelve yards. Then a pass over the middle to the wide receiver for nineteen. West Brainerd gave ground grudgingly. But the drive ended with Billups in the end zone. Doug was on top of him, but too late. The extra point tied the game.

West Brainerd was unable to move the ball consistently. Doug stayed on the sideline, while Tommy played fullback. There were a few good plays. A pass over the middle to Herman Dale went for 17 yards. Henry Warren managed a twelve yard run on sheer determination. But the drive ended in a punt, which went into the end zone for a touchback.

The Brainerd Central machine went back to work, four, five, six, twelve, fifteen yards at a time. The clock moved relentlessly. With two minutes left in the half, Billups made a brilliant, weaving run and scored the touchdown that put Central up by six. Central's extra point kick was no good.

Central 13, West Brainerd 7.

When West got the football, there was momentary excitement as Coach Watkins called a screen pass to Henry Warren that went for 36 yards. But the drive stalled. West Brainerd tried a field goal but Johnny Long didn't have enough leg. The kick fell short.

And the half ended.

Chapter Six
BRAINERD CENTRAL STADIUM, AUGUST 2022

AT THE HALF
IN THE LOCKER ROOM

Steve Watkins, who had been head football coach at West Brainerd High School for the past 12 years, stood next to two of his assistants in the crowded visitors' locker room and studied his players. He was pleased, except with the score. His team had competed. No one had been injured. They weren't slumping from either dejection or exhaustion. He watched as trainers circulated with cups of Gatorade to make sure the team was hydrated.

You can tell they've been in a tough game, he thought. Their white uniforms with russet numbers and trim were wet with sweat and dirty with grass stains. Despite the air-conditioning, rivulets of sweat were trickling down from scalps and shining in the fluorescents. They weren't talking much, yet.

But they're not beaten, he thought. He was sure of that. And it was his job to find a way for them to win. He had been thinking about what he needed to do all the way off the field, and now he had some conclusions. He turned to linebackers and defensive line coach Glenn Murphy, who was standing to his right.

"How's Stump holding up?" he asked.

"Good," Murphy said. "Better than he's ever done, this time of year. I've checked with him every time he came off the field."

Watkins nodded and reached a decision. He turned to his left and exchanged a few sentences with Angelo DeRatt, his offensive backfield and receivers coach. (He coached the offensive line himself; West didn't have the budget for a big staff.) Then he cleared his throat and called to his team.

"All right, people. Listen up."

The buzz of conversation ended immediately. All eyes turned to Coach.

"We're going to win this game," Watkins said. "And we're going to have fun doing it. Now, here's what we're going to do.

"We've been mostly running the ball, but we're really going to mix it up in the third quarter. If we can protect Les, I don't think their secondary can stay with Javon and Herman. Freddie, too, come to it.

"Stump, we're going to need you on offense. Are you ready?"

"Yes, sir, coach," Doug shouted, his voice clear and strong.

"Good. We're going to shuttle Tommy and Freddie with plays. Stump, too, sometimes. We're going to go out of the gun sometimes. But we have to set them up first. Our first play after the kickoff is going to be the sprint draw to Henry. Stump will be at fullback and Tommy at wing. And I want you guys to knock them out of there.

"Our second play…"

IN THE STANDS

Samantha Ashworth and Tiffany Washington were happy their old high school was ahead. Rob and Marc didn't care, really, but were buzzing with talk about Jeremiah Billups and Stump Martin. All four were exiting their seats. Samantha and Tiffany were headed to the women's restroom, a trip that would consume the whole halftime between the lines and their girl talk. Rob and Marc would hit the restroom, too, but also were bound for the concession stand. All of them were still warm, although now, with the sun fully down and the stadium lights on, they knew the second half would be cooler. Rob had decided he was going to buy bottled water and not soft drinks. That would be better.

As they entered the aisle and began to inch their way up the steps, Samantha nudged Rob.

"Eh?" he said. He had been watching the insects circling the lights, and the bats pursuing them. He might as well. The line wasn't moving.

Samantha leaned toward him to speak into his ear. "Honey," she said, "did you feel anything from the field?"

BRAINERD CENTRAL STADIUM, AUGUST 2022

Rob didn't respond right away. "You mean?" he asked finally.

"Yes." Even though no one was likely to hear them above the buzz of other conversations, they didn't want to get specific.

Rob hesitated again. He had felt *something* on the field at times, but nothing definite, and he could be mistaking it in the game excitement. Yet Sam, he knew, had more Sensitivity than he. She was, as Mitch McCaffrey said, "off the charts."

"Maybe," he said. "I'm not sure."

"I am," Samantha said. "I think it's coming from that Martin guy from West. The one they call Stump. I think he made all those tackles because he knew where the ball was going."

Rob considered. He and Marc had already told each other that Central would be ahead by three touchdowns if it hadn't been for Stump Martin.

"I can't tell," he said. "We'll talk about it after the game. We'll see if Mitch picked up on anything."

"What are you two whispering about?" Tiffany asked.

"Tell you later," Rob promised, and they continued to make their way through the crowd.

IN THE PRESS BOX

Danny Jarvis reached his editor at *Tar Heel Sports Weekly*, for whom he was writing the game story, on the third ring. He had to speak loudly into the cell phone microphone. The press box was that noisy.

"Andy? Danny here. Yes, I'm at the stadium. Listen, I'll lodge the game story in the morning. It's a good one. But I'm going to hang around here for a few days. I think there's some human-interest follow-up."

He listened for a few seconds, and continued. "About Doug Martin. Yes, the one they call the Stump. It may not be anything, but I think there might be. No, I can't give you anything specific yet."

He listened again.

"Yeah, I understand you can't agree to pay expenses unless you take the story. I'll eat them. But I think I may have something you'll like."

By the time he ended the call, the second half was about to begin.

Chapter Seven
BRAINERD CENTRAL STADIUM, AUGUST 2022

THE SECOND HALF
THIRD QUARTER

When Doug took the field for the second half kickoff, he realized two things. First, it was noticeably cooler. The last of the late afternoon heat was gone. Second, he felt good. Call it acclimated, conditioned, whatever, he still had plenty of energy. The rest of the team looked the same. There had been plenty of energy in the locker room.

He managed to take out one of Central's kick-coverage guys, then shielded another from Javon Shade, the returner, who had made one of the Central edge "gunners" miss a tackle. Javon took the kickoff out to the West thirty eight yard line. Just twelve yards short of mid-field, it was a good place to start.

The play had been called in the locker room, and West Brainerd didn't huddle. The play was a sprint-draw, in which Les Bronson lined up under center, sprinted to his right as though he would throw a sprint-out pass, and then handed off to Henry Warren running back to the left. Warren then cut slightly right, to take the ball between guard and tackle and then straight up field.

To make it work, Mike Abernathy had to handle the nose tackle, right guard Kenny Mastriano and right tackle Harry Simpson would double-team Markus Caldwell, and Tommy Mason would block down on the defensive end. Doug's job was to block Buster Beck, one of the inside linebackers, while creating enough traffic to make the other linebacker go around. They went on a quick count, hoping the Central team, thinking West would huddle, at least briefly, wouldn't be fully set.

Just before the snap, Doug looked across the line at Buster Beck. Maybe it was body language, maybe he just felt it, but he knew Beck was going to "crash," a run blitz as opposed to one designed to go after the quarterback. Sure enough, that's what Beck did, and ran straight into Doug charging forward. Buster Beck wasn't a little guy, but Doug's 217 pounds of mostly muscle met him, legs driving, and knocked him out of the hole and into the legs of the other linebacker. The other blockers did their jobs, and Henry was through the line. He was finally tackled by the Central safeties at their own 39, a gain of twenty-three yards.

West went without a huddle again, the play that had been called to run second if the first worked. The Redwings lined up in a "shotgun" formation, with Les Bronson several yards behind the center, and Doug immediately to the quarterback's right. Henry Warren was split wide left as a flanker, and Freddie had replaced Tommy at wingback and was split wider out than usual. The whole formation screamed "pass."

But it wasn't. When the ball was snapped, Freddy took a half-step downfield, and then cut back to block the defensive end. He and Harry Simpson were helped by the end and Markus Caldwell running a twist, where the end was slanting to his right, and Caldwell to the left in an attempt to get to the quarterback. Mastriano, only five-eleven but a solid 221 pounds, engaged Beck, who was blitzing again.

Bronson, after feigning setting to pass, stuck the ball in Doug's gut, and Doug was off downfield. The play was a draw, which could be a big gain if it worked, but would lose yardage, or gain little, if not. If this one was to work, Doug would have to make the other linebacker, who wasn't blocked, miss.

It helped that the Central linebacker's eyes had been on Herman Dale, who was slanting across the field as though he would catch a pass; but the guy recovered enough to close on Doug about three yards past the line of scrimmage. Doug had almost a full head of steam by now and drove his left shoulder into the other player's body, while cutting a little to the right. He bounced off the tackle and kept going. He was at full speed in a couple of steps.

The Central defensive backs had dropped into coverage, thinking Dale, Warren, or Shade would be thrown a pass. They didn't close on Doug until he was at about the five yard-line. But they tried to tackle high, and Doug lowered his shoulders and dragged them into the end-zone.

Doug felt his teammates pound his back as he trotted off the field, after first tossing the ball to one of the officials. They were excited, and so was he. He returned to the field to block for the extra point. Not many high school teams had really reliable kickers. West Brainerd's Johnny Long was one of them.

West Brainerd had gone 62 yards in two plays, and now led, 14-13.

But the lead did not last long.

The next series began well enough for West. The defense was jacked, and Central was reeling, just a bit. Billups gained three yards to the left, and two to the right. If the Redwings could hold on third and five, they had a stop. But on third down, disaster struck. Lenny Benfield, the Central quarterback, rolled to his right, and appeared to look downfield for a wide receiver. But instead, he tossed the ball to Jeremiah Billups, who had got behind the linebackers, with no one between him and the end zone. It was the Central crowd's turn to jump up and down. This time the extra point was good, barely, and Central led 20-14.

Doug was angry at himself because his usual sense of where the ball was going to go had failed him. Well, not exactly, but by the time his "sixth sense," as he privately thought it, told him where the play was going to go, he was too far across the field shadowing the fullback to be able to do any good. That had been Doug's actual assignment. Tommy Mason was the one who was supposed to "spy" on Billups. And he'd done his job, but had been tripped somehow in traffic.

He told himself he couldn't be everywhere. But he was still mad at himself. Then he realized he had to shake it off himself, if he was going to help Tommy do it. The game wasn't over.

The next series wasn't good. The coaches gave Doug a breather on offense, which he protested he didn't need. Coach overruled him, though. So, he stood on the sidelines and watched while his team broke Henry Warren for a five-yard gain, and ran a scissors play to Freddie back to the right for six. Then, on first down Les hit Herman Dale across the middle for 14 yards, but the officials flagged Kenny for holding Markus Caldwell.

The next three plays gained eight yards, and West Brainerd had to punt.

The 12-minute high school quarters went fast. The quarter ended with Central still leading.

But there was one good thing, Doug thought as he ran back on defense to start the fourth quarter. He thought Central's guys looked a little gassed. Maybe he sensed it, more than saw it.

But he wasn't gassed. And he didn't think his teammates were. Tired, sure. Steam rose from heads when helmets were removed. Jerseys were soaked with sweat. They breathed hard after plays. Numbers and pants were grass-stained.

But the Central team was the same. And, he thought, more so.

THE FOURTH QUARTER

Central had the ball again, and again was on the march. Billups got the ball on almost every play. They paid for every yard, but the yards piled up. Doug kept telling his teammates to keep hitting hard, and something good would happen. He tried to lead by example, too, and noticed Billups was getting up more and more slowly after each play.

The Central Cougars were on the West Brainerd thirty-four yard-line when it happened. On third down and three, Central lined up in their pow-er-I set, Billups dotting the "I" behind the fullback, who was behind the QB. The West Brainerd defenders dug in.

As the Central quarterback barked the signals, Doug realized the play would be a pass. He didn't stop to think how, whether it was something in the quarterback's stance, or eyes, or what. He just knew it would be a pass to the tall, gangly tight end over the middle, behind the linebackers. Even before the ball was snapped, he was turning sideways and backing up.

The whole stadium watched as Billups slammed into the line, and appeared close to the first down, then gasped as they realized Lenny Benfield still had the ball, and saw him release it toward Jenkins, the tight end. For less than a second, Jenkins appeared to be wide open. Then they saw Doug Martin, the Stump, sprint close to Jenkins, turn, and jump, right arm outstretched.

It helped that Benfield had thrown the ball "on a rope," with not much air under it. Doug was known for many things, but not for his leaping. In any event, his hand found the ball and batted it just before he crashed into Jenkins. The ball turned sideways and came down into Doug's arms, who fell on Jenkins with the ball clutched tightly against his chest.

The officials signaled the change of possession by interception. There was a short delay while the Central coaches protested there had been pass interference. Doug had an anxious minute while the zebras conferred. But the call stood. Doug had batted the ball before making contact.

Coach Watkins held Doug out again, and again told him the team would need him fresh down the stretch. He watched the offense take the field with Tommy at fullback. He didn't know that Javon Shade had told Coach that he thought he could beat the cornerback deep.

The play was a play-action pass, in which Les Bronson faked to a sweep to the right with Henry Warren, kept the ball, and rolled left. Markus Caldwell hadn't been fooled and was coming hard, having beaten Harry Simpson's block. But Bronson's roll-out took him away from Caldwell, and the right side of the Central Defense had bitten on the fake and hadn't recovered. Looking downfield, Bronson saw Javon Shade streaking down the left sideline, all alone, and unleased the pass.

The pass wasn't a perfect spiral. It wobbled a little. Javon had to slow a step to wait for it. He made the catch and turned on his sprinter's speed. Because there had been a second's wait for the ball, Jeremiah Billups almost caught him. But the play ended in a touchdown. The West Brainerd band played a fight song while its crowd cheered.

Watching from the sideline, Doug leaped in the air, signaling the score before the officials. The score was 20-20, and then, after Johnny kicked the extra point, 21-20, West Brainerd. There were six minutes and forty seconds left in the game.

Central had its own speedy wide receiver, Dimitri Jones. It had been Jones that blew the coverage that allowed Javon Shade to be all alone. Offensively, he had been quiet for most of the game, which, from Central's standpoint, had been the Jeremiah Billups show. But now it was his turn to shine, and he returned the kickoff to the West Brainerd 40 yard line. Doug had realized Jones was going to make the cut that freed him, but this time, he'd just been blocked.

On the very next play, Jones got the ball again, a sideline pass that went all the way to the 17 yard line. Then the West Brainerd defenders dug in. This time, the Central offense used their fullback more. Doug realized Billups must be flagging, and slammed into the ball carrier hard on almost every carry. But Central was good, and the yard-marker moved slowly, but moved all the same.

Finally, it was third and goal on the three. Coach Watkins called time out. On the sidelines, he told the team to expect a power sweep with Billups. Doug spoke up.

"I'm not sure, Coach," he said. "I think it may be a pass or a quarterback keeper."

"Son," Watkins said. "We've watched film from all last year. The sweep is their bread and butter inside the five."

The play did appear to be a sweep. But Benfield kept it and rolled right. Doug, sensing it coming, recovered and almost got there. But it was a score. Central led 26-21, and this time made the point after touchdown.

27-21. Just under three minutes left.

"Doug," Coach Watkins said on the sideline, "maybe I'll listen to you next time." He said it with a smile, and then gave instructions to the offense.

Javon Shade returned the kickoff to the 28. The stadium was loud as the teams lined up. The entire Central crowd were on their feet making noise. This possession was likely West Brainerd's last chance.

The formation was the same as one West had used earlier. They lined up in the shotgun with only Doug in the backfield with Les. Henry and Freddie were flanked out. Everyone was sure the play was going to be a pass. There wasn't much time in the game. West Brainerd wouldn't run a draw again.

The play was not a draw, but a toss sweep to Doug to the right. He caught the lateral and turned on the speed. West blocked the play at the point of attack perfectly. Caldwell was not a factor. Harry got under his pads and moved him. Freddie helped. Javon Shade, all 145 pounds of him, cut down Dimitri Cook. Doug was eight yards down the field before a Central player came at him. It was Buster Beck, whom Jack Abernathy had not quite blocked.

Doug had known Buster would be coming, and used his left hand in a stiff arm, putting all his strength into it. Beck's momentum reversed and he flew backward. The safety was next, and Doug cut abruptly left. The defender ran past him. Doug, not slowing, cut back to the right, and put on all his speed. He passed the 50 but Jeremiah Billups had an angle and caught him at the Central 31. Doug put a shoulder into Billups, bounced off and kept going down the sideline. Cook finally recovered and hit Doug at the 20. Doug stumbled, almost kept his balance, but was tackled at the 14 as the rest of the Central team recovered.

Tommy Mason came in, so Doug could catch his breath. The stadium was buzzing. The West Brainerd fans were chanting, "Go! Go! Go!" The

Central stands countered with "Dee-fense! Dee-fense!" Coach Murphy pounded Doug on the back.

"What a run! Coach Watkins wants to know if you can go back in."

Doug took a towel and wiped sweat from his eyes.

"Yes, coach. I want it. I want the ball. We'll score."

Doug watched Henry Warren run the ball to the ten, and then went in for Tommy. The play call was for Doug to slam right up behind Mastriano and Abernathy. As he lined up, he felt it. Central was not beaten, not quite, but now they were doubting. He hit the line, legs churning. When the whistle blew, West Brainerd had the ball on the Central seven. Third and three. The coaches signaled in a sweep to left with Doug and Tommy blocking and Freddie carrying. But Dimitri Cook came up hard, and Freddie was stopped a half yard short.

Coach Watkins sent in Tommy Mason, not for Doug, but for Freddie.

"Coach says give it to Stump until we're in the end zone," he said.

There was a little over a minute left in the game. The Central fans were making noise, but Doug blocked it out. The rest of the game was a blur.

Doug ran left for three yards, and the clock stopped for the first down. Then he ran right for two. The clock was running and the Central players were taking their time lining up. Les Bronson called time-out.

"Can you do it, Stump?" he asked in the huddle.

Doug nodded, and the huddle broke. Doug ran left again and almost made the end zone. West called another time out. Under twenty seconds left. Doug slammed into the line. He was sure he had scored, but the officials said no gain. It was fourth down with seconds left when West Brainerd lined up again.

Doug hit the right side of the line, legs pumping, using all his strength. There was a big pile up. Doug could not see where he was.

But the West Brainerd fans were celebrating a touchdown. The clock said time had expired. Even so, West was allowed to go for the extra point, because the game was tied.

Johnny Long's kick was good again. West Brainerd, the AAA underdog, had beaten Brainerd Central.

And Doug Martin had scored the winning touchdown.

Chapter Eight

MARTINTOWN, NORTH CAROLINA, AUGUST 2022

AFTER THE GAME
IN THE BROADCAST BOOTH

Danny Jarvis pushed his way out of the crowded press box, and picked his way through the exiting reporters to the broadcast booth next door. That booth was crowded, too. Not only had WNCB sent Bill Crowder, together with a retired high school coach whose name Jarvis did not remember, to do the "WNC Game of the Week" on FM, but also the companion AM station, which always had the Brainerd Central game, had a team there. West Brainerd didn't have its own radio broadcast.

There was still plenty of noise. The West Brainerd fans were celebrating on the field, and its band was playing the school song over and over. And everyone, it seemed, was talking about the game as they made their ways to the exits.

Jarvis heard someone yell, "Look, fight!" He turned his eyes to the field and saw Sheriff's deputies separating two men near one of the stadium exits. He supposed something like this was inevitable. The deputies let one of the two go, and then the other, watching them walk away in different directions. They didn't take anyone into custody.

Jarvis finally found his way to where Bill Crowder's team was packing up their equipment. Bill saw him coming and waved. As Jarvis approached Crowder found a handkerchief in a pocket and wiped his face. He had obviously been perspiring, more from tension than the humidity, Jarvis suspected.

"Well, Danny," Bill said, raising his voice to be heard, "how do you like high school football in the foothills?" Crowder's broad face sported a wide grin.

Jarvis stepped closer so he wouldn't have to shout back. "Pretty damned exciting."

"Isn't Billups something?" Crowder asked.

"As advertised," Jarvis said. "Over 200 yards total offense. But I think he wore down a little. He played both ways most of the game. And he's not the big story anyway."

"You mean the Stump?"

Jarvis nodded. "I mean the Stump. If there were any doubts about that kid as a college prospect – and I didn't have any myself, not really, although I thought he wasn't likely to go to one of the 'power' conferences – they're answered now. That guy can play college ball either at running back or linebacker. The big schools will be all over him now."

"What do you know about him?"

Crowder pursed his lips. "Not much. I mean not personal information. I hear he's an only child. Someone told me his mom is a nurse, and his dad works for Simmons in IT. They live in what's called the Glen Arden community. That's on the west side of town toward the lake."

"Do you know if either parent was a star athlete?"

"Not that I've heard."

"Where can I get more information? I want to do a follow-up?"

Crowder removed the handkerchief and wiped his face again before answering. Jarvis saw there were rings of perspiration around his armpits.

"You can ask for an interview with the kid and his folks. You might want to go through his coach."

"Thanks, but I know *that*," Jarvis said. "What I want first is some background, something on what the locals know about the family."

Crowder closed a case he'd been packing. "Well," he said, "I can tell you where to go in the morning if you want to overhear a lot, and maybe ask some discrete questions." He grinned. "They'd better be discreet, or everyone on the western end of the county will know a reporter has been asking questions."

Jarvis grinned back. "I don't know that I care whether they do or not. Where are you talking about?"

"The Bean n' Bacon Café. That's a place outside town on the road up the ridge. More toward Maple Oak than Glen Arden. But everybody goes there on Saturday morning. Good food. Real good coffee. I'd go early if I were you – at least fairly early. Don't wait until eleven o'clock or something."

Jarvis thanked Crowder for the advice and the two shook hands. Then he excused himself to make his way to his car. It was going to take a while to get to his hotel. He hoped the bar would still be open.

ON THE WAY OUT

Mitch and Diana McCaffrey finally reached the exit to the stadium closest to their vehicle. They chatted on the way with other jubilant West Brainerd fans, many of whom Diana knew from the Bean n' Bacon, the breakfast and lunch café she and her mother owned and operated, although they more and more were able to turn things over to their assistant manager, Margaret Truman, who wanted to buy the place from them, and would probably get to do it sooner than later, Diana thought.

Thank goodness, Diana thought, Margaret is going to open tomorrow. There was no telling what time she and Mitch were going to get home. Not with this crowd. She wouldn't have to get up at the crack of dawn.

Diana was in a good mood. She had gone to high school at West Brainerd, after a short and unhappy half-year at Central, thanks to Monica Murray, now Gilbert; and she still carried a grudge. For different reasons, so did most West Brainerd alums and fans. West had been consolidated from the old high schools in Glen Arden and Maple Oak, both of which the Martintown crowd looked down on. The snobbery persisted after decades, and certainly was present when Diana was in high school. That was why she'd had no protection from Monica.

Good enough for some of those jerks, Diana thought. It will just kill them to lose to West. Good.

They reached the parking lot, where the press of people spread out to find their cars, and no one else was trying, at the moment, to talk with them. Diana noticed that Mitch had gone silent.

"Did I tell you that Samantha Ashworth texted me at halftime?" she asked, and then amended, "Oh, I know I didn't. You were too busy discussing the fine-points of the Arrh-Pee-Ohh – whatever that is – with the guy sitting next to you. Anyhow, Samantha said she saw Monica Gilbert was sitting a few rows behind her…I hope that bitch enjoyed watching Central being beat."

"Do you really think Monica cares about who wins the game?" Mitch asked. "I'm surprised she even showed up."

"I don't think Monica cares about anything but Monica," Diana said. "But I'm still glad she was here to see Central lose."

Mitch said nothing.

"Honey?" Diana asked when they reached their car. "Is anything wrong?"

"Eh?" Mitch said, as he opened the car door for his wife. "No. Not really. I was just thinking. You know that West fullback? He plays linebacker, too."

"Yes," Diana said, laughing as Mitch got in the driver's seat next to her. "I think the whole stadium and the whole radio audience knows about him now. What about him, except he's a good player?"

"I think he has the Talent," Mitch said as the car started.

Diana knew her husband didn't mean football talent.

"You mean?" she asked, her voice trailing.

Mitch was waiting to pull into the line of exiting vehicles, and said, "Not spell-casting, not even Sensitivity like Samantha has it. More like, well, ESP. Did Sam say anything about it?"

"Not in the text," Diana answered. "She did say she'd talk with us tomorrow. I thought that was just being polite."

"Well, I want to talk with her," Mitch said, pulling into line. "Alyssa, too, when she and Ben get back."

IN AND OUTSIDE THE LOCKER ROOM

The team had been mobbed by fans coming off the field, and had entered the locker room shouting, back slapping, high fiving and singing the school fight song off key. Coach Watkins had gathered them around and told them how proud of them he was, how they ought to enjoy this moment, and remember this game; but he also reminded them that it was just one game and that they still had a conference schedule to play.

Then the exhaustion set in. Doug sat on the bench in front of the locker for longer than he usually did before removing the uniform and pads and packing them in a duffel bag, and stumbling to the shower. He soaked under the hot water for a while. It felt good, but he would feel the bruises in the morning. He toweled, dressed, and combed his still-damp hair, from which little rivulets of water leaked down past his ears and wet his shirt collar.

Coach Murphy walked up and said, "Stump, there's a newspaper reporter from the Martintown paper who wants to talk with you. And about five college coaches."

Doug groaned. He knew his parents, and Eva and her parents, would be waiting outside. Eva and he were going to be allowed a late date tonight. Curfews were being extended, but not by all that much. He wanted to hug his folks, and spend some time with Eva. And he wanted a cheeseburger.

"Coach, do I have to? Talk with them, I mean."

"Yes, you do, Doug. You don't have to talk long. But if you don't, somebody is going to call you a prima donna, or stuck up, or something. And you're looking for that scholarship, remember."

So Doug answered a few questions, and accepted the congratulations of a few coaches. He hoped his answers were okay. Coach Watkins stood beside him smiling, and didn't interfere, so they couldn't be too bad. Later, he wouldn't remember the answers until he read them in the newspaper.

The coaches were a blur. There was a Clemson coach, an App coach, a coach from North Carolina, and one guy who said he coached at Wisconsin. There were more lined up to speak with him, but he begged off by saying he looked forward to visiting with them all, but right now he wanted to see his mom and dad, and his girlfriend.

He had arranged to leave with Eva instead of on the team bus. When he walked out of the locker room, there she was, standing with her folks and his, all of them smiling. Eva looked almost as tired as he did, he thought, after jumping up and down, turning cartwheels, and cheering the whole game. Her face was shining, and her hair was damp and a little curly from the humidity and from her exertion.

She ran up and gave him a quick, chaste hug, and then he accepted the hugs and handshakes of his mom, hers, his dad, and hers. They all talked for a couple of minutes, and then he and Eva were off for the car her parents had loaned her. She would drive, and he was glad of it.

He was too tired to want to drive. Not tonight, anyhow.

EVA

Eva Martinez stood between her parents and Doug's outside the Brainerd Central visiting team's locker rooms. She had traded pom-poms for a clutch purse her mother had brought her. People were passing by on the way to the parking lot, and several spoke. She answered but didn't try to start any conversations.

Eva was not exhausted, but tired. Really, really worn out. As the only real gymnast on the West Brainerd cheerleading squad, she had been expected to do most of the flips and cartwheels. Not only did that take a lot out of her physically, it had also caused her to miss seeing key plays. She had been starting a backflip when Doug began his long fourth quarter run, and saw only its conclusion. Anyway, she was pooped. She wanted to get on out of there. Her folks had been nice enough to let her use her mother's car this evening, while her mom rode home with her dad. She and Doug didn't have all night.

One of the team managers came out and told them that Doug had been asked to speak with several college recruiters, but would be out as soon as he could. Eva sighed and looked at her watch, ignoring the sly smiles from her parents and Doug's.

She and Doug had a comfortable relationship. Neither knew how long it would last. Neither of them knew, yet, where they were going to college next year; and it might not be the same place. But they found each other attractive, shared many of the same friends and interests, and enjoyed each other's company.

And Doug could take "no" for an answer. Not always cheerfully or gracefully. But he always accepted it. Eva was glad, because, more and more, she really didn't want to say "no," or at least her body didn't. Most of her friends didn't understand why Eva even thought about saying no. Many of them had been sexually active since middle school. Eva had asked her mom more than once for money to pay for a "morning after" pill for one of her classmates. (Her father didn't know about that.)

As for Eva, she was well aware of all the bad things that could happen as a result of promiscuity. She didn't think she was prudish. She wasn't concerned about what the parish priest would say. But she had big plans for her life that she didn't want to mess up. It helped that Doug hadn't pushed the envelope too far. So far, anyway.

Finally the door opened and here he came. They were off.

ROB AND SAMANTHA

The Washingtons had accepted a ride to the game from the Ashworths, and had parked their car at the Ashworth condo while they were all at the stadium. Marc and Tiffany declined an invitation to stay for a glass of wine, pleading how tired they were; and Rob and Samantha hadn't pressed them. They needed to turn in before long themselves. Both had to work a couple of hours Saturday morning. They also wanted to talk alone.

They sat in the kitchen at the breakfast table, Samantha sipping a glass of wine while Rob nursed a Scotch, neat, a taste he had picked up from Sam's father and from Mitch McCaffrey. They talked about the evening, including people they'd run into, for a few minutes; and then Rob, with a glance at his watch, raised what was on their minds.

"After you mentioned it, I felt it, too," he said, both knowing what "it" was. "When are you going to mention this to Mitch, like you said you were?"

"I already did," Sam said. "I texted him from the car. He texted back that he agreed and we'd all talk about it after Ben and Alyssa get back Sunday."

"I guess we're supposed to report this to Major Hutton," Rob said. Fred Hutton was their DIA contact. The entire "coven" was contracted to report anything paranormal to him.

"You don't think you and I should do that, do you?" Samantha asked, her rising inflection betraying her fear.

"Good heavens, no!" Rob said. "Not on your life. Mitch or Alyssa can do that. But I'm sure they will."

"What do you think Hutton will do about the Martin kid?" she asked.

Rob drained his Scotch and set the glass on a coaster. "I don't know. I have no idea, actually."

Chapter Nine
MARTINTOWN, NORTH CAROLINA, AUGUST 2022

AT THE BEAN N' BACON

Danny Jarvis arrived at the Bean n' Bacon about 9:00 Saturday morning. The parking lot was close to full. When he entered the main dining room, which was noisy with clanking plates and flatware, and conversation, he didn't see any empty tables. He noticed that the coffee bar along one wall had a counter fronted by high rise chairs, a couple of which were not occupied. He asked the hostess if it was possible to order food there. She said that it was, and did he want a seat? He did.

He found himself squeezed between two bulky middle-aged men, both wearing jeans, one in a flannel shirt that would be too warm for the day, and the other in an oversized tee-shirt that said, "See Linville Falls." The first was wearing boots and the second, sneakers. Both sported baseball caps, and Danny noticed graying hair peeking out from both. They had been talking, and continued their conversation over Danny while they waited on their food. Fortunately, they were talking about last night's football game, which was what Danny wanted.

A plump, pleasant-faced woman, hair piled in a bun, whose name tag said she was "Margaret," appeared before Danny and asked if he wanted a menu. He told her he did, and asked for a large coffee with cream while he decided what to eat. She placed a laminated menu in front of him, and left, saying "sure, honey." He decided to see if he could work his way into his neighbors' conversation.

"Excuse me," he said, turning to the flannel shirt guy on his left, "but what's good here? I'm from out of town."

If the man was irritated at being interrupted, he didn't show it.

"Just about ever'thing," he said. "I don't like the corned beef hash, but I don't care for corned beef. Eggs're good. They have good sausage. A lot of people like the pancakes. What do you think, Cooter?" The question was directed at the man on Danny's right. The tee-shirt guy.

Cooter didn't mind answering. "I like it all, like Mel here says, but I always get two eggs, over-easy, an' bacon. Biscuits and not toast. They have good biscuits. They have the best coffee anywhere around here."

Just at that moment, Margaret arrived with a steaming mug of the region's best, silverware wrapped in a paper napkin, and two containers of cream. "Ready?" she asked.

"Well, this gentleman recommends eggs over-easy with bacon and biscuits," Danny said, although he really preferred toast. Margaret jotted on a pad, nodded and left.

Cooter decided to pursue the conversation with Danny. "Where're ya from?"

Danny introduced himself. "I live in Cornelius, outside Charlotte. I'm a freelance writer, mostly sports. I came to cover the game in Martintown last night."

Cooter offered a hand and his name. On his other side, Mel did the same. Their food came just then, but the two decided they could talk and eat at the same time.

"That was some kind of game, all right," Mel said, cutting into his sausage. "We were just talking about it."

"I heard you. I take it you were for West Brainerd?"

"Yeah," Mel said. "I went to the old Glen Arden High School, before it consolidated in '82. Cooter here went to Maple Oak. We both live in the Maple Oak area now."

"I heard you talking about the Martin kid, the one they call 'Stump,'" Danny said. "What can you tell me about him?"

"Don't know him," Cooter said around a mouthful of eggs.

"I've met him," Mel said. "Before I retired, his dad used to do some work for the company I worked for. You, know, computers, security system. Darren – that's his dad – worked for Simmons. Still does. I don't know the mama.

"He made a couple of emergency calls for us on weekends, and he brought the boy. Of course, the Stump was a lot younger. Even then, pretty big. Broad across the shoulders."

"Do the Martins have any other children?"

"Don't think so," mumbled Cooter.

Mel had a more detailed answer. "No. Doug is an only. Adopted, too. I remember Darren talking about bringing him home in, let's see, it must have been '05 or '06. He was pretty happy about it. I don't think he and his missus could have children."

That's interesting, Danny thought. It was something he hadn't known.

"Did he say where they got the baby?" he asked.

"It was out of state," Mel said after a moment's thought. "If I recollect correctly, the kid is some kind of kin to Darren's wife. She's from up north somewhere. Originally, I mean. They've lived here in Brainerd County for years."

Even more interesting, Danny thought. He remembered to take a bite of his scrambled eggs, and reflected as he chewed. He could ask for an interview, and he might. But first he could do some digging. There had to be some kind of public record on the adoption papers. A birth certificate or court order or something.

He decided to change the subject. "Is the boy well-liked?"

Cooter laughed, spitting egg back in his plate. "Hell, I don't reckon the Central folks like him worth a shit."

"Probably not," Danny conceded. "But I mean in his own community. Classmates and so on."

"As far as I know," Mel said. "I haven't heard anything bad about him."

"Does he have a girl friend?"

"Cheerleader, ain't it?" said Cooter.

"I think it's Joe Martinez' girl," Mel said. "He's a landscaper. Owns his own company."

"Think he'd talk to me?" Danny asked. "Him or his daughter."

"Ask him," Mel said.

"I will," Danny answered. And he probably would.

But he had some research to do first.

COVEN MEETING

The group Alyssa McCormick, now Callahan, had dubbed "the Brainerd Coven" met at her husband's condominium late Sunday afternoon. (The house they were building on the ridge next to the McCaffreys' new home was not completed.) Not everyone who was "in the know" about their little community was a member. Several lawyers at Melton, Norville, Jennings & Johnson knew the firm had paranormal clients. But only Ben Callahan and Kathryn Turner knew everything. Well, Kat knew *almost* everything, Alyssa thought. Kat didn't know the particulars about what had happened on the mountain last Christmas. The NDA everyone there had signed excluded her.

Alyssa's newly-minted husband had no paranormal abilities. But just as Alyssa was the unofficial chairperson of the Coven, Ben was its unofficial legal counsel. So, he was present. Mitch and Diana McCaffrey were there, as were Bob and Samantha Ashworth. They hadn't asked Aleksandra Tatarkiewicz. She hadn't been at Friday's game, and her now very serious boyfriend Rick Barton, who had just joined the firm in July, knew some things, but not everything. Alyssa would decide what to share with Aleks later. She'd ask Mitch his opinion about it first, she decided.

Everyone had settled into chairs, some brought from the dining table, in Ben's great room. Mitch and Diana had accepted coffee, and Ben and Rob each had a beer. Samantha was sipping a glass of white wine. Alyssa had a wine glass, too. Inevitably, everyone wanted to ask about their honeymoon, and Alyssa let the honeymoon conversation go on for a while before getting down to business.

"All right, everyone," she said, setting her wine glass on a coaster. "Someone please tell me just why it's so important we all get together today."

"Why don't you start, Samantha?" Mitch suggested.

Samantha related what she had noticed about the West Brainerd linebacker and fullback, Doug Martin. Rob and Mitch confirmed her. So did Diana, who added that because she sensed no malice in what she had felt, she hadn't seen the need to use her spell-blocking Talent.

"Although," she added, "I'm not sure I *could* have blocked him. This wasn't a spell. It was…different."

"It was," Mitch said. Samantha and Rob agreed. Everyone was silent while that datum sank in.

Rob finally spoke. "Uh, this has to be reported, doesn't it? To Fred Hutton, I mean." He looked directly at Ben, the senior lawyer, who had had a hand at writing all of the written agreements with the government.

Ben nodded without hesitation. "It does. But I don't think anyone needs to write a report just yet. Someone should just call him. He may not want anything in writing. Ordinarily, I'd say Alyssa should do it. She's our usual liaison. But she wasn't there. Mitch?"

Mitch swallowed the dregs of his coffee, and said, "Why don't Alyssa and I call him together? I don't want to do it tonight. But I'm working remotely in the morning, and can set up the secure line at the house."

"Works for me," said Alyssa.

"There's one other thing," Samantha said. "Monica Gilbert was there. I'm sure she felt the kid's Talent too."

"Maybe not," Mitch said. "Monica isn't as good as she thinks she is."

"Maybe she's not," Alyssa chimed in. "But she's getting better. Someone at the Bureau is giving her training. We better assume she sensed the guy, and tell Fred she was there."

"Do you think she'll report this to her FBI handler? What's his name? Springfield?" Diana asked.

Alyssa snorted. "Monica Gilbert, miss a chance to earn brownie points? Or brown-nose points, more like. Not a chance."

"That's settled, then," Ben said. "Anything else? More wine? More coffee?"

But everyone was ready to go home.

MONICA REPORTS

Monica Gilbert didn't know when and how Mitch McCaffrey and his Gang (as she thought of them) would report on the Martin boy to the DIA, but she knew they would. If she had picked up on his Talent, so would they. She wanted to lodge a report with Dennis Springfield at the FBI as soon as she could because she wanted her contacts to know before theirs.

The problem was that Barry Feldman was spending the weekend with her at her home in Martintown, and she couldn't afford for him to know what she was doing. These days, she spent about as much time in Martintown as she did in Raleigh. The Bureau wanted her to keep an eye on the paranormals in Brainerd County, none of whom except her were in its hip-pocket; and her superiors at the State Board for Community Colleges didn't mind her working remotely. In fact, she suspected some of her co-workers, notably those in the legal department, not counting Barry, would rather she not be around. She didn't care.

Barry had driven in Friday afternoon in time for the game, which had received a lot of attention all over the state, and he wouldn't leave until early Sunday afternoon. So, she had to wait and hide her impatience. Barry was sweet and was good in bed. He had been supportive of her when others had not. She was as close to being an "item" with Barry as she'd been with any man since her divorce. But she didn't see how she could be expected to limit herself to one man. Barry wanted more than that, so she wasn't sure how long this thing they had was going to last.

He left right after lunch on Sunday, and Monica didn't wait long before placing the call. She used the secure tablet the Bureau had provided, and used its proprietary secure software. The tablet was easier to use than her Bureau provided cell phone. There were four levels of urgency to use in the code, and she resisted the temptation to use the highest; but she didn't pick the lowest, either.

Springfield accepted the call. He appeared on her tablet screen wearing a tropical shirt with a pale blue and white pattern, sunglasses perched on his head, and irritation showing in his tight features. She could see beyond to a patio, with a beach and ocean front beyond that. A woman in a dental floss bikini was sunbathing in a recliner on the patio. Another recliner was unoccupied beside her. Monica was sure this was not Dennis' wife. She didn't care, but she mentally filed away the information. It might be useful down the road.

"What is it?" Springfield snapped, his tone implying "this better be important" without his saying it.

She told him. His irritation disappeared.

"Well, well," he said. "This *is* interesting. See what you can find out about this kid."

"How?" Monica asked. "I mean, I can ask some discrete questions, but…"

"That's up to you," Springfield said, irritation returning to his voice. "That's why we pay you. But...I'll put an agent on it, too. Someone will contact you. It may be a day or two. In the meantime, ask, but be careful. Don't let the DIA bunch know what you're up to."

"I won't," she promised.

"All right, then. Now let me get back to my little vacation."

Monica was about to speak, but he had terminated the call.

She walked to the wet bar in her parlor and poured a sherry.

Where should she start? With whom?

Chapter Ten
MARTINTOWN, NORTH CAROLINA, AUGUST 2022

MONDAY
AT SCHOOL

On Monday morning, Doug Martin pulled into the student parking lot at West Brainerd High School. He was driving the used RAV4 he'd bought with savings from work and with a little help from his parents. He'd been able to work part time for Simmons IT and Security, supervised by someone other than his dad. It had mostly been non-technical, helping to install security devices and connect equipment; but he'd learned some things. And earning money had been nice. It did make for busy summers, working and keeping up his running and workouts. But that was good in most ways, too.

The weekend had been nice but a little hectic. On Friday night, after Doug had got his cheeseburger, both he and Eva had been too tired to do anything but sleep; so, she'd driven him home. They'd had a nicer date Saturday evening, and Doug smiled at the memory. It had ended in a torrid necking session in his car, parked on a rise overlooking the lake, featuring unbuttoned and unzipped clothing, but no actual sex. Eva had firmly insisted on stopping short. In a way, Doug was glad. He hadn't really been prepared for that, and he was almost as scared of the bad possible outcomes as she. Still, it was…frustrating.

By the time they'd gone out on Saturday night, the hectic part had already started that morning. He wasn't a stranger to the attentions of college recruiters; he'd heard from several last season, and then over the summer. But nothing like what he'd received Saturday morning. There were only a few phone calls; those were regulated. But text messages mostly were not, and they hit like an artillery barrage. He tried to respond to all of them, but wasn't sure he had.

Sunday was a little better, but not much. He went to mass with his mother, spoke briefly after church with Eva and her folks, and returned home. He wouldn't see Eva again that day, although they were to Face Time Sunday evening. Doug's dad wanted him to help "sight in" a new telescopic sight for his deer rifle, and Eva had a gymnastics lesson. But the barrage of text messages continued. Many promised an offer was coming. Doug's dad said he'd speak with Coach Watkins about getting some order in this recruiting process.

Evidently, the news of what happened Friday night had gone all over the state, and beyond. Some writer named Danny Jarvis had filed a game story with *Tar Heel Sports Weekly*, and they had it on their web site. Jarvis' account gushed about the Redwings and especially about Doug. Coach Watkins and his father had cautioned him about "reading his press clippings," so he hadn't paid much attention to the story. But others had.

Doug had had "fully committable" scholarship offers from both Appalachian State and Elon University since last year. Coach Watkins had explained how to tell the difference between that and a mere expression of interest. Sometimes, he said, a prospect would hear something like "we sure hope we see you wearing our uniform next year" and take it as an offer when it wasn't. But now Doug had offers from North Carolina (that had been one call) and Wisconsin (that had been another). Both had made clear that if he committed, he could make a public announcement anytime he wanted. One caller had asked him if he had a Twitter or Instagram account the coach could follow. Unlike most of his classmates, Doug didn't use Instagram. He was glad of it. He did have a Twitter account he barely used, because Eva had pushed him to have one; and he shared his account information with the coach with some reluctance.

After parking, he exited his car and grabbed his backpack and duffel from the back. Coach had cancelled practice for today, as a reward for Friday's effort. Doug was glad. He had been sore all weekend and was still sore. But he needed to go by the locker room and turn in his pads and uniform, which he'd washed over the weekend. So loaded, he walked across the lot toward the school entrance. Some classmates called out and waved to him as he walked, and he returned their greeting. He was hoping to spend a few minutes with Eva before the first class.

But as he neared the door, he saw Coach Watkins standing outside next to a guy he didn't know. Coach waved and motioned Doug to come to them. He groaned. It was starting again this morning. This was going to be another college coach.

Well, at least Coach Watkins would be with him.

AT THE CLERK'S OFFICE

Danny Jarvis had spent Sunday morning doing research on his computer, and Sunday afternoon walking around downtown Martintown, nosing into the stores that were open and into cafes and coffee shops, hoping to find someone who knew something about the Martin family. He had some success at both.

His research told him that records of adoption, after court approval, were transmitted to the state office of Vital Statistics and placed under seal. But that meant there should be an old court file here with *something,* surely. He's also learned that the high school rules required some proof of birthday to verify a player's eligibility. That might be a birth certificate, or it might be the record of admission to the first grade. So, the school itself might have something. He thought he'd try the clerk of court, because he didn't want to announce himself at the high school, or even at the county central offices. Not yet, anyway.

Sunday afternoon, he got lucky. He had stepped into a Caribou Coffee shop and ordered a medium coffee. On the way to the counter, he passed two women seated at a table. One was about 50, tall and thin with salt and pepper hair. The other was younger, plumper, round-faced with glasses, with shoulder length brown hair. The shop didn't have many customers; so, while he was paying for his coffee, he was able to hear one of them, he thought the one with glasses, say, "I'm sure Lara Martin was just thrilled with the way her son played Friday night. I can't wait to congratulate her tomorrow."

He walked over to their table, and said, "Pardon me. I'm Danny Jarvis. I…" After introducing himself, he continued, "I take it you know the Martin family?"

The woman wearing glasses, who had introduced herself as Mabel Fredrickson, said, "I've worked with Lara for years, ever since they moved here."

"When was that?"

"Oh, about 2004 or thereabouts. We're nurses. Pediatric nurses. At Brainerd Medical Center, in the NICU."

"Do you know her son?"

"Not that well. But he's a sweet boy. Everybody says so. I remember when they brought him home. Way back in '05."

"I'm told he is adopted."

She nodded. "He is. The birth mother is some kin to Lara, she said. I don't remember what."

"Where did they get him? Somewhere around here?"

Mabel's brown hair swayed from side to side as she shook her head.

"Oh, no," she answered. "Somewhere up north." Mabel pursed her lips in thought. "You know, Lara is from Massachusetts, but I swear I don't think it was that far. It was…somewhere in Virginia, I think. No, I'm sure it was West Virginia, but I'll never remember where in West Virginia. It's been a minute."

"Well thank you," Danny said. "I'm just getting background. Where the kid was born really isn't important."

Yet, for some reason he couldn't put his finger on, he had a feeling it really might be important, he thought. But no point telling these ladies that.

He thanked them again and excused himself. He wondered what he might find in the Clerk's office.

It turned out to be not much. The deputy clerk who helped him explained that court files that old were archived and couldn't be retrieved without a wait. She added that if it was an adoption, the file had been sealed and transmitted down to vital statistics in Raleigh.

But, she offered, the old docket books were in the office, and if he'd wait a minute, she'd pull 2005, and see what the docket entry said. She disappeared and returned with a heavy volume bound in leather. She placed it on the counter with a thud, and blew dust off it, causing them both to cough. But they found the entry after checking the alphabetical index in the front of the volume.

The adoption of James Douglas Martin had been approved by Judge David Sinclair on October 15, 2005. Date of birth: September 3. Place of birth: Not in N.C. And that was the sum of it.

Danny thanked her and left. He still wasn't sure why he thought the circumstances of the kid's birth were important. Maybe an interview with the birth mother? No, that information likely wasn't available. Danny shook his head as he unlocked his car and climbed into the driver's seat.

There was just something unusual, almost freakish, about the kid.

HUTTON

Mitch had said he was going to set the remote meeting with Hutton at 10:00 a.m. on Monday morning. Alyssa decided she might as well run over to the McCaffreys' new home and do the meeting sitting next to Mitch, rather than use her own device. It would give her a chance to drop by the construction site for the new Callahan home adjacent to Mitch and Diana's. That way, she could see how close to completion the contractor was. Ben had a court hearing this morning.

The location was not so far from where the McCaffreys' used to live, in Mitch's free-standing unit in High Country Estates. In fact, it was on the ridge opposite, and you could see Mitch's old place, now occupied by his son Carson and daughter-in-law Lisa, from Mitch and Diana's veranda. The biggest issue in building both houses had been the improvement and extension of the old private road leading to the ridge top. They were going to see if they could get Brainerd County to accept it as a public road; but in the meantime, the two couples would share the cost of maintenance. That wasn't as much an issue as one might think when corners could be cut with spell craft.

When Alyssa arrived at the construction site, the contractor himself wasn't there; but his foreman was, and he showed Alyssa around. She was pretty much pleased but had a few questions and some requests, none of which would delay completion much. The foreman said he thought they'd be done this week, so the building inspector could come out and authorize turning on the power. (Getting the power lines extended had been a process, too.) Then Ben and Alyssa could move in.

"Most of what we've got now is cleaning up and seeding the lawn," the man said. "If the weather holds up, that won't take long."

Alyssa drove the short distance to the McCaffreys' home, and found Mitch, as expected, in his new study with the magnificent view of the opposite ridge. It was going to be spectacular in a few weeks. She pulled up a chair beside him as he punched in the connection, using the secure device provided by the Defense Department. They saw Fred Hutton's face appear on the screen, his wide brown face smiling.

"Good morning," Hutton said. "I understand you have something to report."

After returning his greeting, Mitch said, "We do, Major." He quickly told Hutton, their DIA "handler," what he had sensed at the football game, and which had been confirmed by Rob and especially Samantha.

"I wasn't there," Alyssa put in. "Ben and I were still on our honeymoon. But you know how sensitive Samantha is. Mitch is pretty receptive, too. Rob not as much, but if he says he felt it, he did; and that shows the vibes from this boy are pretty darned strong."

Hutton had listened without comment, and his voice showed no emotion when he asked, "What do you know about this young man?"

"Not much," Mitch said. "He's a senior and started getting a reputation in football last season, but I didn't see any of the games last fall. Diana did, but didn't pick up on anything. We don't know the family, but I haven't heard anything bad about them.

"I will say the kid is freakishly strong and a helluva young football player."

"Did you ask Diana?" Hutton asked.

"I did. She said that she doesn't always notice her witch sight, when there's a lot of background emotion, and if she's distracted. She took the boys to games last year, and her ex-husband was with them, so I'm sure she was distracted."

"I met the boy's girlfriend," Alyssa said. "Actually, I already knew her, but I didn't know she was dating the Martin boy then. Sometimes I help a woman here in Martintown who teaches gymnastics. I went yesterday, so I could get in a workout myself.

"The girl's name is Eva Martinez. She's nice and quite pretty. Latina on her dad's side. Not a bad gymnast, either, considering she's only had lessons for a couple of years.

"Her classmates kept asking about Doug, since he'd done so well Friday night. I asked Eva a few questions, but couldn't be too obvious. He's an only child. His mother is a nurse and his dad works in IT for Simmons. That's the company Ben's law firm uses for IT and security. Mitch and Diana use them, too, don't you, Mitch?"

Mitch nodded. Where the kid's father worked was interesting but not a significant data point.

Hutton was silent while he jotted a few things on a note pad.

"All right," he said when he'd finished. "This is an interesting report. Thank you. We'll have it under advisement. You all just keep your eyes and ears open, and report if there's anything significant."

"So, you don't want us looking deeper into this?" Alyssa asked. She supposed her voice betrayed her surprise.

"Not at this time," Hutton said. "If we need anything else, I'll let you know. As I said, contact me if anything new comes up."

"There's one other thing you need to know," Mitch said. "I almost forgot. Monica Gilbert was at the ball game. There's a good chance she picked up on the boy's Talent."

Hutton frowned. His fingers drummed his desk top as he thought. Monica Gilbert had been a thorn in the sides of a lot of people for a while. Finally, he said, "I see. Thank you. But…no additional instructions at this time, except to keep her on your radar, too, and report her activity if it affects this boy."

When the meeting ended, Mitch closed the screen on the device, and turning to Alyssa, said, "Well, that was odd. Didn't you think?"

Alyssa cocked her head and answered, "Yes, but I'll tell you what it wasn't."

"What's that?"

"He didn't act surprised."

Chapter Eleven

MARTINTOWN, NORTH CAROLINA, AUGUST 2022

MONDAY
MONICA AND DANNY MAKE A CONNECTION

Monica Gilbert was sitting at her breakfast table, drinking coffee and nibbling on an English muffin with strawberry preserves, when a ping on her secure phone told her that Special Agent Dennis Springfield wanted a remote meeting. That was surprising; he'd made it clear yesterday that he didn't want any distractions from work. All the same, she didn't want to keep him waiting, and clicked the link to do the conference on her phone, rather than going for her tablet.

She couldn't see much except for Springfield's face and upper body on the small screen. It appeared he was in a hotel room somewhere and was alone. At least, she didn't see or hear anyone in the background.

"I've been thinking, Monica," he said without preamble. "And, by the way, sorry I was so abrupt yesterday. I guess I was a little distracted."

Monica made an effort to keep a smile from her face. The distraction, as she knew, had been a curvy and leggy brunette in a thong bikini. She waited for him to continue.

"For years," he said, "there's been a rumor that the DOD has been experimenting with cloning fossils. Oh, nothing as esoteric as dinosaurs as in *Jurassic Park*. Much more recent stuff, like mastodons and woolly mammoths. In fact, there's supposed to be a herd of mammoths somewhere in the Yukon.

"But more to the point, they're supposed to be working on cloning early humans, including Neanderthals. The idea is that they might be some sort of super-soldiers: Incredibly strong, much greater bone density than modern humans. There is also a rumor they've succeeded. Just a rumor, mind you. The DOD is very, very protective of its secrets and very, very jealous of its tech.

"But this guy you told me about makes me think he's what I've been hearing about."

"I see," Monica said, but didn't add anything. She knew there was more coming.

"The thing is," Springfield said, "we have to be really careful. You and I have already had our hands slapped more than once for what they call meddling with the DOD's assets and trampling on its turf. I can make some discrete inquiries, and I want you to look around, like I told you. But don't – Do. Not. – take any chances you'll get caught. I can't emphasize that strongly enough."

"I understand," Monica said.

"What we really need," Springfield said, "is a source that can't be traced very easily to us. I can't think of one right now. Maybe I'll come up with something. That's all for now. My…friend is waiting for me downstairs."

When the meeting terminated, Monica warmed her coffee and finished the muffin, contemplating as she chewed.

I need to be the one who comes up with something, she thought. I know I'm on double-secret probation with the Seventh Floor, meaning the executive offices of the Bureau. I need something to make them forget it.

But she couldn't think of what. She'd finish up her work e-mails and go downtown. Maybe something would come to her.

Danny Jarvis was at a dead end. Unless he got lucky, he wasn't going to find anything on the Martin family that wasn't already known; and he really shouldn't go around a small community like this asking questions without the subject's, or his family's, approval. Word was going to get back to them.

He supposed he'd better bite the bullet and call the kid's parents and ask for an interview. The boy was 18 and legally an adult, for most purposes, but he'd found from experience that if the youth was still in high school, going around the parents was a bad tactic. Or he could start with the kid's coach. That might be better, although the parents were still likely to be involved.

But by now it was close to noon, and he wanted lunch. All he'd had for breakfast had been coffee from the Comfort Inn where he was staying. He'd heard there was a new bistro downtown attached to a brewery. What was the name? Oh, the Woods Booger's. That was a local name for Bigfoot, he'd been told.

When he arrived at the restaurant, there was already a line coming out the door, with people sitting on outside benches or standing on the sidewalk, and a harried hostess coming out to place names on a list. When he finally had her attention, and told her he was alone, the young woman's face clouded.

"We're sitting singles at the bar, and we won't have anything for a little while," she said. "We could seat you quicker if you had someone to sit with you."

He started to say he'd wait, when he heard a female voice beside him say, "I'm game if you are."

He turned and liked what he saw. The woman was tall, with high cheekbones, a wide mouth, and a nose a little too long and sharp but not bad at all. Enormous green eyes, and long chestnut hair. She couldn't be much over 40, he thought, and probably not even that. Just a few years older than he.

Below the neck, she was, well, spectacular. Deeply bosomed with long legs, both shown to advantage in a snug-fitting green top and tan Capri pants. Thankfully, she was wearing flats, so they were looking each other in the eyes. In heels, she'd be taller.

Danny flushed, realizing he'd been staring. She helped him by smiling, extending a hand, and saying, "Monica Gilbert."

He recovered enough to say, "Danny Jarvis. And yes, I'm game, too."

The hostess was waiting, and her rolling eyes said she was exasperated. When Danny said, "Yes, miss, we'll take a table for two," and gave his name, she jotted it down, and said, "You'll be seated shortly."

And to Danny's surprise, that turned out to be true. They'd barely had time to introduce themselves more thoroughly when they were summoned to be seated. The table they were given in the bar area was small, and cramped between other small tables, but it would serve. Inside, the décor was, like so many establishments around here, rustic, and the restaurant was crowded and noisy. At least, he thought, no one was likely to overhear their conversation. Not that it mattered.

"Tell me, Monica," he said as they studied the menus, "what caused you to ask me to sit with you?"

She studied him for a moment before answering with a smile he could have sworn was lascivious, "You could say I'm hungry," she said. "Or you could say I don't like waiting. Or you could just say I liked your looks. All are true…Now what made you agree to sit with me?"

"Well," he said, fixing her eyes with his, "you could assume I'm hungry. Or you could think I detest waiting in line for anything. Or…you could just say I like your looks. Every word of that is true."

They laughed together, enjoying the flirting. Danny, who had dark brown hair that was slightly curly, a snub nose and a strong chin, and who kept himself in shape, did well enough with women that he believed her interest was sincere.

And she was. But she didn't tell him that she had the strong intuition that he would help her. It wasn't that she sensed he had any Talent beyond the smidgeon that most everyone had without realizing it. It was just a strong feeling. She'd learned from her training to accept such dim clairvoyance. It was one of her Gifts, but not a strong one. And not always reliable, she admitted. She'd see about this time.

Outside, they had time to tell each other about themselves. They picked up that thread, and learned they were both single, that Danny lived outside Charlotte and Monica had a home here in Martintown and a condo in Chapel Hill. She explained her job with the state Community College System and how she was working remotely for another day or so before she went back east.

"Did you happen to catch the big football game Friday night?" Danny asked, expecting her answer to be negative. But she surprised him.

"I did," she said. "I went with a friend." She didn't bother to mention Barry by name. She had another target at the moment. She frowned and added, "The ending made me sad. My dear old alma mater lost."

Danny noticed the friend had gone without being identified, and took that to be a good sign. He said, "I told you I'm a freelance writer. Well, I was here to cover the game. And I've stayed for a day or two to do some human interest follow-up on one of the more interesting players. But I'm having trouble getting background…Hey, maybe you can help me."

"I doubt it, Danny," she said, "But tell me who you're talking about and what's the problem you're having."

Danny explained his interest in Doug Martin and how his investigation into the circumstances of the young man's birth had hit a dead end. Monica cocked her head as she listened.

"I know it sounds crazy," Danny finished, "but I just have a feeling there's more to this kid than meets the eye, and I could find out what if I just knew more about where he was born and who his birth mother is. It's just a" – he shrugged – "feeling. Do you happened to know anything?"

Monica willed herself to hide her excitement. Fortunately, the waiter arrived to take their orders just then. Impulsively, she ordered a bottle of wine. When the server had departed, she said, keeping her voice even, "Not personally, no…But if you want to find out what's buried in that sealed file down in Raleigh, then I think I can help with that. I have…a connection or two.

"We'd have to keep it secret."

She didn't think this was a promise she couldn't keep. With her Power, or those of the other agent Dennis was sending, she could get her hands on those records.

Danny warmed to the idea immediately. He deliberately didn't ask about the legality of what Monica suggested. He knew it probably was illegal to access that information without a court order. But a reporter learned not to look a gift horse in the mouth.

"That's great!" he said. "Wonderful. Look, it will take me another day or so here to try to get some interviews. I guess the Comfort Inn will put up with me for one more night, maybe two. Then, if you'll give me a card or something with your contact information, I'll be in touch. I'd be glad to come to Chapel Hill. Or Raleigh."

"Sounds good," Monica said. "If I get your e-mail address, I'll email you my card. But…" Her smile was full of promise. "Forget this Comfort Inn stuff. You can stay with me. I've got plenty of room. And…I'll even cook dinner for you tonight."

Danny thanked her and eagerly agreed. The wine arrived and they toasted their meeting and their continued acquaintance.

Monica didn't mind cooking. Especially if she were alone when she did it and could use spell craft. She decided to make a pasta with seafood sauce. That required her to stop by a supermarket, but that was okay.

While the sauce simmered, she decided to try Special Agent Springfield again. He answered, but the irritation was back in his voice. Evidently, he was about to be "distracted" again. Well, so was she. She thought he'd have time for this, though.

"You know that unconnected source you wanted?" she asked, and without waiting for an answer, added, "I think I found one."

When she explained, the cloud fell from his face.

"You're right," he said, "this is perfect. An investigative reporter. Yeah, we'll have to give him some help, but he'll never know it's coming from us. You don't even have to tell him how you got it. In fact, you just pass the search to the agent I'm sending and step away. He'll use a fake identity. It should be easy to get that stuff. These state files aren't warded against the Power.

"The Agent's instructions will be to show what he finds to us – me, actually -- first. Depending on what it says, we can decide whether to pass it on to this – Jarvis? – guy, or whether we keep it. If we don't pass it on, our guy will just tell your...new friend... he couldn't get anything. But I think we'll likely let the story, if there is one, break and see what Defense does about it.

"Good work. We'll talk later."

After the call ended, the doorbell rang. No doubt it was Danny Jarvis. The evening was going to be entertaining.

Chapter Twelve

MARTINTOWN, NORTH CAROLINA, AUGUST 2022

INTERVIEWS

After the unexpected and promising (in more ways than one) lunch with Monica Gilbert, Danny decided to try to talk with the West Brainerd coach, Steve Watkins. He drove to the high school, using his phone GPS, parked in the designated visitors' parking, and told the security guard he was a journalist looking for an interview. He reflected that high schools didn't used to have security guards. Changing times, he supposed.

He was escorted to the principal's office, where he was given a chair. He didn't have to wait long before he was ushered into the office of a tall, thin man with sharp features and a receding hairline whose desk placard said he was Dillon Epley and was assistant principal. He presented his press card, and asked if he could speak with Coach Watkins.

"You didn't call in advance," Epley said. His tone was mild, but it was an accusation.

It was something Jarvis had heard before, and he knew how to answer.

"I know," he said. "I'm sorry. I…I've been visiting around the community getting background, and I lost track of time. I was just hoping the coach can spare me an interview. You have a good story here, and my stories and my blog get regional attention. I want to tell your story.

"It would be nice if I could talk with some of your student athletes, too."

Danny watched as Epley considered. The assistant principal knew Jarvis was offering good publicity. If it got out in the community that he had rejected that opportunity, people would be upset. Danny had dealt with school administrators before. He knew that rural school districts carried big chips on their shoulders. They thought they had good schools, and not just good sports teams. They chafed when they read about the bigger systems and larger high schools all the time. He'd get his interview, but likely a lecture with it.

Sure enough, Epley said, "I don't know about the students. They have class. But I think Coach Watkins has a free period coming up. I'll call him in a minute. But let me tell you: We have a good high school here. West Brainerd is not just a football team. We have good academics. Most of our kids go on to at least a community college for a trade, and a lot go to college. We have a fine marching band and a number of student organizations and clubs.

"If you do get to talk to any of our students, I hope you ask them about their overall experience here, not just the game last Friday."

"I promise you I will," Danny said.

Epley picked up his desk phone receiver and dialed a number. He spoke into the phone and nodding, hung up.

"You're in luck", he said. "Coach can see you now. I'll have my assistant take you to his office. It's in the gym."

Epley's assistant was a cute young woman whose name tag said she was "Mrs. Johnson." Jarvis enjoyed watching her butt sway inside her tight skirt as she led him down the hallway, out a door, and over to the high school gymnasium. Nothing was surprising. West Brainerd looked like thousands of other rural high schools across the state, and doubtless, he thought, around the country.

He had checked out Coach Steve Watkins online. Originally from Lenoir County, east and a bit north of here, he had won his letter at linebacker and on special teams from Appalachian State, but never started. He had worked his way up to head football coach at West Brainerd, where he'd coached for twelve years. His teams had been good, and made the playoffs a number of times in West's classification, but not until last year, when the team with Martin, Warren, Mason, Shade and others had gone to the quarter-finals, had the Redwings made any serious noise. If Watkins had ever had offers to move up to a bigger school, or to a college job, it didn't appear from anything Jarvis had read. He was now 47 years old.

Like that of most high school coaches in Jarvis' experience, Watkins' office was cluttered, photographs askew on the walls and trophies on shelves and in the floor, papers littered across the desk, which also featured a family picture of Watkins, his wife, and two kids. There was a computer on a credenza behind the desk, which could be reached by swiveling his chair. The office had a faint musky smell with an underlying scent of liniment.

Watkins rose to greet him, displaying the beginnings of the traditional coach's gut. He smiled, but Jarvis thought the smile a bit forced. Danny introduced himself and was offered a seat. He had to remove a stack of game programs to use it.

Danny decided to ease into why he was really here. He first asked about the game Friday, and got the standard coach-speak that was no different than what Jarvis had read in this morning's Martintown newspaper. Watkins was proud of his team. It was a real team effort. They had given their all, but they had a long season ahead. The East Burke team that was coming to town Friday was no slouch. Jarvis dutifully listened and made notes, or pretended to.

"Coach," he said, "I want to talk about some of your players. And then, if I can, I'd like to talk with them."

Watkins's eyes narrowed. "Okay. Which ones?"

"Let's start with Doug Martin. The Stump."

Watkins took a deep breath, and answered, "I'll talk with you about Doug, but I'm afraid he's off-limits for an interview today."

"Oh?" Jarvis allowed his brows to rise. "Why?"

Watkins sighed. "Mr. Jarvis –"

"Danny."

"Okay… Danny. Doug is worn out from all of the attention. At least three newspapers have called asking for interviews. He's had a barrage of college recruiters texting him and calling him and just showing up. N.C. State came this morning, and Clemson showed up at lunch. He's asked for my help. Jeremiah Billups over at Central is used to this stuff. Doug is not. Not like this. He's asked for my help. I'm going to talk with his parents this evening.

"We're going to have to put some order in this. We have nine more games. He is an 'A' student and has class. He has a girlfriend. We can't allow his life to be disrupted. I can maybe get you a telephone interview later. But not today."

Danny wasn't surprised. Nothing here was new to him. He decided to plunge on and learn what he could.

"I understand, coach. So, let's talk about him as a player, and as a young man. To start, what is his college position, in your opinion?"

Watkins didn't hesitate. "I think he can star at a high level at either line-backer or running back. This 'too short and too slow' stuff is bullshit, and I think you saw it. He hits like a ton of bricks. And he is not slow."

Jarvis nodded. "I saw him. He…well, he's about as broad as he is tall. I know it's an over-used term these days, but he's sort of…a freak."

"He is in the good sense of that word. He's a freak the way Derrick Henry is a freak. Or Rob Gronkowski."

"Do you know his family? What can you tell me about them?"

Watkins frowned. This was getting a little sensitive. "I know his folks. They're nice people, like most…all…of our kids' parents. But Darren and Lara Martin are not helicopter parents. They don't hang around practice. But they're supportive."

"Brothers and sisters?" Jarvis asked, although he knew the answer.

"No, he's an 'only.'"

"I heard over the weekend he's adopted. Do you know anything about that?"

Watkins' mouth worked and he colored. "Yeah, I've heard that. But it's not any of my business, *Mister* Jarvis, or yours, either. Look, that's personal, and I'm not going to talk with you about something like that. Understand?"

Danny was prepared for the reaction, and it didn't faze him. "I do. I was only curious. The young man really is quite a physical specimen. I was just wondering where he got it."

"Well, don't ask me," Watkins said, growling. Then he composed him-self. "As I said, he's off-limits today. And –" he jabbed a finger at Jarvis – "if you ever do talk with him, you better not ask any questions about being adopted or anything like that."

"Of course not," Danny said.

"But." Watkins leaned back in his chair. "I cancelled practice today. The kids need a rest. A lot of them live a pretty long car or bus ride away. Now,

Tommy Mason and Henry Warren don't live far off, and Tommy lots of times gives Henry a lift. Do you want to talk with them? After class?"

Jarvis considered. The kids might let something drop.

"Sure," he said. "Thanks."

Coach Watson insisted on being present for the interview with the two players, and found a small meeting room that smelled of wet socks to do it in. There was a table and a number of folding chairs. He'd rather have spoken with the young men only, but the coach being there, he'd found, was typical.

Both were juniors. Tommy Mason was just short of six feet and weighed about 190 pounds, much of it muscle. His face was slightly rounded, with a nose that had a little dent, and longish dirty blonde hair. Henry Warren was about the same height, but more slightly built; he looked to be about 170. Coach Watkins had told him that the prior year, Warren had been "155 pound soaking wet" and Mason only around 175. Both had worked hard in the weight room to get bigger and stronger, Watkins said.

The kids were smiling but fidgeting when introduced. Jarvis decided he needed to start slowly to put them at ease. So, he started by asking their grade in school, which he already knew; and moved from there to how they were doing academically. Their answers were sheepish, heads lowered; but they answered politely, and called him "mister."

Jarvis moved on to the Central game. He asked them what it was like to play in, and win, such a big game against a bigger school that had such well-known players, like Jeremiah Billups. They warmed up to that question. They agreed it was the biggest sports thrill they had ever known.

"But I knew we'd win," Warren said.

"Huh!" Mason said. "I didn't. But man, I wanted it. We all did."

Jarvis asked them what it was like to play against Jeremiah Billups. They looked at each other and laughed.

"Like trying to catch the wind," Warren said.

"Like tackling smoke," Mason added. "Smoke in the wind."

"But," Jarvis prompted. "You caught him, Henry. And I saw you hit him a few licks, Tommy."

"Not like Stump," Tommy said. "Man, Doug was all over the field."

"We'll talk about your teammates in a minute," Jarvis said, not wanting to appear too eager on that subject with Watkins in the room. "What about you two? Is college in your future?"

"Man, I hope so," Warren said.

"Yes sir," Mason said. "With or without football. Hopefully with."

"Are any colleges interested?" He asked them, although he knew the answer was "yes."

"Some," said Mason. "I talked some with a couple after the game. App State and Elon. I got texts from State and Carolina, and Virginia Tech today."

"About the same," Warren said. "The App State coach told me if I keep on growing and improving, they're gonna want me as a tailback."

They talked for a few minutes about colleges and probable positions. Then Jarvis thought it was safe to move on.

"Let me ask you about some of your teammates. Tommy, you mentioned Doug Martin."

They exchanged looks again. "Yeah, the old Stump," Warren said. "Man ever'body's gonna want *him*."

"Doug is a good friend of mine," Tommy said. "Really, he's friendly with everyone. He's a great player. Good guy, too."

"How does he like his nickname?" Jarvis asked.

More laughter. Finally, Mason said, "Well, he *tolerates* it."

"Likes it better than his first nickname," Warren said.

"Oh?" Jarvis asked. "I haven't heard of that. What was it?"

The two boys exchanged a look again and this time couldn't control their laughter.

"N.B.," Warren finally got out. "Stands for 'Neanderthal Boy.'"

Mason got his giggles under control, and explained, "That was year before last. Henry and I were just freshmen. Doug was a sophomore. The world history teacher, Mr. Conrad, made his class watch this show on the History Channel, or maybe the Discovery Channel. It was about Neanderthals and how strong they were, and big through the shoulders, and so on. Doug and Jack Abernathy were in that class, and Jack's a big cut-up. He started calling Doug 'Neanderthal Boy.'"

"But it didn't stick?" asked Jarvis.

"Nah," Warren said. "Doug didn't much like it. Claimed he's better looking than that. And he's such a good guy, and well, then 'Stump' came along, and ever'body liked that better."

Jarvis nodded in encouragement. "I see. Well, your friend sure seems as strong as a Neanderthal. Or he did Friday night."

"You ought to see him in the weight room," Mason said. "Benches 550 pounds. But I don't know where he gets it."

"Pardon?" Jarvis asked.

"It's not from his dad and mom," Tommy said. "Doug's adopted."

"Oh, I see," Jarvis said, and catching Watkins' warning look, decided he'd better not pursue it – now. He moved on to other players.

But he'd have to find that TV show.

Chapter Thirteen

MARTINTOWN, NORTH CAROLINA, AUGUST 2022

TUESDAY

By Tuesday, August was on its way out, but the heat was still oppressive. Practice had been lackluster, the team sluggish, causing Coach Watkins to call the team together at the end, and remind them that East Burke was coming Friday night, and beating Brainerd Central would mean nothing if the Redwings lost their first conference game. Doug wasn't too worried. He was confident the pep would return as the week wore on.

As he drove home, he was more concerned about how he was going to manage the recruiting process, which was getting insane. Coach Watkins was driving over to the Martin home after supper this evening to meet with Doug and his parents about managing the process. It wasn't as though he hadn't heard from colleges before. But the number of offers had more than tripled since Friday. College coaches were wanting him to visit their campuses. Some were wanting immediate commitment.

The first day in which prospects could sign binding acceptances of grants-in-aid wasn't until December. A "verbal commitment" didn't mean anything, legally. But most prospects kept their commitments, although many committed, de-committed, and then committed to someone else. Some of the coaches who had been in touch had told him he'd better commit now, because offers were limited, and if they didn't get a commitment, they'd move on to someone else. In essence, everyone who had been in a "wait and see" mode about Doug had decided they had waited long enough and seen enough.

Doug was flattered by the attention, but it also confused him. He certainly intended to go to college, and wanted to play football there, but he had a great deal to do in the meantime. He had practice and games. He had schoolwork. He wanted to spend time with Eva. He didn't need being badgered by recruiters.

He also didn't know where he wanted to go to college. His dad had got Doug interested in IT, but he'd received all of his training in the Air Force. His mom had a nursing degree from App, and he had visited the App campus a lot because it was close to home; but she wasn't pushing him toward the Mountaineers. Nor was Coach Watkins. Carson McCaffrey, who had supervised Doug when he worked at Simmons, had studied computer science at Carolina and computer engineering at Virginia Tech, and liked both schools. But he wasn't pushing, either.

Many young men who were being recruited made a big production out of the process. They tweeted every time they received an offer or visited a campus. They publicly announced their top five or ten schools. They scheduled press conferences to announce their commitments, or even waited until signing day to make the announcement public.

Doug wasn't into any of that. He had a twitter account, as well as one on Pinterest, but seldom used them. Many of his friends, athletes or not, seemed to live on social media. Even Eva was into it, but in a smaller way than many of her friends. Doug thought social media a waste of time. He had so many other things to do.

That evening, when Coach Watkins came and sat down with Doug and his parents around the kitchen table, they settled on the rules. All recruiters' visits at school had to go through Coach Watkins. Visits at home were not allowed except by appointment through Doug's parents. They couldn't do much about the text messages, but Coach Watkins would try to discourage phone calls.

To Doug, it was almost surreal to be sitting at the same kitchen table where the family had taken most meals as long as he could remember, the long counter, sink, and dishwasher to one side, the oven and microwave at right angles on the wall next to the garage door, the refrigerator and pantry door on the other side of the sink, wood-grain cabinets above and below the counter, the same table where he had frequently done his homework, talking about his future in this way. He kept thinking if he blinked, Coach would vanish. But that didn't happen.

"How close are you to a decision?" Coach Watkins asked him. "You know a lot of prospects have already committed."

This was true. Jeremiah Billups, for example, although Doug had heard Billups' announced commitment to the Tar Heels hadn't kept other schools from continuing to recruit him.

"Not very close, Coach," Doug answered.

Watkins didn't act surprised, but he said, "Doug, I think you need to visit some schools before you decide anything."

Doug winced. He had known this was coming. "But when do I have time, Coach. We have a game every Friday night, and we're going to be in the playoffs -- "

"We may not be if you guys don't practice better than you did today," Watkins interrupted. But he said it with a smile.

"I know, Coach, I know," Doug said. "But anyway, I don't want to be gone weekend after weekend. That's a lot of traveling. Oh, App would be easy, but I know them already. And I went to one game at Carolina last year, when they played at night. I went by Wake, Carolina and State one week-end last summer. And if I visit Wisconsin or Michigan, I'd have to fly."

"Well," Coach insisted, "you need to think about it. You get five official visits. You don't have to take them all. But you need to decide. If you don't sign in December, you have to wait until February. Some kids do that. Now how many of these schools will hold a scholarship for until then, I don't know.

"Anyway, think about it and I'll get with your folks and work out a schedule with the schools you pick out. We do have one open date."

"Doug, honey," his mother spoke for the first time since offering Coach coffee. "Your father and I are very proud of you. We want you to make the best decision you can, and go where you'll be happy. But Coach Watkins is right. You can't put a decision off forever. You know your dad and I will talk it over with you any time you want."

Doug knew he was getting good advice. He promised to think hard about what he wanted to do.

But he was still confused.

What will Eva say about it? He wondered. He'd call her later.

Eva was propped up on a big throw-pillow in her bedroom, reading from her English literature book, when her cell phone rang. She saw it was Doug and glanced at her bedside clock. 9:30, the clock said, so she could take it. Her father had forbidden telephone calls after 10:00, and it seemed to her he must lurk in the hallway outside her bedroom listening so he could enforce his rule. She thumbed the phone to accept the call.

Doug told her about the recruiting rules he, his parents, and Coach Watkins had worked out. She said they sounded fine to her. Then he shared his frustration with the process and his confusion about where he should go to college. She'd heard much of it before, but she listened patiently for a while. Let him get it out of his system, she thought. And she was sympathetic. She had a choice to make, too. She'd applied to several schools, some of which, such as Duke, she wouldn't be able to attend without a scholarship.

"Honey," she finally broke in, "welcome to my club, the club of confused and uncertain high school seniors. I don't know where I'm going, either. Dad wants me to go to App State. Mom's okay with that, but she likes it that I'm interested in Duke. But Duke is out unless they offer me a scholarship. And" – she sighed – "I like Carolina, too. And Western.

"I don't know. Except I want to study business and finance. I do know that."

"Coach Watkins wants me to visit some schools. He said it will be fun," Doug said. "But I've got all my games, and school, and…and I'd miss you."

Eva was glad they weren't using Face Time, because she was sure he'd see her frown, and she didn't want him to see it. He was sweet. But she said what she had to say.

"Doug, sweetie…we knew this was coming. We agreed we wouldn't try to follow each other somewhere. If we wind up at the same place, that'll be great. But if we don't…." She let her voice trail off.

There was a long pause, and then she heard him say, his morose tone breaking her heart, "I know. I know. But I didn't think it would start so soon."

She decided he needed encouragement. "Oh, cheer up," she said. "We've still got lots of time together. So what if you're gone for a weekend or two. You have been before. It's not the end of the world. We'll see each other tomorrow, and this weekend, and…"

He actually laughed. "Yeah, I know that, too. And…Eva, I don't mean to be a baby. Really. This recruiting stuff just got to be so much, so fast. It makes my head spin."

"It would make mine spin, too, sweetie," she said. "But think how lucky you are. You have choices most of us don't."

He admitted she was right. And then she had to hang up, because 10:00 o'clock was here.

CHAPEL HILL, NORTH CAROLINA, SEPTEMBER 2022

August became September, and Monica was back in her condo in Chapel Hill, and going to work at the office rather than online. Danny Jarvis was waiting to hear from her about what she had been able to obtain from the state archives, and she in turn was waiting to hear from whomever Dennis Springfield had assigned that job. Jarvis wouldn't get anything until she and Springfield had reviewed it – if then.

Her night with Jarvis had been a pleasant diversion. He was a more selfish lover than Barry Feldman; but she liked being selfish and aggressive, too, and had matched his ardent assault on her body with her own on his. He was also younger and more muscular than Barry, and she liked the way he felt against her and in her hands. He had texted her several times in the days since their encounter at her Martintown home, ostensibly to ask for an update on the Martin boy's birth, but with hints that he'd like a return engagement. She would grant him that, but not right away. She liked her men hungry.

Barry was away doing something, some hearing or other connected with the community college in Wilmington, so she was spending her nights alone. That wasn't so bad; she could use the evening to practice the skills she had learned at the Bureau's paranormal training center in Virginia, and to catch up on her professional reading for her day job. But she was starting to wonder when she would hear anything from whoever was doing Springfield's prying for him.

All she knew was to expect to hear from "Sam" when he had anything. "Sam," of course, would not be his real name, which she would never know. Plausible deniability, they called it. Finally, one evening, there was a call from a number she didn't recognize on the secure phone the Bureau had provided. She answered.

"Hello, this is Sam." The well-modulated voice was flat, standard American, the type you heard most of the time on television. His next words were the code words Springfield had given her. She answered with the response he'd also provided.

"I have a package for you," the voice said.

"Oh, good," she replied. "When can I get it? Where?"

"I can deliver it now, if you'll let me in. I'm standing right outside your building."

Monica pushed the button that would release the outdoor lock to the building, and waited by the door to her unit for the doorbell, which rang in only moments. She saw a tall, slender man with ascetic features who was clearly Indian or of Indian descent. Whatever his name, which she was never to learn, she very much doubted it was "Sam." He was dressed conservatively in gray slacks and a blue oxford cloth shirt under a Navy blue blazer. His only jewelry besides his wristwatch was a small, silver pendant on a chain around his neck. She felt a chill when she saw it was a statuette of Kali, the goddess of destruction as well as creation, the fierce aspect of Mahadevi.

The man's Talent was evident, and he made no effort to hide it. This was a powerful mage, for all his calm demeanor and preppy dress. She would treat him with respect, if not deference. She gave him a warm smile.

"Come in, Sam," she said. "I'm curious to see what you have for us."

"Sam" was holding a thin plain manila envelope. There couldn't be much bulk inside, but sometimes good things came in small packages. She closed the door behind him after he entered, and motioned for him to follow her. She led him to her home office, where she seated herself behind her desk and motioned him to a chair across from where she sat.

"Can I get you anything?" she asked. "Water? Something stronger?"

"Maybe in a minute, after I show you what I have," he responded. "Do you have coffee?"

"I can make you a cup," she said. "I have a Keurig."

The man smiled and said, "Thank you. I may take you up on that. But let me show you what I have. I have to tell you, it was hard enough getting it. The state Archives Department now scans everything and destroys the paper file. I had to hack into the system, and take the long way around, and when I got in, I found another layer of encryption for this file that didn't apply to the other files. But it was secured by Ward, so I used my Talent on that."

Monica was impressed. There weren't many magic users who could manipulate electronics. She knew, to her sorrow, that that asshole Mitch McCaffrey could do it, but it had always been beyond her ability. Her spells just seemed to slip off devices.

"What do you mean by the 'long way around,'" she asked.

"Oh, I had to make it look like a Russian hack," Sam told her. "But I got what there was to see. Let me show you."

He leaned forward over the desk, opened the envelope flap, and removed a thumb drive and about four sheets of paper.

"Copies of everything are on the thumb drive, and I've sent a duplicate of everything to our friend by secure transmission," he explained. She knew the "friend" was Special Agent Springfield. "You're supposed to check with him before you do anything, and keep this in a secure place."

She nodded. "I have a safe, and it's Warded."

The first sheet of paper was a docket sheet that recorded the date of the adoption of "Baby Doe, a/k/a James Douglas Martin" by Darren and Lara Martin in October of 2005. The date of birth was September 6th of the same year, "not in North Carolina" to Jane Doe (surrender approved in state of birth, which was not given), father unknown. Danny had found out that much in Martintown. The second sheet was a Court Order that said much the same thing. Monica noted with a wince that the counsel for the adopting parents had been Rebecca Johnson of Melton, Norville, Jennings & Johnson. That group had been a thorn in her side for the past three years.

The next sheet was simply an acknowledgment of receipt by the archive department. But the last sheet was pay-dirt. It was a birth certificate. Monica read it eagerly.

UNITED STATES MILITARY HEALTH SYSTEM

UNITED STATES ARMY MEDICAL CORPS

SPRUCE MOUNTAIN MEDICAL CENTER

CERTIFICATE OF BIRTH

The certificate recorded the birth of Baby Doe to Jane Doe on September 6th, 2005. The father's name was blank. It was signed by two Army officers who were also M.D.s.

"Where is Spruce Mountain?" she asked.

Sam spread his hands to each side.

"That's the curious thing," he said. "I can't find any mention or record anywhere of a 'Spruce Mountain Medical Center.' All of the military hospitals are listed online. This one isn't. There's a Spruce Mountain in Vermont, and one in West Virginia; but there's no Army hospital in either. Not that I found."

"This comes from West Virginia," she said, and noting Sam's raised brows, added, "I have a source."

"Sam" did not ask for more information. He realized, she supposed, that in this matter, it was better if no one person knew too much.

"Well," he said, "that's about it. Our friend will be in touch with you."

He smiled, showing brilliant white teeth. "Now how about that cup of coffee?"

Chapter Fourteen

MARTINTOWN, NORTH CAROLINA, SEPTEMBER 2022

THE SECOND GAME

As Coach Watkins had feared, there was some hangover from the intense game with Brainerd Central the week before, and the Redwings started the game a little sluggish. East Burke had been picked to be a conference contender, and they came out swinging. They were a team with only a few college prospects, and none at major college level; but they had a skinny quarterback named Sid Larkins who could run and throw, and was a nifty ball-handler, and two running backs who ran hard and had some speed. East's offense was a throwback to the veer schemes of the 1970's; and the Quarterback Larkins was slick in the way he ran and threw off of the option.

The West Brainerd team gave them some help early in the game. Henry Warren fumbled the ball when he was hit at West's 25 yard line, and that led to an East Burke touchdown pass. On the next series, Javon Shade slipped as he cut left while running an out pattern, and Les Bronson's pass, which would have been on target, was intercepted by the East Burke safety, who returned it for a touchdown.

The only bright spot in the first half came with only two minutes left. West Brainerd had the ball, third and one, on the East Burke 42 yard-line. The handoff went to Doug, who broke through the line, kept his feet, and ran into the end zone. The half ended with the score East Burke13 , West Brainerd 7.

Halftime was as unpleasant as Doug thought it would be. The whole team received a tongue lashing from Coach Watkins, who told them if they were content with the win over Central and mailed in the rest of the season, it was all right with him, which of course it wasn't. He said some other things that stung, too, and spared no one. Coach then modulated his tone, and he and the assistants calmly pointed out what the East Burke team was doing, and how West Brainerd's guys could clean up their act and turn the game around.

"Henry ought to be able to gain 200 yards, and score touchdowns…if somebody will block," Coach Watkins finished, his eyes sweeping the linemen, Doug, and Tommy Mason. "Their guys are quick, but not that fast; and Javon will be open any time we want to throw to him – if he doesn't fall down." He fixed his eyes on Javon Shade.

Doug resolved then and there that he was going to lay some hits, and knock some people down. He looked directly at Tommy Mason, and they nodded to one another. Then the team exploded out of the locker room and onto the field.

Doug kept his promise to himself and to the team. When he blocked for Henry or Tommy, he knocked people down. On defense, he tackled hard. He let his instincts take over. The East Burke option offense, which had not resulted in points in the first half, but which had burned clock and kept the ball away from West Brainerd, went nowhere in the second half. On one play, Doug, on a blitz stripped the ball from the East Burke quarterback and recovered the fumble.

Henry Warren didn't gain 200 yards; it was only 147, but he scored three times. Javon Shade didn't fall down again, and caught two touchdown passed from Les Bronson. When the final gun sounded, West Brainerd had a 42-13 win, and a happy locker room. Doug had carried the ball only one time, for the first half touchdown. But he didn't care. He had been having too much fun blocking and tackling.

He found another college coach waiting for him outside the locker room. This one was from South Carolina, which had missed sending someone the previous week. It was their running backs coach, a barrel-chested African American with short grizzled hair who had played running back at Auburn, he said.

"And I know you're an instinctive runner, Stump," the coach said, using the nickname without asking. "I was one myself. Look, we want you to be a Gamecock. We want you to carry the rock. And I promise you you'll see the ball more with us than you did tonight."

The coach, whose name was Johnson, tried to get Doug to commit to an official visit. Doug referred him to Coach Watkins, and politely excused himself. He wanted to see Eva.

And he did, but all he had from her there outside the locker room, in front of her parents and his, was a quick hug and a peck on the cheek, with a promise she'd see him Saturday night. Under the circumstances, that would have to be enough. He didn't want anybody's parents, including his, to start making unwarranted assumptions or asking too many questions.

At least, he thought, he'd seen two college recruiters there, both from small or "mid-major" schools, who wanted to talk with some of his teammates, including Henry and Tommy, even though they were only juniors. Even diminutive Javon Shade had a coach from North Carolina Central who wanted to talk with him. That was good. Doug didn't want all of the attention. He didn't even want as much as he had.

CORNELIUS, NORTH CAROLINA, SEPTEMBER 2022

Danny Jarvis spent Friday evening at home, surfing the internet and changing channels on the radio, keeping up with high school football scores. He hadn't found much to write about since his two pieces on the Brainerd Central vs West Brainerd game last week -- one on the game itself, the other on the West Brainerd players, including Doug Martin and the two guys he'd actually interviewed, Mason and Warren. He had talked with some college assistant coaches he knew and confirmed what he already knew – that Martin's star was rising, and its light was attracting attention to some of Martin's teammates. That wasn't going to be good for more than a paragraph on his blog. He needed material for a whole story.

He'd found the West Brainerd vs. East Burke game on the radio, and that had shown some promise. But reception was poor, fading in and out; and then he'd seen that the two teams had reverted to their expected forms in the second half, so that game wasn't going to be a story after all. He saw that Brainerd Central had taken out their frustrations on some no-name team, with Jeremiah Billups running for over 200 yards and five scores. But still another piece about Billups wasn't going to wow anyone. It was worth a sentence or paragraph on his blog, but that was all.

Danny wished he would hear something from Monica Gilbert. Hell, he'd like to *see* Monica again. That night at her house had been memorable. Danny had been engaged, once, but they'd broken it off. Never married. He had been between women for a while, so his encounter with Monica had been a good, good thing. She'd appeared to enjoy it, too; but he didn't fool himself into believing she didn't have other options that she might like better.

More to the point professionally, he really did wish she could find something in the state archives about the Martin kid's birth. He'd found that Discovery Channel show on Neanderthals the two kids had told him about, or maybe it was a different program with the same subject matter. When he'd seen the re-creation of a Neanderthal running into a wild bull with a long spear, he'd immediately thought about how broad-shouldered and barrel-chested young Stump Martin had sprinted down the field, football tucked under an arm.

He knew his thoughts were awfully far-fetched. But still...

He decided to try texting Monica again tomorrow, or maybe Sunday. It couldn't hurt.

OUTSIDE MARTINTOWN, NORTH CAROLINA THE SAME NIGHT

"You're awfully quiet tonight, honey," Eva's mother said. She was looking over her left shoulder back at her daughter, who was seated in the back seat of her father's car while he drove them home from the game; so, Eva knew her mom was talking to her and not her father.

She decided she'd better answer, and tell as much of the truth as she could.

"It's Doug," she said. "He's been sort of down in the dumps. All of these college recruiters are driving him crazy. They all want a commitment. Most of them want him to visit their campus."

"That ought to make him happy," her father said. "Isn't that what he wanted, a scholarship offer. And now he's got several. He ought to be thrilled with that. I would be, if I were in his shoes."

"He is," Eva said. "I think it's that he's feeling pressure from all of it. And it's on top of his games, and schoolwork."

"I do think it'll get better. He said Coach Watkins and his parents were going to help manage the process. But I – I think he wants advice from me, and I don't know what to tell him."

Her mother's over-the-shoulder look was shrewd. "You two aren't hung up on going to the same school, are you? I thought you'd decided against that."

"We had," Eva replied. "Well, not quite against. I mean if we did, it'd be great. But we've said we're not going base our decisions on where the other decides to go. I just think now Doug is looking for some easy way to make a decision. I don't want that to be me. I mean, how do we know we won't break up when we get there?"

"You don't," her father said. "And you stick to your guns on that. Y' hear?"

Eva said nothing, and her father continued, "I don't know why this is such a big surprise. Surely Doug and his parents knew this was coming, didn't they?"

"I don't think they expected it to be like this," Eva said. "Yeah, they knew some schools were interested. But this many, coming on so hard – I don't think anyone expected that. Doug didn't."

"Well, bless his heart," her mother said. "And yours. Well, things will work out. They always do."

Eva left it at that, and her parents seemed satisfied that she did. But she couldn't tell them what was really bothering her.

She was starting to want Doug, physically, pretty badly. It wasn't that he was getting more insistent. He wasn't. This was all her. She was starting to think she was going to lose control of herself, and that scared her.

The worst was there was really no one to talk with. The talk would scare her mom. Her dad would absolutely freak, and forbid her to see Doug, and that would be a scene. Her girlfriends wouldn't understand, and would make fun of her. She didn't trust her parish priest to hear it.

Her dad had an old CD by some country group called the Statler Brothers that he kept playing over and over. One of the songs had a line that said, "Things get complicated when you get past 18." Eva was going to turn 18 in a week.

She sure hoped that didn't mean things were about to get more complicated. She didn't know what she'd do if they did.

Chapter Fifteen
CHAPEL HILL, NORTH CAROLINA, SEPTEMBER 2022

Monica was having a lazy Saturday morning, but also a boring one. Barry was still down in Wilmington. For some reason, he hadn't returned to the Triangle for the weekend. She wondered if he'd found another woman, and couldn't decide whether it would be a good thing or a bad thing if he had. He was sweet, but she was getting a little bored with him. Jarvis had been a refreshing change.

She was caught up at work. She really should be practicing some new spells, but she didn't feel like it. A co-worker named Alice had invited her to go with her to the Duke football game, but she'd declined. She really wasn't much of a sports fan. And Alice could be a drag.

She'd go to the gym later today, but that could wait. She wound up on her sofa with coffee and a Danish looking for something to watch on Netflix. She would limit herself to one pastry. She had learned the hard way about the risks of overeating and using spell craft to control her figure. Damned McCaffrey.

Sometimes she liked to watch the paranormal shows to see how close they came to reality. Usually, not very close; but that made them humorous, at least to her. She found one and was soon chuckling.

Her secure Bureau phone buzzed. There was a text from Dennis Springfield inviting her to a teleconference in 30 minutes. She quickly texted her acceptance. This morning was about to get more interesting.

She went to her home office to do the meeting on her secure Bureau tablet, which had a bigger screen than her cell phone. When Springfield

CHAPEL HILL, NORTH CAROLINA, SEPTEMBER 2022

appeared, it was evident that he also was in his study at home and not in his office at work. He appeared freshly shaved and washed, though, and was dressed in a pale blue golf shirt.

Springfield got directly to business.

"It's taken me a while to decide what to do about the information 'Sam' uncovered," he said. "It's pretty sensitive. I'm positive this guy you saw playing football is a clone from the DOD project I told you about. There's no point in reporting what we found to Hutton over at the DIA or to anyone at the Pentagon. They'd just tell us to keep the lid on and warn us to keep their hands off their business. Hutton would probably report us to the Director, and we can't have that."

"So, we do nothing?" Monica asked. "I can just tell Jarvis we couldn't find anything so he might as well let it go?" She knew her disappointment came through when she asked.

Springfield let a slow smile spread across his face before he answered. "I didn't say that," he told her. "I didn't dare go to the Director, but I had a discrete conversation with the Deputy Director over our division, one that never happened and you know nothing about. Understood?"

"I do."

"Good. Here's the thing. That young man is potentially one hell of a special agent. Think about the Hulk. Better yet, Captain America. He'd also make one more Spec Ops guy for one of the services, but Defense hasn't grabbed him for that – yet. The fact that he has Power of some kind makes him better yet. We'd like to have him as one of our own."

He paused, evidently gathering his thoughts. Monica just waited, saying nothing, but she had the feeling she'd like what Springfield had decided.

"Now," Dennis said, "it's evident that Defense has decided just to observe this kid as he grows up. Let him play football, go to college, maybe even pro ball. Maybe they'll recruit him then, maybe they have another clone or two out there and he is some kind of control. We don't know, and really have no way to find out. Not at this time, anyway."

He paused again. Monica waited patiently.

"The boy -- young man, I should say -- is worthless to us if he's allowed to go on the way the DOD is handling this. If we wait until he's in college to recruit him, they'll beat us to him.

"But if he is outed, now, exposed, what do you think will happen? He won't be allowed to continue as he is. Every self-righteous asshole in the state will scream that it's unfair to allow him to compete with normal kids. Especially if we leak some suggestions that he's not really human."

"I know that'll disrupt his life," Springfield said. "But it can't be helped. Especially since our Division will be there to pick up the pieces. We'll be his saviors. So...I want you to leak what you have to that reporter, but I don't want you involved. All you're going to do is find a way to make sure he runs into 'Sam.'" His mouth twisted in a wry smile, and he added, "Not that he'll be called that, and he won't look anything like the agent who visited you. Our man has more than one face. Even I don't know what the real 'him' looks like."

Monica opened her mouth, but Dennis raised a hand to cut her off.

"Look, Monica. *I'll* know you get credit for this. The Division Chief will know. 'Sam' will know. But nobody else. The Bureau can't be seen to be connected with this. At all. Do you understand?"

She nodded. "Yes, Special Agent. I do." She used his title to convey she was serious.

"Good," Springfield said. "Now let's talk about how we're going to do it. It's important that your reporter friend gets most of what he reports on his own." He grinned. "Or at least appears to."

CORNELIUS, NORTH CAROLINA, SEPTEMBER 2022 LATE SATURDAY MORNING

Danny Jarvis was watching "Game Day" on ESPN when he received a call from Monica Gilbert. He took it eagerly.

After they exchanged greetings, and assured each other they both were well, Monica said, "Danny, I'm so sorry. I did my best, but I wasn't able to get anything for you out of state archives. I did my best, but all my contacts struck out. I was hoping one of them could call in a favor. But they all said it would take either a court order or a request from the young man or his family to obtain the file. Like I said, I'm sorry."

"Well, thanks for trying," Danny said, trying not to sound disappointed but not succeeding. He had been hoping for a reason to go to Raleigh, so he could see her again. And then she gave it.

"Tell you what," Monica said. "The least I can do to make up for flaming out is to buy you a nice dinner. Can you come to Chapel Hill this evening, by any chance?"

Boy, could he ever. But he kept the eagerness out of his voice when he said, yes, he could make it.

"Oh, good," she said. "Let's see. I don't feel like cooking tonight, so let's meet at *Chez Richard*. It's my favorite French restaurant. We can have a nightcap at my place and you can stay over if you want."

Better and better, he thought. "Sounds great," he said. "What time?"

"Let's say we meet at six, in the bar. They have a very nice bar. I do have a meeting at the office this afternoon, and if I'm late, you'll be comfortable. Be patient. I'll be there."

Danny thanked her and they hung up. He hadn't showered or shaved, and he'd have to do that, and throw an overnight bag together. But he had plenty of time to do that. It wasn't a bad drive.

Tonight was promising. It almost made up for not getting information on Doug Martin. Almost.

CHAPEL HILL, NORTH CAROLINA, SEPTEMBER 2022 SATURDAY EVENING

Danny had no trouble finding the restaurant, which was in a shopping village off Highway 54. Entering, he saw the restaurant was airy and open, modern in décor, with no effort to look like a French inn or farmhouse. He liked that.

He walked to the hostess stand, and told the woman there that he was meeting Ms. Monica Gilbert in the cocktail lounge, and thought she had a table reserved for later on. A young woman in a severe black pantsuit and white blouse told him, after checking her list, that Ms. Gilbert had reserved a table for 7:15, that she had not arrived, but that he was welcome to wait in bar, where seating was first come, first served. She pointed directions.

Danny found the bar crowded. Looking around, he did not see an empty seat. He was about to leave and wait outside when he saw a man he didn't know, who was sitting alone at a round high-top table with two high chairs, one empty, waving at him, and then motioning him to approach.

Danny walked up to the table warily. He wasn't there to meet a new best friend, of any sort. As he approached, he found a man a bit younger than he, lean with longish dirty blonde hair, wearing wire-rimmed glasses with tiny lenses, and dressed casually in cargo shorts, sandals, and a purple acrylic golf shirt with "ECU" and a pirate logo on its right breast.

"I saw you looking around for a seat," the man said. He spoke with a slight accent Danny thought might be Eastern European, but couldn't place. "You're welcome to the other seat here."

"Thanks," Danny said, "but I'm supposed to meet a friend here. I can just stand or wait outside until she arrives." He made sure to say "she" just in case his would-be benefactor had a wrong idea.

"Not a problem," the man said. "I will not stay long. When she comes, she can have my chair."

Danny decided the guy was just being nice and sat in the untaken chair. A waiter approached and he ordered a draft beer.

"Jeremy Jones," the man said, extending a hand. Danny saw he had been sipping from a glass with a clear liquid over ice and a twist of lemon. He didn't think the guy's name should be "Jones" and probably wasn't. Danny hadn't missed that "J" in "Jeremy" had a faint "Y" sound when the man said it. But he took the hand and gave his name.

"Meeting a girl friend?" Jeremy asked.

"Ummm," said Danny. "Not exactly. But I hope at least a friend."

"Ahh, I understand," Jones said. "High hopes, eh?"

Danny nodded agreement. "High hopes," he repeated.

"Well, good luck," Jeremy said, sipping his drink. Then he said, "So, Danny, what do you do? For a living, I mean?"

Danny saw no harm in telling him.

"How's it going?" Jones asked.

"Fine," Danny said, "although right now I'm a little frustrated because I can't get information I'd like to have."

"Really. What sort of information?"

Danny considered. Was there really in harm in saying what he was trying to find out? He decided there wasn't, and explained.

Danny's beer arrived, and he told the waiter to open a tab. When he turned back to Jones, he found the man regarding him intently.

"You know," Jones said, "I just might be able to help you."

Danny was immediately suspicious. "Now just how could you do that?" he asked. Jones did not appear to be any sort of state government insider.

"Oh, by doing what I do," Jeremy said, finishing his drink and motioning the barkeep for another. "I'm a hacker, and a damn good one, if I do say so myself, and I do. I could give it a go. For a price."

Danny was suspicious. He could imagine the man taking his money and disappearing. In fact, that was the most probable outcome.

"Oh, I don't know," he said. "How much money are you talking about?"

"One thousand dollars."

Danny could afford that much, but he didn't want to be scammed; and this looked like a scam.

"That's too steep," he said. "I wouldn't pay until you produced something, and then only if I could use it."

"Oh, come now," said Jones. Then he paused, cocked his head, and said, "Look, I know you don't know me; and I can't give references. The ones I could give would have to kill you. But I'll tell you what. I'll offer you this: Five hundred on delivery, after you've inspected what I've found. And five hundred in addition if you get a story out of it. What could be more fair than that?"

Danny considered. This actually didn't sound bad, although the part about killer references was disquieting. Still, he couldn't see any harm in letting this guy try. It bothered him that what Jones was suggesting was illegal. But he wouldn't have to disclose his sources. There was a shield law for journalists.

"O-kay," he said slowly. "I'll bite. What will you need to start?"

Jones didn't hesitate. "I'll need names and dates, so I can narrow the search. And I'll need your mailing address, your e-mail address, and your cell phone number. You'll get instructions on how to get the money to me. We'll arrange a drop, or a post office box I can rent under another name, and do it in cash. No paper trail."

Danny nodded. He had to admit it made sense.

"All right," he said, we'll do it." He gave Jones his contact information, and received instructions on where to e-mail the information he had obtained from the clerk's office. Jones said the e-mail address was not traceable.

"In the Dark Web," he explained.

"Jeremy Jones" left after finishing his next drink, promising results as soon as possible. Danny saw him pass Monica, who was on her way in as Jones was on his way out.

Danny stood. He and Monica hugged and she gave him a peck on the cheek. "Who was that guy who had been sitting with you?" she asked.

"Don't you know him?" he asked. This couldn't be a coincidence. Then again, maybe it could.

Her brow furrowed with a frown. "Why no," she said. "Why should I?"

"No reason," Danny said. "I just thought you might. Anyway, he's just some guy who let me sit with him."

She didn't ask for more information. And Danny wasn't about to tell her.

Chapter Sixteen

CORNELIUS NORTH CAROLINA, LATE SEPTEMBER 2022

THE PACKAGE

The next Wednesday afternoon, Jarvis returned to his modest town-house condo after having driven the short distance to Charlotte to interview the head coach at UNC-Charlotte. It had been a pretty vanilla interview, although Danny had asked some questions about how the coach was going to move the program forward. The answers had been fairly standard, following the basic theme of "we're just going to outwork everyone else."

Still, he would get a column out of it to go out on *Tar Heel Sports Weekly's* online edition, and it would probably get picked up by the Associated Press, too. He'd mention it in his blog. It wouldn't be a scathing column, because writing those was how you got your access cut off by the school. It had been one of those "it's a living" days. He was attempting a book about his life as a freelance sportswriter, and had spent the early morning at home, working on that project without making much progress. He was sure he had a book in him, but he really needed a better subject. He suspected few would find his life very interesting. Sometimes, he didn't himself.

What he needed was a breakout story.

Danny had thought about stopping for dinner, but decided not to. He didn't want to eat out alone this evening, and heating a frozen dinner, spaghetti and meat balls or something, would do him fine. When he pulled into his driveway toward his single-car garage, he noticed a package setting on the front door step to the condo. After parking, he walked around to get it. It was a UPS delivery, addressed in block printing, with no return address, but a label that said the package had been placed with the delivery service in Greensboro. The package was fairly bulky, but it wasn't heavy.

He felt a thrill of excitement. He hadn't ordered anything from anyone. Could this be from Jeremy? Already? He had already retrieved mail from the box outside, and placing it on the package, picked it all up, swearing under his breath when envelopes fell off while he fumbled for his house key. He resolved to calm down and be more methodical. He unlocked and opened the door, and picked everything up and carried the package, with mail stacked on top to the kitchen counter.

He turned on the lights, and deciding to be methodical, poured a glass of wine, sat at the counter, and tackled the mail first. Most of it was junk, as usual. There were a couple of bills, which he sat aside to pay later. No personal correspondence, but he hadn't been expecting any. No one wrote letters anymore, what with e-mail and social media.

Only the package remained. His hands trembled, just a little, as he used his pocket knife to get it open. Under the box, he found another box, and inside that, still another, thin and flat. Opening the third box, he found a slender manila envelope. There was no label on the folder, nor was it sealed. The flap had been closed without adhesive or fastening.

Opening the envelope, the first thing he found was a folded sheet of plain paper with his first name spelled out in letters that had been clipped from a magazine and pasted. He set it aside while he looked at the remaining sheets. There was a docket sheet like the one he had already copied in Martintown. There was a court order that provided little additional information. Reaching the final sheet, his eyes widened. It was the birth certificate.

But all this raised more questions than answers. What were the Martins doing adopting a child born in a military hospital? Where the hell was Spruce Mountain Army Medical Center? Who were the doctors? Could they be located? And who was Jane Doe? That was odd, if the story that the birth mother was some sort of relative was true. Wouldn't it?

He decided he'd better see what was on the folded sheet of paper. He unfolded it and found printing, all in capital letters,that had been cut and pasted like the lettering on the fold. He read it twice, and a third time for good measure, feeling his heart rate quicken with each reading.

"RUMOR HAS IT THAT THE DEFENSE DEPARTMENT HAS BEEN EXPERIMENTING WITH CLONING BABIES WITH DNA FROM EARLY HUMAN REMAINS, POSSIBLY INCLUDING NE-ANDERTHALS. WHERE? YOU CAN FIGURE IT OUT."

Beneath the message, there was additional lettering that gave a post office box in Mount Airy, and another in Salisbury, but no name on either. That was evidently where he was supposed to send his checks.

Danny realized that the documents he'd been sent had not been obtained legally. Whoever had sent them, and Danny was willing to bet his real name was not "Jeremy Jones," was covering his tracks. He was also willing to bet that the only fingerprints anyone would find on the package and its contents were his own, and on the outer "shell" those of UPS personnel, and that the P.O. Boxes were opened under other assumed names.

But that didn't concern him too much. He didn't have to use these documents if they lead him to something else; and even if he did, there was a legal privilege of reporting. It would be someone else's problem to figure out who "Jeremy" was. Danny didn't care. But could he use this? Only, he decided, if he was able to follow the lead and learn something else that was fit to print. That meant he had to accept the challenge to figure out where Spruce Mountain Army Medical Center was located.

Danny took his phone from the holster at his belt and did a quick search. He couldn't find Spruce Mountain Army Medical Center. There was a "Spruce Mountain" in Vermont. That could be it, if the birth mother was a relative of the Martin kid's mother. Wasn't she from Boston, originally?

Wait a minute, he thought. If this kid was a clone, the story the birth mother was a relative had to be false. Where had the lady at the café said they'd gone to get the baby, eighteen years ago? West Virginia, wasn't it? Yes. Definitely West Virginia.

Sure enough, there was a Spruce Mountain, West Virginia, in Pocahontas County, right on the state's eastern border with Virginia. The closest town was Bartow, which was just a wide spot in the road. The county seat was Marlinton, which was no more than a wider spot. But that's where the court records would be. Snowshoe Ski Resort was close, so there should be some hotels in the area, including some that fit his budget.

From where he lived in Cornelius, it wouldn't be a bad trip to Pocahontas County, West Virginia. Not at this time of year. He could get on Highway I-77 not far from where he lived and take it most of the way. He could go tomorrow, right after he filed his interview with the UNCC coach, which he could do tonight or early in the morning. He'd find a hotel online first. That shouldn't be a problem. He'd stay a night and return Friday. He'd know by then if there was anything to find out. And he could always come back if he needed.

The trip would dovetail nicely with the rest of his plans. He was going to cover the Appalachian State football game in Boone on Saturday. He'd picked that game because he'd learned the Martin kid was going to Boone Saturday morning to "unofficially" visit the school. That meant he wouldn't get the full tour with a player-host and all that stuff; it couldn't be done on a game day. But Doug would sit with other "unofficial visitors" at the game, and meet the coaches before kick-off. That information hadn't been hard to find. Colleges announced in advance who would be visiting for PR purposes. Even if there was no information on Martin to be had on Saturday, App State was always good for a human interest story about an athlete or two who had been overlooked by "name" colleges but who were over-achieving at App. It was a recurring theme with them, one that the school promoted.

It would be pretty easy, Friday afternoon, to take I-77 back down to Winston-Salem and then take Highway 421 to Boone. The weather was supposed to be good, and he already had a place to stay in Blowing Rock. He was used to a lot of driving. In his job, it came with the territory.

A little reluctantly, he decided "Jeremy" had earned the first $500. He'd pay by cash and send it to the first P.O. Box addressed to "Owner." If he left early enough, he could do that on the way out.

Danny's heartbeat had slowed, but he found it racing again. Could this be the big story that would make his career? He couldn't tell yet. But it was worth a trip to West Virginia to find out. He had lost interest in his wine, and in dinner, while studying the contents of the package; but now he was hungry. He placed the papers back in the envelope and rose to find a frozen dinner.

He had a feeling this was going to be big.

MARLINTON, WEST VIRGINIA, SEPTEMBER 2022 AT THE COURTHOUSE

Danny Jarvis yawned as he pulled into the parking lot of the Pocahontas County courthouse in Marlinton. He had had a busy evening yesterday;

and even though the digital clock in his Toyota Camry said it was only 3:15, already a busy day today.

The first thing he had done Friday evening was to write and file his story on the Charlotte coach. With that out of the way, he decided he should do some more online research. He learned that in West Virginia, adoptions were handled in the Circuit Courts. That was where he would start. He also learned that land records were kept by the County Recorder's office, and land tax records, including maps, were kept by the County Tax Assessor's Office. He was delighted to find that tax maps could be viewed online.

Sure enough, there was a sizable tract right up against the Virginia line that was labeled "Federal Land – not subject to tax." It appeared that the government had acquired it in 1954. He couldn't find the deed because the electronic records in the Recorder's office didn't go back that far, but he doubted if it would tell him anything.

The Circuit Court also had electronic records, and these did go back to 2005. But the listing for "The Matter of the Adoption of Baby Doe" in September of that year had only the entry, "SEALED; certified copy transmitted by Order to Brainerd County, North Carolina." Beneath that were the names of the judge and counsel for the Petitioners, and he jotted them down. An online search for their names got hits, but apparently both were dead. He'd verify that, though.

Next he decided to look up the two doctors who had signed the birth certificate. But he couldn't find anyone who he was sure was either. He didn't want to dig deeper, at least right now. Even if he found them, they wouldn't tell him anything, and would probably report the inquiry to someone in the Army. He didn't want that. He might have to tolerate it later.

He rose early Thursday morning. Online, he found a modest but clean-looking hotel outside Marlinton and reserved a room for one night. In his line of work, he always kept an overnight bag mostly packed. Because he wouldn't be back until Saturday night or Sunday, he threw in some extra clothes. The envelope he'd received yesterday went in on top of the clothes and toiletries. He grabbed his laptop, and was ready to go.

He stopped at the post office, where he mailed the cash payment to "Jeremy Jones." He didn't include a return address. The postal clerk gave him a quizzical look for wearing latex gloves, but he wore a cloth mask, too; and the man probably thought he was another COVID paranoiac. That was good. He didn't want to leave a trail.

The drive up Highway I-77 past Fancy Gap, and then over and up past Bluefield was pleasant. He passed through pretty mountain scenery, especially in West Virginia. The drive would be still prettier in about a month, he reflected; there wasn't much autumn color yet. It still felt like summer, even though the calendar said fall had arrived.

The state roads over to Marlinton were good, although not interstate highways, of course. But by the time he parked, he needed a stretch of the legs and wanted a beer, which he wouldn't get here at the courthouse. Maybe later, he promised himself. No, definitely later, after he'd finished his business here, he promised himself.

The courthouse was old, but obviously had been recently renovated. He had no trouble locating the office of the Clerk of the Circuit Court. When he went in, he saw it wasn't busy. He was immediately greeted at the counter by a pretty woman who gave him a big smile. She had short-bobbed dark hair, large brown eyes, and a prominent bosom that strained her white blouse and probably need underwire support to make it so upright. She was carrying perhaps ten pounds more than she needed, but the effect was still pleasing.

"Hello," she said, "how can I help you?" She pronounced "help" as "hep." Danny knew that many women found him attractive, and had found it didn't hurt his inquiries as a reporter that they did. He grinned back at her.

"I'm looking for records on an old adoption," he explained.

At his request, she pulled out an old, dusty docket book and helped him find the entry. As expected, it mimicked what he had seen online.

"I don't suppose there's a court file I can see?" he asked.

She shook her head. "Not without a court order, and you won't get one, unless you're the adoptive parents or the child himself. He'll be eighteen now, you know…Why do you want to see it?"

Danny decided to be truthful. "I'm a sports reporter, and I believe this child is now a high school football star down in North Carolina. I'm looking for background."

"Why don't you ask him? The boy, I mean."

Danny still grinned, but he knew it was rueful. That was okay, he wanted her to sympathize.

"I can't get to him past his coach," he said. "The coach is being ver-r-ry protective…I don't suppose I could talk to the judge, or maybe the lawyer?"

The young woman's smile was a bit sad. "They're both dead," she said, "and I doubt they'd talk with you anyway. But…Old Seth Blaylock's daughter Janice took over his law practice. She might still have the file. But I doubt she'd show it to you. You can ask. She's three doors down the street."

By this time, another woman, plump and iron-haired in a gray slack suit, had walked up and was listening. She extended a hand to Danny over the counter.

"I'm Frances Wainwright," she said. "I'm the clerk. I heard what you've been asking, and Sarah here has told you the truth. We can't show you anything, and Janice Williams – used to be Janice Blaylock – won't. Attorney-client privilege still applies."

The clerk didn't sound unfriendly, Danny realized, and clearly wasn't busy. Maybe he should push a little. Very gently, though.

"Were you the clerk here at the time of this adoption, Ms. Wainwright?" he asked.

"I was the Chief Deputy, like Sarah is now," the woman said. She paused, clearly thinking something over, and continued, "I do remember it, because it was so unusual."

"Oh? What made it unusual?" Jarvis asked, mentally crossing his fingers.

"Well," the clerk said, "first off we don't get many transfer of cases to other courts out of state. I can only recall a couple of others, and I've been here for…a while." She smiled. "Then what was very unusual was that the baby was born on that base or whatever it is over near Bartow. It's the only birth from there we've ever had. It was a charity case, I guess. I don't know."

"What base is that?" Danny asked.

Wainwright threw up her hands. "Who knows? I don't. As far as I know it doesn't have a name. Really hush-hush."

Sarah chimed in, "We see vehicles coming through town on the way in or out, but they never stop. I haven't been over there, and if you try to go, they'll invite you to leave. There's only one way in, and it's in the side of a mountain. I guess everything is underground."

"What do they do?"

"No one knows," Wainwright said.

"One of the guys I used to date thinks they have flying saucers in there," Sarah said.

Her boss snorted. "I don't know where he got that. But if you're talking about Fred Smalley, Sarah, he's dumb as four o'clock anyway."

Danny decided to move the conversation off Sarah's ex-boyfriend.

"Did you know the birth mother?" he asked Wainwright.

"No," she said. "I think she was local, but I didn't know her. She was a pretty girl, but she had mousy hair. The baby was a red-head. I remember that….But I'll tell you who might know her."

"And that is…"

"Johnita Simpson, who still works over at the Mountain Grill. That's right outside town. You ought to eat there. Good food." Johnita has been waiting tables there for a good thirty years. She knows everything that goes on hereabouts."

"Does she ever," Sarah put in with a grimace that implied the Simpson woman knew things about Sarah herself that were better left unknown.

Wainwright smiled at that. "And yes," she said, "Johnita will share information. Ask for her, and tell her I told you to."

"I'll do just that," Danny said. "Thank you both so much. Here's my card." Sarah took it with a smile.

"I may be back," he promised.

"Oh, I hope so," Sarah said.

His answering smile held a promise he had no intention of keeping.

AT THE MOUNTAIN GRILL

Danny first tried the Williams law office, but it was already closed. He supposed that in a small town, a law office could close whenever the lawyer wanted. He wasn't too disappointed. Assuming the woman who had inherited the practice still had a file, she wouldn't show it to him; and she might decide to call her father's clients, who had been Doug Martin's parents, and tell them someone had been asking.

He decided to try Johnita Simpson at the Mountain Grill, which he'd passed driving into town and noted wasn't far from where he would be staying. It wasn't even 5:00 o'clock, but he was hungry. He hadn't bothered to stop for lunch, and the bowl of cereal he'd had this morning had already worn off. He hoped the place was open.

It was. The Mountain Grill wasn't very large, and from the age of the building had been in business for a while. But when he entered he found the dining room spacious and clean, with a distinct "steakhouse" feel, tables set well apart, all covered with red and white checked oilcloths. There was a modest bar along the far wall, with four beer taps, and a small selection of bottled spirits on shelves behind. There were two customers at the bar drinking beer, and chatting with an amiable looking middle-aged man in a white apron.

Johnita herself greeted him. She was clearly over 60, with a round cheerful face and hair that was nearly white. She, too, wore an apron over a mauve uniform. Her name tag told her name.

"Just one?" she asked. "For dinner?"

"Yes, and yes," Danny said. "Will you be my server? Frances Wainwright told me I ought to talk with you."

"Really?" the woman asked, and smiled. "The young ones usually ask for Julie."

She motioned to the other side of the room, where a young woman with long black hair that should have been in a bun, and whose uniform, unlike Johnita's, featured a short skirt and was tight enough to show a rather spectacular figure, was wiping down a table. But he saw Julie was about 20 at the most. Way too young for him, and he said so.

"You'd be surprised how many your age and older don't think so," the woman said. "Here, I'll get you a menu."

She took a laminated single sheet from a stand and led him to one of the smaller tables.

"Let me get your order, young man, and then I'll find out what Frances Wainwright said I could help you with. We won't be busy for a little bit," she said.

Danny ordered a draft Yuengling and then asked what was good.

"Honey," she said, "the special today is meatloaf, and it's good; but if you like steak you'll want the strip steak with grilled onions. Don't get fries. The mashed spuds are better. Today's vegetable is English peas."

"Then that's what I'll get," he said.

She returned with his beer in a mug in moments, and took a seat opposite him.

"Jack won't mind if I sit for a minute," she said. "Now, what's on your mind?"

Danny introduced himself, related his conversation with the clerk, and explained what he was looking for, which was information about the birth mother. Johnita was silent for an uncomfortable minute, as her eyes traveled to the ceiling. Finally, she looked back at him.

"Nobody has mentioned poor little Cindy Warfield in years," she said. "Yes, I remember her. Pretty little thing. She grew up in a little house, not much more than a shack, up on a mountain outside Bartow. Her momma and daddy died in a car wreck when she was no more'n ten. One of her aunts raised her from there, but they didn't get along.

"I knew her because my nephew Jim went to high school together, and he sometimes brought her here. He was sweet on her, but finally gave up. She always said she was getting out of Pokey County – that's what she called it – as soon as she could get the money to leave. Problem was, there weren't any jobs to get money.

"She told Jim one day, right after graduation, that she had a way out. She said she was going to sell a baby. He thought she was kidding. And then she just disappeared.

"She came in with Lawyer Blaylock for breakfast one day months later, carrying a red-headed baby. There was a nice looking couple with them. I guess they were gonna adopt the little thing. Seth told me to hold my tongue. Cindy was going to leave right after she surrendered the baby, and there was no use talkin' about her.

"I reckoned he was right, so I didn't. I didn't even tell Jim. Now all these years later, you come in with this. I never knew she had her baby over at that secret base or whatever it is over near Spruce Mountain. That's news to me. Who knows what goes on over there? I don't."

"Do you know how to find Cindy?" Jarvis asked.

Johnita shook her head vigorously. "I do not. She disappeared again."

"Could her aunt find her?"

"I doubted. They didn't get on. And Carrie Lynn – that's the aunt – moved away, too. I don't know where."

Danny wouldn't accept that, so he pressed her. "Johnita, someone has to know something. She had classmates. She dated your nephew."

The woman shook her head with a sad smile. "You don't understand. Cindy was …odd. No wonder. She lived up the side of a mountain. Her clothes were shabby. She went with Jim because he saw something in her and wouldn't take 'no' for an answer. I doubt she had any real friends, and she hated it here."

"Look," Danny said. "There has to be something…What about pictures? A yearbook from school?"

She sighed. "Jim may have a yearbook. I'll ask him. Tell you what. You leave your card with me and I'll call you if I hear something, or have something. You never know. Now, let me go see about your steak."

Johnita took his card, and returned with the steak in no more than two minutes. He thanked her and asked for another beer.

As he ate, he realized he owed "Jeremy" the other $500. He didn't have everything he wanted. But he had enough. Enough to start, anyway. He was already thinking about what he could say about "sources."

Other customers came in. One of them was Sarah from the clerk's office. She walked over and asked if she could sit with him. He said yes.

She wasn't Monica. But this might be another interesting evening.

Chapter Seventeen
MARTINTOWN, NORTH CAROLINA, SEPTEMBER 2022

ON THE ROAD BETWEEN BOONE AND MARTINTOWN

The road through the mountains from Boone to Martintown is a good one, but winding, as are all mountain roads. Darren Martin had to concentrate Saturday evening as he drove his wife and son home from their visit to Appalachian State. As he drove, he and Lara spoke softly about her plans to transition completely to teaching at Carolina Highlands Community College from her hospital work. She had taken her bachelor's and master's degrees at Appalachian online and by commuting so she could do that. Doug sat silent in the back seat.

Darren took notice of their son's silence. The boy had seemed preoccupied ever since they had said their thanks and good-byes to the App coaches after today's game, which Appalachian had won in a squeaker. He hadn't even wanted to stop to eat, claiming he wouldn't be hungry until they got home. Well, after the pre-game spread for visiting players and families, that wasn't surprising – except that Doug usually had the typical appetite of an active teenager.

"I think Doug's asleep," Darren said to Lara, keeping his voice low, so as not to wake the young man.

"Poor baby," Lara replied, looking over her shoulder at her son slouched in the back seat, his chin almost resting on his chest. "It's no wonder, after last night and today."

The previous evening West Brainerd had to travel to McDowell Central. McDowell had been picked in the upper division of the conference and had a solid team. The Redwings couldn't afford to overlook them. Doug had had a great game on both sides of the ball. He'd been all over the field on defense. On offense, Henry Warren, the starting tailback, had been knocked unconscious by a McDowell linebacker in the second quarter. The hit had been clean, but Coach Watkins didn't want to risk any further injury; so Doug, with some help from Tommy Mason, had been required to shoulder running the ball.

Doug's performance had surprised even his parents, who knew their son's physical prowess better than anyone. He had combined speed with power, running over tacklers when he must, and weaving his way through them when he could. He'd also blocked effectively for Tommy, and caught both of the passes Les Bronson had sent his way, one for a touchdown. They'd been proud to hear the stadium buzzing about their son as the game ended.

Then, this morning, the family had risen early to make the drive to Boone, where they met with the App coaches, other parents and their prospect-children, and even some reporters before the game. The reporters had not been fun. There was one, some guy named Danny Jarvis, who had cornered Lara and asked him where her son's freakish strength had come from. She had deflected the question by laughing and saying, "He works out constantly." But the question made her uncomfortable. It was as though the man suspected something. But he couldn't, could he?

Then they'd watched the game, which had gone to overtime, and had gone to the locker room afterwards to watch the Mountaineer team celebrate and have a final word with the coaches.

Now, the sun was low in the sky as they drove home. Even Darren and Lara were tired, and Doug was probably exhausted. No wonder he was sleeping, Darren thought.

But his son was not asleep. He had heard every word of his parents' conversation, including the part about him. Doug really was tired, and actually had dozed a little on the trip; but every turn, and every bump in the road, had snapped him awake, his mind immediately racing about everything going on in his life.

On the field, ever since the second half of the game against East Burke, he had resolved to trust his instincts, the sense of where the ball or the tacklers would be. He wouldn't ignore his coaching, but instead marry it to the sense or senses he didn't understand. That trust had led to his best game Friday night, even if McDowell Central was not, and would not be, the best team the Redwings had played or would play. He'd known he could run over most opposing players at the level he was playing now; but that wouldn't be true next year. Not all the time, anyway. He found he could cut and weave and dodge as well as use power. He'd surprised even himself.

But he had carried the ball, a lot. He'd also played every snap on defense until late in the game. When he woke up Saturday morning, he was still tired and sore; and he had the whole day ahead of him. So, yes, he was pretty exhausted, he admitted to himself. But he still couldn't sleep. There was too much to think about. Maybe it would help to share some of it with his mom and dad. He decided to try.

"Hey, Dad," he said, "I'm awake. I've just been thinking."

He had addressed his father, but it was his mother who responded.

"What about, son?" she prompted.

"Well…part of it is where I go next year," Doug said. "I've been accepted at App, and Carolina, but…I'm not worried about being accepted anywhere. I like App. It's close to home. I know the coaches. I like it there…" he trailed off.

"I hear a 'but' coming," his father said.

"I think it may be a little too close," Doug said. "I think I'd like somewhere a little farther off. But not too much farther off."

"How much is too much?" Lara asked, looking over her shoulder at her son, now sitting straight upright in the back seat.

"I don't think I want to go as far as Wisconsin or Michigan," Doug said. "I mean they're good schools and all, but…it's just too far.…I think I'm leaning to Carolina, but I want to see some other schools. State. Maybe Tennessee." His sigh was heavy, like a steam engine. "That means more visits."

"I think you might be too traditional and conservative for Carolina to suit you," Lara said.

His father spoke up. "That's something Doug will have to deal with just about anywhere, he said, adding, "Including App."

"I know," Doug said. "I can handle it. I can keep my mouth shut when I need to. But…Mom, do you want me to go to Appalachian?"

Lara snorted a laugh. "Because of the degrees I got online? No, son. That's not a problem…But tell me, Doug, you're not hung up on going the same place as Eva, are you?"

Doug took his turn snorting a laugh, but he realized it sounded forced. "I can't, Mom," he said, "She doesn't know where she wants to go…We've talked about it, and, well, it'd be great if it worked out we did go to the same college. But we agree we can't decide based on that."

Darren slowed and hit the turn signal for the turn that would take them from the main road to the road to their subdivision. "That's good," he said. "You two are very young, way too young to close doors just to keep dating. And let me tell you, if it is in the cards, you two will survive being separated."

"I know," Doug said.

"We just want you to make the choice right for you," Lara put in. "And your father and I are here to help…and listen."

"I know that, too," Doug said.

"Well," Darren said, "we're just about home. Son, has this talk made you feel better?"

"It has, Dad," Doug said, truthfully. But he hadn't shared the other thing he'd been thinking about. That was Eva, and not where she was going to college.

There are some things you just can't say to your folks, he thought.

THE WASHINGTON HOME

Marc and Tiffany Washington were having Rob and Samantha Ashworth for dinner Saturday, after which the men would watch a football game on television while Tiff and Sam went to a film they wanted to see, something Marc called a "girl flick," a term Rob found highly appropriate.

Everyone had worked this morning, Sam at her accounting office and the other three at Melton, Norville, Johnson & Jennings. Marc and Rob both handled litigation, but not the same types; and firm policy prohibited his wife reporting to him. So, Tiffany had worked with Rob to compile and label exhibits in one case, while Alexandra Tabarant (whom they knew to actually be named Aleksandra Tatarkiewicz, and to be Polish, not French, although most in the firm did not) came into the office to help Marc compile other documents to be produced in another, different, case.

They had knocked off work in time for Marc and Rob to play a round of golf and then watch some football, and for Tiffany to make her famous three-cheese lasagna. Samantha's contribution was to pick up wine and help slice vegetables and shred lettuce for the salad. Marc and Tiffany had bought a home between the Glen Arden and Maple Oak communities, in the same subdivision, they learned, where their client Mitch McCaffrey had lived during his first marriage. It was an older home, although recently updated, so everyone was seated in the separate dining room.

Over dinner, Marc and Rob discussed the West Brainerd football game from the night before, which they had driven over to Marion to watch. Rob had attended McDowell Central, but they had really gone to see Doug Martin. Tiff and Sam were not really big football fans, but they were interested in the latest report on the Martin kid, and didn't protest the conversation.

"The guy is just uncanny," Marc said. "He runs like Jim Brown or Walter Payton. It's like he has eyes in front, eyes in back, and an eye on each side. But he's got that Larry Csonka style to go with it."

"That's a good way to put it," Rob said. "Maybe he does have eyes all around his head."

"Oh, you don't mean that!" Tiffany said.

"I think I know what he means," Samantha said. "It's what we felt a few weeks ago. The guy has Talent. You can feel it from the stands. And it's some kind I've never felt before. Could you feel it last night, honey?" She turned her eyes to her husband, who was draining a wine glass.

Rob swallowed and said. "I'm nowhere near as Sensitive as you, sweetheart, but I could feel it."

Marc and Tiffany said nothing. They knew what Rob and Sam were talking about, but hadn't experienced it. It was like being blind and hearing someone discuss colors.

"Well, I'll tell you this," Marc said. "The boy is damn good. I just hope some wiseass federal agency doesn't come in and mess up his life.

"Hell, I want to see him play football."

Tiffany's brown eyes, already large, widened. "Do you think that might really happen?" she asked.

"Yes!" said Rob and Sam together.

Tiffany silently reached for the wine bottle. There were things the Ashworths knew that she didn't, and she was glad she didn't.

SUNDAY EVENING
OUTSIDE MARTINTOWN

There were places for young couples to be alone around Brainerd County, Doug reflected, but you had to give it some thought. That is, if you were not completely open-ended about making out in front of people. He and Eva were not, although plenty of their friends were. They made out, or sneaked into bedrooms or bushes for more, at parties or picnics or whatever.

These events were also associated with drinking and frequently with drugs. Doug and Eva did not frequent these gatherings; and when they did, they did not stay long. Neither could say they had never tasted alcohol, but they didn't drink enough to matter. (Well, once Doug had, on a camping trip with some teammates, when Eva wasn't there. But he wasn't anxious for a repeat performance.)

They realized some of their friends thought them prudish, or even stuck up. But this was the way they both wanted it. Private activity was best done in private.

The time-honored way for couples to be alone was in a parked car. There were various places for that. One of the favorites was on a graveled lot on a ridge overlooking the lake. The issue with using it tonight, after they'd shared a pizza at Mario's, was that it was still early. It still didn't get dark until later in the evening, and wouldn't for about another month.

But that was where Eva had wanted to go. She hadn't wanted a movie after pizza. "That will make it too late for us to talk after the show is over," she'd said. "And I want to talk, you know, just to catch up."

That raised Doug's antenna. He sensed that something was bothering her. Was it him? He didn't think he'd done anything wrong. Maybe she just wanted to break up. But why?

So, here they were, parked in the graveled space, the lake in front visible through the trees. There was another car there when they arrived, but Doug parked well away from it. Doug turned off the engine, unsnapped his seat belt, turned toward her, and waited. He didn't reach for her, sensing she didn't want that. He'd already exhausted everything he had to say about the trip to Boone while they were at Mario's and driving.

Eva looked good. She always did. She was wearing form-fitting jeans with holes at the knees, and a cotton, sleeveless shirt. Her hair was loose about her shoulders, slightly curly with the humidity, as was his. She twisted her body away from him, her back almost against the passenger-side door. That wasn't a good sign. She sat there, lips parted, her eyes intent on him. She didn't look angry, but she didn't speak.

Finally, to break the tension, which had come from somewhere he didn't understand, he smiled and spoke. "Okay, honey. What's on your mind?"

"Doug, honey," she said, her voice breaking just a little, "is it all right if we don't make out this evening? I just want to talk."

He was disappointed but tried not to show it. "Sure," he said, "if that's what you want. But what do you want to talk about?"

Eva drew a deep breath, causing him to drop his eyes to where her breasts strained the fabric of her shirt, but he quickly raised them. He nodded encouragement. Then her words began to pour.

"About us," she said. "Us together, when we're alone. I don't trust us. I mean, I do trust you. I don't trust myself. Every time we kiss, every time you touch me, or I touch you, I feel like I'm in danger of losing control. I'm afraid I'll ask you…beg you…to…do it."

Doug squirmed in his seat, suddenly aroused despite himself. This wasn't what he expected.

"I understand," he said, and then gave a rueful laugh. "Believe me, I do understand. But…you know I'd never force –"

She cut him off with a raised hand. "I know that," she said, "that's not what I'm talking about. I said I don't trust myself. I – I don't want to get pregnant."

Doug didn't know what to say. He didn't want that either. He knew abortion wasn't an option for her, and not just because of the Church. He said nothing, and sure enough, she plunged on.

"If I get pregnant," she said, "it will mess up both our lives. I'll have to postpone college to have the baby. I'll have a real issue with my father. You…you."

Doug still said nothing. He knew what she was talking about. It would be a mess for both of them, even…even if they got married. They could. He was 18 and she'd be 18 in another week. He waited for her to continue, and she did as her tears now came.

"If we keep on," she said, "we're going to have sex. We will. We could stop seeing each other…"

"Do you want to?" Doug asked, now apprehensive. Maybe she *was* going to break up with him. "Do you want to see someone else?"

Her sob turned into a derisive laugh. "God, no," she said. "I really do like you…a lot. Anyone else would be worse. Anyone else wouldn't take no for an answer. Not anyone around here."

Relief washed over Doug. He hesitated, and then said, "Well, there's always…"

Her tears were gone. "I know," she said. "Birth control. We could do that…If we got caught, my dad would be furious, but I think Mom would be all right. What about your folks?"

"I don't think it would bother them. God knows I've had enough 'safe sex' lectures from my dad."

"About me?" she asked.

He nodded. "I haven't seen much of anyone else. No one for a while."

Eva started giggling and couldn't stop. "You know," she said, "all my friends think I'm nuts. I turn 18 next week. Most of my friends have been screwing since they were 13. At least, they say they have, and some of them are telling the truth. I've helped some of them get 'morning after' pills. They can't imagine why I would even worry about it."

She paused and gave Doug a long look. "What about your friends?"

Doug said with a curt laugh, "Oh, they think we're having sex," he said.

Eva's face contorted in anger for the first time. "You mean you told them –"

"Oh, no," he said. "I've said we're not. They just flat don't believe me. Well, a few do. *They* think I'm nuts. They think we both are."

"Aren't we?" she asked, giggling again. "We may be the only couple in the country having this conversation."

Both were silent for a while, then she said, "You can kiss me now. If you want to."

Their kiss was warm and long, but somehow not erotic. When they separated, she was all business.

"All right," she said, "it's settled. We'll use birth control. We need to decide what kind."

They spoke for a few minutes and settled on condoms, at least to start. It was simpler than her taking pills, although she allowed her mother might, eventually, help her hide them. Doug privately thought the decision wasn't as momentous as Eva appeared to think it. It wasn't even like the subject hadn't come up before. But he supposed she wanted it to be her decision. He respected that, and was very pleased by it. So, he kept his mouth shut.

Their mood was bright as he drove her home. As Doug said, "Now that we've decided this, everything will work out. I just can't see what else could happen – unless I get hurt, or something."

She shuddered. "Don't even mention that," she said, and then said, "But I can't help feeling the same way."

Chapter Eighteen

CORNELIUS, NORTH CAROLINA, OCTOBER 2022

Danny Jarvis sat in the offset area of the master bedroom of his condominium that he had converted into a home office staring into the screen of his laptop computer while drumming his fingers on his desk. Outside, it was raining, and the dull gray day reflected his mood. A coffee cup, its contents now cold, sat untouched on a coaster to the right of his computer.

September had become October, the leaves had not yet fully turned; and he still didn't have his big story. He'd thought he had it when he wrote the draft, which was now displayed on the screen in front of him. But when he'd let it sit a couple of days, and come back to edit it, it seemed…weak.

His draft started well enough, detailing the exploits of Doug "Stump" Martin, the high school fullback and linebacker from Western North Carolina who had suddenly changed from "possible prospect" to "highly-sought after prospect" following his team's early upset of Brainerd Central and its consensus five-star tailback Jeremiah Billups. The West Brainerd Redwings were still undefeated, and now the only debate about Martin was whether he was better suited for college running back or linebacker.

The most recent game was illustrative. The Redwings had played Canton Pisgah, also undefeated, a team packed with rough mountain boys and which featured its own all-state candidate at fullback and linebacker, six-one, 230 pound Dennis McGrath. Offensively, Martin had spent most of the game blocking for Henry Warren and Tommy Mason, but had carried the ball enough to plunge for three scores. Defensively, he had again been all over the field; but he was only one player, and the Pisgah Bears had scored, too.

As the clock had wound down, West Brainerd led 28-23, but the Bears were driving, matching McGrath's runs with some timely passes. The Redwings had finally slowed and then stopped the advance, so that Pisgah, with just under a minute to play, faced fourth and nine at the Redwing 12 yard line. A field goal would have done the Bears no good. They'd had to try a fourth-down play. The whole stadium had expected a pass.

Instead, the Bears had tried a draw play to McGrath. But Stump Martin, reacting with striking-snake speed, had shoved aside a blocker who had pulled to trap him and met McGrath head on at the line of scrimmage. Four inches shorter and almost 15 pounds lighter than McGrath, Martin had hit the ball carrier with a perfect form tackle, stood him up and driven him to the ground on his back. Ball game.

The next part of the draft was okay, too. Jarvis covered Martin's high school career, his academic standing, the boy's popularity with his teammates, and his former nickname of "Neanderthal Boy". There was a glowing paragraph about Martin's incredible strength and uncanny agility, about how hard he worked in the weight room and his training at home under the tutelage of his father, something the boy's mother had (reluctantly, he thought) told him when he'd spoken with them in Boone.

And then he'd got down to the nitty-gritty in the draft:

There is something preternatural about this young man. The weight training and the exercises and drills with his father can't explain it. Doug Martin is a freak. Watching him, one has to wonder if his teammates came closer than they thought when they named him Neanderthal Boy. And maybe…just maybe, that's what he is.

The draft then related that it was no secret that Martin was adopted. His teammates knew it. Therefore, he must know it himself. But his adopted parents hadn't mentioned it when Jarvis had spoken with them in Boone. Then there was the matter of the birth certificate, which Jarvis inserted verbatim and asserted had been sent to him by an "anonymous source."

A birth certificate from an Army hospital that didn't exist. But there was a government *something* at Spruce Mountain, West Virginia, a facility of which the locals knew nothing and didn't want to discuss. And yet another source who wouldn't give his or her name had told Jarvis that there were secret government efforts to clone Neanderthals for undisclosed reasons.

He had inquired of the Defense Department about the West Virginia facility buried in the mountainside, the draft read, but the government had not responded. The truth was he had sent an e-mail and had received only a link to the Army hospitals. He hadn't followed up. He hadn't tried very hard. He hadn't asked for confirmation or denial of his theory. He'd been afraid to do so. He actually feared that even the e-mail himself had him on the government radar.

Then there were the adoption files that were sealed in both states. There was the story that the Martins had adopted the child of one of his mother's cousins. But she was from Boston, her Facebook page mentioned no cousins, and the adoption had clearly been in West Virginia. That was odd. Wasn't it?

"What if it were true?" he asked his readers. "What if there really is a Neanderthal boy playing football in North Carolina?" He had followed this question with a discussion, based on online research and a telephone conference with a professor at Davidson College who had consented for his name to be used, but to whom Danny Jarvis hadn't given all of the context, making it sound completely hypothetical, of what science knew about Neanderthals, and the dispute about whether they were truly human or only a related species.

"If that's the case," he had concluded, "don't we all need to know? Doesn't the public need to know about the cloning experiments? Do not Doug Martin's teammates, classmates, the players opposing him, the school itself, deserve to know whether they are playing with, educating, going to class with, or playing against, a super-human? Or (and I say this with regret) a sub-human?"

The draft, Danny admitted, sounded wildly speculative. Perhaps irresponsibly speculative. He'd sent the draft to his editor at *Tar Heel Sports Weekly* and received a terse e-mail asking him if he were nuts. He'd replied with a copy of the birth certificate. The editor had calmed down but he still thought Danny didn't have enough to "go to press." But he'd agreed to send the draft to the publication's attorney.

The lawyer had been no help. "No one will take this seriously," he'd written, "except the kid and his parents. And their lawyer. They'll likely sue for libel or invasion of privacy. Take your pick."

So, there he was. He had a story he couldn't use. But he did know, he thought, what he needed.

He needed the birth mother. But as of yet, he had no clue where to find her. An internet search of the name given to him by the lady at the diner had yielded nothing. That wasn't surprising. The Feds had probably moved her, paid her, and given her another name. Something like the witness protection program.

I'm at a dead end, he thought. Unless I get lucky.

And the next day, he did.

CORNELIUS, NORTH CAROLINA, OCTOBER 2022 THE FOLLOWING DAY.

The next morning, when Danny went to his doorstep to retrieve the morning newspaper, he found a Federal Express package. That wasn't unusual. But he hadn't ordered anything, and he wasn't expecting a delivery from anyone he knew.

He took the box along with the newspaper to the kitchen counter. Setting the latter aside, he drew a steak knife from a drawer and opened the box. The first things that fell out was a black and white photograph, something like two by three inches. It showed an attractive teenaged girl with a snub nose and shoulder-length hair that might be light brown. On the back, in a neat, cramped, feminine hand, was written, "Jim – thanks for everything. Cindy."

There was also a folded sheet of paper. The writing was a scrawl, but legible. It said, "Jim wants the yearbook back, so send it back to me. He says you can keep the photo. He doesn't want it. He doesn't know where Cindy is – hasn't heard from her." It was signed "Johnita."

He pulled a high school yearbook from the box. He found the entry for Cindy Warfield in the senior class listings. It was the same picture as on the single photograph. There wasn't much about her in the book. No superlatives. Her signature over her photograph in the yearbook was the same signature as on the other picture. He finally found her entry where she had written in Jim's book, but it said only the same thing as on the photograph.

Danny's pulse quickened, and he went from yawning to wide awake. Now he had a picture. He needed someone who could "age" the photo by 17 years and then use photo-recognition software. The problem was, he didn't have a clue about where to find such a person. Maybe the magazine—

Wait a minute. Monica was some kind of government consultant. He suspected it was the FBI, or maybe the DHS or CIA. Those agencies had lots of experts.

Maybe Monica could help.

CHAPEL HILL, NORTH CAROLINA, OCTOBER 2022 LATER THAT MORNING

Monica was at work in the community college wing of the administration building for North Carolina higher education when her Bureau-supplied cell phone rang. Caller ID said it was Danny Jarvis. This was the number she had given him. His calls couldn't be traced. She didn't want a record of calls to her work or personal phone numbers.

As she thumbed the icon to take the call, she wondered what he wanted, hoping that it was not to see her. Barry was back from his trip, and having Danny coming around would be…awkward. Not that she didn't want Jarvis on a leash. He was an amusing diversion. But she wanted to be the one to yank the leash.

But he didn't start the conversation with a suggestion for a rendezvous. Instead, he told her about the package he had received from West Virginia and its contents. That got her attention. Then he outlined what he thought he needed.

"Monica, I need someone in law enforcement or national security to help me," he finished. "I mean, there might be a private security company somewhere who could do it, but nowhere near as well; and I don't want to be calling around. I know you have connections. Can you help?"

"Hold on and let me think," she answered.

While he waited, she thought. Dennis Springfield would be delighted if Jarvis broke a story about the Martin kid. She knew that. And running Jarvis as a cat's paw would be a feather in her cap. She knew that, too. But he'd also made it clear that nothing Jarvis did could be traced to the Bureau. So, there was no point in asking for help from there, either from standard facial recognition or from one of his division's spellcasters. She'd be turned down. Her own Talent wasn't inclined in that direction, and Dennis wouldn't want her involved even if it were.

"Monica?" she heard Jarvis ask. "Are you there?"

"Still thinking, Danny," she answered. "Hold on."

Then she had it. The IT company in Asheville she had used in the Mc-Caffrey case. True, that hadn't turned out well, but this time there would be no devious Mitch McCaffrey to interfere. They could do it, and they were reliable. The problem was they were also expensive, and she didn't think Jarvis had a deep pocket. She decided to suggest the company anyway.

"I know a company in Asheville that I believe can help you, Danny," she said. "It's an IT, Security and Consulting Company." Checking her data base on her personal phone, she read out the contact information and the name of the person he needed to call. "I have a history with them, and I can call ahead of you so they'll expect your call."

"What about your government contacts?" Jarvis sounded disappointed.

"*If* I have government contacts," she told him, letting frost creep into her voice, "they won't touch this. This is hardly anything they'd be interested in."

"But I thought —" he began, but she cut him off.

"Whatever you thought, Danny, you were wrong…This company can help you, I assure you." Actually, she wasn't sure, but she thought there was a good chance they could. "This is the best I can do," she said, removing the ice from her tone. "Really."

"Okay," he said. "But, uh, how much do they cost?" She could tell he'd been hoping for a freebie.

That was the rub, she knew. "They're not cheap. I perhaps can wheedle a discount for you, but it will still cost money. I can't help that. Can't your magazine pay for it?"

"I don't think so," he said. "They operate on a shoestring, anyway; and based on what my editor and his lawyer think of the story, asking for funding will be a non-starter."

"Can you pay for it?" she asked. Monica had the money, but Springfield would be livid if he found out she financed this project. So she didn't offer anything.

This time Monica had to hold while Jarvis thought it over. She could guess his process. If this paid off, then he would have a big story. Then the magazine would reimburse him. Then he'd have a book deal, and be invited onto podcasts.

"I don't know," he said at last. "I'll need to see the quote…I sure hope you can get me a good price."

"I'll do my best," she promised. "Wait until this afternoon. I'll call in advance this morning and text you."

"Thanks a lot, Monica," he said. "Say, I was wondering if there is a good time to get together."

"Well," she said, "possibly, but not for the next several days. Tell you what. Let me know what you're able to get out of the folks in Asheville. Then maybe we can set something up." She paused, and added, "I do miss you."

"That sounds great," he enthused.

Monica smiled into the phone, pleased that her body remained a good carrot to dangle. "I'll look forward to hearing from you, Danny dear," she said, adding the endearment for further incentive. Then she ended the call.

Minutes later, she was able to place a call to Asheville. When the party answered, she turned on the charm again.

This project was promising, she thought. And she hadn't even had to cast a spell.

Chapter Nineteen
ASHEVILLE, NORTH CAROLINA, OCTOBER 2022

TEN DAYS LATER

Danny Jarvis found the offices of Progressive IT, Security & Consulting Services, LLC in a large converted residence on Merriman Avenue in Asheville. He dropped off the yearbook and photograph, signed the agreement for services, and paid one-half of the fee two days after he spoke with Monica. The payment made a bigger hole in his savings than he had anticipated, and he frowned when he saw the box marked "Other" had been checked, and someone had written "results NOT guaranteed" into a blank on the services agreement.

He consoled himself that he'd owe only the initial payment if the company couldn't make an identification. And his only other option was to give up. He didn't want to do that. He signed the Agreement, handed the check over to the receptionist, and took his copy. The receptionist, a young woman with purple hair and a nose ring, whose name tag said she was "Chelsea," thanked him and assured him that a team would get on the project right away, and he'd be contacted when the results were ready.

Nine days later he received a text that the project had concluded, and asked if it would be convenient to review the results at Progressive's office the next day at 2:00 p.m. His pulse quickened when he read a reminder to bring payment for the balance due. They must have something. He reminded himself that "something" did not mean "something usable for a story." But he texted back that he would be there.

He arrived the next day at 1:30. Maybe they would see him early if he showed up early. But, no, he had to wait. Chelsea, this time minus the nose ring, assured him that Mike and Sally would see him in just a few minutes, and asked if he wanted coffee or water. He declined.

"Did you bring the payment with you?" Chelsea asked.

"Yes, but I want to see the results first," Danny said, not quite able to keep the irritation from his voice. This place might style itself "progressive," and have a reception area that was radical chic, with posters for various left-wing causes as well as paintings of wildlife on the walls; but it was hard-nosed capitalist in dealing with customers.

Chelsea evidently was used to his reaction. "Of course," she said, and then smiled broadly and added, "I'm sure you'll be satisfied, Mr. Jarvis." That got his hopes up, and his heart raced again. Reminding himself not to expect too much, he said, "I hope so," and took a seat.

Mike and Sally appeared from a door to the left of the reception cubicle at 1:55. Based on Chelsea, Danny had expected tie-dyed shirts and tattered jeans. But Mike wore khakis above scuffed loafers, and a blue chambray shirt with sleeves rolled up and a loosened yellow tie with blue shellfish. He was tall and thin, his face saturnine and his unruly dark hair longer than currently fashionable. Sally was almost as tall, a red-head with freckles, and wore a form fitting red dress that showed off a good figure and long, tapering legs.

The woman spoke first. "I'm Sally Collins," she said. "I'm the team leader for your project. Mike Gentry here is the lead technician." Both extended their hands and he took them in turn. "If you'll come with us," she said, "we have some interesting things to show you."

They lead him through the door, down a hall with more paintings and posters, and into a medium sized meeting room with a large screen on one wall, and a conference table with chairs where a laptop computer had been set up. Sally directed him to a chair facing the screen, and took another beside him, while Mike sat in front of the laptop.

"I will go over the steps we took and what we found," Sally said. "Mike will explain the technical stuff. We have a written report for you and a thumb drive." After Danny nodded his understanding, she said, "Go ahead, Mike."

Mike clicked keys, and the photograph of the 18 year-old Cindy War-field appeared on the screen behind him. Danny again saw the mousy-haired young woman with the shy, hesitant smile.

"So," Sally said, "here is the subject 18 to 19 years ago. She would now be about 37 years old. Our first job was to 'age' the photograph in various ways, so we could start looking for a match. We're going to skip the images that didn't pan out, and go to the one that did."

Mike clicked again, and the image changed. The photograph was of the same person. That was apparent. But the hair was longer and much lighter, the face was fuller, the bosom larger, and the smile somehow more confident.

"This is what we called the maximum probability," Sally explained. "Woman who don't like mousy hair typically lighten it. Maturity frequently brings some weight gain, especially if the subject has had children, which we assumed. We also assumed the gain in weight was not excessive. There are others with other assumptions. But this one got a hit pretty quickly... Go ahead, Mike."

Another click, and the image on the screen changed again. It was an entry from a webpage for a firm called "Brentwood Realty" in Brentwood, Tennessee. The picture was amazingly like the photoshopped photograph on the previous screen, except it was in color. It showed a woman with shoulder-length blonde hair, the face a bit round, the eyes hazel. Her smile was wide and welcoming, as one would expect from a Realtor. The head and shoulders shot showed a bright red top under a blue blazer. The scoop neck showed a substantial but not scandalous amount of cleavage.

The woman's name was Veronica Clayton. Her firm bio said she'd been with the company eight years and was a member of something called the "30 Million Club." Danny had dated a realtor for a while and she'd told him the "Million Dollar Club" meant sales of one million dollars in a year. If that concept carried over to the 30 Million Club, it meant this woman was doing very well for herself in commissions. The bio said "Ronnie" handled "high end" homes and commercial properties.

Danny's jaw dropped. Could he be looking at Cindy Warfield?

"Our software gives this a 90 percent match," said Sally. "And there's more."

The next screen was the Facebook Profile page for the same woman. The name was Veronica Porter Clayton. The profile said she was a graduate of Western Kentucky University, that she was originally from some town in Ohio, and lived in Cool Springs, Tennessee. He supposed that was near Brentwood. It said she was "not in a relationship," but the next page, which was her Facebook photographs, showed two children. One was a boy who was about twelve; the other, a girl who appeared three or four years younger.

"She was married to a lawyer in some big firm in Nashville," Sally said. "But she's divorced."

"What happened?" Danny asked, not expecting an answer.

But Sally smiled and said, "Her ex is now married to a woman who was a paralegal with the same firm, so we can guess. Court records in Nashville show that she's getting a nice chunk of child support and a piece of his 401K. Her alimony has expired."

The next screen was a high school transcript from a high school in Ohio. The one after that was an Ohio birth certificate for Veronica Nicole Porter.

"How did you get all of this?" Danny asked.

"It's not that hard," said Mike. "A lot of court records are now electronic, and available for public access. School records are electronic, too; and their system security is not very good."

That meant the school records were hacked, Danny realized. Not that he cared.

"The Feds did a good job setting her up with a new identity," Mike said. "But her Facebook friends don't include anyone from back in Ohio – not relatives, or high school classmates, or anything. They probably inserted the transcript in the school records, and fitted her up with the birth certificate and a driver's license. And I'm sure she got cash.

"But I bet if you go back to that one-horse town in Ohio, no one will remember her. There won't be any yearbook pictures or anything. Anyway, we didn't find any when we looked."

"This is your girl," Sally said. "At least we think so. We're pretty positive... She moved to Nashville after college, and went into real estate. We have her address, her e-mail address, and her phone numbers. It's all in the report." She sounded a little smug, but Danny didn't care.

"Well," Danny said, "I suppose you want your money."

He'd found the person he needed. Now, if she would only talk to him.

BRENTWOOD, TENNESSEE, OCTOBER 2022
THE OFFICES OF BRENTWOOD REALTY

Veronica Clayton sat at her desk going over the settlement statement for a closing scheduled for early that afternoon. The home she had sold was in Franklin, and the buyers were a doctor and his wife who were moving from Chicago. They had been difficult customers, but the commission would make her efforts worth it. The flight from Chicago to the metro Nashville area in the last several years had been good to her, she reflected. It helped pay for the kids' private schools.

She glanced over at the framed photographs of Jimmy and Marcia. Good kids, both of them, and thinking of them made her smile. The smile faded as she thought of her first childbirth, eighteen years ago. The baby had not been hers, genetically, but she had carried him for nine months. Signing the surrender papers had been more of a wrench than she'd thought it would be. Sometimes she wondered what had become of him. But she had been warned not to attempt any contact, and she never had, as much as she'd wanted to at times, and still did. He would be in high school by now.

Veronica turned back to the settlement statement. Everything appeared to be correct. She had sold her own listing and the commission would all be hers, except for the part that went into the company coffers. She'd get some of that, too, because she owned a piece of the company. It was approaching lunchtime, and her stomach growled, but she would skip lunch today. Her pants were getting tight, and it was time to rein in the power lunches.

The telephone on her desk rang, and caller id said it was from Janie, the receptionist. She wondered what it could be about. She wasn't expecting anyone. She hoped no one wanted to reschedule the closing.

She lifted the handset and said, "Yes?"

"There's a Danny Jarvis here to see you," Janie said, sounding a little puzzled. "He says you're not expecting him, but that he thinks you'll see him."

"I have no idea who he is," Veronica said. "I don't know him."

"He – he said to tell you," Janie said, "that he wants to talk with you about Cindy Warfield. I don't know who he's talking about."

Veronica felt as though she'd been punched in the stomach. She certainly did know, and the words made her shiver. She drew a deep breath. She didn't know how this man had penetrated her cover, but she had to find out. Refusing to see him would be the worst thing she could do.

But she couldn't afford to talk with him here. Maybe someplace public.

"All right," she said into the phone, "tell him to wait a minute. I don't know the name he gave you, but it might be a new client. I'm on my way to lunch. Tell him I'll talk with him on my way out."

COOL SPRINGS TENNESSEE, OCTOBER 2022
LATER THAT AFTERNOON

Veronica went home early that afternoon. Somehow, she had made it through lunch with Jarvis and then through the closing. She'd taken Jarvis to a noisy bistro down the street from her office, after declaring in front of Janie that she wasn't familiar with the name he'd given, but if he'd follow her out to lunch she'd let him explain. She could tell from Janie's quizzical look that she knew something was up, but that couldn't be helped.

She walked into the kitchen, poured herself a glass of wine and sat at a high chair at the kitchen island to think. The kids would not be home for a while, and she was glad of it. She needed the time to think. Her hand trembled as she lifted the wine glass. This was something she never thought would happen, had been assured would not happen. But it had.

In a way, she was actually relieved. Her first thought was that Jarvis would try to blackmail her, but he hadn't. Her next thought was that he was a government agent there to test her, but she didn't believe that was the case. She'd realized, as they sat in the noisy restaurant and she picked at a salad, that he really was what he said he was – a reporter who wanted a story. He came over as likable and rather attractive. She was mad at herself for the latter even crossing her mind.

Per the instructions she'd been give so long ago, she had stonewalled him. She didn't know what he was talking about, she said. She told him she assumed he was there to bring her a new real estate client, or she wouldn't have bothered with lunch. She had looked at the documents he showed her and shrugged her shoulders.

"This is crazy," she'd said. "Just nuts."

She hadn't fooled him, though.

"Look, Ms. Clayton," he'd said, "I have enough, or almost enough, for a story *now*. I can go up to New Bedford, Ohio and nose around. No one will remember you, because you weren't there. I can say I contacted you and you refused to talk. This story *will* have legs. Don't you want to have your side of it told?"

"If you do that," she'd warned, "I'll sue." She could tell that got his attention. Her ex-husband had handled some libel cases, and he'd told her that the law looked at libel differently for ordinary folks than for public figures.

But he'd said, "Truth is a defense."

She'd laughed at him. "You can't prove it's true. You just have this weird story you made up."

He'd tried a different approach. "Don't you think the public has the right to know the government is up to things like this?"

That question had pissed her off. The public didn't have any right to know about her personal life. But she'd said, "There is no right to know something that's not true."

But Jarvis had been persistent. "Well, don't you think the boy you carried in your womb has a right to know the truth?"

That jab got to her, but she'd tried hard not to show it. Instead, she'd said, "The truth is that he's someone else's child. Not mine."

Finally, he had appeared to give up. He had pressed his business card and a newspaper clipping about Doug Martin's exploits on the gridiron on her, and asked her to call him if she changed her mind. Then he had abruptly changed the subject, asked her about her real estate business, and had been completely charming. She'd found herself liking him in spite of everything.

"Like I told you," he had said after the check came to their table, "this story will run. Then you'll have to talk with me. And not just me. It's a pity you won't talk now. I probably don't even have to use your name."

For the first time, she had been tempted when he said that. But no, she couldn't risk saying anything to him. That might bring the government down on her, because she'd be breaching the agreement she had signed.

"There's nothing to talk about," she'd said.

Veronica sipped her wine, calmer now. It was likely Jarvis had been bluffing. It was likely that his e-zine's lawyers would kill the story. He really didn't have anything that could be printed.

She told herself that, but...she couldn't be sure. Suppose he did release a story. She could not abide being questioned about it by other reporters, seeing her name in print here in Williamson County. Maybe she should report this to the Defense Department. She still had a number for Fred Hutton.

But that wasn't attractive either. Maybe they'd have Jarvis arrested. Or worse. Maybe they'd have him beaten, or even killed. She knew that her own country could play rough when it had a secret to protect. She'd hate to see him hurt. He was pretty nice. (Damn it, there goes that attraction thing again. Veronica, grow up.) She'd have to think about it before she reported him.

Setting down her wine glass, she removed the newspaper clipping. The baby she had carried to term was now some sports hero. Jarvis didn't know it, but this was the biggest temptation of all.

She'd like to see the boy.

The kids would be home soon. She sighed, replaced the clipping, and finished her wine.

Chapter Twenty
CORNELIUS, NORTH CAROLINA, OCTOBER 2022

Danny Jarvis was home after his trip to Nashville. He had arrived tired, behind in his deadlines, and dejected after getting more or less nothing out of Veronica Clayton. He was certain she was lying. He had done enough interviews to develop a feel for that.

But he should have known that the government wouldn't have supplied her with a new identity and paid for her college education without a pretty strong "gag" agreement. There were bound to be penalties for violating it. He wondered if she would report him to the Defense Department. Somehow, he didn't think so.

He supposed he'd know soon. If she had done that, he'd get a visit soon. From whom, he didn't know. His imagination conjured images of Men in Black or some version thereof.

He decided he needed some rest before he tackled any of his deadlines, and slept for over ten hours. He woke refreshed, and after a shower and shave, made himself and ate breakfast, and then tackled his backlog of work. By early afternoon, he had filed the stories he owed to various outlets. Then he started thinking about the Martin story.

Maybe he had something after all. He decided to rewrite it and add what he'd learned about Veronica Clayton. It took him a while, because he kept his consulting firm confidential, he had to admit the Clayton woman had denied everything, and that he hadn't nosed around in Ohio – yet. A trip to southern Ohio would tax his time and budget, and that was all his editor wanted to be able to run the story, the magazine could damn well pay for the trip.

He went through the manuscript again and corrected some typos. He liked it. He hadn't proven anything, but the piece raised some intriguing questions. He didn't think about the effect of releasing it on the boy himself, or his foster parents. Rather, he did; but that wasn't his concern. News was news. He wasn't in business to protect anyone.

Danny e-mailed the current draft to his editor at *Tar Heel Sports Weekly*. At the last second, he added the report from Progressive IT, including the full set of photographs. Then he got a beer from the refrigerator and waited. While waiting, he decided to call Monica to bring her up to date.

She took the call and wanted a copy of the Progressive report, and he sent it to her. He knew she'd pass it on to whatever shadowy government agency she worked for. It had to be someone other than the Defense Department. But that wasn't his concern, either. She continued to put him off on getting together, but promised they could work something out "soon."

Knowing she had another man, or men, he wasn't too disappointed. Monica was a great lay, but a little intimidating. To his surprise he found himself thinking about Veronica Clayton. Despite the uncomfortable nature of their visit, he thought they'd managed to hit it off. But that wouldn't go anywhere, either, he realized.

He was about to go somewhere for dinner when his computer pinged, telling him he had e-mail messages. One was from his editor, Andy, who wanted a ZOOM meeting in the morning with Danny and the magazine's lawyer. That was encouraging. At least he had Andy's attention now.

He decided to tax his budget by getting a steak somewhere.

CHAPEL HILL, NORTH CAROLINA, OCTOBER 2022
THE SAME AFTERNOON

Monica decided to send the Progressive IT report and attachments to Dennis Springfield in Arlington. Within minutes after she clicked "send," she had a call from him on her secure phone. She closed the door to her office before accepting it.

"Well, well," he said without preamble, "your boy Jarvis has been busy." She could tell from his voice that he was pleased.

"Yes," she agreed, "giving him that lead has paid off. But he's still not sure his editor will run it."

"Eh?" Springfield said, irritation creeping into his voice. "Why not?"

"He's afraid the magazine's editor will kill it as too risky," she said. "He doesn't have any real proof. Just unanswered questions and speculation. He thinks the lawyer will believe it will invite a lawsuit from the Clayton woman, or the boy and his family."

"Well, can't he put it on his blog?" Springfield insisted.

"Then it would all be on him – or his insurance policy," she said. "He told me he doesn't have all that much insurance."

"When did that ever stop anyone from running with a story?" Springfield asked. "Hell, he could send it to the *New York Times* or the *Washington Post*. They print stuff from 'undisclosed' or 'anonymous' sources all the time."

"I could put that bug in his ear," Monica said, "if his editor nixes the story."

"Do that," Springfield said. "It's better if it runs in that dinky little state sports magazine anyway. We'll make sure the national media pick up on it."

"Dennis," Monica asked, "why is this one so important to you. Do you really think the kid will wind up working for the Bureau?"

"I think he might…But I'll be fair with you. I mostly want to stick it to those assholes at DIA. They need to share information like this with the Bureau. And…and they've sure messed with me…with us…over that crowd down in Martintown enough. You know that."

Monica certainly did know. Fred Hutton at DIA had leaned on the FBI to in turn lean on Springfield and Monica more than once to leave Mitch McCaffrey and his coterie alone because they were DIA assets.

"I think I can persuade Danny Hutton to go public," she said.

"No spells, Monica," Springfield warned.

She smiled into the phone. "I have other methods of persuasion," she said. Dennis knew what she meant. She had "persuaded" Dennis himself a couple of times.

"I'm sure," he answered. "But it may not be necessary. My bet says the lawyer won't like it, but will let it go to press. I don't think anyone will sue."

"Why not?" she asked. "You know they'll have to react pretty strongly."

"Sure," he said. "But I don't think they'll go that far. Look, I think Jarvis is onto something. This is real. I'm sure of it. The kid's parents know it's real. The woman in Tennessee knows it's real. Taking it to court gives the lawyers discovery rights. They'd risk proving what they deny is true.

"My money says they'll pooh-pooh it, deny it, and hope it blows over."

"You're not as cautious as the lawyers I've dealt with," she said. "And I think Danny is afraid the Defense Department will come after him somehow."

"I think they'd be hesitant to do that," Springfield said. "He doesn't have any government secrets. Threatening him would be admitting his story has legs. And…they don't like going after American citizens."

Unlike you, Denny, Monica thought but didn't say. "I'll tell him that, if it's okay," she said.

"Sure," Springfield responded. And…maybe we can help some more," Dennis told her, adding, "Strictly *sub rosa*, of course."

"How?"

"We can leak another anonymous source," he said. "And maybe we can get to the Clayton woman. I'll have to think about that. But have your powers of persuasion ready. And I don't mean spells."

"They always are, darling," Monica purred into the phone. "Always."

CORNELIUS, NORTH CAROLINA, OCTOBER 2022
THE NEXT MORNING

Danny Jarvis woke the next morning with butterflies. The ZOOM meeting was scheduled for 10:00 a.m., and he'd find out whether his story would run. He went ahead with his morning toilet, but was too nervous to eat. He settled on making coffee and opened his laptop.

He had an e-mail from an address he didn't recognize and almost deleted it as junk. When he opened it, he was glad he'd decided to read it.

"If you want to know about delivering Neanderthal babies," the message read, "check out Dr. Nathan Valenski. Where? Look online here." There was a link. Then the message continued, "Wonder where the good doctor was in 2005?" Then there was another link.

When he pressed the first link, he connected to a press release from the Pennsylvania State University School of Medicine stating that Dr. Nathan Valenski had been named Professor Emeritus. Valenksi, the release read, had joined the faculty in 2010, after retiring from the United States Army with the rank of Major. He had taught obstetrics and had been awarded grants for research in genetically inherited diseases. He would continue to teach but with a reduced schedule. There was a photograph of a bald, smiling man who looked a bit over 60 years old.

The second link had the same photo and was Valenski's faculty biography. It detailed his service record, including stints at Walter Reed and other Army hospitals. But from 1998 through 2009, it said only, "Genetic Research." The location was not mentioned.

He forwarded the e-mail to Andy. It couldn't hurt. And it didn't.

He also had a call from Monica. She told him, without giving a source, what Springfield had said about the probability of suit and the likelihood of anything but bland denial by the DOD. He thought that might help, and said he'd let her know. She hinted she might be available Friday night. That was good.

The ZOOM meeting went better than expected. Andy had decided he liked the story, and thought it might get national attention. The lawyer, who was a college classmate of Andy's, had already reached the same conclusions as Dennis Springfield (although Danny didn't know about Springfield) about the probability of suit.

"It's irresponsible," the lawyer said. "You'll get criticized. And made fun of. And you'll deserve it. But..." he sighed. "I think the risk of suit is minimal." He suggested the kid's family be asked to comment first, but didn't insist on it. Neither Danny nor Andy wanted to take that step, because, if this were real, as they thought it was, the parents might contact the government, and the government might do something – although they didn't know what.

The lawyer didn't insist, and Andy discussed with Danny running the story next week. There was some discussion of insurance, and Danny was pleased he had more than he thought, counting homeowners and umbrella. They considered asking Dr. Valenski for comment, but decided they didn't have anything definite and that it carried the same risk of Defense Department interference. Andy wanted to send copies to the Associated Press and the Brainerd County TV station, and Danny suggested sending it to the *Washington Post* as well.

The meeting ended on that high note. Danny decided to do two things. One was to call Monica and let her know the decision. Maybe she'd let him take her to dinner that weekend. He'd make that call that right away. The other was to let Veronica Clayton know the story would run. That was for later. Days later. She was a risk, too.

Chapter 21
MARTINTOWN, NORTH CAROLINA, OCTOBER 2022

THE PREVIOUS WEEK

On the Wednesday before the Pisgah game on Friday, West Brainerd High School held a career day for seniors, who were excused from class while they attended 45-minute segments with representatives from regional industries and businesses, all designed to end prior to the conclusion of the school day. A wide variety of professions and companies were represented. These included a local moving company, several departments of Southeastern Electronics, Simmons IT & Security, a restauranteur, an hotelier, a newspaper reporter, a news broadcaster, hair dressers, an engineering firm, an architect, and a law firm. The Highlands Repertory Theater sent an actress.

Both Doug and Eva signed up for exposure to several careers, but their choices did not overlap much. Doug's choices were eclectic. He picked the engineering firm, and chose a session with Simmons (largely out of loyalty and his liking of Carson McCaffrey, for whom he had worked during the summer; he already knew about the company, of course). But he also picked a session with the reporter, because he liked to write, and a segment with the actress, just for fun. He'd enjoyed playing in the junior class play last spring.

He had one session left, and picked the law firm. That was the last session of the day, and the only one he had with Eva. She had picked the broadcaster, the accounting firm, the hotel manager, and the human resources department from Southeastern. She did fine in STEM courses, but not quite as well as Doug. But she was still uncertain of a career choice.

There were only six people in the session with the representatives from Melton, Norville, Jennings & Johnson. Eva couldn't figure out why two of them were there. One was a girl she knew who wanted to study cosmetology. The other was Doug's teammate Kenny Mastriano, who said he wanted to be either a football coach or follow his father in the family restaurant business. Everyone else, she thought, was pretty open to a legal career of some sort, although no one knew anything much about it except what they'd seen on television – which she knew was probably not realistic.

The law firm was represented by Rob Ashworth, one of the younger lawyers, and by a striking young woman with dark hair, blue eyes and a porcelain complexion, who was introduced as Alexandra Tabarant, a paralegal. She spoke with an accent and claimed to be from France, but Eva didn't think the accent was French. Well, it could be, she supposed. She really didn't know European accents. The lawyer called her "Alex."

The two handed out print-outs from the firm webpages, and then Ashworth and Tabarant took turns explaining what various lawyers and paralegals did in the firm's practice. Ashworth said that Tabarant sometimes worked with him, but more frequently with Marc Washington, another young partner.

"Marc couldn't make it today because a court hearing came up," Ashworth told them. "He gets to handle fun stuff like civil rights and discrimination cases. My cases are supposed to be dull."

After Ashworth described working on bankruptcy and business cases, Kenny Mastriano had to agree with the opening remarks. "It sounds boring," he said. But Eva thought the combination of technical issues and advocacy fascinating.

"A lot of people think it is," Ashworth answered Kenny. "I do not. But Marc Washington has to wade through a great deal of detailed information, too, much of the time. Just ask Alex. The point is that most of law practice isn't glamorous. It's hard work."

Alex then explained the types of work she did. Organizing documents. Pulling excerpts from discovery depositions. Online searches. One of the young women attending asked her about divorce cases, and was told the domestic relations lawyers' paralegals did much of the same work. The girl who asked the question looked thoughtful. She obviously hadn't expected the answer, but it made sense to Eva. She could see herself working in an office like this one. And she liked these people. She stole a look at Doug, who was seated next to her. He appeared interested, she decided.

As Rob Ashworth outlined the various areas of practice at Melton Norville, Eva thought she saw Alex Tabarant watching her and Doug intently. She made eye contact with the woman, who made no effort to look away, and smiled at her. Eva returned the smile, but had no idea why Tabarant was so interested. Did she just think they were a cute couple? Was it because Doug was cute? A sports star?

The session ended, and Eva, along with Doug and a couple of others, filed by where the presenters sat at the front of the classroom to thank them. Alexandra Tabarant extended her hand, and Eva took it. The paralegal pressed her hand, and spoke in a soft voice.

"You may have challenge ahead of you," she said. "But don't worry. You will be fine. You are safe with him." She nodded toward Doug, who was talking with Ashworth.

Eva thanked her and mumbled, "I know." But what was the woman talking about? Their relationship? Their love life? It was odd.

But she appreciated the reassurance.

IN ASHWORTH'S CAR

Rob and Alex had driven to the career day at West Brainerd in his car. They had both enjoyed the day, but attendance had been duty imposed by the firm management committee, and had taken both from other work.

After Rob had started the engine, he gave Aleks a sharp glance and asked, "What were you talking about with the Martinez girl? I noticed you were using your Talent."

Aleks didn't respond immediately. That was like her. She always chose her words carefully.

"You felt the boy, didn't you?" she asked, not yet addressing his question.

"Oh, yes," Rob answered. "I'm not as Sensitive as you and not nearly as much as Samantha. But he broadcasts like a radio station. I'm not sure what it is, but it's strong.

"I got nothing from the girl, though," he continued. "Did you?"

"No. Only the little most people have," she said. "Yet there is a bond between the two. And – Rob, I have not said before, but sometimes I can feel something is about to happen when I'm around someone. Not full prescience, no. But a feeling. I felt it today. Both will be affected.

"Yet, I felt they are strong. Strong together. And that he will protect her. I told her."

"That's pretty close to giving yourself away," Rob warned.

"I do not think so," she said. "I didn't say enough for that. But" – she giggled – "the girl may think I am crazy foreign woman. So what?"

"Well, pass this on to Alyssa," he said. "We're supposed to do that."

"*Bien sur*," Aleksandra responded in the language that was her front, and not really her birth tongue. "I will do so."

ON THE MOUNTAINSIDE
SUNDAY AFTERNOON

Eva Martinez lay draped across Doug Martin's big chest, while he reclined on the blanket he'd brought in the trunk of his vehicle. They were not quite naked. Eva wore only the flannel shirt she'd worn for the drive, leaving the shirt unbuttoned, her breasts pressed against the hairless expanse of his hairless pectorals, while Doug had slipped on his boxer shorts. They had just cleaned their private regions with the sanitary wipes she'd thought to bring. Doug had thought to bring snacks, which they'd share soon. That was men for you, thinking of food, but not hygiene.

The day had been perfect. It was a bright, balmy Indian summer day in mid-October, a bit cooler at this elevation than down toward Martin-town, but not appreciably so. Not yet, anyway, and there was still plenty of daylight. The leaves were turning, and already near peak here on the mountainside, the oranges and reds and yellows breaking through the ever-greens and sparkling in the sunlight. There was a slight breeze. It was, she thought, perfect.

Perfect for her first time. His, too. Theirs. They'd planned it carefully. They hadn't been able to see each other Saturday. Eva had a gymnastics meet in Morganton, which Doug couldn't attend. He had to pick some time to catch up on his studies. And to rest, she realized. He was covered in bruises, and she absently kissed one. Football was a rough sport.

Today, he'd had permission to drive up into the mountains to see the leaf cover and have a picnic. Doug was a hunter, camper, and hiker. He'd found this spot a year ago on a deer hunt, a clearing in the woods, not to steep, not too far off the road, but private. Perfect, she thought again.

Their love making had at first been hesitant, a little shy, a little awkward when he fumbled with the condom. And there had been some pain when she pushed herself down onto him and he'd entered her. But their excitement had overcome the hesitation, and they'd moved in rhythm, gasping and murmuring until it was over – all too quickly.

She didn't know if they would go again. Her caressing hand had found he was ready right now, even as their breathing steadied from their first encounter. She wasn't sure she was. She was sore. But she felt her breath quickening again as she squirmed over him. They kissed for a long time.

But she propped herself up with her left arm, feeling the grass yield to her hand under the blanket. She stared down at him, and allowed a soft laugh.

"What's funny?" he demanded.

"Oh, you. Me. Us," she said. "That was wonderful. But it was so… quick."

He laughed with her. "Yeah," he said. "I guess I was like a gun waiting to go off."

"Well, me, too," she said. "But we can go slower next time." Then she gasped. He'd raised his head and his lips had found a breast.

The next time was slower, and even more perfect, she decided, when they lay panting again a few minutes later. Now they would have to clean themselves all over again. She was glad she'd brought plenty of wipes, and a plastic bag for their garbage. This would definitely be the last time today, though, she decided. She really was going to be sore "down there," as her mother called it.

Doug accepted her decision without being told, and soon they were sitting up on the blanket, her shirt partially buttoned this time, wearing her panties now, and thinking of socks and jeans. The breeze had picked up, and she'd had goosebumps when she'd pulled on the shirt. Doug had donned his shorts, but hadn't made a move toward the rest of his clothes, which were still piled in the grass on his side of the blanket.

They talked for a while about all kinds of things. The career day. The game Friday. Next week's road trip over to Tennessee and a date with Science Hill High School in Johnson City. How the meet had gone, and the red ribbon she'd won yesterday. His decision to postpone more college visits until after the season. Her dislike of the French teacher. They always found it easy to talk. She loved that.

She caught him staring at her. Not at her breasts, although they were on display where the partially buttoned shirt gaped, but directly into her eyes. She loved that, too.

"You are so beautiful," he said.

"Ummm," she answered, returning his stare and running a hand across his chest, "you're pretty beautiful, too."

"Hey, cut that out," he said, squirming, and then changed the subject. "Hungry?" he asked. "I am." He reached for the knapsack next to his clothes. But as he pulled it to him, he stopped, suddenly tense.

"Shhh," he whispered. "I feel something." He jerked his head uphill.

Eva opened her mouth, but closed it with an inaudible snap as she saw his face. He hadn't said he'd heard anything. He said he'd felt something. Her eyes followed his up the slope. She saw nothing but pine and laurel. She heard nothing, not even any birds. That in itself was frightening.

Then she heard it, and could see from his face that he did, too. It was faint. She wouldn't have heard anything if the two were not so still. But there it was, in the trees to the right of the laurel thicket. Something or someone was coming toward them. For an absurd moment she thought it was her father, or maybe one of her girlfriends, there to catch them. But... she didn't think this was a man. She couldn't have told anyone why.

Slowly, silently, Doug reached for the backpack. From a sheath on the side he removed a knife. He'd told her it was a survival knife when she'd asked as they walked in from the car. It had broad cross guard and a flattened knob at the end of the hilt. She drew a quick, hissing breath as she watched him slowly get to his feet, motion her behind him, and assume a posture she assumed his father must have taught him. Semi-crouched, the knife in his right hand, pointed down with his thumb pressed against the cross-guard, his left hand, fist clinched, held low for blocking.

And then she could see it, stepping between the edge of a bush and a tree at the edge of the clearing, maybe 10 yards away. It was not a bobcat. It was... Jesus, she thought. It's a mountain lion. I thought all of them were out west.

The lion snarled, showing fangs, but didn't look as if it were prepared to spring. It snarled again, and this time did seem to gather itself.

Doug maintained his posture, and looked directly at the big cat. He made eye contact, which Eva had heard you were not supposed to do. The lion snarled again and remained semi-crouched. Eva's breath came quickly, and she looked around for a rock or anything to grab. But there was nothing.

She didn't know how long Doug and the lion stared each other down. Probably seconds, surely no more than a minute, but it seemed like forever. She suddenly wanted to pee.

Then the lion snuffed and shook its head. Sort of a "well, then, I'll be seeing you," she thought. And it turned and disappeared back into the trees. It made no effort at stealth, and they could hear it moving past the laurel thicket.

She realized she'd been holding her breath, and found herself gulping air. She could see and hear Doug breathing heavily, too. He straightened, but held a finger to his lips, and stood while they heard the cat's movement subside.

Finally, he said. "I think it's all right now."

Eva stared at her boyfriend – lover, now, she knew. "What did you do?"

Doug's features clouded. He looked puzzled. "I-I don't know," he said. "I just knew…I just knew I could back it down. That it would know me."

"Know you? How?"

"Don't ask me," he said. He sounded lost. "I don't know how. I just knew."

Eva reached for her wool socks and sat to put them on. "Are we going to tell anyone about this?"

He was suddenly teasing. "About what? The sex or the mountain lion?"

She threw a sock at him. It missed. "The mountain lion, dummy."

"We'd better not," he said, reaching for his tee shirt, followed by his hoodie. "You know, there's been stories about catamounts in these mountains for years. But Wildlife Resources says there aren't any."

"Catamounts?" she asked.

"Same thing as mountain lion," he said, pulling on the hoody.

"Well," Eva said, "we just saw one. Okay, I'll be quiet about it. But I have two things to ask."

He pulled on his hoodie, his eyes still up slope. "What are they?"

"One," she said, "as pretty as it is here, let's find some other place to screw." She gave him a wicked grin. "If anything is going to claw your back, it's going to be me."

He laughed and picked up his jeans.

"Okay," he said, "I agree. What's the other one?"

Her voice was plaintive this time. "Can we eat in the car? I don't want to stay here with that lion around."

When they reached his vehicle and seated themselves, doors locked and windows only cracked at her insistence, she leaned over and kissed him on the cheek.

"Thank you," she said, "for keeping me safe."

He grimaced. "I don't know what I would have done if the lion had sprung," he said. "I was just hoping you could get away while I kept it busy, if that happened. But I thought it was just curious and I could back it down."

"You'd have done something," she said. Then she laughed. "You ought to have seen yourself there with the knife. It was right out of Edgar Rice Burroughs."

"Huh?" he asked. "What are you talking about?"

She handed him a sandwich from the knapsack in her lap, took one for herself, and said, "My Dad has a whole shelf of old books by Burroughs. I've read most of them. You know – Tarzan, John Carter, and so on. They're pretty good. I'm surprised you haven't read any."

"I've seen some movies," he said.

"Not the same thing at all, my dear," she said. "And you were right there in one of the stories – fiercely protecting your mate."

Her voice sounded teasing, but he realized it was a front. She was actually proud.

Chapter 22
BRENTWOOD, TENNESSEE, OCTOBER 2022

TUESDAY, THE FOLLOWING WEEK

Veronica Clayton was sitting at her computer going through her e-mails. Most were routine. There was the weekly bulletin from the local Realtors' Association on recent home sales and housing construction starts. She knew most of the information already, and skimmed it. A client had e-mailed her to ask when a pending contract would close – again. For the third time, she replied that they were waiting on the buyers' bank to finish the loan paperwork and title insurance. But she made a note to prod the buyers' agent – again.

She almost deleted the next one. It was probably something her spam filter hadn't caught. She didn't recognize the address. But the title, which appeared to be the first part of the message, caught her attention. "If you want to see your oldest son…" She opened it and read the rest.

"If you want to see your oldest son play football, he'll be in Tennessee Friday night when his team plays Science Hill High School in Johnson City."

There was nothing else. There was no signature. She wasn't familiar with the domain, so she googled it and found it was one of the domains used to send anonymous e-mails. The rest of the address was nonsensical. "friendgirl@." Definitely not a friend, and maybe not even a girl. She considered forwarding the e-mail to the company's IT contractor and asking them what they could find out. But no, they wouldn't be any help, and they'd ask questions she didn't want to answer.

She googled "Science Hill High School football schedule" and sure enough, it said that this coming Friday, the Hilltoppers would play West Brainerd High School from Martintown, N.C. at home. Yes, that was the high school in the newspaper clipping she'd been given by Danny Jarvis.

This had to be from him. Didn't it? She couldn't think of anyone else. She still had the man's card. She should call him and tell him to leave her alone. But no, that was another bad idea. He'd know he had hit the mark with her and had her on his hook.

The worst of it was that she was tempted. She had carried this child in her womb for nine months, and had felt the wrench when she had given him up, never mind that she wasn't the biological mother and was being paid to carry the baby to term. She wanted to see him.

That's another bad idea, she thought. This is bait and someone wants me to take it. Besides, Johnson City was a good four or five hours from Brentwood, depending on traffic and how willing was one to exceed the speed limit. She'd miss a half day's work, have to stay overnight, and find someone to stay with the kids. Her *real* kids, she reminded herself. She'd have to think of something to tell them, and….Oh, it was impossible.

Still, the thought persisted. She wouldn't have to have any contact with the young man. She could just watch. She could wear a bulky sweater and a hat and no one would recognize her. No one would have to know.

"Ronnie, you're nuts," she said aloud; and when she realized she had, she looked around to be sure no one else had heard her. No, she was alone in her office; and although the door was cracked open, she wouldn't have been heard over the usual office buzz outside.

She made up her mind. I can't do this, she thought. I won't.

But maybe she would.

JOHNSON CITY, TENNESSEE, OCTOBER 2022
FRIDAY NIGHT THE STADIUM

Kermit Tipton Stadium, also known as Steve Spurrier Field after the high school's best known alumnus, held a sell-out crowd as the teams took the field. The weather was clear and cooler than usual for Mid-October. West Brainerd had brought a sizable crowd for a school its size, including its marching band, which had dueled with the Science Hill band all during warm-ups. The drive up the mountain and over into Tennessee wasn't that bad. Redwing fans were used to drives as long or longer.

Doug felt the usual pre-game butterflies, but he felt good, too. Earlier in the week, he'd been a little concerned that last Sunday's tryst with Eva would distract him from preparing for this week, but it hadn't. Instead, it felt like they had passed a milestone, and could quit worrying about when they would claim each other's virginity. He'd practiced well all week. The whole team had. They were ready.

The Johnson City high school they were playing was, like Brainerd Central, a much bigger school. It had a bigger budget, a bigger stadium, a larger student body, and a larger team. Classifications were a bit different in Tennessee from North Carolina; but if Science Hill were in North Carolina, it would be about two rungs up from West Brainerd. The headline in the Martintown newspaper that morning had been, "Can the Redwings be Giant Killers again?"

The Hilltoppers had a good team. They had a robust quarterback named Bellamy who could run and throw, and a tailback and wide-outs with speed. Both lines were big. At this point in the season, they were undefeated, with big wins against two Knoxville area teams, but hadn't yet faced traditional powers in Kingsport and Greeneville. They had definitely heard about West Brainerd, based on the signs on the home side of the field: "Beat the Giant Killers" and "Pluck the Redwings."

Defensively, Doug's job tonight was to "spy" on Bellamy, which meant he was to be aware of the quarterback on every play, blitz him when he dropped back, and deliver hard tackles when he kept the ball. "If he goes to the locker room to pee, Martin," Coach had said, "I want you to go with him. I want legal hits, but hard hits. Make him feel it. Light him up!"

Offensively, the plan was to use Doug as a decoy and a blocker, with Henry Warren getting most of the carries, and Les Bronson throwing more than usual. Coach thought Javon Shade could get behind the Hilltopper secondary. Because Doug was going to be so active on defense, Tommy Mason would spell him frequently at fullback. Doug didn't mind. He just wanted to play.

The Hilltoppers were as good as advertised. They hit hard, and were seldom out of position. With the defense keying on Bellamy, they hurt the Redwings with the tailback, whose name was Stringer. Doug continued to "tag" the quarterback every time he had a legal shot, but Science Hill still gained ground, and scored.

But the Redwings scored, too. Bronson found Shade for two quick strike touchdowns. The Hilltoppers evidently had decided to treat Doug the same way he was treating Bellamy, because he was hit on practically every play when he was in at fullback. But that opened the way for Henry, and when Tommy was in at fullback the 'Toppers looked confused, not knowing whom to key on. By the middle of the fourth quarter, the game was tied 21-21. Doug had powered in from the one yard-line for the third score, on one of his few carries for the night.

Science Hill had the ball in its own territory, and Bellamy tried a down-the-line option with Stringer as the trailing back for the pitch. But he never got to pitch it. Doug had sensed where the play was going, shed a blocker with a forearm and nailed Bellamy with a classic form tackle before the quarterback could make a decision. It was like the hit the previous week on the Canton fullback, but Bellamy was smaller and the hit that put the Canton guy on his back sent Bellamy sailing backward with Doug on top of him. Better still, the ball went bouncing across the turf. Little Javon Shade, playing corner, beat a Science Hill back to the ball, scooped it up, and ran it in.

The Science Hill fans were booing the tackle. The Hilltopper coach ran out of the field, yelling "targeting!" But the official, to his credit, would not call a penalty. "Legal hit, legal hit," Doug heard him say. Bellamy was slow getting up. Doug helped him, but he fell over again. His teammates pushed Doug aside to assist their quarterback. Bellamy finally made it to his feet and walked the sideline. He was a little wobbly. The boo's continued, competing with the cheers from the West Brainerd fans.

One of the Hilltoppers shoved Kenny Mastriano on his way off the field, but Kenny wouldn't take the bait. West Brainerd lined up for the extra point, but the kicker missed it, wide right. The score was 27-21 with a half quarter to go. Plenty of time for Science Hill to win.

But the Hilltoppers never got going after that. Bellamy returned to the field, but his passes and runs were tentative. He fumbled the center exchange once and handoffs to Stringer misfired twice. The 'Toppers recovered both times but the mistakes killed their drives.

The game ended with the Redwings leading 27-21.

BEFORE, DURING, AND AFTER THE GAME

Veronica Clayton found her seat in the crowded stadium after getting some help from an usher. It wasn't the best seat, but it wasn't bad. Her connection at the Northeast Tennessee Association of Realtors, who had helped her get a ticket, had apologized that it was on the visitors' side; but that suited Veronica perfectly. It gave her a better view of the sideline and of the one, certain person she was there to watch.

She was still surprised at herself that she was here at all. She had decided to take the whole day, and use the excuse that she needed to meet with her connections at the Northeast Tennessee Association as the reason. She did have some state association business with them, but it could have been handled by teleconference. She couldn't even convince herself that her brief meeting with the local association staff at their offices in Gray was the reason for the trip. She realized it was an excuse.

The trip wasn't hard to arrange. She had just the person to stay with the kids overnight. All of her other meetings could be moved or handed off to an associate. She left Friday morning and had interstate highways the whole way, slowed only by road construction just west of Knoxville. She met with the Northeast Association staff early in the afternoon, picked up her game ticket there, and then drove to Johnson City and checked into the Carnegie Hotel across the street from East Tennessee State University. The hotel had arranged for its shuttle to take her to the stadium, and she could call for it to pick her up after the game.

Surely, she thought, this won't do any harm. She didn't know anyone around her. No one would recognize her. The cool weather helped. She wore a bulky sweater, boots, a jacket, and a warm cloth hat that shielded much of her face. That was paranoid, she admitted to herself. No one would know her, or why she was there, anyway.

She just couldn't help herself. She wanted to see the young man her baby had become.

He wasn't hard to pick out. Her first thought was, my, he's big. Not tall, but freakishly broad in the shoulders and across his chest. No wonder they called him "Stump." Short, muscular legs. Big biceps. When he came off the field and removed his helmet, his head, steaming in the cool air, showed a dark red shock of hair, slightly curly from his damp sweat. Veronica had brought a pair of field glasses and studied him closely. Why, he's handsome, she thought, and felt an irrational thrill of pride she couldn't help.

Veronica wasn't a dedicated football fan. She sometimes went with friends or business associates to the Titans' games at LP Field; and when she'd been married, her husband had insisted they go to some Vanderbilt games. She watched part of a game on television every now and then. But it was all casual.

She'd picked up enough to be able to follow the game. And Doug Martin was easy to follow. She found herself standing and cheering when he made a big hit, or when he ran the ball. This gained her some sidelong glances from those seated around her, who were mostly home team fans. There weren't enough West Brainerd fans to take up the whole visitors' side. But the only comment she got was from a man who asked in a friendly tone, "Hey, lady, how'd you get seated here with us?" Everyone figured she was just a misplaced West Brainerd fan.

She stood and moved with the crowd toward an exit when the game ended. She realized she had to get a closer look at the boy she'd come to see. She watched the West Brainerd fans filing out, and followed them. Surely some would go by the visiting team's locker room. It will be all right, she told herself. I won't speak with him. I won't get too close.

The line of fans walking out moved slowly. Not everyone close to her was a visiting team fan. She found herself walking next to two men who had evidently come together. One was short with a grizzled beard and wore a denim jacket. The other was taller and wore a dark blue sweatshirt with a University of Tennessee logo on the front. She could hear their conversation.

"That 'Stump' guy plays dirty," the one with the beard said. "They oughta thrown him outa the game."

Veronica felt herself stiffen. "Her" boy did not play dirty!

The other man said, "Yeah, well, I know this. The Vols are after him hard. Real hard."

"Hummph," the first man responded. "I hope we get him. He's good."

Veronica looked down, hiding a smile. Apparently it didn't matter how dirty someone played if he was going to play for your team, she thought. But…the boy didn't play dirty anyhow.

Angling to her left, now that the line was thinning, she found a clump of fans whose colors said they were Redwings supporters. She found a tall, blocky, dark-haired man, maybe in his thirties, who kept a wide grin who'd been calling out to others, and fell in beside him.

"Excuse me, sir," she said, "are you going to the West Brainerd locker room? Is this the way?"

"I am and it is," he said, looking down at her and extending a hand. "Bob Mastriano. My kid brother is Kenny. He plays guard. I don't believe I know you."

"I'm Ronnie," she said, deliberately not giving a last name, and not explaining herself.

But he persisted. "Do you have someone on the team?"

"N-no," she said. "I – I just have a friend who told me I ought to check out the game. He...said this team is special."

"Who's the friend?" he asked as the line moved, more quickly this time.

"Danny Jarvis," she blurted. Damn! She swore silently. Why did I say that?"

"The Reporter?"

"Uhh, yeah," she said.

"I read his blog," Mastriano explained.

"That's nice," she said, and added, "He's more like a friend of a friend. I don't know him all that well."

By now they had arrived just outside a building that evidently housed the locker rooms. There were buses parked outside. Veronica could see young men in letter jackets exiting, carrying duffels. They were being greeted by friends and family.

"I see," said Mastriano. "Well, there's Kenny. He's going to ride home with me. Are you waiting for anyone."

"N-no," she said, not knowing what else to say.

He looked puzzled, but to her relief, said only, "Well, nice to meet you," and walked away toward a boy who was waving at him. She breathed a sigh of relief. That had been awkward.

Her eyes roamed the crowd. Doug Martin was easy to find. His blocky form stood out. He was standing just outside the double doors to the building, his duffel propped against a leg, talking to a big black guy wearing an orange blazer. She supposed the man was a college scout or something.

Walking closer, she saw a group of five people who appeared to be waiting for Doug to finish with the man in the orange blazer. There was a dark, Latino looking man with a brown-haired wife and a pretty young woman in a Redwings cheerleader outfit. That must be the girlfriend and her parents, she guessed. The others...were these the foster parents? Her memories were vague. The man was large and well-built, his hair nearly all gray. The woman was blonde and much younger. They were chatting amiably with the girl and her parents, but she couldn't hear the conversation.

I'd better not get too close, she thought. She didn't think she'd be recognized, but she shouldn't take any chances.

She jumped and squealed as a voice behind her said, "Hello, Veronica."

Turning, she saw Danny Jarvis, his good-looking face marred by an infuriating smirk.

"You- you startled me," she accused, her mind racing. She realized she'd given herself away, no matter what she'd said or would say. She resolved to stay the course. He couldn't prove anything, as bad as this might look.

"Sorry," he said. "But fancy seeing you here. An unexpected pleasure… Here to see your boy?"

Veronica made what she hoped was an exasperated face. "No. I was here today on business, and I was curious. That's all."

"Curious enough to come over here for a closer look?" he asked, keeping the maddening smirk.

"I was looking for a good spot to call the hotel shuttle," she said with gritted teeth. "Not that it's any of your business."

He ignored the jibe. "You don't need to do that. I'll be glad to run you over to your hotel. Where are you staying?"

"The Carnegie." She might as well tell him.

"Nice," he said. "The real estate racket pays better than writing. I'm down the road from you at a Comfort Inn." His voice losing the bantering tone, he added, "Look, I'm going to try to get a quick interview. I'll take you for a drink, and then back to your hotel. We need to talk, anyway. What about it?"

Veronica considered. This evening was already a disaster, and was unlikely to get worse. She needed to have it out with him, anyway. And he was kinda cute, she thought, immediately angry with herself as she thought it.

"We-ll," she said. "Okay. But you're still barking up the wrong tree."

"We'll see," he said. "C'mon. I'll introduce you."

She hung back, shaking her head, and then decided it would be worse if she didn't brazen it out. She followed him to where Doug was now talking with his parents, girlfriend, and her parents.

Danny walked up and re-introduced himself, and then Veronica, whom he called "my friend." Ha! She thought. Not likely. But she was about to have a drink with him. How weird was that?

If Mr. and Mrs. Martin recognized the young woman who had birthed their son, they gave no indication of it. Well, 18 years had passed and she was all bundled up. They greeted her politely and shook hands. They introduced their son and the other couple, whose name was Martinez. The girl was their daughter Eva. Veronica noticed the way Eva looked at Doug managed to convey both worship and ownership.

Veronica willed her hand not to shake as she shook hands with the young man. My baby, she thought. My first. But all he said was, "How do you do, Mrs. Clayton?" But of course he'd have no idea of whom he had just met.

Doug's father allowed Danny one question before they had to leave for a late snack and trip home.

"Are you any closer to deciding on a college, Doug?" Jarvis asked. "I saw you talking with the Tennessee linebackers coach."

"No, sir," Doug said. "I'm not."

"Is Tennessee in it?" Jarvis asked.

"That's two questions," the boy's father said. "But – okay."

"I'm considering a number of schools," Doug said. "Tennessee is one."

"But do you…" Jarvis began, but the senior Martin cut him off.

"I said that's all," he warned. His eyes turned to the rest of the group. "Let's go, people."

Veronica stood with Jarvis and watched them walk away, then followed him to his car.

She felt trapped. And she'd stuck her own head in the trap.

Chapter 23
JOHNSON CITY, TENNESSEE, OCTOBER 2022

AT THE CARNEGIE HOTEL

The restaurant cocktail lounge at the hotel was still open, but not busy. There was a man drinking alone at the bar. A couple was having a late snack and wine at a high-topped table. Otherwise, the lounge was empty.

Veronica and Danny found another high-topped table at the opposite end of the room from the other couple. The bartender came around to take their orders, and Veronica asked for a double vodka martini with a twist. This was not her usual style, but damn it, she needed a drink right now. Jarvis ordered Scotch and soda. The bartender left a bar menu and departed to fetch their drinks.

"Do you want anything to eat?" Danny asked.

"Not right now," she replied. Actually, she *was* hungry, or would have been if the post-game events had been less upsetting. "Maybe later," she said.

"All right, Veronica," Danny said. "Let's talk. I know you gave birth to that kid. You're much better off talking with me about it. The story is going to break anyway, probably next week. Don't you want your version to be told?"

"My 'version' is I still don't know what you're talking about," she said. "And if you print something, my name better not be in it."

"You don't expect me to believe that, do you?" he asked.

151

"I don't care what you believe," she said.

The bartender appeared with their drinks, and asked if they wanted food. "I'll be here until midnight," he explained, "but the kitchen closes in thirty minutes. If you want something, you'd better order it now."

Jarvis scanned the menu and ordered a Reuben with fries. Veronica started to decline anything, but realized she wouldn't get another chance to eat until morning. She glanced over the menu, and asked for a turkey sandwich.

When the man was gone, Jarvis took a sip of his drink and tried again. "Look," he said, "suppose I guarantee your name won't be mentioned. Will you talk with me if I do?"

She didn't hesitate. This slope was entirely too slippery, and she'd slipped far enough as it was. "There's nothing to talk about," she said.

Jarvis made a shrewd guess. "NDA?"

She knew what he meant. "Non-Disclosure Agreement."

There was a non-disclosure provision in the agreement she'd signed so long ago, and its liquidated damages provision was pretty steep. She didn't think she'd violated it already. But she wasn't going to give him anything. She said nothing.

"Look," he said. "I don't care what the penalties are, they're nothing compared to the book deal I can get you if you'll tell me the whole story. They're not going to *kill* you or anything."

Veronica suppressed a shudder. She didn't know what the DOD might do to cover up if it thought its secret was jeopardized.

But she smiled and asked, "With you as my co-author, I suppose?"

He smiled back. "Of course."

Veronica took a healthy sip of her drink, and said, "I told you. There is no story."

Jarvis sighed. "All right," he said. "I give up. You have my card if you change your mind." He finished his drink and added, "By the way, I'm meeting with Dr. Nathan Valenski next week. "I'll tell him you said 'hi.'"

She couldn't catch her sharp intake of breath. That was the doctor who had delivered the baby who was now Doug Martin. She remembered him. But she caught herself and said, "I don't know that name."

Jarvis didn't argue, but his smug smile said he knew he'd scored a hit. Where had he got that name? Someone was already talking, she realized, or feeding him information somehow. That was troubling. She finished her drink, and Jarvis waved at the bartender for re-fills.

"You'd better be careful with the Scotch," she warned him. "I don't have to drive anywhere tonight. You do."

His grin was infuriating, but somehow appealing.

"Well," he said, "I was sort of hoping…"

She laughed out loud. "Forget it."

But she was tempted. She didn't know why she was drawn to this man. His looks? His persistence? But she sure wasn't going to sleep with him.

Not tonight, anyway. When this thing blew over…

She had his card.

"Can we talk about something else while we eat?" she asked, seeing the bartender on the way with plates, fresh drinks, and water glasses.

"Sure," he said, looking directly into her eyes.

Oh, hell, she thought. But she decided she didn't want to completely change the subject. She wanted his answer to something else.

"Have you ever stopped to think about what publishing this crazy story you keep talking about is going to do that boy?" she asked.

Jarvis kept the eye contact, but shifted in his seat. Good, she thought. He ought to squirm a little.

"I don't see that it will do anything to him," Jarvis said. "If anything, it will help him. He can make money off of it. Cash in on the attention."

"I can see you don't remember what it's like to be a teenager. Some people will shun him. Some will make fun of him. He may lose friends. And a bunch of so-called news hounds like you will harass him. That's a lot to put on a kid."

"I don't think that will happen," Jarvis insisted. But she saw him hit his drink pretty hard. But he rallied.

"Veronica, if what I think really happened – and you know it did, better than I – doesn't the public need to know what the government has been up to in secret. I mean, cloning ancient humans! Doesn't the public have the right to know?"

"Give me a break," she said. "This is about your career and nothing else. Don't bullshit me."

She watched him finish his drink and pick up his Reuben without answering. She was glad she'd gotten his goat, for a change.

But damn it, she still thought he was cute.

ON THE ROAD IN TENNESSEE AND NORTH CAROLINA, OCTOBER 2022 SATURDAY

On Saturday morning, Danny Jarvis woke early in his hotel room in Johnson City. He showered, shaved, brushed his teeth quickly, anxious to get on the road and back to work. He briefly considered calling Veronica Clayton to ask if she'd join him for breakfast, but decided to leave well enough alone. She'd certainly made herself clear last night that she was not looking to hook up with him.

Actually, he was mad at himself for hitting on her. It was not very professional, he admitted to himself. In fact, it was not professional at all. She was the subject he was investigating for a news analysis. Well, not the main subject. That was Doug Martin and his antecedents. But she was connected, no matter what she said. That made any personal relationship, well, inappropriate.

He couldn't deny her attraction, and he could have sworn it was mutual. That didn't matter. He should have had better self-control. Now maybe, later – but no, he corrected himself. The story, once it broke, would go on for a while. Besides, there was too much distance between them, and she had her own life, her acknowledged children, and her own career.

But, he thought as he checked out of the hotel and loaded his overnight bag and computer into his car, she suited him better than most women he'd been around. To his surprise, that included Monica Gilbert. Monica was quite the looker. She had a killer body, and was a deranged mongoose in bed. He knew, though, that he was just a diversion. She had someone else, maybe more than one someone. And she treated their coupling like a contest she was determined to win. He was sure Veronica would be…different.

Jarvis found a Bojangles near the hotel where he could get a coffee and a sausage biscuit for the road. He would eat in the car to save time, because there was much to be done when got home. He had the game story to write. And then he had to revise the big story. Its release had already been delayed so he could do some edits, and hopefully find out some more information. So, he needed to get his mind off women and onto what he had to do.

He decided not to take the route over the mountain that the West Brainerd team and fans had used to get to Johnson City. That was shorter as the crow flies, but winding and tiring to drive. Taking Highway I-26 to Asheville, I-40 to Statesville, and I-77 from Statesville to home was longer; but the roads were excellent, and it was the type of brainless drive that enabled him to write his stories in his head while he drove. He did that a lot.

He couldn't file the re-write until Monday anyway. He had one more call to make, the one he'd promised Veronica he'd make to Dr. Valenski. It would probably come to nothing, but he had to try. If he actually learned something, he'd have to revise some more. What he wanted to think about today was what to say about Veronica, and also how to soften the story's coverage of the boy.

Despite what he'd said to Veronica last night, there really was something to what she'd said about the impact of the story on Doug Martin himself. None of this was his fault. By all accounts, he was a good kid. He already had some abnormal things to think about in addition to the usual teenage stuff. Not many kids had so many colleges clamoring for his services as an athlete. He had that to deal with in addition to all the usual things with school, his ball games, his girlfriend, and so on.

Danny didn't consider for a minute not running with the story. That was too big, too important, to let go. But maybe he could emphasize the young man's humanity more, make people think of him as a person and not just a freak in a football uniform. That was worth writing, he decided as he drove. That part of the piece should be beefed up. He would delete the word "sub-human."

What about Veronica? He didn't think he ought to use her name. The lawyer didn't think she'd sue, but she might. She surely would issue a loud and scathing denial. Personally, he was certain she was Doug Martin's birth mother; her showing up for the game in Johnson City had clinched that for him. But he still couldn't prove anything over her denial. He thought her explanation was lame, but some people wouldn't. It might actually be better, he thought, to leave the birth mother's identity a mystery for now. He could write in such a way to tempt her to come forward, or to inspire a bigger news operation, with a bigger budget, to follow up and find her themselves.

By the time he reached Morganton, he thought he had it. He reached for his phone with one hand, and turned on the voice-recorder application. He spoke as he drove:

"Douglas MacArthur Martin is a good citizen, an outstanding student, a good teammate, a good friend, and a good son. He is also a freakishly talented young athlete. These talents may be the result of traits directly inherited from an ancestor immediate to him but remote to us. Or they may not. In any case, having such talents is not his fault.

"There is reason to believe, but no firm proof, that his physical prowess derives from the genes of a man long dead. And if that is the case, do not Americans deserve to know whether their government is engaged in the creation of, for lack of a better term, supermen, perhaps with unanticipated consequences? In Martin's case, the trail becomes cold in the mountains of West Virginia, where a young woman who cannot be named and cannot be found bore a child eighteen years ago. She is out there somewhere now, and has at least some of the answers."

He liked it. It would salve his conscience and avoid any trouble with Veronica. And he would have his story in print within days.

When he arrived home, it turned out he didn't have another call after all. When he opened his computer, he found another anonymous e-mail from an untraceable domain. He read it twice.

"Rumors persist that the Defense Department has cloned early humans as well as fossilized animals. Most have been brought up in secret, but one was selected to be reared as a 'normal' child. Nathan Valenski knows who that child is, and you can guess. But don't try to contact him now. Let the story break, first. A word to the wise."

Danny didn't know who was sending him these e-mails. He suspected he didn't want to know. He was aware there was competition among different branches of government, even different branches of the armed services. He'd take the advice. But he'd delete the e-mail.

He could remember what it said.

CHAPEL HILL, NORTH CAROLINA, OCTOBER 2022 SATURDAY AFTERNOON

"I sent the e-mail you wanted to Jarvis," Monica said into the telephone, "and got back a receipt it had been delivered."

"Good," Dennis Springfield replied. "After I thought about it, I realized Valenski would be on the phone to someone at Defense, maybe our 'friend' Fred Hutton, as soon as Jarvis spoke with him. The DOD might've tried to block the story. They have contacts here and at Justice. Not everyone is on the same page, as you know."

"Do you think they can trace the e-mail to me?" Monica asked.

"I doubt it, but if they do, we can wipe your computer before they can do anything," he said. "Hmmm, we may need to do something about Jarvis' computer, too; but we'll have a little time after the story breaks…Has Jarvis been in touch with the host mother?"

"I don't know," she said. "Do you want me to find out?"

"Why don't you ask him for an advance copy of his story?" Springfield asked. "If he doesn't out her, we may have to take…additional steps. But wait a day or two. I don't want you calling him today. He might put two and two together."

"I'd better not wait past Monday," she said. "I don't know when he'll release it. And don't worry. I won't call him today. He might want to see me this weekend, and that would be…awkward."

She could imagine Springfield smiling into the phone, but she didn't care. Dennis knew how she operated with men.

"Whatever you think," Springfield said. "We've almost pulled off our little *expose'*. Good work, Monica."

She thanked him and ended the call. She needed to finish with her hair. Barry would be here soon.

Chapter 24
MARTINTOWN, NORTH CAROLINA, OCTOBER 2022

Coach Watkins cancelled football practice on Monday. His team was coming off two tough non-conference games, and was headed into the stretch run in first place, looking for a spot in the playoffs. Coach wanted the team rested.

Doug Martin was glad of the time off. It was just a day, but another day to let the bruises heal was welcome. He could enjoy class today and hang out with his friends for a while after school without needing to gear up for physical activity. He wouldn't be able to hang out with Eva after the final bell, because her cheerleading practice had not been cancelled, but he and Kenny and Javon and Harry could go watch. And he had two classes with her.

The first was advanced math with Mrs. Miller, a middle-aged, dumpy woman from Georgia, whose accent he loved and who was a really gifted teacher. The official name of the course was Algebra III and Trigonometry, but everyone called it "advanced math." They'd even get into calculus before year's end. He liked it.

He liked the next class even better. It was one of the courses taught to seniors by professors from Carolina Highlands Community College as part of its "early college" program. Depending on where you went, you'd get college credit for early college classes. This one was English Composition with Mr. McCaffrey, who spiced up the class by sneaking some of the English literature he taught to sophomores into the class as a way of sparking essay writing.

Doug took his seat next to Eva with anticipation. Class with Mr. McCaffrey was almost always fun. There were all kinds of rumors about Professor McCaffrey (who disliked being called "professor" and preferred "mister"). He was an Enduring Freedom veteran. He'd been the subject of a hearing at the college two years ago, when somebody (it wasn't clear who) had been after his job, and last year had been, everyone said, the subject of an FBI investigation. Some students thought he was secretly still in military intelligence. His wife was the pretty coffee lady at the Bean n' Bacon.

Right now, his class at West Brainerd was reading "Romeo and Juliet", and Mr. McCaffrey had promised he'd explain Renaissance fencing when they discussed the duels between Mercutio and Tybalt, and Tybalt and Romeo. Doug thought that would be way cool.

He and Eva sat next to each other. She liked the course, too; and being active herself, also looked forward to the explanation about swordplay. Both listened raptly while McCaffrey explained the origins of the word "swashbuckler," took a yardstick to demonstrate how the swords were used, and explained the convoluted politics of the Italian city-states in the 1500's. McCaffrey even asked for a volunteer to help him demonstrate swordplay, and Doug raised his hand. Their slow-speed sparring earned a round of applause, and McCaffrey followed up with a lecture on how some of the audience at the Globe Theatre would have known something about sword fighting, so that the actors had needed to be at least a little realistic.

After class, he and Eva went to the school cafeteria for lunch. She contented herself with a salad, while he got the Salisbury steak and vegetable. He needed lots of fuel. They talked about their classes, and especially how much they liked McCaffrey as a teacher.

"That reminds me," Eva said, her face solemn. "I've been meaning to tell you. I...I think I'm going to go my first year, maybe my first two, to Carolina Highlands. It won't cost much, and...well, I'm interested in going to law school, we're not rich, and I need to save money somewhere. I just wanted you to know there's no chance we'll be at the same place next year."

Doug had been expecting something like this. He'd known they have to face their college decisions sooner or later. In a way, he was relieved she'd put it on the table. He reached across the table and covered her hand with his.

"I understand," he said, hesitated, and then let himself smile. "At least I know where you'll be when I come home."

Eva smiled quickly, and then the solemn mask returned. "That won't be often, will it? I mean, I don't see how it can be, with your games and practices and all."

"Maybe you can come to visit me," he offered.

"It depends on how far I'd have to go," she said. "Do you know where you're going, yet? Or what you'll study?"

Doug shook his head. "I really don't. I don't think I'm going to decide until after the playoffs." He took a final bite of steak, chewed, and said, "I do know this: Whatever I go into, I want to do something active. That might be a lot of things. Civil engineering, maybe. But I can be active doing a bunch of stuff. I'll have to think some more.

"Anyway, you and I will work things out. I'm sure we will."

He squeezed her hand. She smiled across the table. He thought she looked relieved.

CHAPEL HILL, NORTH CAROLINA, OCTOBER 22 MONDAY AFTERNOON

"Sure, Monica," Danny Jarvis said into his phone, "I can send you a copy of what we're going to run as soon as I have the final edits. The plan is for the web version to be up Friday morning, and the print newsletter to be mailed Thursday afternoon, so most of the print subscribers will have it early next week. I'll do a teaser on my blog this week, without giving away anything, and update the blog Friday morning, with a link to the story.

"Of course, if whoever clicks on the link doesn't already have a sub-scription, they'll have to sign up before they can read the whole story."

"What about the mainstream press?" Monica asked. "Are they going to be informed?"

"Oh, yes," he said. My editor will send copies to the AP, to the newspapers in Charlotte, Asheville, Raleigh, and Wilmington, to the Washington *Post* and the New York *Times*. He'll send it to the networks and cable news people, too. With any luck, we'll get some national attention."

"How do you think it will be received?" she asked.

Jarvis hesitated. That was the 64 thousand dollar question, to use an outmoded term. "Well," he said, "I hope someone will take it seriously, or at least see the human interest in the story. We'll just have to wait and see."

"Did you ever get the birth mother to come clean?" she asked. "You did find her, didn't you?"

"I…I think so," he said, immediately uncomfortable with bringing Veronica into this. "But we can't prove anything, and – well, the story won't use the name we have. Maybe she'll come forward on her own."

Or maybe she won't, Monica thought. The woman is probably too scared of the consequences to do that. God knows what the DOD told her or had her sign. Well, maybe she needed some help. She'd talk with Dennis about that.

But all she said was, "I see. Well, thank you. I'll look forward to reading it…Of course, my name is nowhere near any of this, is it?"

"Of course not," he said. "I didn't get anything from you."

"I just wanted to be sure," she said. "I did try, but I couldn't get anything."

"I know," he said. "Thanks for trying."

"No worries," she replied. "I'll let you know what I think when I read it."

When the call concluded, Monica was sure of two things. First, Jarvis suspected she'd been the one who found the agent who'd hacked into the state archives for him; but would keep his mouth shut, because he couldn't prove anything. Second, Jarvis hadn't leaned on the Clayton woman all that hard. He was protecting her. She thought she knew why.

It was telling that Danny hadn't pestered her for a return engagement. She didn't really care, but the omission was still annoying. She liked men who were on her hook.

Well, she thought, there was something else Dennis' contacts could do: they could find a way to leak to the big news outlets that this story might be real. Danny didn't know it, but he was about to get some major help.

MARTINTOWN, NORTH CAROLINA, OCTOBER 2022 AT THE MCCAFFREY RESIDENCE

Mitch McCaffrey sat on a stool at the central kitchen counter, watching Diana slice tomatoes, cucumbers, and onions and toss a salad, while he sipped a glass of merlot. A pot of the Bean 'n Bacon beef stew was simmering on the stove. Paul and Steve were supposed to be doing their homework, but were probably sneaking video games, knowing their rooms were too far away for their mother and step-father to hear them.

Mitch had been telling his wife about how much fun he'd had with the course at West Brainerd this morning, including his recount of the sparring with Doug Martin.

"I'm telling you, honey," he said, "that boy is quick as a cat and strong as an ox. We weren't even at full speed, he'd didn't know the first thing about fencing, and he almost touched me with his yardstick twice and knocked out my hands once. And I don't think I'm a weakling."

Diana put down the utensils she'd been using to toss the salad and gave her husband, who she knew to be a physical fitness fanatic, a fond look. "No, darling," she said, "no one would call you that."

If he knew she was teasing him, he didn't show it. "And his anticipation was just unreal. It was as though he knew where I would try to tag him. His Talent was broadcasting clear as a bell, even if he didn't know it."

"Is anybody going to tell him about that?" Diana asked.

"No," Mitch said with a headshake. "Fred Hutton said definitely 'no.' We're just supposed to watch him and report anything unusual."

"So, the government is just going to leave him alone?" she asked.

"For now," Mitch agreed. "That could change if…"

"If what?" she prompted.

"If anything happens," her husband said.

"What could happen?"

"I don't know. But," he continued, "I have a little prescience, too; and I don't have a good feeling."

"I hope it's a false alarm," Diana said, and pushed the intercom button to summon the kids for dinner. "But if it's not, I'm betting Monica Gilbert is behind it."

"Huh?" her husband said.

"She's been behind everything else that's gone wrong around here," his wife said. "No reason to think she's reformed. And she knows about this boy. She's bound to."

Chapter 25

MARTINTOWN, NORTH CAROLINA
OCTOBER 2022

FRIDAY MORNING

Darren Martin returned to the offices of Simmons IT & Security from a service call to a regular client just after 11:30. He had started to stop for lunch on his way back, but decided he needed to complete his billing time entries and enter his call report first. He had just seated himself in his cubicle, when there was a knock on the side panel. He looked up to see Carson McCaffrey standing there holding a tablet.

"You need to see this," Carson said, his tone almost apologetic. "It's about Doug." He handed over the tablet. The screen was open to the first page of the weekly electronic version of the *Tar Heel Sports Weekly* newsletter. Darren took the proffered device and began to read.

Darren was used to seeing a lot of wild speculation about Doug, mostly involving where his son would wind up going to college. But it was immediately obvious that the lead story in front of him was different. It had been written by Danny Jarvis, whom Darren had never trusted, and the headline was, "Is a Neanderthal Clone Playing Football in Western North Carolina?"

Darren felt as though he'd been punched in the gut. This was what he'd thought he would never see, been assured he'd never see. But there it was. Where had this guy got his information? There had to be a leak somewhere in the government. Hutton had told Darren and Laura that everything was sealed and encrypted. The story was speculative, and admitted it was; but it came uncomfortably close to the mark. No wonder Jarvis had kept asking him and Lara where their son got his physique and talent. He'd been working on this all along.

At least, the piece wasn't hostile or derisive toward Doug. That was something. But it would attract a bunch of attention; and if that happened, who knew what else might happen?

Darren finished and looked up at Carson. "Can you send this to me?" he asked.

"Sure," McCaffrey said, then added, "This is nonsense. And it's irresponsible. Are you going to call a lawyer?"

"Maybe," Darren said, and amended it to, "Probably."

But first he had to call Lara. And he'd have to send this story to Fred Hutton.

CHAPEL HILL, NORTH CAROLINA, OCTOBER 2022 FRIDAY MORNING

As promised, Danny Jarvis had sent Monica the links to his blog and to the *Tar Heel Sports Weekly* newsletter early Friday morning. He'd already sent her an advance copy of his story. She'd sent everything to Dennis Springfield as soon as she had it, and was now on the secure line to him.

"Well, I've done my part," she said. "Now we'll see if this goes anywhere."

"Oh, I think I can assure you that it will," Springfield said. "We do have our own contacts in the media. They'll get messages that the story is 'real'. You know, the usual 'anonymous sources' they love so much. And…we do have *some* friends inside Defense. This cloning thing they did was done by a prior administration, one they didn't like. There are some people there who wouldn't mind some other folks getting a black eye.

"But," he continued, "I'm concerned about what this man Jarvis has on his devices. Hutton's group has some pull with the Director, and with Justice, as you know. We do our share of infighting, too. I wouldn't want a raid to find something that would cause us to be suspected. And Hutton and his people might have enough pull to get a raid on the guy and confiscate his devices."

"I thought you told me nothing could be traced to us," Monica said, suddenly alarmed.

"I said nothing they'll find can be proven to have come to us," Springfield said. "I'd rather nothing be suspected. Well, Fred will suspect us no matter what, but without evidence, it won't matter."

"What are you going to do about it?" Monica asked.

"I think we can arrange for someone to pay a little visit to your buddy Danny Jarvis," Springfield said. "Call it an unfortunate burglary."

"You're not going to hurt him, are you?" she asked. She felt nothing for Jarvis, but he had been a good bedmate. She really didn't want to feel responsible for his being hurt.

"Oh, no," Springfield said. "Scared? Sure. Hurt? No. Come to think of it, I don't we'll need to do that just yet. Whomever Defense is talking with at Justice won't want to get a warrant and raid Jarvis right now. If they did that, claiming Jarvis has illegally accessed documents 'essential to national security,' everybody would know the story is true. So they won't do anything of that sort until the cat is well and truly out of the bag. So we've got time.

"And don't worry. You won't need to be involved. I've something else in mind for you."

"What is it?" she asked, wary of what he might want from her.

"You'll enjoy this; it's right up your alley," he assured her. "This Martin thing will be a finger in the eye to the DIA no matter what. That's good. But we have a better shot at recruiting the kid if he's not playing football.

"Here's what I have in mind…"

As she listened, Monica started smiling. Dennis was right. What he wanted really was her "line of country," as the Brits say. And it would all look so innocent, so…responsible. So…correct.

MARTINTOWN, NORTH CAROLINA, OCTOBER 2022 FRIDAY AFTERNOON

In a few minutes, Darren and Lara Martin would need to leave for the stadium to watch Doug's ball game. They knew he was bound to have seen the Jarvis article, and would have questions after he came home tonight. But now they were gathered around Darren's laptop in his home office, looking at the image of Major Fred Hutton on their screen. Hutton had sent them an encrypted link for a video conference after he and Darren had talked.

They were all 18 years older than they'd been when they'd arranged for Doug's adoption. Hutton was a little heavier and a lot grayer, but otherwise had not changed a lot.

"I don't think there's that much to worry about," Hutton said. "I read the piece twice. So far, it's only in that local sports newsletter. I can't tell that anyone else has picked up on it yet. I doubt they'll pay much attention if they do."

"But what if they do?" Lara asked. "I'm sure we'll be contacted by at least the local media."

"My recommendation is to laugh it off as ridiculous," Hutton said. "There's no real proof. Yeah, I know the guy has guessed right; and that's upsetting. I get that. But all his stuff sounds like wild speculation."

"What concerns me is that he found out Dr. Valenski's name," Darren said. "It sounds to me like you have a leak somewhere."

Hutton frowned. "Yeah, that bothers me, too…I'll see what I can find out. But that doesn't change my recommendation. I promise you that the Defense Department will issue a 'don't be ridiculous' denial if anyone calls us. And don't worry about Nathan. He'll do the same. I talked with him already."

"Should we sue, or at least threaten to sue?" Darren asked.

"I wouldn't. That just dignifies the claim. And it also opens you up to giving depositions and so forth. Suing might make everything worse.

"If it will make you feel better, you can talk with a lawyer. Do you have anyone in mind?"

"I'm sure we'd call someone at Melton, Norville, Johnson & Jennings," said Lara. "They're supposed to be the best around here."

"I'm familiar with the firm," Hutton said, and smiled as he saw the Martins exchange a look. He was sure there had to be some rumors swirling in Brainerd County after the last two years.

"Do you think Jarvis has found the birth mother?" asked Darren.

"Well," Hutton answered, "you read the article. It doesn't look like it… If he did, she didn't give him anything. She's under a non-disclosure, too. I have her contact information. I'll call her and remind her of her obligations."

"There's something else," Lara said. "What do we tell our son?"

Hutton frowned again, considering. "What does he know now?"

"He knows he's adopted," Lara told him. "And that his birth-mother is a local girl and not a relative. Nothing else."

"What have you planned on telling him?" Hutton asked.

"At some point, the truth," Darren said. "We've talked about waiting until he was eighteen. He's eighteen now, but we haven't told him, because, well, we wanted to talk with you, first, and then, he's had enough on him with all this college recruiting attention. Now…now, he'll have more on him. But we've been thinking about it."

"We don't like lying to Doug," Lara said. "He *is* our son, in our hearts."

Hutton's sigh was like a steam engine winding down. "I know," he said. "But I wouldn't tell him just yet. That will put even more pressure on him. You know we'd have to put him under an NDA, too.

"I'd wait. Chances are, this will blow over."

"I hope," said Darren.

"I pray," Lara added.

But they were worried.

COOL SPRINGS, TENNESSEE, OCTOBER 2022 FRIDAY AFTERNOON

Veronica Clayton was home after an upsetting day. It hadn't been work. That had been routine. It was reading and re-reading the article Danny Jarvis had sent her that morning.

Jarvis had really done it. He'd really gone to press with the story. For some reason, she didn't believe he would. But he didn't mention her name, and from reading the piece, you'd think he had no idea of the Martin boy's host mother. She was grateful for that. No one was going to call her. She wouldn't have to say anything to anyone.

For now, she reminded herself. But if Danny could find her, someone else might, too, if somebody read Danny's article and got interested. And some of the big papers, and the networks, had a lot more resources than Danny freaking Jarvis. The idea scared her.

Veronica didn't know what to do. Probably nothing, she told herself. Just wait and hope. She'd started to e-mail or call Jarvis and thank him for leaving her out of the story, but caught herself before she could click "send" or press the call icon. That would be the worst thing she could do.

She was supposed to meet some friends for dinner at a local restaurant, and busied herself in repairing her make-up and changing clothes. She hoped she could relax this evening.

She jumped when her cell phone rang. Caller id said the caller was from somewhere in Washington. She decided she'd better answer. It was Fred Hutton.

Ten minutes later, she ended the call and grabbed her purse to leave for the restaurant. She'd said all the right things, told Hutton what he wanted to hear. She acted as though she hadn't seen the story. Hutton promised to send it to her. And she didn't tell him Jarvis had found her. But that wasn't too bad a lie. She'd given Jarvis nothing, and promised Hutton she'd stonewall anyone who called, and contact him immediately if someone did.

So far, so good. But there were still two problems.

One was that she wanted to see the boy to whom she'd given birth again.

The other was that she wanted to see Danny Jarvis again.

Chapter 26
MARTINTOWN, NORTH CAROLINA, OCTOBER 2022

FRIDAY EVENING AT THE STADIUM

Doug Martin sat alone on a bench in the locker room. Every now and then, a teammate would walk over, slap him on the shoulder pads, and offer an encouraging word. He always gave them a smile and a thumbs up. But, sensing he wanted to be alone with his thoughts right now, they mostly gave him space.

Today had been a blur. Everyone at the school had a smart phone. The school's wi-fi was good. The story in *Tar Heel Sports Weekly* had spread all over West Brainerd in an hour. Most of his classmates had considered it a colossal joke. Javon Shade had gone around calling him "Caveman Stump." Doug noticed some students sneaking sly looks at him and whispering, but not all that many.

His problem wasn't them. It was him. The story felt right to him. It made sense to him. He couldn't explain his own body, the barrel chest, the massive shoulders. He didn't understand why he could bench press more weight than anyone on the team, and more than most collegiate athletes. It didn't make sense that he'd inherited his physique from some unknown girl and boy from West Virginia.

The Jarvis story was accurate. He believed it. And his parents had never told him. He didn't blame them for that. They probably had been required not to tell. But he sure hadn't wanted to learn the truth this way, on the internet from the keyboard of some freelance reporter.

As planned, he hadn't gone home after class, but hung around the locker room with food his mother had packed. He didn't eat all of it. He hadn't much appetite. He'd see his folks after the game. He dreaded that.

The only real lift he'd had that day was from Eva...

They were sitting in the cafeteria, Eva with her usual salad and he with a plate of baked chicken and vegetables he wasn't eating. They were at a rear table, at a corner to themselves. Doug didn't miss the sly looks they were receiving from other students. More than usual.

Eva had to notice it, too; but she was concentrating on her boyfriend.

"Aren't you going to eat anything, Doug?" she asked. "You have a game tonight."

Doug took a bite of chicken. One bite, and set his fork in his plate.

"I get it," she said. "It's that silly e-zine report. Get that out of your head. Nobody believes that crap."

Her jaw dropped when he said nothing in response.

"Oh. My. God. *You* believe it, don't you?"

His head jerked in a quick nod. She saw him blink. Was that a tear?

Eva bit her lip and leaned across the table.

"Let me tell you something, Doug Martin," she said. "I think it's nonsense. But if it's true, so freaking what? *I* don't care. You're still you. You're the guy who backed off a catamount. You're the same guy you were yesterday. My guy. Mine."

Sitting on the bench, Doug smiled at the memory. Lifting his head, he saw Coach Watkins' eyes were on him. Coach nodded and smiled. Then he called to the team to gather around him.

"All right guys," Coach said. "Three more games, and then the playoffs. If we win. We can't let up. Those guys we're playing don't care that we're favored. They'd just love to come in and embarrass us."

Watkins, paused. His eyes roamed the room, and settled on Doug.

"Stump," he said. "We've all read that Jarvis guy's story about you. We all know it's bullshit. Pure bullshit."

The team laughed, and then roared approval. "Damn right," someone said.

"Get that out of your mind," Watkins continued. "I want you focused. I want you all focused." He dropped his head and said, "Now let's all say a little prayer for a good, clean game, and nobody gets hurt."

The team shared a moment of silence, and then ran shouting on to the field. Doug ran with the rest, realizing he owed it to the team to do as Coach Watkins told him.

But despite his resolve, Doug couldn't focus. Not like usual. He mistimed and missed tackles and blocks. He fumbled and the other team recovered. And he never missed blocks. He never fumbled. But he did tonight. The coaches kept telling him to shake it off, but he couldn't. It didn't help that the opposing players kept calling him "Clone-boy."

At the half, the visitors led 14-13. It would have been worse if Javon hadn't taken a kick off all the way to a touchdown. Doug knew he'd get a tongue-lashing from Coach in the locker room.

But he didn't. Coach just called him over, heaved a noisy sigh, and said, "I swear, Doug, you're the only person on this team who seems to be taking that bullshit seriously. I don't get it."

Doug lowered his head and mumbled, "I'm sorry, Coach."

"Don't be sorry," Watkins said. "Just go play. Believe in yourself. Your teammates believe in you. I believe in you. Go do it. I want you to knock people down. Run through them. Run over them."

That helped, but not as much as his memory of what Eva had said at lunch. He realized he was still himself. He was still Doug Martin. He was the same player as he'd been last week, the same person he'd been yesterday. He owed it to her, and to Javon, Tommy, Kenny, Les and the rest to act like it.

The second half was different. Doug allowed his instincts, all of his natural senses, including those he didn't understand. If they came from a man 50 thousand years gone, it didn't matter. They were his.

His tackles were hard and sure. So were his blocks. When he had the ball, he ran instinctively, weaving through and then powering over tacklers. He sacked the opposing quarterback three times on blitzes. He ran for two scores. The final score was 40-14, punctuated by a final, long touchdown run by Henry Warren, in which Doug knocked down a defensive end, then took out a linebacker, and escorted Henry into the end zone.

The locker room was happy but not jubilant. The team knew they were supposed to win this game over a middle of the conference opponent. But they embarrassed Doug by surrounding him and shouting, "Cave Man!" over and over.

Coach Watkins finally intervened. "Hey," he called out. "Leave Stump alone. He's had enough bullshit today!"

After he'd showered and dressed, and spoken with the ubiquitous college coaches who managed to make their way into the locker room, Doug made his way outside. He knew his folks, and Eva and her parents, would be waiting.

And there they were, except for Mr. Martinez. He wasn't with Eva and her mom. Eva walked up, stood on tip-toe, and kissed him on his cheek.

"Where's your dad?" he asked, anxious.

"He…couldn't come tonight," Eva said. She sounded nervous. "I'll call you tomorrow."

That was odd, he thought. They already had a date tomorrow, didn't they? Then she stood on tip-toe again and kissed his cheek again. "You're still my guy." That made him feel better.

Doug turned to receive hugs from his parents.

"We'll see you at home, son," his father said, his face solemn. "Good game," he added. "Great second half."

His mother just smiled and hugged him.

Doug said "bye" and started toward his car, dreading what he might learn at home.

MARTINTOWN, NORTH CAROLINA, OCTOBER 2022 AT THE MARTIN HOME

Doug sat at the kitchen table across from his mother. He still wore his letter jacket. His father had removed his coat and hung it from a peg on the wall in the hallway. He was now leaning against the refrigerator.

All our family meetings are here at the kitchen table, Doug thought. Just like all of our meals except when they had company or when it was a special occasion like a birthday or Christmas. And this was going to be a family meeting. He could tell. You could cut the tension with a knife.

"Are you hungry, son?" his mother asked. "I can get you something to eat."

He actually was famished, but said no. He wanted to talk first. He had to know.

"I'll make coffee," his mother said, rising.

Doug said nothing. He didn't drink coffee, not at night, anyway.

His father turned and opened the refrigerator door. He removed two Heinekens, and opened them with an opener nailed to the wall. He set one in front of Doug.

"I could buy these when I was 18," he said, "so I guess you can drink one now. At home," he added.

Doug noticed his mother looked surprised, but she didn't say anything. She continued to pour coffee into a filter. Doug took a sip of the beer.

"It's good," he said.

Silence. There was an elephant in the room, but no one wanted to talk about it.

Finally, he said, "It's true, isn't it?"

He noticed the look his parents exchanged. Then his father said, "Why would you think that?"

"Dad." Doug said. "Come on. Take a look at me. Some miscellaneous kids in West Virginia couldn't have produced me. I can't explain how I'm built. I have…instincts, things I haven't even told you about, I can't explain. They show up on the football field, and….elsewhere." He was thinking about the mountain lion. He hadn't told his folks about that.

"I'm a freak," Doug said, knowing he sounded helpless, and hating it. He started to cry, and he hadn't cried since he was a little kid.

His mother stopped filling the coffee maker and rushed to him, crying herself, and hugging him. "My little boy," she sobbed, and then pulled back and said, "You're not a freak. Don't ever say that."

He looked past her to his father, who had set his beer on the counter and was looking at his son and wife with wide, comprehending eyes. His father straightened his shoulders. Doug knew his dad always did that when he'd reached a decision.

"Lara," Darren Martin said, "our son is becoming a man, is a man. It's time we treated him like one. He needs the whole story."

Lara, always practical, wiped her eyes and said, "Let me get the coffee going."

The three sat at the kitchen table while his parents told him about his adoption, about the papers they had to sign, what they knew about the host-mother, which wasn't much. They told him about Dr. Valenski, and what he'd said.

"I'll never forget what the doctor said," Lara told him, her tears starting again. "'Your son will be a short, strong, normal human boy.' And you are. You're our son."

"And that's it," his father said. "We'll have to tell Major Hutton you know, and you'll have to sign papers, too.

"But you are our son," he continued. "You always will be. You're a Martin. And Martins are tough. We're fighters."

Doug's eyes were dry now. He was still processing all of this, but he knew Darren and Lara Martin were his parents in every way that counted. And he knew something else.

"I'm hungry," he said. "Can I still get something to eat?"

Both his parents laughed. "What do you want, son?" his mother asked.

MARTINTOWN, NORTH CAROLINA, OCTOBER 2022 THE MARTINEZ HOME

"I said that's final," Joe Martinez said. "I don't expect to tell you again. You are not to see him anymore. I won't have my daughter consorting with that…animal."

There had already been one blow-up at the Martinez home that day, when Eva had returned from school, and her father had refused to go to the game. Now Eva and her mom had returned, and it had started again.

They were in the den, where they had found Eva's father watching television and sipping a drink. Eva was still in her white wool cheerleader's outfit with russet lettering and trim, pleated short skirt and all; her mother had removed her coat and stood next to Eva, her arm protectively about her daughter's shoulders.

"Joe," Loretta Martinez said, her tone somewhere between pleading and warning, "the boy is not an animal."

Joe was not in a mood to back down. "I read today he is not human," he said. "Not completely. I don't see a difference."

Eva shifted in discomfort. During study hall, she had done some online research herself, and was aware that how close Neanderthals had been to modern humans was a controversial subject. But she defended her guy.

MARTINTOWN, NORTH CAROLINA, OCTOBER 2022

"But Dad," she said, "most scientists now think the Neanderthals were very close to us. Surely you read that, too."

"I told you the subject is closed," her father said.

"But, Dad," she pleaded. "Doug is…human. I don't think the story is even true. But if it is, we know Neanderthals were human. I mean…they and other humans could have children."

She realized immediately that she'd said the wrong thing. She watched her father's pale face turn crimson. He half rose from his chair.

"Don't tell me that you and that…whatever he is, have…"

Eva felt heat creep up her face. "No, I didn't say…I mean we haven't…" she trailed off.

Fortunately, her mother came to her rescue.

"Joe Martinez, you ought to know your daughter better than that," she said, and added, "And before you start talking about anyone's ancestry, I haven't seen you taking a DNA test."

Martinez flushed again, but not so brightly. Despite his dark hair and eyes, his complexion was pale; but being *Cubano,* it was more than a little likely his ancestors included Native Americans and Africans. Loretta didn't care, but she knew there were still folks who would.

"Well," Martinez grumbled, "I guess…I know we can trust Eva." Actually, Eva knew, her blush continuing, they couldn't, but if there was ever going to be a time to tell them, this was not it.

"But," her father finished, "I am not going to change my mind. Now please let me watch this show."

Eva broke into tears as she left the den. Her mother caught her in the hallway.

"Your father will come around," she said. "Just give him time. In a day or two, he'll realize just how ridiculous this whole thing is."

Eva nodded and choked out, "I hope so."

She dreaded having to call Doug tomorrow and break their date. And she really, really hoped her mother was right, about both her dad and the whole thing blowing over.

But, as she washed away tears and make-up, preparing for bed, she feared her mother might be wrong. On both counts.

Chapter 27

MARTINTOWN, NORTH CAROLINA, OCTOBER 2022

SATURDAY

Doug's mom and dad let him sleep late on Saturday morning. He wandered down to the kitchen about ten o'clock, following the smell of brewing coffee. He found his parents sitting at the kitchen table. He had heard them talking on the way downstairs, but hadn't been able to follow the conversation.

"I guess I'd better get Doug up," his father was saying, "we'll need to – oh! There you are son. Sleep well?"

Doug mumbled, "Uh-huh," and made straight for the coffee. He had already spoken with Eva; she'd called about thirty minutes ago, just as he was coming fully awake. She'd broken their date for this evening, but she hadn't been tearful about it. She'd sounded angry.

"It's my father," she'd told him. "He gets like this sometimes. Worked up over nothing. Or almost nothing. You know how protective he is about me. Sometimes I get tired of it.

"Mom says he'll get over. I hope so…." Then she added with steel in her voice, "He'd better. He'd just better…Anyway, he can't follow me to school. As far as I'm concerned, nothing has changed. Nothing. I don't care what anyone says."

"It's just that guy Jarvis," Doug had said.

"Not anymore," she'd whispered. Then she told him there were stories in the Asheville and Charlotte papers parroting Jarvis' speculation; and her mother had told her the networks had the story, although Eva hadn't seen anything.

"Anyway," she finished. "It will be old news before we know. Dad will move on when everything quietens down. And besides…I love you."

That last statement brought him up short. She'd never said that before. Neither of them had said it. All their talk had ended with not knowing what the future held. And, now, if anything, it was more uncertain.

"Doug…honey," she'd said, "Did you hear me?"

What the hell, he'd thought. If she was going to go there, so would he.

"Yeah," he'd said. "I heard you. And I love you, too."

"What do you want for breakfast, Doug?" his mother asked, bringing him back to the future.

He asked for bacon and eggs with toast, and said "sure" when his mother offered grits. He sat at the table with his father while his mother bustled about. His dad told him about the news reports, and he pretended he didn't know. He didn't want to talk with them about Eva and her father. Not right now.

"I've already spoken with Fred Hutton," his father said. "He's going to e-mail a non-disclosure agreement for you to sign this morning. Thank goodness you're 18, so we don't have to worry about your signature being legal. He's set up a meeting with us by whatever the government uses instead of ZOOM or WebEx later this morning, because he wants to talk with you.

"The networks and some of the newspapers have already asked the Defense Department about the Jarvis story," Darren continued. "Hutton said they will issue a short and sweet statement later today. They'll send us a copy. He thinks we ought to issue something, too, along the same lines. Maybe even have a press conference."

Doug's mother pushed a plate in front of him. It smelled wonderful, but he was too curious to eat until he learned more.

"What is the government going to say?" he asked his father.

Darren started ticking points off on his fingers. "One. There is an Army installation near Spruce Mountain, West Virginia. Two. Research does go on there. The particulars are a matter of national security. Three. Yes, the base does have a small hospital. Four. In 2005, a young local woman approached the base and told the security guard she was about to have a baby and needed help. Five. As an act of charity, the Army doctors delivered the baby and facilitated the adoption."

He switched to the second hand. "Six. The Army does not know what became of the young woman, and has no idea of the identity of the baby's father. Seven. As for the rest of the Jarvis story, don't be ridiculous."

Doug started eating. Between bites, he asked, "And they want us to say the same thing?"

"Yes," his father answered. "Are you okay with that?"

"Do I have to take questions?" Doug asked.

"No. In fact, he advised us not to."

Doug chewed bacon and swallowed, then said, "Then I'm okay. Is there anything else?"

"Yes, he thinks we should get a lawyer, just in case."

"In case of what?"

"He didn't say. But someone might try to mess with you…somehow. I think Major Hutton is right. Your mother and I have talked, and we want to call the Melton Norville firm. They're the ones who have represented Carson's dad. He's mentioned Kathryn Turner, and then she had some young guy helping her. He also mentioned a guy named Ben Callahan."

Doug mopped up yolk with a piece of toast. "Dad," he asked, "how do we pay for a lawyer? I mean, I know we're not rich."

His father nodded. "We're not. But Hutton told me not to worry about it. He'll find a way to cover the cost."

"How?" Doug asked.

Darren Martin grinned and responded, "How does the government pay for anything they don't want anyone to know about?"

MARTINTOWN NORTH CAROLINA, OCTOBER 2022 SATURDAY AFTERNOON

Marc Washington had worked at the office most of the morning, and then he and Rob Ashworth had played racquetball at the gym. Tiff had gone into the office, too, to help Rob prepare a motion and supporting documents; and she had left with Samantha for Asheville to go shopping.

He really ought to do some yard work, he thought. But he really didn't want to do that today. Not after working all morning and sweating to beat Rob on the court. Instead, he'd invited Ashworth to come over and watch football with him, and they were settled into the living room with beers, flipping channels from game to game.

His cell phone rang. Caller identification said it was Kathryn Turner. She wasn't yet 40, but she was the senior partner to whom he reported; so, there was no question that he'd better take the call. He told Rob who was calling and muted the TV.

"Marc, I hate to bother you, but something has come up; and I need you to baby-sit a matter for me," said Kathryn.

"Okay," he said, knowing that "baby-sitting" had a way of evolving into "primary responsibility," but also knowing that Tuesday she was starting a trial that would likely take several days. "What is it?"

"Have you been following this Doug Martin thing? You know, the football player at West Brainerd?" she asked.

"Well, yes," he said. "But I think Rob here has been following it more closely."

"Oh, Rob is with you? Good. You can get him to help if you want. Put your phone on speaker."

When Marc had done so, Kathryn continued, "I got a call this morning from Darren and Lara Martin. They're the kid's parents. They are issuing a statement to the press denying all of this nonsense about their son being a Neanderthal clone or whatever. They think that'll be the end of it, but they want to be able to get legal advice 'just in case.'

"I think that's smart of them; but my trial will run all week and maybe into next. Ben is in Charlotte in depositions in a tax case. So, I told them you'd be available. They have your number. If you need Rob to help, that's okay. Aleks, too." Tiffany was not ordinarily allowed to assist him because they were married. Besides, she was with Callahan for his multi-day depositions, while Jenny Jackson would be in trial with Kathryn. That left the relative newcomer, Aleksandra Tatarkiewicz, a/k/a Alexandra Tabarant, to work with Marc and Rob. But Aleks would be fine, Marc decided.

"Do they need anything right away?" Marc asked.

"No, they just want someone on retainer. You can work up an agreement for them Monday morning. As I said, this may turn out to be nothing."

Marc had read the Jarvis story, and thought it nonsense. He was inclined to agree and said so. She thanked him and ended the call.

"I don't think there'll be much for us to do," he said. Rob didn't answer. He looked thoughtful. Marc decided not to push him.

Marc turned back to the television and turned on the audio. They had tuned to ESPN and it was half-time. The studio hosts had interrupted covering scores of games in progress, and were discussing the Martin story. They played a short clip of Doug running the ball and making tackles.

"The Defense Department denies the report," one of them said. "But other sources and government suggest it may be true. This is a developing story."

"It does raise a question," his co-host responded. "If this really is true, is there a safety issue for other players?"

"He hasn't injured anyone," the first man said.

"Not yet," the other replied. Then they went back to the scores.

Marc muted the sound again.

"It doesn't look like this story is going away," he said. "I hope no one is going to create trouble for the kid."

"Don't count on it," Rob said. "And…"

"And what?"

"I think the story may be true," Rob said. "I've sensed something about him. So has Sam. So has Mitch McCaffrey. We've been watching him."

Marc stirred uneasily. He and Tiffany knew more than most in the firm about some of their clients, the ones he thought of as "the McCaffrey Group." But there was a lot they didn't know. Now it appeared they were about to be sucked in deeper.

But, he thought, what the hell.

"One thing about working here," he said. "You can count on strange things happening."

"Amen," said Rob.

They returned to watching football.

CHAPEL HILL, NORTH CAROLINA, OCTOBER 2022 SUNDAY AFTERNOON

Monica had spent Friday and Saturday morning making as many calls as she could squeeze in. She had connections. There was a woman here in Durham. Sylvia Sonenberg back in Brainerd County. Other people she knew from political fundraisers. She knew some reporters for the Raleigh and Charlotte papers. She really wasn't supposed to do that on the state's time; but Dennis Springfield wanted it done. Besides, it wasn't as though most of her co-workers weren't politically active, even though they were not encouraged to be.

Finally, Saturday afternoon, she had reported to Dennis that she thought her mission had been accomplished. After she'd explained what she'd done, he'd thanked her, but had said, "But there's something you lack. We need something from people who, well, you can't reach."

"Who are they?" she'd asked him, curious.

Then he'd told her. Hearing what he said made her smile. There was a use for some of those funny fundamentalists after all.

"I'm surprised you have *those* connections," she'd said.

He'd laughed into the phone. "We have many connections."

Now she could relax. Her condominium development had an indoor pool, and she was lounging beside it with a magazine. Barry was going to come by later, and she'd let him find her there. He liked the way she filled a bikini.

And tomorrow, or maybe the day after, it would all hit the fan. Even she had been surprised at how quickly the machinery had fallen into place. She'd had to make a contribution, of course; but she'd find a way to tack most of it onto her Bureau consulting fee.

Chapter 28

MARTINTOWN, NORTH CAROLINA, OCTOBER 2022

MONDAY

Josh Fulkerson shifted the telephone receiver against his ear, and scratched his bald spot, something he always did when he was stressed. Fulkerson was 46 years old, and had been principal of West Brainerd high school for the past eight years. He had the degrees and certificates for advancement in school administration, but so far had had no opportunities to move into an associate superintendent's job. He wasn't sure he wanted to do that anyway; he liked the interaction with students – seeing them in the hallways, handing out awards for academic achievements, going to the school plays and concerts, and following the sports teams.

There were headaches. Managing teachers was sometimes a chore. There was the occasional problem student, but he hadn't had many. Dealing with reports and budgets were no fun. But all in all, he liked his job.

Most of the time.

Today was an exception. He'd followed the news reports about Doug Martin, including the statements released by the Department of Defense and by Doug's parents. He'd thought that was the end of that. The whole thing was silly, anyway.

But at mid-morning today, a news crew from the local network affiliate, led by Mary Marletti and accompanied by some another reporter sent by the network, had showed up insisting on an interview with Doug Martin. Josh and his assistant principal, Bobby Simpson (who was also an assistant football coach), had managed to intercept them and deny them access to the student. Then they'd insisted on a statement from Josh.

He hadn't been sure of the protocol for giving media interviews, or even if there was one. Acting on the spur of the moment, he'd agreed to a brief appearance before the camera. Maybe he shouldn't have, but he'd done it.

"Doug Martin is a student in good standing at this high school," he'd said. "As a matter of fact, he is an honors student. He is a member of the football team, and is actually a captain. The Brainerd County Schools respect his privacy, as we respect the privacy of all students. If you want an interview with him, I suggest you speak with his parents. We will not allow that here. I have read his parents' statement on this…crazy rumor. I have nothing to add to it."

That was his statement and he'd refused to take questions. He'd called Doug to the office and told him what had happened. He'd advised the boy to be careful about being cornered after practice that afternoon, and had managed to reach Doug's father to suggest he might want to be present at practice today, or at least when practice ended. He'd informed Coach Watkins about what happened. He hadn't needed to do so; the whole school was buzzing about the TV crew that had showed up. Finally, he'd made an announcement over the intercom, counseling all students to avoid talking with the news media without parental guidance.

He'd been rather proud of how he had handled everything. But evidently he hadn't made the Superintendent, who was now on the phone with him, very happy.

Superintendent Larry Winston was not Fulkerson's favorite person anyway. Winston had been hired two years before to replace a woman who had held the position for years. A divided school board had brought Winston in from a small county in Eastern North Carolina. Winston didn't know Brainerd County. He and his wife lived in Martintown, and Fulkerson thought they were altogether too chummy with those who thought they were Martintown "society" and whose kids went to Brainerd Central.

"What in the hell were you doing, Josh, giving an interview to the TV people without going through this office?" Winston demanded. "And to make it worse, you spoke for the 'Brainerd County Schools.' You don't. I do. The Board Chair does. But you don't."

"Mr. Winston, I'm sorry. I didn't remember any policy about this…"

"Well," Winston snarled, "if there's not, there soon will be. I promise you that."

"But don't we respect our kids' privacy? I thought we did."

"Josh, we don't know what we're going to do about this boy, and you told the media he was a student and player in good standing."

"But he is," Josh insisted. "He hasn't done anything."

"He…he…" Winston was foundering, but finally found his tongue. "Well, let me tell you, I've had calls about this all day. I haven't been able to do anything else but take these calls. The Board Chair called, because *he's* being called. Jeremiah Billups' mother called and said it's a wonder 'that brute' – that's what she called him – hadn't hurt her baby, and wanted to know what we were going to do about him to protect other kids. Sylvia Sonenberg called…"

Fulkerson frowned into the receiver. Sylvia Sonenberg was an heiress who was a big deal in what passed for Brainerd County 'high society.' She was a member of more clubs and charities than he could count. And she was, or thought she was, influential in local and state politics, mostly on the Democratic side. Fulkerson thought she was a professional busy-body. She believed she knew the answer to everything.

"…and she said," Winston was saying, "the same thing as Billups' mother. She said funds were being raised and a statewide committee is being formed to protect other athletes from Martin. Some of the Board members want to call a special meeting on this. Some of them want West to forfeit their games."

"What?" Fulkerson asked. "Why? We haven't done anything wrong."

"That remains to be seen. If your guy isn't even human…Well, whatever they decide, I'll have to be there. I'll be in the middle of it."

"And then *you* make a statement to the media, as though this is nothing!"

"As far as his class standing is concerned, isn't it nothing?" Josh let ice creep into his tone.

"Of course, it's not 'nothing!'" Winston practically shouted. "I don't know what it is, but it's not 'nothing.'…Look, don't say anything else publicly. I mean that. I'll be in touch."

The call ended. Fulkerson didn't know what to do next. Should he call the boy's parents? Maybe, but not now. Nothing had happened, and he'd scare them, and the boy, too. But he'd better tell Coach Watkins.

He needed an aspirin.

CORNELIUS, NORTH CAROLINA, OCTOBER 2022
TUESDAY

Danny Jarvis was surprised at how fast the story had taken off. It had been picked up by the state and national media, and some had backed up his claims with their own references to undisclosed "sources." He wondered who those sources were and how the contacts had been made so swiftly.

He also wondered whether Monica Gilbert had had anything to do with spreading the story. He knew she had wanted copies of everything, and that he'd obliged. She had said she had "connections." Who were they? He thought about calling her and asking, but he didn't.

In any event, he'd been interviewed by network affiliates in Charlotte and Raleigh, who'd also played brief highlights of the Martin boy's performance on the gridiron; and excerpts of the interviews had made it to national news reports. Of course, the networks had also reported that the Defense Department and the Martin family denied the story; but that was what he had expected.

He had been careful to avoid any mention of Veronica Clayton. He had sent her the link to the original story, so she knew it was out there. He had half-expected her to call and thank him for omitting her name. But no such luck. He'd reach out to her eventually, but now was not the time. He was too busy.

And today he was about to be on Jimmy DuGard's podcast. DuGard had a national following and did a podcast twice a week, a short one on Tuesday and a longer one on Friday. He covered everything from politics to entertainment to sports. His opinions were eclectic. Sometimes he sounded almost right-wing; at others, very progressive. A lot of people scorned him, but many liked him.

And the podcast had video as well as audio. That was good. He could sit in his home office and sign in, and subscribers would see him and DuGard as well has hear them. There was going to be another guest, too, some semi-retired professor from Duke named Herbert Sikorski that DuGard had found. The guy was supposed to be some kind of expert on early humans, including Neanderthals.

The Podcast began at 11:00 a.m., Central Time, so it was noon for Jarvis. He didn't have any trouble logging in, and waited patiently to be admitted to the virtual "meeting room." When that happened, he saw DuGard himself and the head and shoulders of a be-spectacled, wizened, white-haired man wearing a tweed coat and bow-tie that had to be Sikorski. DuGard welcomed the online viewing audience, and then introduced Danny as a "well known freelance journalist" and Sikorski as an "Emeritus Professor of Anthropology and expert in paleo-anthropology at Duke University." Jarvis hid a smile at his introduction. Until the past few days, he really hadn't been well known at all.

DuGard then shared a screen that contained an excerpt from Danny's story, and then played a clip of Doug Martin running the football for West Brainerd. He explained that Martin was a "highly sought after" college prospect, and "to be fair," he said, shared screens with the statements released by the Defense Department and the Martin family.

"So," DuGard continued, "let me start with you, Dr. Sikorski, and let me cut right to the chase. Do you believe Mr. Jarvis' report? Do you think this young man down there in North Carolina is a human-Neanderthal clone?"

Sikorski, without hesitation, replied in a rather high-pitched but strong voice that contained little old-age quaver.

"Oh, yes," he said. "I think it's almost certainly true. In fact, it really must be true. Here, I'll show you."

He shared a screen and played an animated re-creation of a Neanderthal holding a long spear, who lowered it and ran toward a bull aurochs, thrusting the spear into the animal's side. Then he had DuGard replay the clip of Doug Martin running over a would-be tackler and running hard downfield.

"Now, this boy's head does not look Neanderthal," Sikorski said. "It looks fully modern human. That comes from his human parent, I think. But the torso is fully Neanderthal. You can see it clearly. A little taller than typical. But it's clear.

"Of course, it would take a DNA test to completely verify the ancestry," Sikorski concluded. "But the physiological evidence is so strong, I really have no doubt what the results would be."

"Do you know whether Doug Martin has given a DNA sample to be tested?" DuGard asked.

"No, Mr. DuGard. I don't know," the professor answered.

"Well, if he and his family deny the report, wouldn't the easiest way to prove it's false is to submit to a DNA test?" DuGard asked.

"I'm not the one to ask," Sikorski said. "But I have little doubt that a test would support my conclusions."

DuGard was clearly enjoying the interview. "Let me follow up on this," he said. "I'll get to you in a minute, Mr. Jarvis. But first I need to ask Dr. Sikorski. Professor, if you are right, is Doug Martin fully human?"

Sikorski looked sad, but he said, "No. Not fully. One of his parents was fully human, yes. *Homo sapiens sapiens.* But the other was not. *Homo neanderthalensis.* Related certainly. Genus *homo,* of course. Fully inter-fertile with human beings obviously. But a separate species."

"Is your view universally accepted in paleoanthropology?" DuGard asked.

"Not universally," the professor admitted. "But many, I think most, agree with me. I'm not sure how it breaks down."

"Aren't there some who claim that the Neanderthals were not a separate species?" DuGard persisted. "Don't some say they were an offshoot of modern humans, but fully human?"

"Some, yes," Sikorski said. "*Homo sapiens neanderthalensis.* A sub-species. I do not accept that view. The differences were too profound."

DuGard appeared to lean forward. "I thought it is accepted that we all have some Neanderthal genes," he said.

Sikorski shook his head. "Not all of us. Caucasians and Asians yes. But very attenuated. A tiny, tiny fraction of our genetic make-up. Africans have no Neanderthal ancestors."

DuGard nodded. "Final question, Doctor. If you are right, should Doug Martin be schooled with, and play sports with, human adolescents?"

Sikorski continued to present as sad, but maybe, Danny thought, that's how he always looked. "I'm afraid not," the professor said. "The young man is so unnaturally strong. He could hurt someone."

"He hasn't yet," Danny interrupted, earning a dirty look from DuGard.

Sikorski ignored Jarvis' comment. "As for schooling, he ought to be in a special school, where he can be studied, and his talents explored and developed. That's my opinion."

"All right," DuGard said. "Now it's your turn, Mr. Jarvis. What do you think of what our friend the professor has just said?"

"I think he's wrong," Jarvis said. "The young man is very talented, yes. But we let big kids play football with smaller ones all the time. He's no more dangerous to others than some of the 300-pound lineman we see in college and pro football, and sometimes even in high school ball.

"And as for being specially schooled, why? He's well adjusted. He's a good student. He has a girlfriend. Why take that away from him?"

"But you released the story," DuGard prompted.

"I did." Danny was starting to be ashamed. He knew that he had been thinking first about his own career. But he decided to defend himself. "I did that because I think the public has the right to know what their government is up to, especially with respect to human genetics. I believed that, and I still believe it.

"But that's the government. I never intended, and do not intend, to use that story to discriminate against the young man. He doesn't deserve that."

"Well, viewers and listeners, there you have it," DuGard said. "Let me hear what you think. I'd like to thank our guests for appearing. We're out of time today, but I will take your calls on Friday."

When the podcast was over, Jarvis found himself torn and more than a little disturbed. He knew it would help his career if this went viral. Yet for Doug Martin's sake, he hoped it did not.

But, as it turned out, it did.

Chapter 29

WINSTON-SALEM, NORTH CAROLINA, OCTOBER 2022

THE OFFICES OF THE NORTH CAROLINA HIGH SCHOOL ATHLETIC ASSOCIATION
WEDNESDAY, MID-MORNING

Jessica Morton had been Commissioner of the NCHSAA for six years, after having been hired by the Board of Directors from a job as director of athletics at large high school in Winston-Salem. She'd been involved in youth sports ever since graduating from Winston-Salem State. She supervised a staff of seven that included four Deputy Commissioners with varying areas of oversight. These years had not been free of issues, as her staff looked at player eligibility, oversight of officials, and the like.

But the issues had always been expected, familiar. Now, hanging up from the Chairman of the Board of Directors, she was dealing with something she hadn't seen before. She e-mailed the Deputy Commissioners for Compliance and Eligibility that she wanted them in her office in an hour, and that they should read the email messages she would forward in the meantime.

They convened at the circular conference table in her office only five minutes later than she'd requested. Roger Farley, the Deputy Commissioner for Eligibility, was late, begging off because he'd been printing out his own stack of e-mail messages. He and his counterpart Deputy Commissioner for Compliance, Bill Morgan, were most of a decade younger than her 42 years. The Association jobs didn't pay particularly well, and staff turnover was higher than she preferred. Jessica wondered how long she'd keep these young men, before they moved on. She liked both of them.

She thumbed through the stack of e-mails Roger had produced. Most of them echoed the ones she'd received, and many were from the same senders. All of them demanded the Association declare Douglas Martin of West Brainerd High School ineligible for interscholastic competition in North Carolina. She had ignored the ones she had received at first. But she couldn't ignore the phone call from the Board Chair.

"Gentlemen," she began the meeting, "I guess you know why we are here. I take it you've seen the DuGard podcast? Read the newspapers?" After seeing them nod, she went on, "Chairman McConnell called me this morning. He's received the same complaints we have. So have a number of Board members. Some of the Board members are complainers themselves. There's going to be a virtual meeting of the Board this afternoon. McConnell wants me to attend. He thinks they're going to vote to have an eligibility hearing, and he wants us to hold it before the playoffs."

"That's unusual," Farley said, and, she thought, he was right. The usual way in which issues of eligibility were resolved was for the Association staff to make an administrative determination, which could be appealed to the Board. Actual hearings were rare. Everything was decided on paper.

"I know," she said. "But it's in the operations manual that a hearing can be held at the direction of the board, either before a board committee or the Association staff, if the Board so directs."

She paused and looked from Farley to Morgan, two open-faced young men who had never dealt with anything more controversial than censoring an official or approving a suspension for a rule violation. Come to it, she hadn't either. She sighed and plunged on.

"McConnell doesn't want the Board involved. He says more than half think the whole thing is ridiculous, drummed up by sore losers and potential playoff opponents. The other group, not a majority but very vocal, are convinced, or claim to be convinced, that this guy has no business playing high school football. Some are under pressure at home. You know most of them are coaches or local administrators.

"Chairman McConnell says he's had a call from the Brainerd County Superintendent, who is all upset." She smiled. "He would be. The political power in Brainerd County is in Martintown, and their team lost to West Brainerd. Anyway, their BOE is going to meet Thursday. There's a chance they'll handle it there, and make their own determination. If they say the kid can't play, that will take this off of us – unless the boy gets a lawyer and takes it to court. But the Chair doesn't think that's likely. He wants us to get ready for a hearing, probably late next week."

"I don't know what there is to hear," Farley said. "Our eligibility standards are academic standing, rule violations, and age. That's it. I'm sure the Martin kid passes all three."

"Isn't it an assumed qualification that the player be human?" Jessica asked, keeping her tone even.

Farley colored, but said, "Well, I guess. But it's not in writing that I can see."

"It's not in writing that we wouldn't let a mountain gorilla or a grizzly bear play," Jessica said. "But we wouldn't, would we?"

"Well, no. But there's no evidence I can see that Doug Martin isn't a human being," Farley insisted.

"This expert at Duke said he's not," Jessica reminded him. "And let me tell you, people have picked up on that." She scrolled through emails on the tablet in front of her. "A woman from Durham says her transgendered child isn't allowed on the girls track team, because of this law the legislature passed last year. She's screaming it's horrible her child can't compete but this ape-man can. Yeah, that's what she wrote. She's formed a group of parents of transgendered kids demanding action.

"Parents of players have called or written the Board, claiming their kids aren't safe playing against the guy. Some people have formed something called the 'Committee for Fairness in Athletics' and they've hired a lawyer from Charlotte. I don't know where they're getting their money, but they're getting it.

"And," she smiled, "there's a whole group of pastors, mostly from country churches, who claim the Martin boy bears 'the mark of Cain,' and that his appearance is of demonic origin." Seeing the shocked faces of her deputies, she said, "I know, I know. But these people vote."

Morgan spoke for the first time. "What bothers me," he said, "is that most of what I've seen comes from school districts that either have lost to West Brainerd or who may face them in the playoffs. That just…smells."

Jessica nodded. "I know that, too. With all of the media attention, this whole thing has become a political football. And we're probably going to get the ball."

She straightened in her chair, and her eyes darted from Morgan to Farley.

"I want a plan for conducting a hearing, including a proposed date and location, on my desk by ten o'clock tomorrow morning," she said. "You two are in charge, and it's your top priority. Assume the three of us are the hearing panel. See to it."

The meeting ended, and everyone departed for lunch.

MARTINTOWN, NORTH CAROLINA, OCTOBER 2022
CAROLINA HIGHLANDS COMMUNITY COLLEGE
NOON WEDNESDAY

Mitch McCaffrey pushed his chair back from his office at the college and glanced at his watch. It was almost time for the meeting with Fred Hutton and Alyssa Callahan that Hutton had messaged this morning to schedule. He hadn't disclosed the subject matter in the text, but Mitch supposed it had to be about Doug Martin, the West Brainerd student and football player. Hutton had asked the "coven" in Martintown to keep an eye on the kid, but the exploding story in the news media had overtaken and passed their observations.

Still, he wondered what Hutton might want of him and Alyssa concerning the situation. Mitch was morally certain the Martin story was true, based on what he'd seen of, and felt emanating from, the young man. But it didn't seem as though the problem could be solved with his Talents, or hers. He supposed he'd find out shortly. Hutton wanted to meet in person in his office and had promised lunch. Alyssa was smewhere training special forces on portal spells, so Mitch would meet her there. He didn't have any training obligations until after the semester, when he was supposed to train some DIA and FBI personnel on manipulation of electronic devices. He really didn't like including the Bureau people, but that was in the amended contract, so he'd do it.

Mitch rose from his desk and locked the door to his office. He turned back toward his desk, and chanting in a whisper, walked through mist into Hutton's office. Blinking, he first saw the sideboard with sandwiches and a coffee urn in front of him, and then more mist to his right, from which Alyssa appeared, clad in jeans and a fluffy Navy blue sweater, her dark shoulder-length hair showing a bit of natural curl. He wondered briefly just how much advanced portal spell craft Alyssa was actually teaching. She was better at portals than he was, and he suspected there was much she hadn't yet taught him.

"Good afternoon," said Hutton from behind his desk, which was to Mitch's left. Mitch turned and saw the man rise and extend a hand, which he and Alyssa each took in turn. Hutton asked them to be seated and promised they'd get to lunch as soon as possible. Mitch and Alyssa both took chairs facing the desk. Hutton sat behind it again.

"I'm sure you have followed the Doug Martin story," he began.

They had.

"The first thing I have to do is to remind you that this conversation falls under your confidentiality agreement. Understood?" Seeing them nod agreement, he continued, "Okay. You've probably figured out the story is true."

Nods again.

"I didn't want to tell you earlier, because I thought we could keep the whole thing under wraps. But now I think you need to know, because – even though I hope we can still stonewall this thing – I'm afraid we won't be able to do it."

He paused, and Mitch saw Hutton's face work as though he was pained with indigestion. Then the man composed himself, and he went on, "Someone here in government wants this to come out. I'm not sure who it is, but whoever it is, has some allies here at defense. I…I guess you know, there's a lot of infighting here in Washington."

"Can't you guess?" asked Alyssa. "I mean, who's been behind all the trouble we've had where we live?"

Hutton chuckled without real humor.

"I know," he said. "Springfield and that Gilbert woman. Yeah, probably, although I haven't been able to confirm it, and I have no idea who they have on the inside here. But what I can't figure out is why. There's really nothing in it for them…unless they just want to give the DIA a bloody nose. Meaning me. But is that enough for them to want to make this thing public?"

"It would be for Monica Gilbert," Alyssa said. "I don't really know about the other guy."

"Yeah, well," Hutton said. "Maybe him, too."

"What do you want us to do?" Mitch asked. He only had a little over an hour before he'd be missed, and he wanted a sandwich.

"Two things," Hutton told them. "First, the Martin family has hired counsel. They're going to use the same people who have represented you two."

"Yes, Ben told me something about that," Alyssa said. "But it's not going to be my husband or Kat Turner. They're tied up." Alyssa had been able to be home every night while doing the training, Mitch knew. That's what you could do with Portal spells.

"It's going to be the Ashworth guy," Hutton said. "I know he's one of you. And the lead lawyer will be Marc Washington, Mitch."

Mitch nodded. Washington had been involved in both cases where the firm had represented him, or him and Alyssa. "Marc's good," he said. "And I hear Rob is, too. But what does that have to do with us?"

"I was coming to that," Hutton said. "I told Darren and Lara Martin not to worry about legal fees, that they'd be covered. I can't afford for the money to come from DIA, not now. I'm working on some contingency plans in case this all blows up, but I can't talk about them now.

"Anyway," he concluded, "I want one of you to cover the fees for now. Sign a guaranty or something. I'll take care of you later. We'll figure out something."

"I'll do it," said Mitch. "There's no need for both of us to be involved," he added, looking at Alyssa, who nodded.

"I don't mind helping," she protested.

"I'll let you know," said Mitch. He understood what it was like to take a chance on incurring legal fees and not know if the money spent would pay off. He sympathized with the Martins and wanted to help, now that he could afford it. He turned back to Hutton. "What else do you need?"

Hutton frowned. "Just…keep track of what goes on. I – I just have a feeling this is about to get out of our control. There might be some kind of public hearing or something.

"Just be ready if someone tries anything cute," he finished. "Now get a sandwich."

Mitch and Alyssa ate quickly. Both had other things to do.

"Tell Diana I might drop over this evening," Alyssa said to Mitch as she dabbed her mouth with a napkin. "When Ben Callahan is getting ready for trial or depositions, he's worthless as company."

They all laughed. Mitch and Alyssa rose and shook hands with Hutton again. Then they both walked through mist back to their respective jobs.

CHAPEL HILL, NORTH CAROLINA, OCTOBER 2022 AT MONICA'S OFFICE

Monica was on the secure line to Dennis Springfield again. Both were pleased at how quickly things were developing.

"I was able to get the Committee up and running faster than I thought," Monica said. "Yes, they all know to keep my name out of it. I had some help from Sylvia Sonenberg. I knew the group here that's all upset about how this is a slap in the face of transgendered competitors."

"It helped that I gave the lawyer money when he ran for Congress," she continued, "even if he didn't get the nomination, much less win election. His firm is doing the paperwork to incorporate the committee and get tax exempt status now. And he said he'd handle the legal work. That will get him back on camera. He loves that."

She was referring to Alex DeBruhl, who was a litigator at a big firm in Charlotte and one of her political connections.

"Where's the money coming from?" Springfield asked. "We can't put anything into this, not directly. You haven't committed the Bureau, have you?"

"Oh, no," she said, letting some offense creep into her voice. "Give me *some* credit, please! I told you I know the folks at the NCFEF – the Foundation for Equity and Fairness. They're fine to fund the Committee…Of course, I had to make a sizable donation to the Foundation; so, most of the money is coming from me…No one will know except you. But surely… *surely*…you'll find a way to reimburse me."

"I'm sure Santa Claus will know," Springfield said. "Just how much are we talking about, though?"

She gave him a number, and added, "This is what Alex said it would take."

She heard him cough into the receiver, which was a bad sign, but then he said, "Okay. I can handle it. Just give me time."

"Oh, good," she said, deciding not to press him now on how much time he'd need. "But let me tell you something else. One of the girls here at the office has a friend over at the high school athletic association. She was able to give me a list of the coaches and school administration that called in to protest the kid playing. Alex said he's going to push for an eligibility hearing. He said he'll have more witnesses than he needs, and his staff is making contacts now."

"Excellent," Springfield said. "Good job." Before she could answer, he added, "There's one thing I don't like, though."

"What's that?"

"Your boy Jarvis is acting kind of squishy. Did you hear what he said in the podcast?"

"Yes, and it surprised me," she admitted. "The last time I talked with him, he was excited about how this story would make his career. He wasn't worried about the kid. He said the boy will wind up making a pile of money himself, so he'd be all right.

"But do we really care now? I mean, Danny has served his purpose. Hasn't he?" Jarvis had quit calling her for dates, which both pleased and displeased her. More the latter. Continuing to see him would be inconvenient.

There was a pause on the connection, and then Springfield said, "'Yes' and 'No.' I still think the best thing for us would be to take away some of the Martin kid's choices, and recruit him for the Bureau later. Jarvis 'switching sides,' so to speak, wouldn't help that.

"But my main concern is that he might start talking about where he got his information. He might even mention your name."

"I thought you said that his source material can't be traced to us," Monica said.

"It can't, by ordinary forensic methods. But what if it gets in the hands of one of the DIA's paranormal contractors, someone really good like McCaffrey? No, I think we better remove the evidence, and probably put a good scare into him in the process. But it still can wait. We'll see what he does. Maybe this 'Lady Macbeth' moment he's having won't last."

"His what?" she asked. She didn't get it.

"You know, from Shakespeare. 'All the perfumes of Arabia would not sweeten this little hand.'"

Monica stifled a derisive snort. She wasn't impressed with references to dead, white, privileged males.

"Anyway," Springfield said, "whatever we do, don't worry about it; you won't be involved."

This is getting too complicated, Monica thought. And what are we gaining by it? She decided to voice her concern.

"Do you think all this is worth it, Dennis?" she asked. She still wasn't convinced there was anything in it for the Bureau.

"It is, if it gives Fred Hutton and his bunch some comeuppance," said Springfield. "He hasn't hesitated to jump in *our* shit, as you know. And the cross-training they promised has been half-assed."

"I know," she said. Hutton's team, which included Mitch McCaffrey and Alyssa Callahan, was supposed to provide training in managing portals and other spells to the Bureau. But so far there hadn't been much. And they had absolutely refused to train Monica, even had that exclusion put in writing. That rankled her.

"And," Springfield said, reading her mind, "your 'friends' in Brainerd County won't like it, either, I'm willing to bet. Don't forget that part of it."

Monica felt a wide grin spread over her features, although Springfield couldn't see it, of course.

"There is that," she said, "There definitely is that."

Chapter 30

MARTINTOWN, NORTH CAROLINA, OCTOBER 2022

AT THE OFFICES OF MELTON NORVILLE JENNINGS & JOHNSON
LATE WEDNESDAY AFTERNOON

Marc Washington, Rob Ashworth, and Alexandra Tabarant sat side by side at the long mahogany table in one of the firm's conference rooms, Marc in the center, Rob to his left, and Alex to his right. They made an interesting contrast, Marc thought. He, with his blunt African American features and short, wiry hair. Rob, with his freckled, boyish face that always seemed to be looking for a sunburn and his coppery hair, today in need of a cut. And finally Alex, her hair as dark as Marc's, but her skin almost as pale as a snowfall in her native Poland.

Spread on the table before them were the materials they had accumulated in preparation for the meeting with Doug Martin and his parents. These included Danny Jarvis' original story, print-outs from follow-up entries on his blog, copies of newspaper stories, and a transcript of yesterday's DuGard podcast. They also included Rob's notes from his telephone conference with Jarvis, and Marc's of his call to Principal Fulkerson. Alex had a laptop open in front of her. She'd use it to type notes and to pull up anything else they'd want to see.

"Well, the clients are here," Marc said. "Are we ready for them?"

Both of his colleagues said that they were. This meeting was later than Marc would have preferred. They'd scheduled it at 7:00 so that Doug could finish football practice and the clients could grab something to eat. But Marc hadn't had dinner and his stomach was growling. Well, it couldn't be helped.

"Alex, can you go bring them in?" Marc asked.

She rose and left the room to fetch the clients, whom she had admitted only minutes earlier, leaving them in the reception area at the front of the building. They'd had to call her on her cell phone to arrange for her to unlock the office, which was closed, for them. Moments later, she returned with Doug Martin, wearing his letter jacket and his red hair, which was quite a bit darker than Rob's pale copper locks, still damp from the shower, followed by his father in a sport coat and tie and his mother in nursing scrubs. Neither, evidently, had had time to change from what they'd worn to work.

Alex seated the clients at the table across from the legal team and offered water, soft drinks, or coffee, which they all declined. When she'd seated herself next to him, Marc introduced himself and the team, and then got right down to business.

"The first thing we need to do is to go over the engagement agreement for our services," he said, and watched Alex slide three copies of the agreement across the table. "You'll notice that all three of you are shown as clients. The document has places for all of you to sign. Note that Doug must sign for himself because, being over 18, he is legally an adult. Take a minute to look it over. We'll answer any questions you may have."

The clients had one question.

"This form has a space for Mitch McCaffrey to sign as guarantor," said Darren Martin. "We understood our costs would be covered, but Mr. McCaffrey's involvement wasn't discussed."

Marc had to think, because he'd been told by Mitch himself that he was going to front the fees. Evidently, no one had filled in the Martins.

"I see," he said. "We were given to understand that Mr. McCaffrey's guarantee would be explained to you. I suggest you sign and circle back to that issue later. Is that satisfactory?"

Darren opened his mouth to speak, then closed it with a snap. Marc saw his wife lean over and whisper something to him. Darren nodded and turned his eyes back toward Marc. "It is. We'll check with...whoever we need to."

Marc had questions about that but didn't ask them. Usually it was better if the lawyers knew everything, but not always. This might be one of those times. He watched while the clients signed, using pens Alex provided them.

When the signing had been done, Marc said, "Now we can move on to what you're facing. The newspaper this morning reports there will be a specially called board meeting tomorrow evening about, well, about you. At least one member of the board wants you suspended and disqualified. At least, that's what he told the newspaper."

"That's Jerry Dixon," Darren said, "the president of the Central Boosters' Club."

"He's just one member," Marc soothed. "Rob and I have been counting votes. There are three members from Martintown, and two from out in the county. The board member from your district will be on your side. We think the one from the South Brainerd District will, too; the story is he dislikes Dixon and the Board Chair, Don Crabtree. That leaves Dr. Watkins.

"That's the new member the County Commission appointed to fill an unexpired term this past spring, when old Joe Betterson had to step down for health reasons. I know Watkins' younger daughter, Lottie. She's the one who made the complaint against Mitch McCaffrey two years ago. Well, she turned over a new leaf, and is now off at college at App State. The word is her daddy is thrilled."

"What does that have to do with Doug?" Lara Martin asked.

"Nothing, directly," Marc said. "But, well, you know Mr. McCaffrey is a regular client?" Seeing them nod, he went on, "Well, somehow Mr. McCaffrey and Lottie's dad hit it off. Mitch says Watkins is a level headed guy. So does Kathryn Turner. Her husband is a surgeon who knows Watkins pretty well. Dr. Watkins knows our firm and that we shoot straight. That helps.

"But the real clincher is that we've talked to the School Board attorney, Gary Sanders. Rob called him this afternoon, while I was occupied with someone I'll tell you about in a minute. He's going to recommend that the School System punt this issue to the high school athletic association. Its board voted to hold a hearing on Doug next week, unless the Brainerd County Board of Education takes action that would make the issue moot. We'll get to that this evening, I promise. Gary doesn't want the Board to do anything.

"Dixon and Crabtree won't like that. But we think it'll appeal to the Superintendent because it gets the issue off his desk. The members from outside Martintown will like it. And we think Dr. Watkins won't want to buck a recommendation from Board counsel. But…we'll have to show up for the meeting tomorrow night."

"Uhhh," said Doug, shifting in his chair as though it had grown uncomfortable.

"Yes, Doug," Marc said. "What is it?"

"I've got a math test Friday. I really need tomorrow night to study."

Rob hadn't spoken since the initial greetings, but now he had a suggestion.

"I'm not sure Doug has to come," he said. "There's not going to be any testimony. We – the lawyers – have to be there. I think it would be good if Doug's parents came. But Doug staying home to study hits a good note, doesn't it. He's acting like a regular student. Which he is, and that's our point."

"I like it," said Marc. "Can one or both of you come?" he asked the parents.

They could.

"Now let's get on to where we really have to win this," Marc said. "The NCHSAA."

He found another paper in the stack in front of him. "Late this afternoon, the NCHSAA e-mailed out a notice of hearing to your high school, Doug," Marc said. "It's set a week from Friday beginning at 9:00 a.m. at a location to be determined. Both you and Brainerd Central are respondents. They're overnighting a copy to you at home.

"We got a copy because we asked for one. The purpose of the hearing is to determine whether your eligibility to play interscholastic sports in this state ought be revoked, because you are a 'direct threat to the health and safety of teammates and opposing players' and -- they really tortured this one – because you are 'not qualified to be a student athlete' due to your 'unhumanity.' Not 'inhumanity.' 'Unhumanity,' as though you're a Martian or maybe an ape."

"How did you find out about it?" Darren asked.

"Good question," Marc replied. "You know that the newspaper reported their board had voted to direct 'the Commissioner and two deputies of her choice to hold a hearing.'" Seeing the clients nod, he continued, "While Rob was contacting school board counsel, I called the Commissioner, a woman named Jessica Morton, introduced myself, and asked for more information. She referred me to the lawyer who is general counsel for the Association, a guy named Frank DuLaney. He's an older guy with a middlin' sized firm there in Winston-Salem, and he's been the Association's lawyer for years.

"DuLaney was cooperative. He told me the date of the hearing and said the location would be determined later. He was inclined for it to be somewhere in Winston-Salem."

"If I have to be in Winston-Salem next Friday," Doug said, "I'll miss the final game. No way I can get back in time."

Marc thought his client had worse problems than missing a single football game, but realized Doug was still a teenager. Anyway, he had a solution.

"I understand, Doug," he said. "More to the point, it would make it practically impossible for us to bring in your coach and teammates as witnesses. I pointed that out to DuLaney, and said that holding the hearing anywhere except Brainerd County on such short notice would be an effective denial of due process. In other words, it would give you grounds to challenge the ruling in court.

"Bottom line, I think I've persuaded him to recommend holding the hearing here. When he asked where, I told him I thought we can get a suitable room at Carolina Highlands – the same room where the McCaffrey hearing was held. I called Mitch McCaffrey and he thinks he can make it happen, and I e-mailed the information to DuLaney."

Marc paused and let the smile fade from his face. "That's the good news. Now for the not so good. I asked DuLaney how the hearing was going to work, and he said the Commissioner was inclined to let that Committee those people formed to remove Doug from football proceed with the case to do so, and then we could respond."

"I protested that it is completely inappropriate to let a private entity prosecute an eligibility issue, but I couldn't move him. So we have to figure that this will be like a real trial, with Alex DeBruhl presenting the case they think they have against Doug, and then we'll put on our response."

"Could we get a court order stopping this?" Darren asked.

"No, we don't think so," Marc said.

"Who is this DeBruhl guy anyway?" Darren asked.

"None of us know him, but I'm sure Bill Norville, who knows everybody, knows him and Ben Callahan likely has met him. Kathryn Turner knows him by reputation," Rob responded for Marc. "He's supposed to be a good, very good, trial lawyer. He's with a large law firm in Charlotte.

"He's handled a number of 'advocacy' cases, some of them *pro bono*, some not. You know, environmental groups, abortion advocacy groups, and so on."

"Does going up against him intimidate you?" Darren asked.

"No!" Marc and Rob answered at once.

"Anyway," Marc said, "we have to plan our defense. That's why we're all here tonight. So, let's get started. Rob?"

Rob cleared his throat, and began, "We think the best approach is to continue what you've been doing. Not admitting anything and daring them to prove it."

When only silence greeted him, Rob added, "Of course, we'll have some evidence. You, Doug. Your principal with your school records. Your coach. Probably a teammate. It would be nice to have an opposing player, but that's probably too much to ask."

"I have some nice text messages from several," Doug said.

"Let us see them," Rob responded. "Anybody close?"

"There's one from McDowell," Doug said, "that's not real far." Then he swallowed hard, and added, "But I don't want to testify."

"Hold that thought," Marc broke in. He assumed that what he was hearing was just natural fear of the witness chair. "We'll talk about it some more. What else, Rob?"

"Wel-l-l," Rob began, "we hesitate to bring this up, but you heard that Duke professor bring up a DNA test. Have y'all thought about getting one for Doug and removing all doubt about how ridiculous this thing is? We have some connections, and might be able to get an expedited report."

The suggestion was greeted by stony silence and uncomfortable shifting in chairs. The seconds ticked away while the legal team waited for their clients to say *something*. Then it dawned on them.

"Oh," said Rob.

"Oh, hell," Marc whispered.

Aleksandra said nothing, but her wide eyes showed she understood, too. The clients knew what a test would reveal.

The clients continued to say nothing. Finally, Rob broke the silence.

"It's true, isn't it?" he asked, exchanging a glance with Marc and Aleks. This explained so much about what they'd seen and sensed.

"We're not allowed to say anything," Darren said.

The lawyers again exchanged knowing glances. Of course the government would have required non-disclosure agreements.

"Do you have copies of what you signed?" Marc asked. "We'd like to see them."

"We'll ask," said Darren.

"Please do," Marc replied. "By the way, anything you tell us is covered by attorney-client privilege. We're not allowed to disclose anything you don't authorize us to disclose. But what the agreements say may be important. I can't believe they would require you to refuse to answer questions under oath before a duly constituted tribunal."

"Why does it matter?" Lara asked. "Can they make Doug give a DNA sample?"

"I don't think so," Marc said. "There's no procedure in the NCHSAA by-laws for anything like that, and we can argue the Genetic Information Non-discrimination Act prohibits it if they try. But I don't think they will, or will need to."

"I don't understand," Lara said. "Can't you just follow your plan, except none of us testify?"

"We can try that," Marc said. "But suppose DeBruhl calls you as adverse or hostile witnesses. The hearing panel will probably let him do that. Don't you see? If you tell the whole truth, then Doug has to admit he's a hybrid clone. If you decline to answer, claiming you're bound by agreement not to reveal official secrets, then the Commission will know the truth even if you haven't said it."

All three clients looked stricken.

"We'll pass that on to our contact," Darren said.

"We'll be glad to talk with him," Marc said. "In fact, we need to."

"Well, he said he was familiar with the firm," Lara said.

"It's not Fred Hutton is it? Major Hutton?"

"Why, yes," she answered. "Do you know him?"

Marc watched his colleague color. Rob knew he was close to revealing too much, himself. But Rob recovered nicely.

"We-we've been involved in a couple of remote meetings," Rob said, "in connection with our work for Mr. McCaffrey and Mrs. Callahan."

That satisfied the clients. It was pretty common knowledge that McCaffrey and Callahan, formerly McCormick, had agreements with the government as a result of last year's prosecution in federal court. Ben Callahan, Alyssa's husband, and Kat Turner had represented them.

Marc decided to reassert charge of the meeting.

"All right," he said. "We needed to know that critical information. Thank you. It tells us what we need to be prepared to do at the hearing."

"What's that?" Doug asked.

Marc's face split in a grin that showed more confidence than he really felt.

"Why, prove that you're human," he said.

"How are you going to do that?" the boy asked.

"You, Mr. Doug Martin, are Exhibit A," Marc said. "Here you are. You walk. You talk. You read. You study. You have friends. Just a normal high school student who is also a good athlete. You're being persecuted because you're a winner...By the way, there is another piece of good news."

"Which is?" asked Darren.

"Late this afternoon, I had a call from Danny Jarvis," Marc said.

"That son of a..." Darren said, and caught himself. "He started this mess."

"He did," Marc agreed, "and now he regrets it. Or regrets the effect on Doug. Anyway, he said he'd help anyway he can. After watching the podcast, I think we ought to put him on our witness list...What's the matter, Doug?"

At the mention of Jarvis name, Doug Martin's eyes had widened and his face had turned pale.

"It's just...it's just a feeling," he said. "But when you said Mr. Jarvis name, I got this feeling he's in some kind of danger."

Marc's eyes darted from Rob to Aleks, but he said nothing.

AT THE OFFICES OF MELTON NORVILLE JENNINGS AND JOHNSON LATER THAT EVENING

When the clients had departed, after some additional discussion of witnesses, including Doug's assessment of which teammate would be best, the legal team met to make their checklists.

"Do you think we really can use Danny Jarvis?" Rob asked.

"Yes, I think we might," Marc said. "The guy who broke the story wants fair treatment for his subject. I know Darren Martin doesn't like the idea, but I do."

Marc paused and tapped his teeth with his pen. "And something he said in the podcast give me another idea."

"What's that?" Rob asked.

"He said Doug is being discriminated against. I think we probably can make a decent argument that suspending him would violate the racial discrimination provisions in Title IX of the Civil Rights Act of 1964."

Rob's face slowly spread into a wide grin. "Makes sense," he said. "We can at least have some fun with it."

"By the way," Marc asked. "Were either of y'all bothered by what Doug said about Jarvis being in danger?"

"Yes," said Aleks and Rob together.

"Why?"

"What Mitch McCaffrey calls our 'spidey sense' – knowing we're in the presence of the paranormal – went off with me the moment Doug said that," Rob said. "What about you, Aleks?"

"Yes. Definitely," she said. "I think we felt...prescience. Being able to sense the future."

"We'd better pass that on to Alyssa," Marc said. "Mitch would be fine, too; but he might be a witness next week, because he teaches our client. Aleks, can you reach Alyssa?"

"I will find way to do so," she promised. She still dropped her articles sometimes.

"There's something else we need to do in a hurry," Marc said. "We need to find an expert witness to contradict that Sikorski guy. Any ideas?"

"Well, there was this professor on television the other night, I think on Fox but it could have been CNN," Rob said. "Young guy, but a PhD. He said that even if the kid is a full-blooded Neanderthal, this whole thing is a tempest in a teapot."

"What's his name, and where is he?" Marc asked.

"I think Western Michigan, and I can't remember the name," Rob said.

"Well, find him. Find him tomorrow. We can bring him in remotely, I think, no matter where he is. While you're doing that, and Aleks is finding Alyssa, I've got to set up a conference call with DeBruhl and Dulaney."

Chapter 31
BRENTWOOD, TENNESSEE, OCTOBER 2022

THURSDAY MORNING

Veronica Clayton's thoughts were jumbled as she drove to work. They had been ever since she'd returned from Johnson City, and really, even before, ever since she'd read Danny Jarvis' story about Doug Martin and the other pieces that quickly followed.

All of this mental chaos was not like her. She usually lived inside her efficient career woman persona, making sure Tommy and Marie Elise were off to school, dressing and doing her make-up carefully, drinking a single cup of coffee and eating exactly one dry toasted English muffin, and checking off inside her head the various things scheduled for the coming day.

An external observer who did not know her well would have noticed no difference this morning. The kids got their cereal and were out the door to catch the bus on time. She had dressed appropriately for this morning's closing and this afternoon's showing. But she had selected the garments mechanically, not taking her usual pleasure in dressing exactly right. She had no memory of applying her makeup. She'd gulped down her coffee and skipped the English muffin. She hadn't had much appetite for the past week. That part was all right, she thought. Dropping a pound or two wouldn't hurt her.

Usually, she reviewed the coming day while driving. Today's drive was a jumble of images that flashed through her head. The birth of the baby eighteen years ago. Re-inventing herself afterwards. Seeing the young man who had been her baby last week. Wanting to see Danny Jarvis again and at the same time never wanting to even read the name again. Thank God, she thought, her office was only a short drive from her home, and the drive didn't require getting on the interstate. That would have been more hazardous than usual this morning.

She knew what was driving the anxiety. Fear. Fear that she'd be outed as the Martin boy's birth mother. Fear that the exposure would explode her carefully constructed persona and the career that came with it. Jarvis hadn't mentioned her name in his story. No one had contacted her. But she still feared the other shoe would drop.

And then there was the guilt. Guilt that she'd given up the baby she'd carried, even though she had no genetic connection to him. Guilt that she'd done so for money. And, somehow, guilt that her "son" was going through this mess, and she wasn't doing anything to defend him. She had this impulse to stand up in front of someone and scream, "What are you doing? This isn't his fault!" Rationally, she knew that probably wouldn't help. But the impulse continued to eat at her.

Veronica pulled her Lexus coup into the parking lot at the offices of Brentwood Realty promptly at 9:00 a.m., as usual. What she saw made her heart sink. Right there in front of her was a news van of a local network affiliate, and two reporters and a cameraman. She recognized one, a young dark-haired woman she saw frequently on the local news. The other, a tall, thin guy, she didn't recognize. She could guess why they were there.

She parked and exited her vehicle, fighting sudden nausea. She tried to walk past them into the offices, but the two reporters moved to block her. The videocam was already rolling. That angered her.

"Ms. Clayton?" said the woman. "We're from your news channel and network news." She quickly gave their names. "May we talk with you?"

Veronica stopped and snapped, "About what?"

This time the man spoke, "About Doug Martin."

"Who's that?" she asked.

"I think you know," the reporter said. "But just to be clear, he's the high school student in North Carolina that reports say is a human-Neanderthal hybrid clone."

Veronica did her best to feign puzzlement. "I think I saw something about that on the news," she said. "What does that have to do with me?"

"We know you're the birth-mother," the reporter said.

Veronica was at once stricken and white-hot with anger that these newshounds would jump her this way. She gulped, fighting nausea that threatened to overwhelm her, and then mastered herself and said, "*What?* Don't be absurd."

The tall reporter bit his lip and motioned for the cameraman to quit filming.

"Look," he said, "suppose you sit down with Nicole here and me for just a few minutes. It can be off the record. No camera. We can do it in your office behind closed doors. We'll tell you what we know and then you can decide whether to give an interview. If you won't do that, we'll run the story anyway, including this film. Your choice."

"If you show this, I'll sue," Veronica threatened.

His response was a skeptical frown. "Our lawyers don't think so. And if you do, the network has a large budget."

Veronica swallowed hard, and nodded. "All right. Whatever it takes to get you off my back. But you're barking up the wrong tree."

The reporters sent the cameraman back to the van, and the two reporters followed her into the office. Veronica told the receptionist to hold her calls and led the two to her corner office. Then she excused herself to visit the restroom.

Once there, she entered a stall and then threw up the morning coffee and some of last night's dinner. After that, nothing else would come up. She felt awful, but she knew she had to go back to her office. She drank a cup of water and it stayed down. Then she used mouthwash and checked her make up and hair. Thankfully, she hadn't cried, so she looked okay, if a little pale.

She took several deep breaths and returned to her office. She closed and locked the door behind her. The reporters were seated in front of her desk. She walked to the desk and took the chair behind it.

"All right," she said, "tell me what you think you know."

The man, whose name was Tom something, took a pocket notebook from his jacket and flipped to a page he had dog-eared. Nicole removed a folder from her shoulder bag. Tom began by explaining he was a science reporter and editor for the network, which made a practice of partnering with local affiliates like Nicole's in pursuit of stories of national interest.

Veronica listened patiently, although she could have cared less about the man's job title or the network's practices. She kept waiting for some mention of Danny Jarvis, but there wasn't one.

Then the two launched into an explanation about how the network's analysts had used facial recognition software to identify her as the girl in the yearbook. The images Nicole removed from the folder all looked similar to what Jarvis had showed her earlier, but again there was no mention of Danny. Veronica did her best to look bored.

"The thing is," Tom said, "your resume doesn't make sense. Your trail into the past runs out prior to your enrolling at Western Kentucky. Yes, you produced a transcript of your grades in high school. Yes, there is a record of your receiving a high school diploma from that high school in Ohio. You even have a birth certificate on file in the Ohio archives.

"But no one back in your so-called home town remembers you. Not any graduates of your class. No teachers. The guy who was principal at the time is retired, but our investigators found him, and he has no explanation. The yearbook for that year doesn't include you. It's as though you appeared out of nowhere in 2006 when you showed up at WKU.

"So, what do you have to say to that?"

Veronica wondered exactly how they found some of what they showed her. It couldn't all be public information. But she didn't ask; doing so would imply they were on to something. She still was bound by the NDA, and she remembered Fred Hutton's instructions. She had to stonewall.

"Nothing," she said.

"Nothing?" Tom repeated. "Are you sure?"

"I'm sure."

"This story is going to be run," Tom said. "This is your chance to tell your side of it. Are you still sure?"

"I am," Veronica said.

"There's something else you should see," Nicole said. She removed a photograph from the folder and handed it across the table. The photo was a little dark, because there was light only from street lamps. But it showed her standing outside next to Danny Jarvis.

"What were you doing in Johnson City last Friday?" Nicole asked.

Veronica tried to remain calm, but wasn't completely successful. She should have denied the photo was real, but she asked, "W-where did you get this?"

"I'm from close to Johnson City," Nicole said. "I still have plenty of friends up there. One of them had read Jarvis' blog, thought he recognized the man, and sent this to me because he knew I had network connections. He had no idea who you were. But we do. Now what were you doing there?"

Veronica bristled. "I don't have to tell you anything," she said.

"You don't," Tom said. "But that photo is clearly you. Our experts say 100 percent certainty. Now that you've seen this, won't you change your mind and tell us the whole story."

Veronica realized it was too late for a complete stonewall. Thankfully, years of dealing with unexpected home inspection reports had trained her to think of an explanation quickly. She straightened and allowed what she hoped was a sincere sigh.

"Okay," she said, "I will. Danny Jarvis came by a couple of weeks ago with the same cock-and-bull stuff I just heard from you. I told him the same thing I told you: you all may think you have something, but you don't.

"Last week, I found out the kid's high school was playing up in Johnson City and went to see him play out of curiosity. I saw him play and came home the next morning. That's it. Well, I did run into Jarvis on the way out of the stadium and we walked together for a while. I told him then just what I told you.

"Now you know everything. I have nothing more to say...I don't know what Jarvis told you. But if he said anything different, he's lying."

"He hasn't told us anything," Nicole said. "When we called him, he said he hadn't been able to confirm anything about you, so he didn't print anything."

"When was that?" Veronica asked.

"Oh," Nicole said, "this morning. We called him from the van while we were waiting for you."

"So, Ms. Clayton, what will it be?" asked Tom. "Do we run the story with or without your cooperation?"

BRENTWOOD, TENNESSEE, OCTOBER 2022

"You've heard everything I have to say," Veronica told him. "And now I'm going to have to ask you to leave. I have a closing at 10:30. And you need to know I'm going to call my lawyer about this."

"Go ahead," Tom said, smiling.

The reporters kept their promise. They pressed their business cards on her and left.

The receptionist and the two realtors who were there at the office, as opposed to out showing property, all descended on her as soon as the two were gone, demanding to know what was going on. She told them all to go back to work, and closed her office door again. After she returned to her desk, she noticed a message light blinking on her land line. It was from Danny Jarvis, saying he needed to speak with her urgently. She decided not to call him back right away. She'd better talk with Hutton before talking with anyone.

But at least Danny Jarvis hadn't ratted her out. She didn't understand why she was glad of that, but she was.

BRENTWOOD, TENNESSEE, OCTOBER 2022
IN THE NEWS VAN

The cameraman doubled as van driver, and his camera was on the passenger's seat. Tom and Nicole sat behind him on a bench seat, with more audio-visual equipment, which would have been taken out if Veronica Clayton had consented to an interview, stored behind them.

"So, Tom," Nicole asked as they turned onto I-65 back toward downtown Nashville, "does the network run the story?"

"I think so," Tom said. "Probably as a segment on the weekly news 'magazine.' We'll start with something from the prior reports, and see if we can get more out of the Jarvis guy. He's clearly protecting Veronica Clayton, but I don't know why."

"Maybe the two have something going on," Nicole suggested.

"Yeah, maybe," Tom said. "Anyway, we'll end with what Clayton told us and show a clip from what we filmed outside. We'll have to get a quote from the defense department. They'll officially deny everything, of course. Like a UFO story, at least the way they used to be handled."

"I thought our meeting with her was off the record," said Nicole.

He shook his head. "No, we offered it, but she didn't insist on it before we started." He stopped and grinned. "You'll be mentioned."

"Thank you," she said. Any mention on the network would help her career. "She said she'd call a lawyer. Does that bother you?"

"Not much," he said. "I do have to double check with legal. But I don't think they'll kill the story. A couple of them over there is concerned with where we got some of the information like the school transcript and birth certificate. But we didn't steal anything. It was all leaked by our 'sources'."

"Who were they?" she asked.

"I really don't know," Tom said. "Someone inside the government, I suspect. But we aren't doing anything wrong by using what we have."

"Does this story really have legs?" she asked.

He shrugged. "It's news."

Privately, Nicole wondered whether this really was important news, compared to some stories the local station and the network had decided to soft-pedal, such as the rising crime and homelessness in downtown Nashville. So the kid was a big strong football player. So what? There were a lot of them running around. Nicole should know; her sister had married one.

But all she said was, "I guess it is." She knew where her bread was buttered.

Chapter 32
CORNELIUS, NORTH CAROLINA, OCTOBER 2022

AT THE JARVIS HOME
THURSDAY

Danny Jarvis was having an interesting day, but he wasn't getting much done. He had submitted his weekly column to *Tar Heel Sports Weekly*, which for a change wasn't about Doug Martin; but he was behind in his blog posts and had wanted to use today to catch up. It wasn't happening.

First, early this morning, he received a call from a number he didn't recognize but showed a 615 area code, which meant Nashville. He had a flash of excitement because he thought it might be from Veronica Clayton. But no, the call was from two people who said they were Tom Harrison and Nicole Bradley, and who claimed to be with a news network and its Nashville affiliates. They said they were outside Veronica Clayton's office building and would interview her shortly, and asked if he had a comment on whether she was Doug Martin's birth mother. He wondered where they got their lead on Veronica, because it hadn't been from him. The only person to whom he'd given the information connecting Veronica to the Martin matter was Monica Gilbert. But he didn't ask them, and didn't comment. He kept to his published story that the trail he'd followed had grown cold in West Virginia.

After the call concluded, he tried to call Veronica and give her a head's up. The only number he had for her was her office land line, which probably wouldn't do any good, but he tried anyway. His call went to voicemail, and he left a message he hoped wasn't too garbled.

Disconnecting the call, he wondered if Monica had leaked anything to the network. Why should she? But she'd said she had "connections." Who were they? He decided he really didn't want to know. On reflection, he realized the network had a lot more resources, and a bigger budget, than he; so, it really wasn't a surprise that they'd found Veronica, probably armed with more damning information than he'd been able to acquire. But he was glad he hadn't exposed her.

He went back to his blog, and the telephone rang again. He didn't recognize the number, but the area code was 828, which covered Martintown. He decided to answer. The caller identified himself as Rob Ashworth, a lawyer with the same firm where Marc Washington worked. Ashworth said he was helping Washington with the Martin matter, but Marc was tied up and had asked Ashworth to call for him. Well, Danny reflected, he'd offered Marc his help, so he couldn't complain about the call. He'd asked for it.

"How can I help you, Mr. Ashworth?" he asked.

"Marc told you we think there'll be an eligibility hearing next week before the high school athletics association, didn't he?" Ashworth asked.

"He did."

"Well, we think it'll be next Friday," Ashworth said. "We're not sure where, but we think it will be here in Brainerd County, probably at the Community College. We'll have to disclose witnesses in advance, and we want you on our list. And we'll likely want you to testify. Will you agree to that?"

"It depends on what I'm supposed to say," Danny said. Now that the prospect of involvement was real and not theoretical, it made him nervous. When he'd offered help, he hadn't realized he'd be asked to testify. *I should have known*, he thought.

"What do you expect from me?" he asked.

"Pretty much what you said on the DuGard podcast," Ashworth said. "Maybe with a few specifics about other big, strong, fast high school athletes whose eligibility isn't being challenged."

"Can't you just play the podcast?" Jarvis asked.

"No. At least we can't count on it. The podcast recording would be considered hearsay. And it wouldn't make the same impression as live testimony."

Jarvis didn't answer immediately. He was nervous about testifying, but not because of what Ashworth wanted out of him. He was afraid he might be asked about where he'd got his information. But...he hadn't obtained it personally. He didn't know the guy who did. The only name he had was Monica's, and he doubted it would come up.

The clincher, though, was that, damn it all, it just wasn't right to keep this kid from playing ball. He'd never intended that.

"Mr. Jarvis?" Ashworth's tone was anxious. "Are you there?"

"Uh, yes," Danny said. "Yes, I am. And yes, I'll do it. Can I do it remotely?"

"Maybe," Ashworth admitted, "but we'd rather you be there in person. Look, I can't promise anything, but we may be able to cover travel expenses. And...I don't know if it makes a difference, but you'll be able to write about your experience testifying. We can't keep you from that, and won't want to."

"Can I sit in on the rest of the hearing?" Danny asked.

"I doubt it," Ashworth said. "They'll probably exclude witnesses except for the one testifying. But you'll have access to the transcript. That will be a public record."

"Will the hearing be recorded? On videotape, I mean," Jarvis asked.

"I'm not sure," Ashworth confessed. "But if it is, I feel confident we can get you a copy."

"Well, you can put me down as a witness if you think I'll do the boy any good," Jarvis said. "And yes – I'll be there. Will I get a subpoena?"

"No. The hearing panel won't issue subpoenas," Ashworth explained. "They're not a court. Now let me be clear. If you're not going to be there, we have to set up a video link. If we can. So if you commit to being there, you need to mean it."

Danny realized he'd crossed a line, even if the line was in his head.

"I'll be there. Just tell me when and where," he said, surprised at the conviction in his own voice.

Ashworth obtained his e-mail address and promised to be back in touch to confirm the date, time and location, and to prepare his testimony. He said the prep session would probably be by ZOOM, if that was okay with Danny. Danny said it was, and the call ended.

Danny looked at the screen in front of him with distaste. Only 50 words. He sighed and placed his hands over the keyboard. Then his phone rang again. This time the screen showed a New York exchange. What the hell, he thought, I might as well take this one, too. If they're trying to sell me something, I'll hang up.

The caller turned out to be an executive with ESPN, who asked Danny if he would be interested in becoming an ESPN contributor. Of course he was, but he asked the obligatory questions on what the position would require, how much the pay would be, and whether he'd be allowed to keep up his local writing and his blog. The answers were all satisfactory.

The guy asked him for his e-mail address and told him he'd receive a contract by e-mail, which he should review with his lawyer. He said the contract would require him to confirm his commitment to "diversity, equity and inclusion." That terminology had become popular after Jarvis had finished school, and he wasn't sure exactly what it meant. But the words didn't sound dangerous, and Danny suspected the guy was just checking off his list. Danny said he understood.

"If we seal this deal with you," the man said, "we'll want you on a show next week, or more likely the week after, for 15 or maybe 30 minutes, about this Martin guy down your way. We can pipe you in remotely, so you won't have to travel. But we'll need the signed contract first."

That was okay with Jarvis. Maybe, he thought, by next week he'd have something important to say. He didn't tell the caller he was going to testify; it would be better to get forgiveness than permission for something like that. He thanked the guy, promised to review the contract ASAP, and ended the call.

Danny went back to his blog, did another 50 words, and realized it was lunchtime. He decided to knock off for a few minutes and make a sandwich. Twenty minutes later, he finished his salami with lettuce and tomato from his refrigerator, the lettuce only slightly wilted, and went back to the computer.

At another 50 words, his post was finally nearing completion. He decided he'd go for a jog around the condo complex when he was done.

He needed the exercise. Then his phone rang again. The screen showed another Nashville number. He didn't think it was the same one as before.

He took the call.

"Danny?" He recognized the voice immediately, and felt his heartbeat increase.

"Hello, Veronica," he said. "What can I do for you?"

"Nothing," she said. "I was just calling to say thank you. Thank you for not ratting me out. And thank you for trying to warn me."

She told him about the reporters' visit. "I don't know if they'll run anything or not. I guess they will. I told them I would call my lawyer, but I haven't, yet. I did call – oh, never mind."

"You called whom?" he asked.

"I can't tell you," she said.

He decided to let that question drop. She obviously was calling someone with the government, and he wasn't sure he wanted to know about that.

"So, what are you going to do?" he asked.

"I don't know. I guess I'll wait and see if they air anything," she said. "What about you? What's next for you?"

Danny wasn't sure he ought to tell her about his commitment to testify, but he did.

"Maybe I can somehow make up for bringing all this on the kid," he said. "I didn't mean for this to happen to him."

"You knew it would change his life," Veronica accused. He knew she was right.

"Yeah, I guess I did," Danny said, "but I thought the publicity would actually do him good, that he'd actually end up making money for himself out of it. And I – I can't change it now."

Yeah, he thought, and if I keep telling myself that, I might start believing it. Well, it still might be true. It could turn out that way.

"Well," Veronica said, "I do want you to know I'm proud of you for trying. I was proud of what you said on the podcast. And, like I said, I'm grateful to you for trying to keep my name out of it, even if it didn't work."

"Maybe…" he began, hesitated, and then said in rush, "maybe, when this stuff quiets down, maybe we can…see each other?"

He expected her to tell him to go to hell, but she didn't.

Instead, he heard a sigh, and she said, "Maybe we can…If I can forgive you for disrupting *my* life."

"Oh, please," he whispered into the receiver, surprising himself with the feeling in his voice.

"We – we'll see," she said, "Bye, Danny."

She disconnected the call. He continued to hold the phone to his ear.

She didn't say "no," he thought. She didn't say "no."

MARTINTOWN, NORTH CAROLINA, OCTOBER 2022 AT THE OFFICES OF THE BOARD OF EDUCATION THURSDAY EVENING

Marc Washington decided that what they were watching this evening was theater. He even wrote the word on his legal pad, added a big exclamation point, and passed the pad to Rob, who sat next to him in the gallery seating of the Board of Education meeting room. Rob took the pad and with his own pen, wrote a cautionary "probably" beneath Marc's message, and passed the pad back. He and Rob made a pretty good team, Marc reflected. Marc himself was more intuitive, but also more impulsive. Rob was more cautious, and thorough to the point of obsession.

Rob was telling him that no matter what they thought would happen, the meeting was just beginning, and the Board had yet to vote. Their services might yet be required, so they had to be on their toes. So far, they had only been introduced as the lawyers for the Martin family. Lara Martin, who had been introduced as Doug Martin's mother, sat in a folding chair on Marc's other side, trying to keep her face impassive, but swallowing hard from time to time. She nudged Marc to see what he and Rob had written, and he showed her.

"Is that good?" she whispered to him.

"We think so. We hope so," he whispered back.

Right now, Superintendent Winston was droning on about how the safety of students, including student athletes, was of paramount (he really had used that word) importance to the Brainerd County Schools. For that reason, he said, he had recommended that the Board call this special meeting to address the concerns of numerous parents and citizens, many of whom were here tonight. That part was correct, Marc thought. All seats were taken, and those who had arrived late were standing along the walls at the rear and sides of the room. A fair number of those present, though, were reporters, including two videographers from different television stations.

The superintendent then plunged into a completely unnecessary but harmless recitation of the low, low number of athletics injuries of students during his tenure as superintendent, a record he was determined to maintain. While he read off statistics, Marc glanced past Rob to look across the central aisle to where Sandra Sparkman sat.

Sparkman was a senior associate with Alex DeBruhl's law firm, and would assist him in representing the Committee for Fairness in Athletics in the Martin matter. She was a tall young woman, attractive but not unusually pretty, with a long, sharp nose and short, burnished blonde hair. Marc thought it a good sign that DeBruhl had sent her to this meeting, and hadn't come himself. She sat there now, wearing a stylish red dress made of some shiny fabric, one leg modestly crossed over the other, her purse and a small notebook in her lap.

Marc had had a fairly contentious video conference with Sparkman, DeBruhl and NCHSAA attorney Frank DuLaney that morning, while Rob was working with Aleks on finding an expert. Marc thought her an ice princess who looked down her long nose at the world. DeBruhl was more friendly, but still condescending. They'd spent much time wrangling over the location of the Martin hearing, assuming there would be one, something Marc had thought settled.

Thankfully, DuLaney had ended the discussion by announcing he had spoken with Claire Daniels at Carolina Highlands, who had confirmed a hearing room was available, and the hearing, if necessary, would be there. They had agreed on a follow up virtual meeting with the legal teams and Commissioner Morton tomorrow afternoon, and agreed to exchange witness lists by close of business tomorrow.

Winston finally finished his speech, and the Board Chair, Don Crabtree, thanked him.

"As you all know, this meeting has been specially called, because of reports concerning a student athlete at West Brainerd High School, Douglas Martin," Crabtree said. "It has been suggested by some authorities that this young man, because of his…hereditary make up, should not be allowed to compete against normal students. The Board will find in its packet a transcript of a recent podcast featuring Professor Sikorski of Duke University. I am sure we have all seen that podcast or read that transcript.

"There is presently no motion on the floor. Before calling for motions, though, I want to open the floor for comments from the public. Several have contacted Superintendent Winston asking to speak, and we will hear from some of you, although time will not permit us to hear from you all, I'm afraid. We will also hear from the Martin family and from the Committee for Fairness in Athletics.

"Superintendent Winston, will you call the first person to speak?"

The first person called to the podium was Jeremiah Billups' mother, who repeated what she had told the media about her fears. Listening to her made Marc squirm. He ached to cross-examine her, but he wouldn't be allowed to do that tonight. The next person was the Brainerd Central coach, who piously echoed what Mrs. Billups had said. Both speakers provoked approbation from the Central fans present and growls from the West Brainerd contingent.

The next speaker provided the evening's only real drama. It was the Reverend Arthur Conley, the pastor of the True Faith Freewill Baptist Church. Marc and Rob had managed to snag the list of people who would speak prior to the meeting, and their phones gave the church's location as out in the country south of Martintown, in the South Brainer district. They'd never heard of the man.

Conley was skinny, and looked to be about 50 years old, with thinning and graying dark hair and dark-rimmed spectacles. He stood at the podium, his eyes darting from board member to member, and cleared his throat. Marc hoped they were not going to hear a sermon. He had sat through enough growing up back in Orangeburg.

"Brothers and sisters, Board members," Conley boomed in a voice surprisingly deep for his stature, "we are here tonight to protect our children. You all have seen or read the words of Doctor Sikorski. Our schools are for human beings. This hybrid child of the apes is not human. He bears the mark of Cain!"

Dr. Watkins had sat poker faced for the first two speakers, but now he leaned forward and spoke into his microphone.

"Just a minute, Pastor," he said. "You do realize, don't you, that what you just said about this young man are exactly the words that were used to justify keeping black people as slaves? You know that, don't you?"

Conley gaped like a fish. Clearly, he had not known that.

"It-it's not the same thing," he finally got out.

"Isn't it?" Watkins probed, but Conley said nothing. A hush had fallen over the room at Watkins' questions. Even Mrs. Billups, seated two rows in front of the Martin group, shifted uncomfortably in her chair. Conley thanked the Board for its time and sat down.

The Chair then called on West Brainerd principal Josh Fulkerson. Superintendent Winston glared at Fulkerson as he approached the podium. Fulkerson had told Marc that Winston would rather he have stayed away, but didn't dare direct it with the whole county and the media watching.

Fulkerson thanked the Chair and raised folder over his head in his right hand. "I am holding Doug Martin's school records," he said. "We are talking about an 'A' and high 'B' student, a student who has presented no disciplinary problems to our school, who competes on the baseball as well as the football team." Fulkerson stopped, and turned to the spectators with a smile, and then turned his face back to the board and continued, "Coach Watkins has told me Doug Martin hasn't even been penalized this year except for one 'motion' penalty. He has hurt no one. He is in good standing academically. And athletically.

"We are here tonight only because of some irresponsible reports in the media. It would be a shame to let them disrupt this young man's life any more than they already have done."

Fulkerson sat, and Marc resolved to congratulate him after the meeting. Josh would make a good witness next week.

At this point, Board attorney Gary Sanders, who was sitting next to the Chairman, cleared his throat and spoke up. "Mr. Chairman, pardon me; but before we hear from anyone else, or receive any motions, possibly I can help simplify things."

"Please go ahead," said Crabtree.

"As I understand it, no one is suggesting that this student ought to be expelled from school. Am I correct?"

No one said anything. Marc thought some of the members looked embarrassed.

"All right," said Sanders. "If that's the case, then all that we are talking about is athletic eligibility. All of our schools are members of the North Carolina High School Athletic Association. Its rules govern eligibility. I understand the Association is prepared to conduct a hearing on this very matter. I suggest this Board defer to the Association. Simply put, I don't think this Board has jurisdiction in this case."

Superintendent Winston looked relieved. A couple of the board members looked sour. Marc saw that three of the five, including Watkins were nodding. That was a good sign.

"Thank you, counselor," said Crabtree. "Now, before I call for a motion, perhaps we'd better hear from the other attorneys present tonight. Ms. Sparkman is here for the Committee for Fairness in Athletics. Ms. Sparkman?"

Sandra Sparkman uncoiled from her chair like a self-conscious python, Marc thought. He really didn't like her.

"Mr. Chairman," she said, her head high and looking down her nose, "we think this Board certainly has joint jurisdiction with the athletic association, should the board see fit to exercise it. However, if the will of the board is to defer to the association, we are ready to show this hybrid athlete presents a direct threat to the safety of others at any hearing the Association may convene."

"Thank you," Crabtree said. "Mr. Washington?"

Marc rose, handed his pad to Rob, and said, "Mr. Chairman, the Martin family's position is exactly as Mr. Fulkerson so ably summarized the matter this evening. But as their attorneys, Mr. Ashworth and I agree with Mr. Sanders. This is a matter for the NCHSAA."

After Marc sat, Dr. Watkins moved to defer any action on Douglas Martin to the NCHSAA. The member from the West Brainerd district seconded the motion. The chair called for discussion, and while Crabtree and the other member from Martintown, Jerry Dixon, looked sour, there wasn't any. The motion carried without dissent, and Crabtree adjourned the meeting.

Marc, Rob, and Lara Martin pushed their way through the crowd, declining to take questions from the reporters who tried to collar them. Outside, they escorted Lara to her car, made sure she made it away without interference, and turned toward their own.

"Like I said," Marc grumbled. "Theater. What a waste of time and money."

CORNELIUS, NORTH CAROLINA, OCTOBER 2022

"Not entirely," said Rob. "We got a window into what DeBruhl and Sparkman will do next week. She said our client is a 'direct threat.' Now they have to prove it."

Yeah, Marc thought. He and Rob were a good team.

Chapter 33
MARTINTOWN, NORTH CAROLINA, OCTOBER 2022

AT THE OFFICES OF MELTON NORVILLE JENNINGS AND JOHNSON
FRIDAY MORNING

Marc, Rob, and Aleksandra were not able to convene until 11:00 a.m. Both lawyers had had early court appearances they couldn't duck, Marc in Superior Court, and Rob at a Bankruptcy Creditors' Committee meeting. Aleksandra found them a conference room they could use until 1:30, and had the receptionist order sandwiches from the coffee shop next door to be brought in at noon. They'd have the remote meeting with opposing counsel and the NCHSAA Commissioner at 3:30. Now they had to compare notes and plan their evidence for the hearing.

There was a white board on one wall of the conference room, and Marc walked to it and opened it, as he'd seen Kat Turner do in similar meetings. He picked up a marker and wrote "OUR WITNESSES" in block capitals.

"Let's list our witnesses first," he began. "Bear in mind that the hearing is scheduled for just one day, and we won't have time for many; so we have to pick our best."

"Marc, while we're on this topic," Rob said, "I'm concerned that De-Bruhl will try to run the clock, and leave us without time. We talked about that the other day. What are we going to do about that?"

"Glad you brought that up, Rob," Marc answered. "Here are my thoughts: DeBruhl wants opening statements, but I'm going to suggest this afternoon that both sides file pre-hearing briefs by Wednesday at close of business at noon, and not allow opening statements except for the memoranda. That's one thing.

"The other thing I'm going to suggest is that the hearing panel put both sides on a 'chess clock,' so that Debruhl has to start promptly at nine and finish by 1:30, with a 30 minute lunch break. That means we'd start at 1:30 and finish by 5:30. There would be 30 minutes, 15 for each side, after that. So we'd all get out by about 6:00. You weren't on the call yesterday, but I think Frank DuLaney will like the idea. He told us twice that the Panel wants to finish in one day. He has a lot of pull with Commissioner Morton."

"Will he be on call today?" Aleks asked.

"Yes, and at the hearing. He will be the hearing panel's 'legal advisor.' I think that's a good thing. He won't let DeBruhl snooker the panel...I hope.

"The other thing that does is get the hearing over before the ball game that night. The game starts at 8:00. It lets us call one of Doug's teammates, and maybe the coach."

Rob agreed Marc had a good plan and they went back to witnesses. They all agreed that Doug Martin had to testify, if only to let the panel see him and hear how articulate the young man was. But should he be the first witness? Rob didn't think it would matter because he was sure Alex DeBruhl would call him as an adverse witness, and Marc tended to agree. But they couldn't be sure, and had to plan for both eventualities.

The biggest question was whether Doug should admit he was a hybrid if DeBruhl didn't ask him. Marc observed it probably didn't matter because DeBruhl was sure to ask.

"It's still important to make a decision," Rob said. "What if DeBruhl decides to wait until cross examination? If we don't bring it up on direct, then the panel may think we're trying to hide it."

"I'm worried about his non-disclosure agreement, if we bring it up," Marc said. The Martin family had received permission to show their agreements to their lawyers; and sure enough, the agreements did not preclude them from truthfully testifying before a duly constituted state or federal tribunal. "But," Marc said, "My sense of the agreement is it doesn't preclude answers to someone else's questions. Answering his own lawyer's questions is too much like volunteering information."

They decided that, if DeBruhl did not call Doug to the witness chair, their client would be their first witness, and his focus would be on his academic standing, his high school social life, and his nearly penalty-free athletic performance. They wouldn't go into his genetic heritage. When it came up on cross examination, they'd address it in re-direct by explaining he had an NDA. Marc would handle the questioning.

"We'd better get him in the morning to go over his testimony before we run out of time," Marc said. "Can you set that up as soon as we're done here, Aleks. Just call his mom."

Marc wrote down four names on the whiteboard: Teammate, Coach, Principal, and Jarvis. They agreed they had to use Principal Fulkerson, because they wanted to emphasize the client's academic standing. As Rob observed, "Ape-men don't make straight 'A's'."

"Except at N.C. State," Marc deadpanned, and the two lawyers laughed, neither being Wolfpack alumni. Aleks didn't understand, and they had to explain. Anyway, Marc would also take Fulkerson.

If possible, they would call both Coach Watkins and a teammate. But what if they were running out of time. Which was more important?

"I think the teammate," said Rob. "Watkins would be a good witness, but everybody knows he's fighting to keep his star player. The teammate's testimony is predictable, too; but we want to emphasize our client is popular on the team and at school."

"I agree," said Marc. "If that's our priority, I'd like an African American. The Commissioner is African American herself, and I think a black guy highlights our position that even if the allegations about the client's being a hybrid clone are true, kicking him out of sports is race discrimination. So what about Javon Shade or Henry Warren?"

"Makes sense," Rob said. "We'll ask Doug which he prefers in the morning. Aleks, make a note to be sure we cover that."

"Rob, I want you to take this witness," Marc said. "We want to plant the 'this is racist' seed in the minds of the Panel, but we don't want to be too obvious."

"You mean black guy questions black kid?" Rob asked.

"Yeah."

"I'll do it," said Rob. "I'll have to find time to prep whomever we pick. What about the coach?"

"I'll take him," Marc said, "if we can squeeze him in. Now what about Jarvis? I still want to use him, even if we have to forego the coach. Fulkerson and Watkins are a little duplicative. Does anyone disagree?"

Rob rubbed his chin and said, "No. No one much outside North Carolina had heard of him before this broke, but he actually has a following here. I usually read his blog myself. This was his only step into anything controversial. One thing about it – he's seen lots of high school games, all over the state. If anyone has seen lots of big strong players playing against smaller guys, he's one of them."

"That's why I want him," Marc said. "That, and the fact I think his buyer's remorse may sell pretty well. Can you take him?"

Rob agreed and then Aleksandra spoke up.

"Do not forget client's concern that he may be in danger somehow," she said. "If we put him on witness list, we need to offer protection, somehow. Do we not?"

"Great point, Aleks," Marc said. "Let's put him on the list, bring it up with the client tomorrow morning, and then see what Alyssa thinks."

Marc then returned to the board, erased it, and wrote, "EXPERT."

"Tell us who it is," Marc said to Rob.

Rob passed over a copy of a *curriculum vitae* to each of the others.

"This is not the guy we contacted first," he explained. "When I talked to the guy at Western Michigan, he sounded very supportive, but he has to be at a convocation at his university next Friday. He gave us another name, someone he'd gone to graduate school with, and set up the contact. Here's the c.v. The new guy's name is Howard Mortenson. Dr. Howard Mortenson.

"Creds are pretty good," Rob continued. "And he's close to local. Just got tenure at East Tennessee State in anthropology. Pretty good list of publications, but not nearly as long as the Duke guy's. College at Washington & Lee, Master's at Tennessee, PhD. from Virginia. Anthropologist but not a geneticist, but I don't think that's critical.

"The best thing is his opinions track what his buddy said on T.V. They're just what we want. And he'll come in person if we advance a retainer and travel expenses."

"Can he get us an expert's report by Wednesday?" Marc asked. They'd likely need to exchange experts' reports in advance of the hearing.

"Says he can," Rob said.

"Sold," Marc said, adding, "You talked with him, so he's your witness."

Seeing Rob nod, he went to the whiteboard again, erased it again, and wrote, again in block capitals, "THEIR WITNESSES."

"We'll know by late this afternoon," he said. "Right now, this is guess-work, but I think we can pretty well anticipate what they'll do."

He wrote, "Doug Martin" on the board, and said, "We've already covered this one." Then he wrote, "Mrs. Billups."

"I think she's a near certainty," Marc continued, "and I'll take her on cross."

"I hope they call that crazy preacher," Rob said.

"Nah," Marc replied, "they won't let that dumb bastard near the hearing panel." He made a face and added, "But I'm sure they'll take money from the folks who think like him."

His colleagues responded with grim nods. They couldn't yet determine where the "Committee for Unfairness in Athletics," as Rob was calling it, was getting their money; but the rumor mill was saying they were raising plenty.

Marc wrote again. "Opposing coach or player."

"Doesn't that look too much like sour grapes?" Rob asked.

"Yes," Marc said, "but I think they'll call one. I think they have to, be-cause that's where most of their money is coming from. Plan on doing the cross, Rob. If you need ideas, see me."

Rob said he would, and then Marc wrote one more name: "Sikorski."

"I know you have our expert, Rob," he said. "But I want to cross this guy. I want at him badly."

"Fine by me," said Rob. "I'll ask our witnesses about some publications you can use in cross and get them to you."

Marc nodded and erased the board again.

"Now let's talk about our panel," he said. He wrote three names: Jessica Morton, Roger Farley, and Bill Morgan. As though on cue, Aleks passed around copies of their biographies from the NCHSAA website.

"The Commissioner, the Deputy Commissioner for Eligibility, and the Deputy Commissioner for Compliance," he said. "Their board is split and won't touch this. They're doing the hearing to appease the faction that wants our client disqualified."

"That's good, but they probably think there's no evidence our client is what the media reports say he is," said Rob. "How do they react when they find out that it's true?"

"I don't know," Marc said. "We'll just have to convince them it doesn't matter."

Rob and Aleksandra said nothing, and Marc continued, "Jessica Morton has been in athletics administration ever since she finished at Winston-Salem State. The other two got all their athletics experience, if you don't count participating in high school sports, in their present jobs. Their college degrees were in business. They're both pretty young."

"Farley has made a bunch of eligibility determinations. Every one of them was based on age or academics. Our client doesn't present any issue on either count. We'll need to hammer that in our memorandum, in the Fulkerson testimony, and on cross examination when we can. As near as I can determine, no one has said he was unfair.

"Morgan runs compliance, so all of his enforcement has been on rule violations. Not an issue here either. We'll need to point that out.

"Morton." Marc paused in thought. "She's held her job for ten years. That means she's at least a good politician. And she's the boss. But I think the discrimination aspect of our case will get her attention."

"Didn't she make a public statement supporting the transgendered males competing in girls' sports?" Rob asked.

"She did," Marc said. "But I don't think that has to hurt us. We're not trying to exclude anybody. We want our client included.

"Incidentally, that's why I don't expect the transgender activists to testify for them, even if they've been making a stink. The cross examination is too obvious."

"Yeah," Rob said. "'You don't really want our client excluded from competition, now do you? What you really want is your folks to be included?' And if the answer is they do want to disqualify Doug, the question is, 'So you're saying two wrongs make a right?'"

"You got it," Marc said. "So, if one of them does testify, you've got the cross."

"Gee, thanks, pal," Rob said.

Then their food arrived and they continued the discussion while eating.

LENOIR, NORTH CAROLINA, OCTOBER 2022
HIBRITEN HIGH SCHOOL STADIUM
FRIDAY EVENING

The West Brainerd High School football team made the bus trip to Lenoir Friday afternoon. The drive was not too bad, Doug thought. This was the last away game of the season, and the last major obstacle to a conference championship. Next week was the final home game, but the opponent was the last place team in the league.

We can beat them, even if I don't get to play, he thought as the team exited the bus. That means I'd better give it all I've got tonight.

For some reason, ever since his emotional session with his parents that night, Doug had remained calm and determined. He wouldn't give up hope, and he refused to let all of this mess distract him from football. He owed coach and the team his best, and they would get it. He was worried about what would happen; but so far, he'd been able shove it out of his mind when the game started. He'd focus on the legal case tomorrow morning when he met with the lawyers.

When the team had dressed, Coach Watkins approached Doug and said, "Stump, I know you're facing – hell, the school is facing – some scary stuff next week. I feel for you. And I'm mad about it.

"But don't let that affect your play. We need this win tonight. I need you to be focused."

"Don't worry, coach," Doug said. "I'm focused. I promise."

Doug was true to his word. He didn't play his best game, but he played a good one. His tackles were sure. His blocks were crisp. He ignored the taunts of "Cave Boy" and "Ape Man" he heard from some of the players on the other team.

His blocks helped free Henry Warren for two long touchdown runs. He didn't get that many carries, but he made them count. And that week, Coach Watkins had put in a new play that he called, "Stump in the flat." The play at first looked as though Doug was leading the blocking off the right side for a quarterback keeper or a pitch to Henry Warren. The Hibriten defense got out of Doug's way to avoid being blocked. But then Les pulled up and tossed a short pass to Doug, who was alone in the flat – the area close to the line of scrimmage outside the right end. The play worked for two scores.

When the game ended, the score was West Brainerd 32, Hibriten 12.

Doug showered and left the locker room. His parents were waiting to take him home, because he had to meet with the lawyers early the next morning. He looked around and saw Eva, who was waiting to board a van with the other cheerleaders, and blew him a kiss. That lifted his spirits, but he noticed her parents were not there.

No one at school knew it, but Eva's father had not relented. He had even called the Martin home, reaching Doug's mother, to insist they keep their son away from his daughter. Lara Martin's tongue could be sharp when she wanted it to be, and she used it on Joe Martinez. He found that out from Eva, because he didn't hear the conversation and his mother didn't tell him about it. Eva said that the episode had provoked another blow-up between her parents.

She was miserable, but so far, she was sticking with Doug. That was something to hold onto, he told himself as he got into the back seat of his parents' car to return home.

Chapter 34
MARTINTOWN, NORTH CAROLINA, OCTOBER 2022

THE OFFICES OF MELTON NORVILLE JENNINGS & JOHNSON
SATURDAY MORNING

Doug's parents let him sleep on the drive from Lenoir back to their home outside Martintown, and then let him sleep as long as possible Saturday morning before rousing him to wash and dress for his 9:00 a.m. meeting with the legal team. His mother made him an egg sandwich he ate in her car as she drove him into town, and didn't fuss this time when he left crumbs on the car seat.

His mother drove him on a roundabout route and dropped him off at the rear door of the law office, where the pretty, dark-haired young paralegal whose name, he remembered, was Alexandra admitted him. The idea was to avoid the reporters and photographers who had dogged him for the past several days. This morning, it worked. Doug had thought the barrage of attention from college recruiters was irritating enough, but it paled next to being accosted by what his mother called *paparazzi*. (He'd had to look up that word on his cell phone.) Thankfully, the recruiting attention had abated some while the coming hearing was pending. He suspected that was temporary, but for now, he was glad of it.

Alexandra led him to a conference room where Marc Washington and Rob Ashworth waited. Marc asked him to sit, and Doug yawned as he did so, causing Marc to offer coffee. He hadn't developed a taste for coffee, so

Alex (that's what they called her) brought him a Coke. He didn't drink a lot of soft drinks, but today the caffeine was welcome.

The first thing the lawyers covered with him was their plans to call witnesses on his behalf. He thought it all sounded good. They asked him to suggest a witness from among his teammates, preferably an African American, and he suggested Henry Warren.

"Javon is a really good dude," he explained, "but you never can tell what he'll say. He loves his jokes. Henry is a pretty serious guy. He'll answer your questions and shut up, and he'll think before he answers the other lawyer's questions."

He saw his lawyers nod in approval. They had told him to pick the most thoughtful witness.

They brought up Danny Jarvis, and he felt another twinge he couldn't explain. He didn't say anything.

"What's the matter, Doug?" Marc asked. "Do you object to using him?"

Doug hesitated. "I – I didn't really like him when he tried to interview me and my folks," he said. "But it's not that. I know he wants to help. I just have this feeling that if he's involved, something bad will happen to him."

His legal team exchanged glances, and Marc said, "Alex, see if you can help him."

The paralegal walked around the table and sat next to Doug. She turned toward him and said, "Doug, give me your hands. Please."

Doug obediently took the young woman's hands. She closed her eyes and sat very still. Finally, she released his hands and said, "Thank you."

"Alex, what did you get?" Rob Ashworth asked.

Alexandra rose and walked back to her chair, not speaking. The other two waited for her to say something. She sat, opened her mouth, closed it, and finally spoke.

"Nothing for sure. Nothing certain. But I think his vision is true."

Marc tapped the conference table with his pen, and then said, "Doug, give us a minute."

The three left and went out in the hall to confer. They weren't gone long. When they returned and resumed their seats, Washington said, "Mr. Jarvis is already on our witness list. We're not going to remove him. But… we'll take steps to protect him. Trust us."

Doug said nothing, only nodded. He really didn't have any choice.

Then his lawyers moved on to his own testimony. The first topic was what he was allowed to say. They asked him if he'd spoken with anyone about it.

"Major Hutton," he answered.

"What did he say?" Marc asked.

"He said it was okay to talk with my lawyers. He said it was okay to tell the truth under oath. But he said he couldn't tell me everything, like my host-mother's name, and that was for her protection, and mine."

"What else?" Marc prompted.

"I – I asked him if I'm human," Doug said. "Mom and Dad say I am, but I wanted to hear it from him."

"And what did he say?" Marc prompted.

Doug allowed a smile. "I almost remember his exact words. He said, 'Yes, you are. Without a doubt. And you yourself are the best evidence I can think of, of that.' I asked him what he meant.

"'Look at you,' he said. 'Brought up in a normal home, with normal parents. Taking the same classes other people take. Doing well. Having friends. I can't think of anything more convincing than that.'"

He noticed his lawyers smiling and making notes, and heard the paralegal's keyboard clicking. They must have liked what they heard.

"Have you had contact with Major Hutton?" he asked.

He saw them hesitate. Finally, Marc said, "He got word to us that it was okay for you to tell us things, so we could prepare."

Doug started to ask additional questions but decided not to do so.

The session moved on to Doug's testimony. They went over two plans. One was if he was called as a hostile witness, the other was if his lawyers put him in the witness chair. He now understood why Eva thought a legal career might be desirable. These people were so methodical, so organized. But he didn't think it was for him.

By the time they finished, it was a few minutes after noon. He called his mother to come get him. Alexandra led him to the back door.

When he exited the building, there was a car waiting; but it wasn't his mom's. He recognized it as Eva's mother's Prius.

And Eva was in the driver's seat, waving to him.

MARTINTOWN, NORTH CAROLINA OCTOBER 2022 THE OFFICES OF MELTON NORVILLE JENNINGS & JOHNSON

When Doug had gone, Rob observed, "Well, that went pretty well. I think he'll hold up okay."

"Yeah," Marc said, "except for one thing: What should we do about his feeling that Jarvis is in some type of danger?"

"It is real," said Aleks, who had just re-entered the room from escorting Doug outside. "I felt it."

"What kind of danger, Aleks?" Rob asked. "Could you tell?"

"No," she said, "I could not. But…I did not feel someone would hurt him, necessarily. But something unpleasant, perhaps frightening."

"And it's connected with his testimony?" Marc asked. "Are you sure of that?"

Aleksandra (there was no pretense it was "Alexandra" when no outsider was with them) hesitated. Then she said, "Not completely, but I think so. Nothing is felt except when he is discussed as witness." She also was not as careful not to drop her articles when the meeting was private.

"We have to warn him, somehow," Marc said. "But I wish we knew what to warn him about."

"We could just drop him from the witness list," Rob suggested.

"I don't want to do that," Marc responded. "For two reasons. One, I don't like caving to witness intimidation. Two, we can't be sure that would solve his problem."

"So what do we do about it?" Rob asked.

"Fred Hutton might be able to help," Marc said, "but he's made it clear that he can't have a direct pipeline to Doug's lawyers. So we have to go through Alyssa, or Mitch if we can't reach her."

"I can reach her," Aleks said. "I feel sure."

"Well, we need to talk with her about this ASAP," Marc said. "Today if possible. Set it up, Aleks, as soon as we break."

They spoke for a few minutes about hearing nuts and bolts, including finishing the pre-hearing memorandum for the panel, contacting Coach Watkins about his testimony and Henry Warren's, their ZOOM meeting with Jarvis scheduled for Tuesday afternoon, and their virtual prep session with the expert they'd scheduled for Wednesday. They were preparing to break for the afternoon when Marc's cell phone rang.

"It's Danny Jarvis," he told the others. "Speak of the devil. I'll put him on 'speaker'."

"Hello, Marc?" Jarvis sounded apprehensive. "Something just happened you ought to know about."

"Go ahead," Marc said. "I have our team here. Tell us."

"I got a text from some unknown number just a few minutes ago," Jarvis said. "Let me read it to you: 'You better think before you testify for that kid. We know where you got your information. This is a word to the wise.'"

"You have no idea who it's from?" Marc asked.

"None," Jarvis said. "And I don't know what he means by where I got my information. Hell, *I* don't know who the guy is or where he got it." He explained about the man who had contacted him and brought him the documents from state archives.

"Who else knows about what you obtained?" Doug said.

"No one, really," Jarvis answered. "Well, there is one person. It's someone who works for the state and told me she'd tried to help but couldn't. And then this other guy showed up out of the blue. I have to admit I always thought that was suspicious."

"Who is that?" Marc asked.

There was a pause, and then Jarvis said, "I'm not supposed to say, but under the circumstances, maybe I'd better." There was another long moment of silence, and then Jarvis said. "Her name is Monica Gilbert. She works for the state community colleges."

"We know her," said Marc.

"You do? How?" Jarvis asked.

"Let's just say she's been involved in some of our prior cases," Marc said. "Look," he continued, "we still want your testimony. Are you still in?"

They heard him sigh into the phone, and then Jarvis said, "Yeah. Yes, I am."

"All right, then," said Marc. "Forward that text to me, and we'll work on getting some hearing security. And…call your local police. They can at least send a cruiser around to your house every now and then."

"I'd…rather not," Jarvis said. "See, I don't know how that guy got my source material from archives. I don't want too many questions."

"You didn't steal anything yourself?" Marc asked.

"No, but I paid him for the information," Jarvis admitted.

"Well, use your best judgment," Marc said. "But send us that text. We're going to stay in touch with you every day from here on out. And we'll see you on the ZOOM Tuesday."

When the call concluded, Marc, Rob, and Aleks all exchanged a long look. Monica's involvement could only mean one thing. Somehow, the FBI was involved in this.

"But why?" Marc asked.

"Maybe to get back at Defense," Rob said. "The Bureau and the DIA… don't always get along. We know that."

Yeah, Marc thought, and Rob probably knows better than I do about that, considering the events of last Christmas and this spring. I didn't have anything to do with all that. But anyway…

"Aleks," Marc said, "I'm going to send that text to you as soon as I get it. Be sure Alyssa sees it and make sure she gets it to Fred Hutton. Make that a priority."

"I will," she promised.

Then they really did break the meeting. But they didn't think they'd get much relaxation this Saturday afternoon. They'd be texting and calling one another.

OUTSIDE THE LAW OFFICE

Doug stood with dropped jaw when he saw Eva laughing in the driver's seat of her mother's car, waving to him to get in. She rolled down a window and called to him, "What are you waiting for?"

When he was seated beside her, he said, "We need to wait. My mother is coming."

"Actually," Eva told him, "she's not. My mom called yours and it's all arranged. I'm taking you to lunch, and then we can hang out for a while."

"How -- ?" That was as far as he got.

"I brought it up to Mom last night, after you told me yesterday you weren't going to drive yourself here," Eva said. "We haven't had much quality time lately, and Mom's being a real sweetheart about it."

"What about your father?" Doug asked, as Eva pulled out of the parking lot.

"Oh, he doesn't know," Eva said. "He's up at one of those subdivisions on the ridge that looks over the lake. Somebody wants a water feature installed before the weather turns cold. He'll be there all day.

"But," she added, "he's getting better. Mom can be pretty persuasive when she wants to be. But what I think really did the trick was when that country preacher showed up on our doorstep Thursday night."

"You didn't tell me about that," he said.

"I didn't want to distract you on game day," she said, "and we didn't have much time. Anyway, our doorbell rang, Dad answered and it was some minister from a little church up on Jonah's Ridge saying he was there to save my soul and keep me away from the corruption of the Beast." She giggled. "I think you are supposed to be the Beast. Dad ran him off and then went into the den and sat by himself for a long time. He didn't say anything to me, but Mom said this morning they talked for a long time. I think he may be coming around."

That was good news. And, Doug thought, I can sure use some right now. Eva wanted to know how the meeting had gone, and he said he thought it went pretty well. He told her was impressed with how organized his legal team was.

She drove to Bill's BBQ, a popular barbecue joint on the edge of town, where she parked and made a phone call. Moments later, Bill himself walked out with a brown bag that held two large chopped pork sandwiches and two bags of potato chips.

"Good game last night," Bill said, as he handed the bag to Eva. "This is on the house. Good luck next week."

They thanked him, and then Eva started the car and drove away. "If you're wondering what we're going to drink, I have a cooler with water and lemonade in the back seat."

"Where are we going?" he asked.

"You'll see," she promised.

She drove to a picnic area next to a middle school. Today, no one was there. She parked under the branch of a maple tree that still had some bright leaves.

"Well, Mr. Martin," she said, turning to him. "Aren't you going to kiss me?"

Chapter 35
ARLINGTON, VIRGINIA, OCTOBER 2022

AT THE HUTTON HOME
SUNDAY AFTERNOON

Fred Hutton and his wife Marianne were seated on their back patio, enjoying the cool but clear and breezy weather. The logs in the fire pit in front of them crackled and warmed them, the only drawback being that when the breeze changed, smoke from the fire pit came their way. They were dressed for the weather in warm sweaters. Marianne sipped a glass of white wine, while Fred nursed a brandy. Marianne had commanded Alexa to play "cool jazz," and the music, not too loud, poured from the speakers at their back. The Huttons were now empty-nesters, their two children living across the country from them, so it was only the two of them. They were outside because October was well on the way to becoming November, and there wouldn't be many more nice afternoons.

Rogan, their German shepherd, lay panting on the patio, under the table between them. Sometimes he would get up to chase an imaginary rabbit across the back lawn, which was fenced in for both privacy and his roaming, but he'd come back and lie down again after a few minutes. Most of the trees in the back yard had lost their leaves, but there was one maple whose branches held orange glory. (He'd been able to coax the leaves fallen from the others into trash bags yesterday. Fred didn't have the Talent of a McCaffrey or a McCormick-Callahan; but he'd perfected that spell after some coaching from Mitch.)

It was an altogether fine day, except he was going to have to get back to work for a while in a few minutes. The message from Alyssa Callahan had convinced him it was necessary. He'd offered a video conference, but she'd said she'd just come in person after her workout and run.

"Alyssa is due here just about now," he said to his wife.

Marianne Hutton taught music at a private school in Arlington, and gave piano lessons on the side; but she had a security clearance Fred had worked to get, although not nearly as high as his. She knew a fair amount about his work, and was used to the comings and goings of, well, *unusual* people at their home.

As though on cue, mist formed in a small cloud on the lawn in front of them, and Alyssa McCormick-Callahan walked through. Her hair was pinned up, with some stray locks escaping, and her curvy figure was partially hidden by a sweatshirt and pants. She wore jogging shoes, and her face was flushed, evidently from recent exercise. Rogan immediately ran to her and jumped up in her face, barking; but the two knew each other, and Alyssa knew he was just saying "hello."

After Alyssa walked up and greeted them, Marianne stood and said, "Here, Alyssa, take my chair. I need to go in and check on the soup. We've got a pot of vegetable-beef going. I hope you'll stay to sample it."

Alyssa thanked her but declined, saying she and Ben had plans later; and Marianne, after expressing regret, offered a glass of wine, which Alyssa said would be nice. Marianne left and return with a full glass in a few minutes, and then excused herself again.

Alyssa seated herself and sipped. "Ummm, that's good," she said, and then added, "Fred, we need to talk about this Jarvis thing."

"We do," he agreed, "but first, how much do you know about the Martin matter?"

"Enough," she said. "Enough to guess the rest of it."

He nodded, thinking. He decided not to elaborate. Alyssa's security clearance would probably cover more information, but he didn't need to push the envelope.

"What they're trying to do to that poor boy is awful," Alyssa said. "Are you going to be able to do anything to help?"

"I'm trying," he said. "I've told my superiors that we're about to be outed, despite our denials, and Defense needs to get out ahead of the story and present the truth – well, as much of it as possible – in the best light. I've put that recommendation in writing."

He paused and sipped cognac. "But getting any movement out of the bureaucracy is like pulling teeth. As you know, we have our factions, too; and they seldom agree. Somebody suggested we kick it up to the White House for approval."

"And what does the White House say?" she asked.

"So far, nothing," he said. "The only thing I know is that they're making sure the president doesn't answer any questions about it, yet, until they have a script for it. You know that if he answers off the cuff, nobody knows what he'll say."

"What do you think they'll do?"

Fred finished his brandy. "I don't know," he said. "They're probably trying to figure out what will help the most, politically. It's likely they haven't decided.

"Some idiot Congressman got on TV and said this is proof that a prior administration cooked up a plan to create a secret race of white super-soldiers to take over the country, and it's still being covered up. Another one said she thinks it's just terrible that this guy who isn't even human gets to play sports while transgendered biological males can't play girls' sports in some states.

"There is absolutely nothing to what the first guy said. Nothing. And the second honorable member has it wrong about the kid's humanity. Not to mention she can't explain how putting down the hammer on Doug Martin is going to alleviate her transgender concerns. But both of them have political clout.

"Look," he said, "I've convinced my boss. I *think* my recommendation is going to be accepted. I am hoping we'll be able to issue a positive statement. I think we will, sooner or later. I think we'll have to. But when? In time to help at that athletic association hearing down in North Carolina? I hope, but I can't promise."

"At least we know who's behind this," Alyssa said. "Fucking Monica Gilbert."

"More likely Dennis Springfield," Hutton said. "The Gilbert woman is just his stooge."

"Well, she's a stooge that mobilized this committee they formed to disqualify the kid," Alyssa said. "The lawyer is one of her buddies. So are some of the people who are raising money."

"I didn't say she is an *ineffective* stooge," Hutton replied with a humorless chuckle. "But Springfield hasn't forgotten how we got his hand slapped over you and Mitch. And he keeps saying the training you two are giving his agents is insufficient."

"That's not true," Alyssa said. "But…it would help if his people went after real bad guys instead of the ones they make up or exaggerate."

Hutton held up a hand. "We can talk about that later," he said. "Right now, let's talk about Danny Jarvis. I agree that the threatening text came from the Bureau, or one of Springfield's contractors. But we'll never prove it."

"Do you think he'll have Jarvis hurt? Send someone to work him over?"

Hutton considered for a moment and said, "No. That's not the Bureau's style. If we were talking about the Company, yes. They might do that, or worse. But the FBI prefers to keep things nice and legal. At least they need to look like that's what they're doing.

"I think what they'll do is get one of their tame U.S. Attorneys to issue a search warrant, claiming he's got classified information or committed some improbable federal crime. Make a dawn raid with body armor and M-4's. Scare him good, and confiscate his computer and cell phone, and anything else that might have his source material.

"Of course," he added, "if the guy resists and gets hurt, it won't be *their* fault."

"That could happen any time," Alyssa mused.

"It could. But I don't think they'll do anything right away. If they do it too quickly, it would give the Martins' lawyers time to react, or at least adjust. It won't be tonight or tomorrow. Probably not Tuesday night or Wednesday morning. Friday morning would be too late; Jarvis will be in Martintown for the hearing Friday; they won't raid him at a hotel.

"Early Thursday morning is my best guess. At his home."

"Anything you can do to prevent it?" Alyssa asked.

"No," he said. "Nothing I dare do about it. What I'm doing here is too delicate. I can't afford to try to push and shove over at Justice. But…" He allowed a sly grin to spread over his flat features. "But I can't prevent you and Mitch from doing something."

Alyssa said nothing, thinking. Finally, she nodded and got to her feet.

"Thank you for the wine," she said. "Thank Marianne for me."

245

As she started walking away, Fred said, "Oh. I almost forgot. There's something else you need to know about."

Alyssa turned. "What's that?"

"The birth-mother. Host-mother, I should say. One of the networks found her. I was afraid that might happen. After Jarvis found her, I knew CNN or Fox or somebody might do it, if they tried. I suspect our friend Springfield had something to do with that, too."

"I didn't know about that," Alyssa said, her tone mildly accusing. "I haven't seen anything about it on the news."

"You didn't have the need to know," Hutton responded. "And I think the network with the information is just waiting for the hearing Friday to decide whether to run it. Anyway, it's something I have to deal with. Or try to."

"Well, good luck," Alyssa said, and walked off into mist.

BRENTWOOD, TENNESSEE, OCTOBER 2022
SUNDAY EVENING ·

Veronica Clayton made sure the kids were in bed, or at least preparing for bed, and walked to her kitchen, where she removed a bottle of Pinot Grigio from the refrigerator and poured a large glass, a bigger pour than she usually permitted herself on a night before a workday. And tomorrow was going to be unusually busy. She had two closings and four showings.

She had watched the network news magazine this evening. There was nothing about her. That was a relief, but Fred Hutton had cautioned her the last time they'd talked that the network was likely waiting on the outcome of the Martin hearing next Friday before deciding to run anything. So she wasn't out of the woods yet.

She'd asked Major Hutton what he could do to help her or protect her. He'd told her he had no control over the network and that the government trying to kill a story would be counterproductive.

"But what can you do to help?" she'd asked.

All he'd said was, "I'm working on it. In the meantime, honor your agreement until we tell you it's okay to say something.'

That advice was no help. She'd already known to do *that*.

Veronica took a healthy slug of her wine. For some reason, she wanted to speak with Danny Jarvis. But she really shouldn't, should she?

Hutton hadn't told her not to. Not that she'd asked about it.

Then again, how could it hurt? She didn't have to admit anything. And he might know something about the hearing.

Her cell phone was on the counter in front of her. She picked it up and brought up Danny's number. She hesitated only a second, and then pushed the icon for "dial."

Danny sounded glad to hear her voice, but also nervous. He didn't press her for more information, and she was glad of that. He confirmed he still wanted to see her, which for some reason she liked hearing, and that he was planning on testifying at the hearing Friday.

"Where is the hearing?" she asked.

"In Brainerd County," he answered. "They found a room at the community college."

That's not so far to drive, she thought, shocking herself. Surely she wouldn't go. Why had that thought leaped into her head?

"And, uh, Veronica?" Danny said, almost whispering.

"Yes?"

"We'd better not talk anymore, at least with me using this phone. I'm afraid I might be wiretapped, or bugged. Or something."

Oh, my God, she thought. What if somebody is recording this call? They'd ask her why she was calling *him*.

"Tell you what," he said. "I'll buy a burner phone tomorrow and call you. Why don't you buy one, too and we can exchange numbers?"

She agreed that was a good idea, but was afraid the horse was out of the barn.

"Bye for now," he said. "I'll call you."

"Okay, 'bye," she said. Not exactly an affectionate good-bye, but not hostile. If only they'd met some other way than this, she thought. But then, how would that have happened?

She finished her wine and went upstairs to prepare for bed. There wasn't anything else to do.

MARTINTOWN, NORTH CAROLINA, OCTOBER 2023 THE MCCAFFREY HOME SUNDAY NIGHT

"Anyway," Alyssa said to Mitch and Diana McCaffrey, "like I told Fred, now we know who's behind this stuff."

They were seated in the downstairs family room of the McCaffreys' new home. The Callahans had finally been able to move into their new home, and now lived next door; so, Alyssa had walked over. No need to open a Portal. Ben was home in his study, working on the depositions that had gone over into the following week.

"Fucking Monica," said Diana.

Alyssa laughed. "I think I said the same thing," she said. "And I think I know how to help the Jarvis guy," she continued, "but I'll need your help, Mitch."

"What do you have in mind?" he asked.

When she told him, he sat quietly for a long moment, then said, "All right. I'll do it. But Alyssa, nothing too…creative."

Alyssa permitted herself a grin, and said, "Aww, you're no fun. But… sure. Nothing too creative. I promise."

"Does anyone want coffee?" Diana asked. "Or a drink? I should have offered before."

"I'd better not have caffeine this late," Alyssa said. "But…do you have Campari?"

"We do," Mitch said. Seeing Diana rise from the couch where they sat, he added, "Honey, it's in the liquor cabinet on the left. I'll take Scotch."

"By the way," Alyssa said, "I'd like Diana to be near the hearing Friday. Di, can you swing that?"

Diana placed bottles on a sideboard and said, "I guess I can. I'll have to have Martha cover the restaurant, but she's used to that. But why?"

"Because I think Monica might show up and pull something. I'd like your spell-blocking Talent handy," Alyssa said.

"If it will frustrate Monica Murray, I'm in," Diana said. She still thought of Monica as "Murray," which she'd been in high school.

"You can sit with me in the witness room," Mitch said. "But bring something to work on. Or read."

"Why?" Diana asked.

"Because waiting to testify is massively boring," Mitch said. "If you don't believe me, ask the lawyers."

Mitch helped Diana bring the drinks to the seating area, and they talked of other things until Alyssa thanked them and left for home.

Chapter 36
CORNELIUS, NORTH CAROLINA, OCTOBER 2022

OUTSIDE THE JARVIS CONDOMINIUM
THURSDAY MORNING, JUST BEFORE DAWN

Danny Jarvis lived in the last building on the right on his street, just before a cul-de-sac. Unlike many units in the development, it was not part of a duplex, but stood alone, like the home where Mitch had lived in High Country Estates, before they'd built the new place. Not a true condominium, Mitch thought, but – what was the term? – part of a Planned Unit Development, or PUD.

He and Alyssa stood against the fence that surrounded the development at a place between the Jarvis unit and the next unit before his, concealed by the darkness and by carefully landscaped shrubbery. All of the units were still dark. The only light was from the street lights, which did not reach to where they stood. No one was likely to see them, but they had a good view of the street.

It was a cold morning, the chill made more biting by a thick fog, which would help them in what they planned to do. They were dressed warmly, but Alyssa hugged herself against the cold. They were glad of the toe-warmers they'd inserted into their boots. There were spells that would help against the cold, but spells took energy they needed to conserve.

Alyssa had brought Aleksandra here Monday night and again on Tuesday. Both times Aleks had sensed danger ahead but nothing immediate. But last night, she had turned wide-eyed to Alyssa and said, "Tomorrow. I feel it. Dark, but dawn not far off. Three black– what do you say? – SUVs." Alyssa had whisked Aleksandra back to Martintown and then called Mitch.

So here they were, shivering. All they had to do was wait.

Special Agent Richard Smalley sat in the passenger's seat of the lead vehicle. He wore a Kevlar vest and a black jacket, both with the FBI logo. His badge hung at his waist opposite his sidearm, and the search warrant was folded in an interior pocket of the jacket. Two agents sat behind him, and there were four, all armed with side arms and M-4 carbines, in each of the two SUVs behind them. Jarvis would get a good scare as well as an early morning surprise, and that was the point.

They had passed a Cornelius PD patrol car on the way in, which had slowed as it drove by in the opposite direction, but then had speeded up and driven on. That was good. He didn't want to deal with local cops this morning. The little caravan dimmed their lights as they turned into the PUD where Jarvis lived. They didn't want to wake anyone. The FBI vehicles drove slowly and close together. Visibility in the morning fog was poor.

As they neared the Jarvis residence, the fog thickened. The mist swirled, but they drove on. Smalley felt a jolt. He hadn't expected a pothole, but they'd hit one. There was a bump and another jolt. The SUV had driven over something. The driver stopped without being told.

The mist started to clear. Smalley could see the other two vehicles behind his. He looked ahead, and then outside. His jaw dropped. The caravan was stopped on flat, rocky ground. To one side, he could see where the rock gave way to grass and animals that appeared to be sheep. There was no more fog. Overhead the stars blazed in an array of constellations, without any light pollution.

"What?" he said aloud. "Where the hell are we?"

The driver, whose jaw had dropped but not yet closed, pointed silently at the GPS screen on the dashboard. The vehicle's GPS had a direct satellite connection that didn't depend on Wi-fi or cell towers. As they watched, it went black, and then white, as it re-set. The image showed their location, but was a big blank with no landmarks. There was a road in one corner of the image, but it didn't show where it led in any direction. That was no help.

Richard Smalley's team was reporting to Special Agent in Charge Springfield this morning. Smalley knew Springfield was in charge of "Special Assets," but he didn't know what that meant. He was completely mystified, and truth be told, a little scared. He heard doors slam on the vehicles behind him. One of the agents pounded on the window, demanding to know what had happened.

He rolled down the window and told the agents outside to stop shouting. There were no cell phone towers anywhere nearby, he felt sure, but there was a satellite phone in the satchel in the floorboard at his feet. He decided he'd better use it. He'd wake up Springfield, but he didn't care.

Alyssa and Mitch watched the three-vehicle caravan slowly approach the Jarvis unit. As it neared, she grasped Mitch's hand and began a whispered chant. He added his power to hers to keep the portal wide enough and remain open long enough for all three SUVs to pass through it. They watched as the mist cleared, with only the natural fog remaining. There were no vehicles on the street.

"Where are they?" Mitch asked.

"Oh, somewhere," Alyssa said with a wide smile. She was no longer shivering. The energy of the spell had warmed them.

"Alyssa, I told you not to be too creative," Mitch said. "Now, tell me. Where are they?"

"Oh," she said, "somewhere with clear, open skies. Lots of fresh air. And sheep. There'll be sheep. And…oh. Probably camels. Two-humped camels."

Mitch was silent as he searched his memory for where she could be talking about.

"China?" he asked. "You sent them to China?"

"No," she said. "I didn't want to create that much of an incident. I sent them to southern Mongolia. The Gobi."

"You sent them to fucking *MONGOLIA*?" Mitch asked. "You sure didn't pay much attention to what I asked you to do."

"I did, too," she protested. "They'll be all right, although it may take a while for them to get home. You ought to see where I'd planned to send them before you asked me not to be too creative."

"And where was that?" Mitch asked, and immediately regretted asking.

"Oh, somewhere I know that has trees and flowers and flowing streams and meadows," she said.

"And?" he prompted.

"Teeth," she said. "Lots of teeth."

Mitch shook his head and exhaled loudly. He decided not to push the issue any more. But Alyssa had just confirmed that her use of Portals was way more advanced than anything she'd taught anyone else, including him. But they had other things to do.

"Okay," he said. "Forget I asked. Now let's go wake up Danny Jarvis."

"Do we really need to?" she asked.

"Yes," he said, his voice firm. "We do."

THE JARVIS HOME
THURSDAY MORNING

The doorbell was ringing incessantly, and Danny Jarvis decided he couldn't ignore it. He rose from bed, tried to rub sleep from his eyes, pulled on a pair of jeans, and stepped into his bedroom slippers. He couldn't help but think about the threatening text he'd received, and considered grabbing the snub-nosed revolver from the drawer under his nightstand. But no, he decided, anyone who was there to assault him wouldn't ring the doorbell first.

He stumbled down the hall and into the vestibule. He flipped on the outside light and squinted into the peephole to see who was outside, and saw a warmly dressed man and woman, unarmed as far as he could tell. He opened the door.

"Wha-what do you want?" he asked, and then asked, "Who are you, anyway?"

"Think of us as friends of Doug Martin," the man said, adding, "And your friends too, come to it."

"May we come in?" the woman asked. "It's bloody cold out here."

Danny stood aside, let them enter, and closed the door. Spurred by adrenalin, he was starting to come awake.

"Would you please tell me what you want from me at 5:30 in the morning?"

"We'll be glad to," the woman said. "But can you make some coffee? Please."

Without a word, he led them to the kitchen and turned on the coffee maker, which he'd filled before he went to bed, so he could brew it quickly this morning. His visitors produced photo-IDs showing they were contractors with the Defense Intelligence Agency. The cards looked official and genuine, but he wouldn't have recognized fakes, he realized. He actually recognized the man's name, Mitch McCaffrey.

"You're that professor who got in trouble at your college a couple of years ago, aren't you?" He asked.

The man nodded, and Danny studied the woman more carefully. Then he recognized her, he thought.

"And aren't you the lady who was prosecuted last year?" he asked her.

The woman smiled and said, "I am. The charges, as I'm sure you know, were dropped. But congratulations on recognizing us. I didn't think you would...Oh, and before you ask, I assure you the identification we've showed you is quite genuine."

He saw the man smile quickly at her last remark. He couldn't know Mitch's thought, which was that Major Hutton hadn't given express permission to show the IDs to Jarvis, but hadn't told them not to.

"But what are you doing here?"

The woman, whose card said she was named Alyssa McCormick-Callahan, turned to her companion and asked, "Do you want to explain, Mitch, or shall I?"

"Why don't you do it?" McCaffrey suggested. Turning his head to Jarvis, he said, "Maybe you'd better take a seat. And let's get coffee first."

Danny poured cups of coffee, and offered cream and sugar. They all seated themselves at the small breakfast table in his kitchen while Alyssa explained about the search warrant and their diversion of the FBI team that was on his way to serve it. Actually, she didn't say how that had been accomplished, only that the SWAT team had been "intercepted and diverted" and wouldn't be paying him a visit this morning.

Jarvis lowered and shook his head. "I don't understand," he said. "How --?" He remembered Marc Washington saying they were going to work on security for him. Was this it?

"It's classified," Alyssa said.

Jarvis continued to try to process everything. "Oh, shit," he said, adding, "Oh, hell. Maybe I shouldn't testify."

"Actually, that's exactly what you should do," McCaffrey said. "We're confident this raid we aborted was cooked up by someone rogue at the Bureau to scare you. If it doesn't work, and you go ahead, they'll likely let it go."

Jarvis still didn't understand, and said so.

"I'm not tracking this. You two say you're DIA, but you're at odds with the FBI. Doesn't make sense."

Alyssa said, "Oh, it makes complete sense once you realize that federal agencies don't always agree on everything."

Danny decided to accept that. He wasn't sure he had much choice.

"What do I do now?" he asked.

McCaffrey had an answer ready.

"We suggest that you get dressed, pack, and drive up to Martintown early. We don't think they'll take another crack at you, but it's more likely they will if you stay home alone. Where are you staying?"

Danny told them. He'd booked a room at the big new hotel on the south side of town that catered to visitors to Southeastern Electronics. No more flea-bags for him now that he had his shiny new contract with ESPN. If I keep it, he thought.

"Good choice," Mitch said. "It's very unlikely they'd try to serve a search warrant there. What they wanted to do was trash your house. Just be sure you are not alone any more than you can help. Hang out in the lobby or the lounge. Stay around people."

"Okay," Jarvis said, feeling better. Well, a little.

"And something else," Mitch said. "Give us your laptop or tablet and cell phone. We'll take them with us and have them imaged, so you can recover everything if someone does take them from you. We'll get them back to you this afternoon. Scout's honor."

Danny did not want to give up his devices. He opened his mouth to say "no" and thought he heard Mitch humming something. He felt a quick flash of pain pass through his forehead and winced. Suddenly he was convinced he ought to change his mind and found himself saying, "Well, okay. But how do I do without my phone?"

McCaffrey reached inside his jacket and removed something wrapped in cloth. "Here," he said. "This is a burner phone. My secure number, and Alyssa's are written on a post-it note we've attached. Call one of us when you need it. We'll reach you on that, and arrange to get your stuff back to you. If anyone manages to…steal…your laptop or phone, we'll replace them.

"Do you have anything on a thumb drive or something besides your laptop?"

"I have a thumb drive," Danny mumbled.

"Go get it, and your computer, and your phone," McCaffrey said. "Alyssa and I have to get back to Martintown right away."

"How?" he asked, letting his voice trail away.

"It's classified," Alyssa said again.

The two left with his devices a few minutes later after thanking him for the coffee. He didn't try to see where they went.

Guess I'd better clean up, load up, and get on the road, he thought.

MARTINTOWN, NORTH CAROLINA
THURSDAY MORNING

Mitch and Alyssa walked through a Portal she had opened into the McCaffrey kitchen. Mitch had promised her he'd make breakfast. Diana would already be at the Bean 'N Bacon. The kids doubtless were still asleep, and he would have to wake and feed them soon.

"Why did you use a compulsion spell on Jarvis?" Alyssa asked. "Didn't you think you could talk him into letting us have his devices?"

"Mostly so I could get a good handle on his brain pattern," Mitch said, removing eggs and bacon from the refrigerator. "You see, I've got one more thing to do after I have Simmons image his devices."

"Which is?" Alyssa prompted.

He cracked eggs into a bowl before answering. Then he said, "I'm going to hex his laptop, and maybe his phone, so that only he can use it. That way, if Springfield's boys do seize it, they won't get anything. Nothing but gibberish, anyway."

"What if Springfield brings in a spell caster to remove the hex?" she asked.

Mitch smiled as he whisked eggs. "He can try," he said.

Alyssa said nothing. We both have our secrets, she thought.

MARTINTOWN, NORTH CAROLINA
THE HOTEL LOBBY
THURSDAY AFTERNOON

Veronica Clayton stood in line to check in. The hotel was not packed, but there were more guests than she had expected on a Thursday. She had noticed media trucks in the parking lot. Maybe the hearing was attracting people. Well, why wouldn't it.

Veronica's mind was made up as soon as she woke that morning. It certainly hadn't been when she went to sleep. The subconscious was a funny thing.

She was going to Martintown. She would see for herself what they would do to her baby. She had to. That was it and all about it.

She told her kids that Mommy had another business trip she had to make. She didn't say what it was, and thankfully they didn't ask. She explained that Mrs. Cardiff would be staying with them again, and that she'd be home sometime Saturday. She made sure they were off to school, and then packed quickly. She had things to take care of at the office, including arranging for Mrs. Cardiff to sit with the kids.

The weather was fine, and the drive was more tedious than difficult, almost a straight shot on I-40 once she turned onto it in Nashville. It was tiring, though, and she looked forward to a quick drink and a long tub soak after she checked in.

"Hello, Veronica," said a now-familiar voice at her left elbow. She wheeled and there he was. Danny Jarvis, good-looking as always in cord pants, pastel shirt, and blue blazer. Her jaw dropped in surprise, but then, she thought, of course he'd stay here. She should have thought of that. Then she realized she was glad to see him.

"I hear you'll testify tomorrow," she said.

"Umm-hmm," he said. "Will you be there to watch?"

"I will," she said. She didn't explain why. He knew.

"Better get there early," he said. "I hear seating will be limited, what with all the reporters and cameras. Do you want to follow me over?"

"That would be nice," she said, as she stepped forward in line. "Thank you."

"Not to worry. And," he leaned close to her ear and whispered, "Dinner tonight? Here? How about it?"

She hesitated only a moment, and said, "Why not? Sure."

He rewarded her with wide grin. "Does this mean I'm forgiven?"

She allowed a coy smile. "Maybe. I'll think about it." But she already had thought. She had worked it all out in her head on the drive.

They settled on a time to meet in the cocktail lounge and he walked away, explaining he was expecting a package delivery at any time.

And we'll see how it goes tonight, she thought. And tomorrow.

Chapter 37

MARTINTOWN, NORTH CAROLINA, OCTOBER 2022

CAROLINA HIGHLANDS COMMUNITY COLLEGE
FRIDAY MORNING

Monica Gilbert pulled into the parking lot behind the administration building at Carolina Highlands earlier than she would have preferred. The parking sticker on her car from the State Board for Community Colleges was enough to get her past the security guards, who moved cones so she could find a space. The lot was already more full than usual, with several media vans from local stations and networks. She had pulled strings with her superiors in Chapel Hill, so that she could attend the hearing. The excuse, which was so that the State Board could observe how well a local college handled security and safety issues, was flimsy; but she had her pass.

Strictly speaking, her presence was unofficial, both from the standpoint of her state job and her secret consulting position with the "Special Assets" department of the FBI. Dennis Springfield had consented to her being there, so she could give her own confidential report of what would happen later; but he hadn't required it. She was there out of curiosity and also to protect herself.

The items filched from the state archives that had enabled Danny Jarvis to break his story could not be traced to her. She was pretty confident of that. Her only connection was to Jarvis himself. Even if he gave her name to someone, she hadn't kept anything she'd seen; and she'd deny seeing it.

Everything had gone to Springfield, and he would protect her. She hoped. She'd learned not to trust anyone too much.

But Jarvis was going to testify today. That concerned her. She didn't know what he'd be asked, or what his answers would be. It was unlikely that her name would come up, she knew, but she was still a little nervous about it. Well, because she would be there, she might find a chance to do something. Maybe not, though, because she knew that hound Mitch Mc-Caffrey would be there, and maybe even others of his little coterie. But it was certain that she wouldn't be able to do anything if she wasn't there.

Springfield had been no help. His plan to confiscate Jarvis' computer had come to nothing. One of her contacts at Quantico, one that Spring-field didn't know about, had told her that Dennis had exploded yesterday when he learned, first, that the SWAT team dispatched to serve the warrant had disappeared, and second, that they'd turned up in Mongolia in the custody of some very suspicious Mongol security police. Dennis had told her last night that the Bureau had handled that situation, but not before he'd suffered through a very uncomfortable session with the Deputy Director to whom he reported. It was okay with him if she went to the hearing, he said, because he couldn't afford to send anyone else.

Monica walked quickly from her car to the door to the building set aside for faculty and staff, the spiked heels of her shoes clicking on the asphalt. The weather was cooler than usual, even for late October, and raised goosebumps on her bare legs. She really should have worn slacks to-day, she thought; but her legs were among her better features, and it would have been a shame to conceal them. They might distract someone to her advantage, after all.

She found the hallways crowded when she entered the building and made her way to the hearing room. That room did not hold good memories for her. It was the scene of her humiliation when she had tried to force McCaffrey off the faculty two years ago. That fiasco had resulted in her transfer to the offices in Chapel Hill and had almost cost her having any position at all. And McCaffrey and his crowd had been thorns in her sides ever since. Especially his wife Diana, whom Monica had despised ever since high school, and that slutty little McCormick woman. She'd heard the latter was now married to a lawyer in the firm that always seemed to appear for McCaffrey or anyone connected to him.

They were all now under the protection of the DIA. That made dealing with them harder. She had no doubts that McCaffrey and McCormick had been behind the diversion of the FBI SWAT team yesterday. Neither did Springfield. Who else was as good at creating portals and holding them open? But she and Dennis also knew that they wouldn't be able to prove a thing. That was frustrating.

She entered the hallway that led to the hearing room, grimacing with the memories of two years earlier as she did so. The hallway was packed and chaotic. College security guards and a couple of state troopers were attempting to assert some order among the media and onlookers pushing for admission, and the lawyers and witnesses trying to find their assigned rooms. She saw Danny Jarvis standing with a slightly plump blonde against a wall, but did not try to get his attention. Jarvis was talking with a lawyer she remembered, the black guy who had assisted Kathryn Turner two years ago.

All of these people from the past keep turning up like bad pennies, she thought. She hoped some of them would get their comeuppance today. She finally made it to the security station outside the hearing room door. She showed the letter authorizing her admission to the troopers there, and made her way in to find a seat.

CAROLINA HIGHLANDS COMMUNITY COLLEGE PRESIDENT'S OFFICE
FRIDAY MORNING

Mitch McCaffrey stood in front of Claire Daniels' desk, Diana next to him. Daniels was the college president, Mitch's ultimate boss, and at the moment a very unhappy administrator.

"I wish I hadn't let you talk me into having this thing here," she said. "This is a zoo."

She had a point, Mitch knew. So many reporters had asked to be credentialed for the hearing that granting all the requests would have meant no one else could attend. Three networks and two local stations wanted to bring television cameras, which would have been unworkable. A resolution had at last been hammered out that Court TV (even though this wasn't court) would be allowed to televise the proceedings and would share film with everyone else. No other cameras would be allowed. There would be a wire feed into the movie screen in the college theater across campus, where most of the reporters, as well as the overflow crowd, would sit.

The solution would work, but it required additional security for the theater, and had required technicians to make the connections last night. These people had to be paid; and it would come from the college budget, unless the NCHSAA would reimburse the school, which was probable, although getting the money was another headache she didn't need. Another problem at the moment was that the announcement of how the crowd would be handled had come late in the day yesterday. Many who wanted to watch it had come to the administration building. Crowd security and Claire's staff were working now to sort them out and send most to the theater.

Daniels' complaints went on and on. Out at the main entrance to the campus, there were two groups of protestors carrying signs. One was a group from a coalition of small rural churches protesting a child who "bears the mark of the Beast." Another was a group of supporters of transgendered students who were protesting the unfairness and inequity of allowing Doug Martin to play high school sports. So far, both groups had been well behaved; but it had meant sending for still more security, this time from the Brainerd County Sheriff's Department.

No, Mitch understood why Claire was unhappy. But he and Diana hadn't really come to listen to her complaints. Their business was related, but different.

"Claire, I just wanted to thank you for the use of the spare office today," he said. "I'm what the lawyers call a back-up witness, which means I probably won't be called unless one of the other witnesses can't make it for some reason. But I still have to be able to get to the hearing room fast if they ask for me, and my regular office is two buildings over, as you know. Being able to work here in Administration helps a lot."

"We still have to pay for the adjunct who took your classes today," Daniels said, her tone accusing.

"I know," said Mitch, "and I'm sorry. But look at it this way. Because Doug Martin is enrolled in my 'early college' class, he'll get transferrable credit here. So, this hearing really does affect a student in good standing at Carolina Highlands."

Daniels didn't look impressed. She eyed Diana.

"What about you, Diana?" she asked. "Why are you here? Mitch doesn't need to have his hand held, does he?"

Diana ignored the jibe. She couldn't very well say that she'd been asked to come and stay close-by the hearing in case her spell-blocking Talent was needed. But she had an answer ready. She hefted a black ledger book tucked under an arm.

"I'm going to work on the restaurant's books this morning, while Mitch does other things," she said. "And yes, I am curious about the hearing and want to be close if something interesting leaks out. I hope you don't mind."

Claire opened her mouth as though to say she did mind, but hesitated and asked, "What if a student comes by to meet with your husband?"

"Then I'll sit outside in the hall while they meet," she said.

Daniels sighed like a steam engine and said, "Well, okay. I've got to go outside and make sure everything is okay. You two get to your temporary office."

Mitch and Diana hid smiles as they did as Daniels asked.

CAROLINA HIGHLANDS COMMUNITY COLLEGE
THE HEARING ROOM
FRIDAY MORNING

Marc Washington sat at the improvised counsel table and scanned the hearing room, which was nearly full already, even with the security guards screening those who were admitted. Aleks sat immediately to his left. She had custody of their copies of the hearing exhibits. Doug Martin sat beyond him, farther from lead counsel than Marc would prefer, but it couldn't be helped. They could pass notes, and Rob could squeeze behind Doug and Aleks to whisper to Marc if need be.

Their client's parents sat directly behind Doug, and they were whispering encouragement to their son while everyone waited for the hearing to commence.

There were microphones positioned in front of Marc and Rob, which they could turn off while conferring. Marc had his hearing notebook, along with his pad and pen; and Rob was identically equipped. Aleks had her laptop. They were ready. *As ready as we could get on short notice*, he thought.

Marc thought about the McCaffrey hearing that had been held in this same room almost two years earlier, when he'd been Kat Turner's second chair counsel. They'd been serious underdogs in that one, he remembered; but it had turned out all right. He hoped that was a good sign. Actually, the hearing that was about to begin was one he honestly thought they ought to win. But that, he thought, makes it worse, in a way. It adds to the pressure.

And today he didn't have Kathryn Turner. Now he was the first chair counsel. And in a matter that was about to make national television. Kat and Ben Callahan had finally finished with the trial and depositions that had taken both out of this case, and both had dropped by his office and Rob's yesterday to assure them they had the firm's full confidence. But neither he nor Rob had missed the other implication: They wouldn't be doing this if more senior litigators had been available.

Now, the witnesses, except for Doug himself, were all in witness waiting rooms off the hallway outside. There weren't many for the Respondent right now. The principal, the coach, and the teammate would come this afternoon. Their expert was there, as was Danny Jarvis. And, thank goodness, Tiffany was there to coordinate. Callahan had released her for that duty yesterday.

Marc took a few moments to look around the room. The Complainant's legal team sat to their right at another counsel table. Minutes ago, he and Rob had shaken hands and exchanged a few words with Alex DeBruhl and Sandra Sparkman. DeBruhl had come over to Marc as too friendly and at the same time condescending. Sparkman had come over as just condescending. They'd introduced their client's board chairman, a gawky, skinny guy in a checked suit and bow-tie, who was a principal at some high school down east, and who probably wouldn't testify.

"I think we have visitors from Olympus visiting Earth today," Marc had whispered to Rob as they went back to counsel table.

"Don't worry about it," Rob had whispered back. "They did the same thing to me and Jack Melton last year." At Marc's raised eyebrows, he'd added, "Same firm. Different lawyers. They think that stuff is intimidating. They did it all through bankruptcy court, District court and the 4th Circuit. Didn't work out for them. They kept losing."

That did make Marc feel a little better as his eyes continued to scan the hearing room. The court reporter was directly in front of them, and the witness chair and table was across the room directly facing the court reporter. There was a television screen for remote testimony on the wall behind the court reporter. The raised bench behind which the hearing panel would sit was just before the far wall, with the North Carolina Seal centered and a door to the right, from which they'd enter. There was a podium with a microphone between the counsel tables.

The Court TV camera took up part of two rows in the seats behind De-Bruhl and Sparkman. The camera crew thought that better than blocking the central aisle. Most of the crowd behind the camera, and behind where the Martin team sat, had pads and pens. They must be reporters. But there were some others. Marc had noticed a short, curvy woman, pretty if a bit too broad in the beam, with shoulder length platinum blonde hair, who had come in, taken a seat at the rear of the room, and hadn't taken her eyes off Doug. He wondered who she was.

He was about to look away when he saw another woman, this time one who looked familiar seated several chairs away on the same row. It was Monica Gilbert. He remembered her from the hearing two years ago, and smiled before he could catch himself. She saw the smile and looked away, coloring. Now why is she here? he thought. She's not on the witness lists. He'd have Aleks text Mitch as soon as he had a chance.

Marc heard a noise from the front of the room and turned his head to see the door to the right of the bench open and the hearing panel file in, followed by Frank DuLaney, the Association lawyer who would advise the panel on legal questions if any came up. Which they will, Marc thought. Everyone stood while the panel entered. The four were followed by Commissioner Morton's secretary, who stood behind a chair at the far right. She cleared her throat.

The room quietened and the woman said, "Please be seated."

There was the scuffling of chairs as everyone sat. Then Jessica Morton, the Association Commissioner, leaned forward toward her microphone.

"Good morning," she said. All counsel responded with the same greeting.

"We are here today by direction of the Board of Directors of the Association to conduct a hearing into the eligibility of Mr. Douglas M. Martin to play interscholastic athletics in the North Carolina public schools. We have determined that the case for ineligibility will be presented by the Committee for Fairness in Athletics. Mr. Martin has his own counsel, who will respond. Are his parents also present?"

Darren and Lara Martin stood and both said, "Yes."

Morton gave Doug's parents a warm smile and said, "Mr. and Mrs. Martin, your son is now legally an adult, so it is not necessary that he appear through you. But I know how interested you must be. The panel has determined you may be present throughout the hearing. Do you understand?"

They said they did. We covered all of this with them yesterday, Marc thought.

"Very well," Morton said. "All other witnesses will be sequestered unless testifying. They are not to discuss the evidence given in this hearing with any other witnesses, except that expert witnesses may be present while the opposing expert is testifying.

"The panel wishes to thank all legal counsel for collegially helping us create the hearing protocol."

Marc said nothing, and hid a smile. All of it wasn't collegial, he thought. But thankfully, he and Rob had got most of what they wanted. They had Frank DuLaney to thank for that, he thought.

"By agreement of counsel and order of this panel," Morton said, reading from a script Marc would bet DuLaney had written, "there will be no opening statements. So, let's begin.

"Mr. DeBruhl and Ms. Sparkman, call your first witness."

Marc swallowed hard.

The hearing had begun.

Chapter 38
MARTINTOWN, NORTH CAROLINA, OCTOBER 2022

CAROLINA HIGHLANDS COMMUNITY COLLEGE
THE HEARING BEGINS

DeBruhl stood and said, "Madame Chair, we call Douglas M. Martin as an adverse witness."

So there it is, Marc thought. Right out of the box. They had prepared Doug for this. He hoped the young man remembered what they'd discussed.

Doug rose slowly from his chair. Marc and Rob whispered encouragement as he slid past them and walked to the witness chair. Chairwoman Morton administered his oath and advised DeBruhl he could proceed.

DeBruhl asked his questions from his seat at counsel table, as was customary in North Carolina. As Marc expected, DeBruhl kept his voice well-modulated, his tone friendly. He bid the witness good morning, asked him to state his name, and to identify his parents. He asked Doug his address and his age, where he went to school, what year he was in, and whether he planned on college. All of this was designed to put the witness at ease and put him off guard before the hammer landed. Marc and Rob had warned Doug about this approach. DeBruhl was not Doug's friend, and he shouldn't believe that DeBruhl was for a moment.

Then the other shoe dropped abruptly.

"Mr. Martin," DeBruhl asked, "do you recognize you are not fully human?" His tone was still conversational. He's smooth, Marc thought. I'll give him that.

Marc decided not to object. Doug should be able to handle the question. They had prepared him for it, or something like it.

Doug, looking apprehensive but under control, leaned forward toward the microphone on the table before him and answered, "No, sir. I don't recognize that. I am human. Fully human."

"Well," DeBruhl said, keeping the same easy-going tone of voice, "let me ask the question this way: Do you deny that you are the clone of a hybrid modern-human and Neanderthal union?"

Following instructions and looking more up at the hearing panel than at DeBruhl, Doug answered, "No, sir, I don't deny that. I believe that I am. I've been told that I am. But I also believe that both are completely human."

There was an immediate stir in the hearing room. Hushed whispers and the clicking of cell phones from the spectators, a smug exchange of glances between DeBruhl and Sandra Sparkman. Marc was watching the hearing panel and saw their jaws drop, followed by the rapid scratching of notes on the pads before them.

"Can you tell the panel your basis for that belief?" DeBruhl asked. That was a sort of "why" question, which lawyers were cautioned not to ask an adverse witness. Marc guessed DeBruhl thought it was worth the risk to handle whatever answer he'd get now, and not wait for Marc to cover it on cross-examination.

Now came the acid test of how well they'd prepared the client. Marc crossed his fingers below the counsel table.

Doug came through. He actually smiled before answering.

"Mr. DeBruhl, I think I'm my own best evidence of that. I mean, look at me. I can understand and answer your questions. I go to school. I make decent grades. I have friends. I've held part-time jobs. Some sub-human wouldn't be able to do any of that, I don't think.

"And I've been told the same thing," he added.

"All right," DeBruhl said, allowing his tone to harshen, "let's talk about what you've been told, and who told you. You said you've been told you're a clone. Who told you? Your adoptive parents?"

"Yes, sir," Doug said.

"All right? Anyone else?" Now DeBruhl's questions were much more waspish, as Marc and Rob had predicted they'd become.

"Yes, sir," Doug said. Marc wished more of his clients paid attention to what they were told in preparation the way Doug did. As they'd advised him, he was answering the question asked, and stopping to wait on the next question.

"Who was that?" DeBruhl snapped.

Doug swallowed before he answered. This was where it would get difficult.

"I – sir, I'm not allowed to say," Doug said.

"Not allowed by whom? By what?"

"I signed a confidentiality agreement," Doug answered. "I haven't been released from it. Not yet, anyway."

"With whom did you sign it?" DeBruhl asked.

"The United States of America," Doug answered, causing another stir in the courtroom.

DeBruhl smiled like a cat who just caught a mouse. He has what he wanted, Marc thought – confirmation the story that caused his mess was true.

But DeBruhl decided to press the witness. "What department?"

"I haven't been released to say," Doug said. Marc heard another stir behind him. The hearing panel continued to scribble notes.

"So let me get this straight," DeBruhl said. "You concede you are a hybrid Neanderthal clone, but you insist you are fully human; and you're just asking this panel to take your word for it, based on what you think and someone else told you. Is that correct?"

"No, sir," Doug said. "I have other evidence, too, that my lawyers will present."

"What other evidence?"

"You know, the witnesses and exhibits on our list. You got a copy, didn't you?"

"Don't get smart with me, young man!" DeBruhl snarled.

Marc rose to his feet. "Objection, Madame Chair. Argumentative and needlessly disrespectful."

"The objection is sustained," Morton said. "Mr. DeBruhl, you realize you are arguing with an 18-year-old, don't you?"

The room erupted in laughter, and DeBruhl's face reddened. But he quickly recovered his composure.

"My apologies, Madame Chair," he said. "May I continue?"

"Yes."

Turning his eyes back to the witness, DeBruhl asked, "Mr. Martin, you realize your genetic heritage from the Neanderthal gives you an advantage over other players, do you not?"

Marc crossed his fingers again. This was another question they had anticipated and prepared Doug to answer.

"Mr. DeBruhl," Doug said. "I realize I have God-given abilities. But so do many other athletes. I don't think I'm all that different."

DeBruhl's smile was predatory. "Who is the strongest player on your team?"

"If you mean bench press, I guess I am." Doug answered.

"How much do you bench press?" DeBruhl asked.

"I've done five-fifty."

"Five hundred and fifty pounds?" DeBruhl clarified.

"Yes, sir."

"Do you know of any other high school football player in this entire state that bench presses that much?"

"There…may be. I don't know," Doug answered.

"Can you give me a name?"

"No, sir."

"And you don't deny, do you, that using your great strength, you broke another student's nose in a fight, do you?"

"That was seven years ago," Doug said. "And he was older than me. And I wasn't as strong then. But yeah, it happened. I haven't been in a fight since."

"Thank you, Mr. Martin," DeBruhl said. "We pass the witness."

"Do you have cross examination, Mr. Washington?" Morton asked.

"Yes," Marc responded. "A little."

The price DeBruhl had paid for calling Doug as an adverse witness was that Doug's lawyers would get to cross examine him, which meant they could use leading questions, as long as they stuck to the same topics DeBruhl had covered. But Marc knew that he ought to avoid leading questions as much as possible. If the panel thought he was putting words in his own client's mouth, they wouldn't pay much attention to the answers.

"Mr. Martin," Marc began, "Mr. DeBruhl asked some questions about your...attributes. Let me ask a few more."

Marc paused, then continued, "You're a senior at West Brainerd High School, is that correct?"

"Yes, sir."

"Are you in good standing at the school, as far as you know?"

"Yes, sir?"

"Have you ever been in trouble? Had any disciplinary issues?"

"No, sir?"

"Ever hurt anyone?"

"No, sir."

"What about your grades?"

"They're...pretty good," Doug said.

"Are we talking about 'A's' and 'B's'?"

"Yes, sir."

"Is it mostly 'A's'?"

"Yes, it is."

"Let's go on to football. As far as you know, do you meet the state eligibility standards?"

DeBruhl objected. "That's why we're here, Madame Chair. This panel will decide that."

Morton overruled the objection.

"Do you need me to repeat the question?" Marc asked.

"No, sir," Doug said. "I can answer it. Yes, as far as I know."

"Do you know what they are?"

"Well," Doug said, "you have to pass a physical."

"Did you pass?"

"Yes, sir."

"What else?"

"Uhh, you have to be under 19 years old."

"And how old are you?"

"Eighteen."

Marc glanced up at the panel, and saw that Roger Farley, the Deputy Commissioner for Eligibility, was nodding. Good.

"You said you were planning on college," Marc said. "Have you applied anywhere?"

"So far only to App State, and I've been accepted," Doug answered. "But I have several applications filled out. I'll send one of them in after I've made my decision on scholarship offers."

"Do you have athletic scholarship offers?" Marc asked.

"Yes, sir."

"How many?"

Doug frowned, his brows creasing. "I don't remember exactly. Between 30 and 40, I think."

"From what schools?"

"I think from all the major schools in the Carolinas, and then there are others."

"Please give the hearing panel some names." They had rehearsed this. He hoped Doug remembered what colleges to mention first.

He did. "Let's see," he said. "There's Michigan. Wisconsin. Notre Dame. I think Stanford. There's several. There are more."

"That's enough," Marc said. All of these were highly rated academic schools. "Have you had any indication you might not be accepted if you decided to take the scholarship offer?"

DeBruhl objected as asking for hearsay, but Morton overruled the objection.

"No, sir, not that I can think of."

"Let's go on to the football field," Marc said. "Have you been penalized?"

"Yes, sir, a couple of times."

"For what?"

"Offsides, once or twice. Backfield in motion, once."

"Any personal fouls?"

"No, sir."

"You said you are the strongest guy on the team. Are you the biggest?"

"No, sir. Several guys are bigger."

"Are you the fastest?"

"No, I'm not. Nobody can touch Javon Shade. And Henry Warren has maybe a half-step on me."

"Are you the best running back?"

"Well, I guess Henry and I are sort of tied. But Tommy Mason is good. And Freddie – he's the wingback – can carry the mail, too."

"Are you the best receiver?"

"No, that's Javon. And Freddie has really good hands. He doesn't drop many. Herman Dale –that's the tight end – has really soft hands, too."

"Are some of these guys white?"

Another objection, also overruled.

"Yes, sir."

"Some of them black?"

"Yes, sir."

"Any other half Neanderthals?"

"Not that I know of."

"But you all have your talents?"

"Yes."

"Thank you, Doug," Marc said, using his client's first name for the first time. "We pass the witness."

"Any other questions, Mr. DeBruhl?" Morton asked.

DeBruhl asked for a moment to confer with Sparkman, and said, "Just one, Madame Chair."

DeBruhl gave Doug a long look and asked, "Mr. Martin, you have testified you are a modern human-Neanderthal hybrid. If this panel determines the Neanderthal side is not human, do you concede you would not be eligible?"

Marc objected, and Morton sustained the objection. DeBruhl's smile was wicked, but he didn't press the point.

"Nothing further, Madame Chair," he said.

Marc had no more questions, and Doug returned to counsel table. Marc studied the panel. He thought the questioning had gone well, but he didn't get any signals from any of them. They just looked expectant.

The next witness was Jeremiah Billups' mother.

Mrs. Billups appeared to be in her late 40s. She was a handsome, well-coifed woman, dressed in a modest white blouse with a brooch at the neck, a dark sweater, and tan slacks. She identified herself as a single mother, and said she was a nurse employed by Brainerd Memorial Hospital.

After these preliminaries, she repeated what she'd said at the School Board meeting the previous week. She was deathly afraid that this…whatever he was…might injure her baby or someone like him.

"Jeremiah said nobody ever hit him that hard," she said at DeBruhl's prompting. "He had bruises all over him the day after that game. Who knows who that…boy…might hurt?"

Marc realized he must be careful with this witness. DeBruhl had not been careful enough with Doug, and his appearing to pick on a teenaged high school student had, Marc thought, helped Doug's cause, at least a little. Marc did not want to be perceived as badgering a concerned mother.

But yet he had his job to do.

"Mrs. Billups, has your son been bruised in other games?" he asked.

"He has, but not like that. I'm telling you his body was a sight to behold."

"But he was not, I take it, actually injured?" Marc insisted.

"He was sore for a week," she said.

Marc picked up a newspaper clipping and appeared to study it, although he knew what it said.

"I'm looking at a newspaper report of Brainerd Central's game with Asheville High last year," he said. "You remember it, don't you?"

"He's played a lot of games," the witness hedged.

"But I think you'll remember this one," Marc said. "The report says that Central's star tailback, Jeremiah Billups, sprained a knee while being tackled and would miss the next game. You remember that, don't you?"

The witness' face worked. *She doesn't want to answer,* Marc thought. After a long silence, he prompted her, "Mrs. Billups? You need to answer."

"Yeah, I remember," she said.

"Any clones on the Asheville team?" Marc asked.

"Not that I know of," she said through gritted teeth.

"Thank you. Now, this year, didn't Jeremiah play the week following the West Brainerd game, bruises and all? Didn't he run for three touchdowns against West Charlotte?" He held up another clipping.

"He did, but he was hurting," the witness admitted.

Marc decided to change the subject.

"Mrs. Billups, does your son have a teammate named Markus Caldwell?"

The witness' frown was replaced by a wide smile. "He does. Markus is a dude."

"I agree," Marc said. "He is. How big is he?"

"Uhh, pretty big," Mrs. Billups said.

"Six-five," Marc prompted. "Two hundred and eighty pounds?"

"That's about right," she said. "Markus might go 290."

"Does your son compete against Markus Caldwell in practice?" Marc asked.

"He does."

"Do they let Markus tackle him?"

"Sometimes."

"Markus hits pretty hard, doesn't he?"

The witness finally saw where the questions were going, and answered, "He does. But he's never bruised him like that cave boy."

"Has your son played against other big guys?"

"He has."

"In fact, it was a 270 pounder that tackled him last year up at Asheville, wasn't it?"

"I don't remember," she answered.

"Well, it says so in the newspaper report," Marc said, picking up another clipping. "Do you want me to show it to you?"

"I guess that's so if the paper says so," the witness answered.

"But Mrs. Billups," Marc said, "I don't see you trying to get those players declared ineligible. Do I?"

DeBruhl objected as argumentative. Morton overruled the objection. In court, that would have been a good sign; but Marc's experience in administrative and arbitration hearings, where the rules of evidence were not strictly followed, made him realize that the presiding officer usually let just about everything in.

"No," the witness answered. "But they're not cave men."

Marc drew a deep breath. He was at the point where the next question was risky, but had to be asked.

"Isn't it true, Mrs. Billups," he asked, "that you wouldn't be here at all if Doug Martin were a black kid?"

DeBruhl leaped to his feet, practically shouting his objection. This time, Marc realized, the ruling would be important. It would tell him whether the panel had read the pre-hearing briefs. He saw Morton conferring with DuLaney.

"The objection is overruled," she said. "The witness may answer...But Mr. Washington," she admonished, "be careful in this line of questioning."

Mrs. Billups didn't wait for the question to be repeated. "I don't understand. This boy here isn't black. And black folks can't be Neanderthal. I saw that on television."

Marc kept his tone gentle. "But what about the African Americans who have some white ancestors?"

"Well, they might have some Neanderthal blood," she said, "a tiny bit."

"How much is too much?" Marc asked, his voice soft but penetrating.

Mrs. Billups threw up her hands in exasperation. "I don't know. But… but I know this young man has too much. He's half. Look at him." She flung an arm to where Doug Martin's almost unnaturally wide shoulder took up space at the Respondent's counsel table.

"And that's why we're here," Marc said. "Not about injuries. It's about ethnicity. About race."

"That's not a question," DeBruhl fumed. "Objection!"

Morton sustained the objection, as Marc had known she would. It didn't matter. He'd made the point.

"Thank you, Mrs. Billups," he said. "We pass the witness."

DeBruhl had two questions on re-direct. He asked whether Mrs. Billups' concerns were sincere. She said they were. Then he asked if race had anything to do with them, and she said it didn't.

Marc had no re-cross. Morton excused the witness and called for a morning recess. The hearing room broke into a buzz. Marc had to enlist security guards to help them push through the crowd to the restrooms, and to fend off the reporters who kept trying to speak with them.

"Good job," Rob whispered to Marc as they stood at the urinals. "So, far, so good."

"Yeah, thanks," Marc whispered back. "But I still don't have a feel for the panel. Do you?"

"No," Rob admitted. "Not yet."

THE HEARING ROOM
AFTER RECESS

The next witness was the football coach at Canton Pisgah High School. Sandra Sparkman did the questioning, and used the podium, looking down her long, pointed nose at the witness the whole while. She looks down at the world, Marc thought. She'd look down at the panel if they weren't seated above them.

The witness said he was very concerned about the safety of players who had to play against Doug Martin. He told the panel that his star fullback had suffered bruised ribs when Doug had tackled him near the end of the game, and had to wear a protective pad under his jersey for the next two games. That was news to the Martin team.

Rob handled the cross-examination from where he sat. This was like shooting fish in a barrel, Marc thought as he watched. The coach admitted his team had lost to West Brainerd, and might face the Redwings again in the playoffs. He admitted his team's chances of winning would go up if Martin did not play. Marc was looking at the panel when the witness said that and saw Bill Morgan, the Deputy Commissioner for Compliance frown and make a note.

The coach also admitted he hadn't brought a medical report on his fullback to verify his testimony about the injury, that he'd had other players with bruised ribs in other games, games in which Doug Martin had not played, and that he'd had players who had suffered more grievous injuries than those he'd blamed on the Respondent.

"In fact, Coach McCarthy," Rob suggested, "you wouldn't be here at all if your team didn't stand to lose to West Brainerd in the playoffs with Doug Martin in the lineup; isn't that correct?"

The witness disputed the suggestion, his body language and tone implying outrage, but Marc didn't think the panel believed him. The bias was obvious.

Marc saw Rob lean forward and look down the table at him, his brow raised in a question. Marc nodded and mouthed, "Go ahead." It was time to water a seed they'd already planted.

Rob drew a deep breath and turned his face toward the witness.

"And as another matter of fact, Coach," he posited, "you wouldn't have the nerve to raise any objection at all if Doug Martin were African American or Latino, would you?"

"Eh? What?" McCarthy said, obviously surprised. Marc had thought the opposing counsel had tried to prepare Mrs. Billups for this line of questioning, with partial success; but they either hadn't done so with this guy or the coaching hadn't stuck.

The witness' startled exclamation was almost simultaneous with Sandra Sparkman's shrieked objection. DeBruhl shouts, Marc thought. She shrieks. Lovely.

"We'll allow it," Morton said. "But as I advised Mr. Washington, be careful, Mr. Ashworth."

Rob assured her he would, and repeated the question: "You wouldn't have the nerve to be here if Doug Martin were African American or Latino, would you, sir?"

"But he's not," McCarthy said.

"No, he certainly isn't," Rob said. "We pass the witness." The point had been made.

Sparkman tried to rehabilitate McCarthy on re-direct by getting him to say race was not a factor in his concerns. But, Marc thought, it sounded lame.

DeBruhl announced that the Complainant's final witness would be Dr. Herbert Sikorski, who would testify remotely if he were permitted to make the connection, and the court reporter would assist in projecting the images on the big screen. This had been arranged in advance, but it took a few minutes to get the connection right. DeBruhl would use a laptop Sparkman had brought, while Marc would use the one Aleks slid over to him. The panel would see everything on the large screen on the wall opposite the witness chair and behind the court reporter. The connection was set for "speaker view," rather than "gallery," so the panel would get a good look at the witness.

Sikorski was slight, stoop shouldered, and white haired. He wore round wire-rimmed glasses that gave him an owlish look, and was dressed in tweed jacket and bow-tie just as he'd been in the podcast. DeBruhl began his examination by laboriously going through the witness' c.v., covering all of Sikorski's teaching positions, awards, fellowships, books, research grants, and journal publications. Marc offered to shorten the process by stipulating the witness' expert qualifications, but DeBruhl declined the stipulation, saying it was important that the panel understand Sikorski's stature.

Marc understood what DeBruhl was doing. The Respondent's expert was much younger, with a shorter resume and fewer publications, and taught at a "directional" university rather than a nationally known school like Duke University. DeBruhl was going to argue that the Complainant had given the court a seasoned scholar, and not some whippersnapper who taught an inferior and strictly "regional" school. Marc would do the same if he were on the other side.

But, he remembered, Farley and Morgan had gone to UNC-Asheville and East Carolina, while Commissioner Morton had studied at Winston-Salem State. DeBruhl might lay it on too thick and overplay his hand. Marc hoped so, anyway. Sometimes there could be too much credentialism.

After DeBruhl qualified the witness, a process Marc hoped the panel would find boring, Sikorski's testimony was a replay of what he'd said in the DuGard podcast. Neanderthals were related to us, as were the earlier *homo erectus* and *homo habilis* (Sikorski had artists' images of both, looking very ape-like), but were not human, not *homo sapiens*. They were a separate species, an offshoot, perhaps one of nature's failed experiments. They may have been, certainly had been, able to interbreed with humans; but who knows? Perhaps that had been true of *erectus*, too. (He flashed that image again.) In any event, they were not human as we understand it.

There was no doubt that the subject of the hearing, Doug Martin, showed strong Neanderthal physiognomy. The abnormally broad shoulders, the huge chest cavity, the relatively short but powerful legs. And those were only what was visible. An observer couldn't see the bone density that enabled him to withstand blows that would cripple one of us.

Marc objected to that on the grounds that there was no evidence of the client's bone density in the record, but Morton overruled the objection, saying only, "Noted." He supposed that meant he had made his point, but the panel had heard the evidence all the same.

Sikorski then opined that all of these factors gave Doug Martin an "unconscionable" advantage with opposing players when engaged in athletic competition, an advantage that enhanced their risk of serious or even fatal injury. At DeBruhl's prompting, he replayed the recreations of a Neanderthal charging a wild bull and then a wooly rhinoceros with a long, stone tipped spear, and then played clips of Doug's gridiron exploits.

"You can see the Neanderthal characteristics very clearly," he said. "The burst of speed in the charge, the incredible strength at the point of impact. The same characteristics that allowed the man from whom he was cloned to hunt formidable prey in forest and tundra."

Great, Marc thought. Now the panel has the image of our client attacking teenaged boys as though they were enormous, extinct animals.

"And so, Dr. Sikorski," DeBruhl concluded, "do you have an opinion as to whether Mr. Martin should be allowed to compete against modern teenagers in athletic competition?"

"I do," the witness answered.

"And what is that opinion?"

"That he should not. It would be most unfair. In fact," Sikorski continued before DeBruhl could cut him off, "this young man should not be in regular classes at all. It was a disservice, even to him to place him there. He should have had special schooling in an environment where he could be studied by men, er, people of science and where he could be taught to control and use his incredible strength."

"Thank you, Dr. Sikorski," DeBruhl said, realizing his witness had strayed into an area with which the panel would likely be uncomfortable. "Now…"

But Sikorski was on a roll. "You see," he said, "there is so much we don't know. Is this young man prone to fits of primitive rage? There is no database to consult. If so, what might he do to others if his rage were to be unleashed? That's why he should be studied. There is so much about Neanderthal psychology we do not know."

We've finally caught a break in this testimony, Marc thought. I'll be able to work with this, I think.

DeBruhl paused, and then asked, "Well, Dr. Sikorski, it may be too late for that. But it's not too late to exclude this man from athletic competition with those he might hurt. Should that be done, in your opinion?"

Marc objected as asked and answered, but was overruled.

"Oh, yes," the witness said. "That certainly should be done."

DeBruhl passed the witness, and now it was Marc's turn.

"Dr. Sikorski," he began, "it appears from your c.v. that most of your published work about Neanderthals came out 30 to 35 years ago. Is that correct?"

Sikorski was prepared for the question. "Yes, I'm pretty old." This produced smiles and muted laughter in the room. "But I think my work holds up pretty well."

"All right, sir," Marc said, picking up a thick folder from the table in front of him, "I'm going to hand up to you a collection of documents that has been pre-marked as an exhibit in this matter." He turned to DeBruhl, and said, "Respondent's No. 3."

Morton looked at DuLaney, who mouthed advice, and asked, "Any objection, Mr. DeBruhl?"

"No, Your Honor, I mean, Madame Chair," he said.

One of the security guards took the folder from Marc and took it to the witness, who opened it.

"What I have handed you," Marc explained to the witness, "is a collection of studies, reports, journal publications, and book excerpts that have been published over the past 25 years, some as recently as last year. My question is, are you familiar with them?"

"Most of them, yes," Sikorski answered. "But I do not agree with them."

"Well, let's talk about them," Marc said. He led Sikorski through a number of the documents, which bore such titles as "Rethinking Neanderthals" and "New Evidence Shows Neanderthals More Articulate and Artistic than Thought."

"Most of these have been peer-reviewed, have they not?" Marc asked.

The witness conceded that was true.

"So, Dr. Sikorski, you must concede, do you not, that at least the current trend, and apparently a majority view, among anthropologists, is that Neanderthals were not a separate species, as you have testified, but rather a division or sub-species of humanity – *homo sapiens neanderthalensis*, and not *homo neanderthalensis*?

Again, Sikorski was prepared for the question. "I grant that there are those who hold that view," he said, trying to sound confident but coming over (Marc hoped) as pompous. "There are always those who go for trendy theories. But I do not share their view, which I do not believe they've proven, and I don't concede they are a majority. I don't believe anyone has taken a poll, not that a poll would prove anything."

Marc and Rob had decided in preparation that there was no point in getting down in the weeds and arguing technical points with the witness. The odds were that they would lose the argument. He tried a different tack.

"Thank you, Dr. Sikorski," he said, as though the witness' answer had been his dearest wish. "We can agree there are differing opinions, differing theories. And yet...and yet...you, on the strength of your *theory* – which you concede a substantial number of your peers dispute – are willing to take away from this boy, this young man, his ability to play the sport he loves. Aren't you?"

Sikorski obliged by continuing to sound pompous. "I think my opinion is more than a theory, young fellow," he said. "And I do think that step is regrettably necessary for the protection of other athletes."

"Dr. Sikorski, Doug Martin has been playing high school football in the state of North Carolina for almost four years," Marc said. "Just how many teammates, and how many opposing players, has he injured in that time?"

"That's not the point," the witness said.

"It's exactly the point," Marc said. "Let me tell you the answer to the question. Exactly none. Zero. Zip. Do you accept that as true?"

"I can neither accept it nor reject it," Sikorski answered. "I don't know, and as I said, that's not the point. It's the potential we must be concerned about."

"Do you know how many high school athletes have suffered injuries requiring surgery playing football in this state during that time?" Marc asked.

"I'm sure you can enlighten us," Sikorski said, smiling.

"Thank you. I can." Marc showed him the pre-admitted exhibit that was taken from reports published by the association. "We can agree, can't we, that all of these players managed to get injured playing football without any help from Neanderthals, can't we?"

"As I said," Sikorski answered, "that's not the point."

"Isn't it?" Marc snapped. "You're willing to exclude this young man from playing football based on your theoretical concerns, when in fact we all know that football is a hazardous sport anyway. Isn't that correct?"

"As I told you, I don't consider my concern theoretical," the witness answered.

Marc left that answer alone and pressed on.

"And, Dr. Sikorski, you don't stop there, do you? In your opinion, this young man should be removed from the public schools and taken somewhere where he can be studied. Isn't that correct?"

For the first time, Sikorski looked startled and unconfident.

"I – I didn't say that," he protested.

"Didn't you?" Marc snapped. "Do you want the court reporter to read back your testimony? Just a few minutes ago you said Doug Martin should not be educated in public schools but placed in special education where he could be studied by – I believe you said, 'men of science.' Don't you recall that?"

Sikorski's image on the screen trembled a bit. Evidently he only now realized the enormity of what he'd said.

"Well, I – that is…" Sikorski said, struggling for words.

Marc didn't give him time to find them. "Is that how you see Doug Martin, Dr. Sikorski? A curiosity, a lab rat to be poked and prodded and studied by *scientists* like you?" Marc hoped his tone conjured visions of "scientists" like Dr. Frankenstein or Dr. Moreau.

"No. No, of course not," Sikorski said, his voice high and tremulous. "But…I mean the young man does present a unique opportunity for study."

Now, Marc decided, was the time for the final blow.

"Dr. Sikorski, have you ever thought that your view of our client is *racist?*" he asked.

DeBruhl objected, but Morton overruled the objection.

"What?" Sikorski squeaked. "That's outrageous. How dare you suggest…"

Marc shook his head. "Dr. Sikorski, I'm not implying you are a racist in the sense that you're biased about skin color, linguistic heritage, or national origin. Nothing like that. I'm talking something even more fundamental."

When Sikorski responded with nothing but a blank look, Marc continued, "Think for a minute. We know that one-half of Doug Martin's ancestry is modern human. The other half is from a branch of our species that has contributed genes to most of us. Are you with me?"

"Yes, but that doesn't make me a racist," Sikorski responded.

"Oh, Doctor, but it does. Aren't you suggesting Mr. Martin be treated differently because of his *ancestry?*"

"Oh, well, but it's not the same thing. The differences are too profound."

"However profound they are, they haven't prevented Doug Martin from making friends, going to school, making 'A's', or holding a part time job, have they?"

"I-I don't know," the witness answered.

"Nobody told you that? How interesting." Marc mused, and when DeBruhl objected, said, "You don't need to answer that question…We pass the witness."

DeBruhl had one question on cross: "Dr. Sikorski, has anything Mr. Washington suggested to you caused you to change the opinions you gave the panel when I asked you a while ago?"

"No," Sikorski responded, looking relieved.

After DeBruhl had passed the witness and Marc stated he had nothing further, DeBruhl announced that the Complainant rested.

Jessica Morton looked at her watch.

"We're running 10 minutes ahead of schedule," she announced. "But we'll still break for just 30 minutes. We're now in recess."

Chapter 39
CAROLINA HIGHLANDS COMMUNITY COLLEGE, OCTOBER 2022

THE HEARING: PART TWO
LUNCH BREAK

As soon as the panel chair announced the lunch recess, all of the broadcast media rushed out to the front of the building to record their morning report for broadcast. In contrast, the print journalists hung around, hoping for interviews they didn't get, as the lawyers and their clients broke for their assigned rooms. They would file their stories when the hearing was concluded.

The network had sent Tom Harrison to cover the hearing, and he had "borrowed" Nicole Bradley from the Nashville affiliate just in case something happened related to the local story in which she was helping Tom – meaning something connected to Veronica Clayton. There was not room for both of them in the hearing room, so they'd decided they'd split the day, with one in the hearing room and the other in the theater in the morning, and trading places in the afternoon. Nicole drew the short straw and got the morning, and Tom would get the afternoon when something was finally going to be decided.

While the camera crew was setting up for Tom's midday report, Tom and Nicole stood together, nibbling on sandwiches the crew had provided. Nicole swallowed a bite and said, "Tom, there's something you ought to know that I don't think you could see from the theater broadcast."

"Oh?" he said. "What's that?"

"She's here."

"She -- ?"

"Veronica Clayton. She's sitting in the back of the room."

Tom had been lifting his sandwich for a bite, but lowered his hand when he heard what Nicole said.

"Well, well," he said. "We need to be sure to get a shot of her today. This is good news. Risk Management and Legal surely won't make us sit on the story any longer if we document she came all the way from Nashville for this hearing."

They had had more trouble getting approval to run the Clayton story than anticipated, and Nicole was rather glad of it. "Tom," she said, "don't you think we ought to leave her alone?"

"Huh?" He lowered the sandwich again. "Why would we do that?"

"What do we gain by running it? We'll just disrupt her life."

"Oh, that's bullshit," Tom said. "She's been a part of a government cover-up. That's news."

"Is it?" Nicole asked. "All she did was give birth to a child."

"It definitely is," Tom said. "But…it would help if she were more visible. Let me see. The Martin kid's team won't be any help. I think I'll give a tip to Alex DeBruhl. They might do something with it.

"Now, please hold my sandwich. I've got to get on camera and give my two-minute report." He noticed Nicole's wide eyes and open mouth, and added, "No, I'm not going to say anything about Veronica Clayton. Not now.

"But I'll tell you, you'd better think about what you're going to say about it to your station. They'll be pissed if you do nothing."

Nicole watched her colleague position himself in front of the camera. She didn't feel good about exposing Veronica. But what could she do about it? Should she warn the Martins' lawyers? No, that wouldn't help, she realized. They couldn't stop whatever the Complainant's counsel were going to do.

And maybe they won't do anything. They have bigger fish to fry, don't they? She hoped.

It was crowded in the Respondent's witness room, now that the hearing team had showed up. Josh Fulkerson, Coach Steve Watkins, and Henry

Warren had all arrived just minutes ago. Tiffany DeRatt Washington, Danny Jarvis, and the expert, Howard Mortenson had been there all morning. Ten people made a crowd. Twelve, when Doug's parents were added, made a bigger one. They were in a large conference room, but still a little cramped. Thankfully, there was a chair for everyone.

When Marc, Rob and Aleks walked in, Tiffany rose from her chair, went to Marc, and hugged him, saying, "We're married" when she noticed some raised eyebrows. Then she distributed bottles of water and sandwiches from a cooler. Thirty minutes was not a long break, and they would have to eat and confer fast before diving back into the hearing.

"You know we can't discuss what has happened in the hearing," Marc said between bites. "We can tell you we think it has gone well enough so far. But it's very important that our evidence go in well this afternoon. I'm sure all of you remember what we've discussed.

"We'll start with Mr. Fulkerson, and then call Coach Watkins and then Henry, so all of you can get back to school. Then, Danny, we'll get to you. Our last witness will be you, Dr. Mortenson. We're on a chess clock – that's a strict timetable, so we'll have to be efficient. Any questions?"

There were none. Rob covered a couple of final points with the expert, Mortenson. Then it was time to go back to the hearing.

THE HEARING ROOM

Chairwoman Morton called the hearing back to order precisely on time, and asked Marc and Rob to call their first witness.

A security guard escorted Josh Fulkerson into the room, and showed him to the witness chair. Marc thought Fulkerson looked apprehensive, but not panicky. A little of the former was a good thing; the latter could be disastrous. The hearing chair swore the witness and Rob began direct examination.

He showed the witness Doug Martin's school records, and went over his class standing, grades, and athletic eligibility, including his birth date and physical examination records. The records had been pre-marked and were admitted without objection. Rob also covered Doug's student activities, including club memberships and membership in the National Honor Society.

"Is Douglas Martin a student in good standing at West Brainerd High School?" Rob asked.

"He is," Fulkerson said.

"Based on his school records now in evidence, has he met the eligibility standards for athletic participation?"

DeBruhl objected on the basis that it was the panel's job to make that determination. DuLaney whispered to Morton, and she overruled the objection. "We'll allow the testimony, which is confined to records," she said.

Rob passed the witness. For a moment, he thought DeBruhl might forego cross examination. But no such luck.

"Mr. Fulkerson, does it make sense to you that an implicit requirement of eligibility be that the player be human?" DeBruhl asked.

Rob objected for lack of foundation, but Morton overruled him.

Fortunately, they had prepared Fulkerson for something like this.

"I haven't seen anything about it in the regs the Association sends us," he says. "That's what we go by…And besides, I have no reason to believe Doug Martin isn't human."

"Are you aware he has admitted being a modern human-Neanderthal hybrid in his testimony earlier today?" DeBruhl asked.

"I don't know what was said this morning," Fulkerson said.

"Would that make a difference to you?"

"No. It would not."

"Really?" DeBruhl asked with a smirk.

"Really, because I've seen him as a student for more than three years. He's human enough for me."

"But then," DeBruhl asked, "it's not up to you, is it?"

"No," Fulkerson admitted. "I'm just stating my opinion."

DeBruhl changed the subject. "You testified that your records show that Doug Martin has passed his physical examinations, is that correct?"

"Yes."

"Did you note anything unusual about those examinations?"

"I didn't see anything unusual?"

"You know the team physician, Dr. Jordan, do you not?"

"I do."

"Did he ever tell you anything remarkable about Doug Martin's examination?"

Rob objected as asking for hearsay, but Morton, after conferring with DuLaney, overruled the objection on the grounds that the rules of evidence did not strictly apply, and "what the team doctor said to the principal, if anything, seems sufficiently reliable."

Marc had an uneasy feeling. Preparation had been a rush job, and they hadn't asked Fulkerson about discussions with the team doctor. DeBruhl's team must have a source. They must have learned something.

At Fulkerson's request, DeBruhl repeated the question.

"No, sir, nothing other than he said Doug has unusually high bone density," he said.

"And?" DeBruhl prompted.

"Just that he could take a lick that might injure somebody else, but not get hurt," Fulkerson admitted in a low voice. He's finally figured where DeBruhl is going, Marc thought.

"And wouldn't that give Doug Martin an advantage over other players in football? An unfair advantage?" DeBruhl asked.

"I guess an advantage. I don't think unfair," Fulkerson said.

"That will be for the panel to decide," DeBruhl said. "Pass the witness."

To Marc's surprise, Rob was immediately ready on redirect.

"Mr. Fulkerson, did Dr. Jordan tell you that the other students' bone densities, the ones other than Doug Martin's, were uniform or identical?"

This time DeBruhl objected to hearsay, but Morton overruled the objection, saying, "This is a door you opened, counsel."

Marc saw relief pass over Fulkerson's face.

"Why no," the witness said. "He said there was fairly wide variation, depending on age and diet and so forth. He said that Doug was at the upper end."

"Did he say Doug's bone density caused him to be concerned about other players?"

"No, he didn't say that."

Rob let the witness go. There was no re-direct.

Good for Rob, Marc thought. He must have got that stuff about bone density from Mortenson. Well, Rob had spent more time with the expert than Marc.

The examinations of Coach Watkins and Henry Warren went quickly, with Rob handling both. Watkins confirmed Doug was not a dirty player and had never been in trouble on the team. The youngster said Doug was popular with the team. He added that Doug hit hard, but said other guys did, too. Yes, he said, Doug had hit him hard in practice, and sometimes he'd been sore; but no, Doug Martin hadn't hurt him.

DeBruhl didn't do much with either. He made them admit that they were biased in favor of their player or teammate, and wanted him available to play on the team, something the panel would assume anyway.

Marc supposed DeBruhl and Sparkman just wanted both out of the witness box as soon as possible, especially the likable Warren.

Now it would be Marc's turn again. They were running a little ahead of schedule, and were down to Jarvis and Mortenson.

When Monica Gilbert heard Danny Jarvis' name being called, she perked up immediately. She wasn't a lawyer, but she didn't think the hearing was going all that well for the side she'd helped to finance. Maybe... maybe she might have a chance to disrupt the other side, and to get back at Jarvis, or at least disrupt his composure. She could feel the Powers of others in the building, including from Ashworth and the Tabarant woman here in the hearing room, and others, stronger, at a short distance. She assumed the latter were McCaffery and probably McCormick (or Callahan, as she now called herself). But no one was blocking her. Maybe she could do something before she could be blocked.

She looked down the row toward the door to the room. The seating was in four tiered rows, with each successive tier above the other. Folding chairs had been placed in each row. She noticed the blonde she'd observed earlier look expectantly toward the door. She must be Danny's present squeeze, Monica thought. A thick cable led up the steps from the first level, where the television camera was located, and under and out the door. There was just enough of a crack between the double door and the floor to accommodate it.

A security guard ushered Jarvis into the room. As soon as he entered, he looked around the room until his eyes found and locked with the blonde's. He continued to look back toward her as he walked to the first step. Monica saw her chance and acted, humming a spell.

Few observers saw the television cable curl and bunch and lift in front of Danny Jarvis as he raised his foot to take the first step down. But they saw Jarvis trip and fall head-first down the steps, unsuccessfully wind-milling his arms for balance. The small crowd collectively gasped.

Then something even more surprising happened. A gust of air, a strong but confined wind, seemed to rise out of the steps and catch Jarvis squarely in his chest. It lifted hair from the heads of those seated closest to the stepped aisle. Jarvis' fall stopped, and then the gust pushed him upright and he found his feet. Shaken but not harmed, he made his way down the steps and to the witness chair.

Monica realized what had happened. Someone had countered her spell. Looking down toward the Martin team's table. She saw Ashworth and Tabarant, whose hands had been clasped under the table, release their handclasp, and the woman begin furiously tapping on her cell phone. A moment later, Monica felt another force around her. Someone close by was blocking spells. That Corcoran bitch, again, she thought, still thinking of Diana McCaffrey from back in high school.

Well, she thought, maybe I at least threw him off his game. Maybe he'd be scared to say everything they wanted.

Before she swore Danny Jarvis, Chairwoman Morton asked him, "Mr. Jarvis, are you all right? You had a close call." Actually, she appears shaken herself, Marc thought. Well, no one here can explain the fall and recovery the way it happened. No one except us.

"Y-yes, ma'am," the witness said. "Just let me catch my breath and get a sip of water."

When those steps had been taken, Morton administered the oath and tendered the witness to Marc.

The plan was for Jarvis' testimony to be as brief as possible, to save as much time as they could for the expert. Marc covered the witness' background, including the number of high school games and players he'd observed through the years, and then got down to the important stuff.

He had the witness identify his original story in *Tar Heel Sports Weekly*, and also his original blog post. Both had been pre-admitted as exhibits.

"Tell me, Mr. Jarvis," Marc asked, "do you have any regrets about releasing this story to the public?"

DeBruhl objected as irrelevant, but after brief consultation with DuLaney, Morton overruled the objection. Marc reminded himself not to put too much hope on the ruling. The panel chair was letting just about everything in.

"Yes, I do," Jarvis said. "I never intended anything to happen like what's going on here today."

"What do you mean by that?" Marc asked.

"Well, I thought that the public ought to know what their government is up to with genetic engineering. I still think that. And…" He looked down. "And I admit I thought breaking the story would be good for my career."

"Didn't you know the story would have consequences for Doug Martin and his family?"

Jarvis took a deep breath, and then looked directly at Doug and beyond him to his parents. "Yes," he said. "I can't say I didn't. But I thought they'd be manageable, even beneficial, in the long run. I didn't expect anything like…like this." He took another sip of water, and added with a rush, "And…Doug, Mr. and Mrs. Martin, I want to say again that I'm sorry."

DeBruhl moved to strike and was overruled.

"Tell the panel what you find objectionable about this hearing, if anything," Marc asked.

Another objection was overruled.

"The idea that this young man's athletic career could be ended. You asked me earlier about how many games I've seen. Like I told you, it's been a bunch. Anyone who follows football at any level knows that we let a bunch of big, strong, bulky, fast athletes play against others who are smaller, slower, and weaker.

"Doug Martin is no more of a risk than any number of other players, some of whom are a lot bigger than he is. He's a good student. He has friends. Whatever we might think about government transparency, there's no reason to disrupt *his* life."

That will do it, Marc decided, and passed the witness.

DeBruhl immediately reminded Jarvis of his speculation in the original story that Doug Martin might not be human. "Isn't it concerning to you, Mr. Jarvis, that other young people may be being asked to compete against some who is not…fully…human?"

"Not after doing the research I've done on Doug Martin," Jarvis said. "You can see him yourself. Big shoulders, sure. Strong, yeah. But fully socialized at school. Popular guy. Anything 'unhuman' about him is strictly theoretical."

"Isn't that for the panel to decide?" DeBruhl asked.

"Yeah, I guess so," Jarvis said. "But it looks like a no-brainer to me."

DeBruhl left that alone, and asked Morton for a minute to confer with his co-counsel. When permission was granted, he turned to Sandra Sparkman and they exchanged whispers. Then he nodded and turned his face back to the witness and his mouth to the microphone.

"Mr. Jarvis, isn't it true that you have withheld information from the public and are still withholding information from this panel?" DeBruhl accused.

Jarvis looks genuinely puzzled, Marc thought. I sure as hell am myself.

"I can't imagine what you're talking about," Jarvis said.

"I'm talking about the identity of Douglas Martin's birth mother," DeBruhl said, his tone indignant as though this was a matter of the utmost importance. "You know it, and you know she's in the hearing room today, don't you?" He stood, wheeled and pointed to a woman in the top tier with shoulder length blonde hair.

Marc immediately objected as irrelevant. The objection was drowned by the general stir in the hearing room, the Chair's gavel banging, Jarvis' startled, "What?", and by a clear voice from the woman who now stood, staring at DeBruhl and his accusing finger.

"Yes, it's true," she was saying. "I'll probably be sued for saying this, but I did carry this young man in my womb for nine months. For eighteen years I've felt guilty, knowing I did it for money and silence; but now I'm not. I'm proud of him, and I want him to know it.

"And I'm proud I did something fine, in bringing this young man into the world where he could grow up in a fine and loving home. Danny Jarvis didn't know it was me for sure until now, so don't jump on him. He suspected but he didn't know. He couldn't."

Morton had to use the gavel again, and gradually the babble subsided.

"Any further questions, Mr. DeBruhl?" she asked.

"Uhh, no, Madame Chair," said a subdued DeBruhl.

Marc asked the witness to step down, and Morton called for a short afternoon recess.

"Well, that went well," Rob whispered to Marc. "Shows what careful planning can do."

Since the woman's revelation had taken them both by surprise, Marc had to chuckle.

"I guess DeBruhl thought they could discredit the witness," he whispered back. "Good break for us – I think…Are you ready for the finale?"

Rob nodded. They had one witness left and it would be Rob's.

Then it would be Marc's time to argue.

In most respects, Marc and Rob liked Howard Mortenson as an expert. His opinions were what they needed. He had produced on short notice a really good expert's report, complete with photos, charts, and tables. He had interviewed and rehearsed well.

They had only two reservations – credentials and apparent youth. His resume was fine but couldn't match Sikorski's. He really wasn't all that young; he'd hit forty before long. But to look at his gangly, spare frame and his boyish features, one would think he was much younger. As Aleks had said, "He looks like kid." Rob had suggested that Mortenson skip his contact lens and wear his thick spectacles to testify. That would help some.

As Marc listened to the testimony, however, he grew more and more pleased with it. Mortenson was amiable, articulate, and knew how to engage with the panel, maintaining just the right amount of eye contact, and treating them as he would a graduate class and not talking down to them.

Rob took pains to qualify the witness, empathizing the Neanderthal experts under whom he had studied at Tennessee and Virginia, the classes he taught on human evolution at ETSU, and the way he kept up with the latest studies on the subject because of personal interest as well as professional, teaching requirements. Finally, Rob tendered the witness as an expert.

"Do you have any objection," Chairwoman Morton asked. DuLaney has coached her well, Marc thought.

After a whispered exchange with Sparkman, DeBruhl rose to his feet and said, "No, Madame Chair. In the interest of the panel's time, we'll wait for cross examination."

Rob's direct examination was by the book. He asked the witness to describe the scope of his engagement and the steps he took to fulfill it. Mortenson said the steps had included review of Doug Martin's school records, a short telephone interview with Doug himself, and review of the most current studies and findings on Neanderthals and Neanderthal hybrids.

"Now," Rob said, coming to the ultimate issue, "Do you have an opinion, within a reasonable degree of professional certainty, as to whether Douglas Martin is human?"

"I do."

"And what is that opinion?"

"That he is. Definitely, he is."

"Please tell the panel the bases of your opinion."

Mortenson launched on a detailed explanation of the most recent findings in archaeological and genetic research. He illustrated his points with charts and tables, and with photographs from recent digs in Europe and Asia. He engaged with the panel as though he were teaching a class; and the panel, Marc thought, looked interested and entertained.

"You see," Mortenson concluded, "for years we had Neanderthals all wrong. Early researchers thought they were stooped and bow-legged genetically, without realizing the skeletons they were studying were from individuals who suffered from dietary deficiencies and arthritis.

"Later on, there was a school of thought that Neanderthals, despite their larger brains, couldn't think clearly. There were those who thought they could not talk. Their voice boxes were wrong. Their skulls were shaped wrong. It was supposed they had no artistic ability. But the most recent findings show those earlier theories to have been based on insufficient information."

"Is that why you disagree with Professor Sikorski?" Rob asked.

"It is."

"Can you relate these findings to Doug Martin?"

"I can." Without waiting for another prompt, Mortenson continued, "Doug's skull is modern human. That's typical in hybrids and means his human parent was likely a woman. His physiognomy clearly shows the Neanderthal strain. His 'father' was likely somewhat shorter and even more broad-shouldered and big-chested than he.

"And as for the way he presents, well, the panel has seen and heard from him themselves. When I interviewed him, he was modest, articulate, and gave intelligent answers to abstract questions. From his school records, he appears to be well-socialized.

"No doubt he's a big-shouldered, strong young man. But he's as 'human' as you or I."

"Thank you," Rob said. "We pass the witness."

Sandra Sparkman rose and asked permission to ask from the podium, which Morton granted. That's so she can look down her long nose at the witness, Marc thought. Questioning from the podium was unusual in North Carolina, but Marc remembered she had joined DeBruhl's firm from a prior position in Louisville. I guess this is what she's used to, he thought.

"Looking at your c.v., Doctor Mortenson," she began, "I notice that you have contributed to three books, but as yet have no published volumes of your own. Is that correct?"

"Yes," the witness responded. "I'm working on one now."

"Oh? What's it about?" she asked.

"Early Native American migrations in the Southern Appalachians."

"Hardly about Neanderthals, is it?"

"No, ma'am. It's not. There are no Neanderthal sites in this area, I'm afraid."

"You haven't personally been to any Neanderthal sites, have you?"

"No," the witness answered, and then threw in, "But neither has Dr. Sikorski. His published works were based on the archaeological findings of others."

Sparkman responded with a wicked smile. "I didn't ask you that, did I?"

"No," Mortenson admitted. "But I thought the panel ought to know."

"Well," she said, "let's talk about Dr. Sikorski. Can you look at his c.v.?" When the witness had it before him, she asked, "Do you agree he has published seven books, two on Neanderthals?"

"Yes," Mortenson said. "About 30 years ago."

"Do you agree he has published many articles in scholarly journals?"

"Yes."

"More than you?"

"Yes."

"Do you agreed he has held tenured positions at Northwestern, Texas, and Stanford, as well as Duke?"

"Yes."

"How many teaching positions have you held, Dr. Mortenson?"

"Well," Mortenson said, trying not to look sheepish. "I was a T.A. at Tennessee and Virginia. And of course my present position at East Tennessee State."

"How long have you been tenured?"

"One year," he admitted.

Marc was watching the panel. He hoped this snob appeal wouldn't sit well with them. Their faces were impassive, but he noticed they weren't taking notes. Was that good? You could never tell.

Sparkman had been leaning on the podium, but drew herself to her full height.

"Dr. Mortenson, are you really expecting this panel to believe you're as qualified to give expert testimony in this matter as Dr. Herbert Sikorski?" she asked, her voice dripping disdain.

Mortenson didn't back down. "In this instance, yes, because his are out of date, and would result in injustice, in my opinion."

"Really?" she asked, her tone contemptuous.

"Yes, really," Mortenson said.

"Well, the panel will be the judge of that," she said. "We pass the witness."

Rob had no re-direct, and Mortenson was excused.

"Anything further, Mr. Washington, Mr. Ashworth?" Morton asked.

Marc rose to his feet and was about to rest their case when he felt Aleks tugging on his sleeve. Looking down, he saw she was holding up her cell phone. He asked the panel for a moment, which was granted, and read quickly. He turned back to the panel.

"Madame Chair," he said. "It has just been brought to my attention that 30 minutes ago the United States Department of Defense released an official statement that has some bearing on this matter. We ask permission to show its transcript from the Associated Press to the panel."

DeBruhl rose in protest. "This is blatant hearsay, Madame Chair. We can't cross examine this alleged statement."

"Neither can the Respondent," Morton said. "But let us confer for a minute."

They waited while the hearing panel whispered among themselves and DuLaney. Finally, the whispering ceased and Jessica Morton turned her face to her microphone.

"The formal rules of evidence used in the courts do not strictly apply to this panel," she said. "After consultation among ourselves, it appears to the panel that the Defense Department may have information pertinent to the issues we are considering. We will see its statement."

It took a couple of minutes for Aleksandra to bring up the press release on her laptop, and synchronize it with the big wall screen. The release came into focus, and everyone started reading.

The heading was "Washington, D.C.," followed by today's date, and the caption, "FOR IMMEDIATE RELEASE." Beneath the heading was the Great Seal of the United States and the words, "DEPARTMENT OF DE-FENSE." The text then followed:

There have been recent reports in the media concerning a young man in North Carolina who is said to be a modern human-Neanderthal clone resulting from experiments by this Department. These have been coupled with other reports that are wildly speculative.

For example, some outlets have reported that there are numerous such clones, and that the government of the United States has been raising them in secret to become super-soldiers. These reports are altogether false.

However, in light of present circumstances, including present proceedings in which the privileges and immunities of an American citizen, to wit: Douglas M. Martin of Martintown, N.C. have been brought into question, the Department believes that justice requires clarification of the prior reports and its own statements.

It is true that over 18 years ago, federal researchers were able to recover sufficient DNA for a single clone. The decision was made to place the cloned infant for adoption by a suitable family to be reared as a normal child. That child is Douglas M. Martin.

From the Department's point of view, the decision made in 2005 has been a complete success. We now know that such a hybrid child is fully capable of functioning in the 21st Century. We do not know what this individual will do with his talents. But that will be his choice as a free American citizen.

For now, the techniques used in cloning must remain classified information. We can answer no questions at this time. But the Department asks that this young man's privacy and rights, and those of his family, be respected.

The printed signature of a Deputy Director of Defense followed. Marc and Rob exchanged a look, and Rob mouthed, "Hutton." Marc nodded agreement that they could see Fred Hutton's hand in this statement. He rose and moved the release's admission into evidence as "an official publication of the United States." DeBruhl objected but was overruled.

Then Marc rested the Respondent's case.

Morton looked at her watch and asked for closing arguments immediately.

DeBruhl gave a good effort, Marc thought. He reminded the panel the hearing was about the safety of student athletes across the state, a concern that, he said, outweighed the preferences and ambitions of any single individual. He hit the disparity in seniority and credentials between Sikorski and Mortenson hard. He was doing a good job, Marc conceded to himself, but he saw the panel sneaking looks at their watches, and decided his best approach would be to cut his argument as short as possible.

They've made up their minds, he thought. There's not that much the lawyers can do now.

When DeBruhl had finished, Marc rose and moved to the podium. He shuffled papers until he found the page he wanted.

"I don't think I need to remind the panel of the evidence it has heard today, but to review it quickly, there is no evidence that Doug Martin fails to qualify by the published standards of this Association. There is no evidence that he has violated any rule, either athletic or academic.

"Instead, the case against him is the assertion that Doug Martin is not a human being, as though he is a beast, or a Martian. That is based, as we have shown, on outdated theories and outdated studies.

"We hear a lot about 'inclusion' these days. The Complainant's case is about exclusion, based on Doug Martin's genes, his ancestry. That's wrong. That's racist.

"As the Department of Defense has reminded us, Doug Martin is an American citizen, and, I remind us all, he is also a citizen of the state of North Carolina. If the Department of Defense, a department of the United States government, treats him as fully human, a free American and not a freak or laboratory rat, can this panel do any less?

"We submit the answer is 'no.'"

DeBruhl declined to offer rebuttal. He, too, must sense the panel's impatience, Marc decided. Morton asked that everyone remain seated while the panel retired to confer. Marc thought that a good sign, but reminded himself that the panel had already made up their minds.

Minutes later, the panel returned. Marc noticed they first looked at Doug. That would be a good sign if this were a jury, he thought. Would it be true of this panel?

"We want to thank all counsel for their skillful presentations," Morton began, then continued, "This panel determines that it is bound by the published eligibility standards of this Association. We find no evidence that the Respondent, Douglas M. Martin fails to meet those standards. Any contrary assertions based on his ancestry are speculative and of no concern to us.

"The petition of the Complainant is dismissed. Mr. Martin is eligible to compete. And we are adjourned." She banged her gavel.

The room erupted into a babble of conversation and a flurry of motion as the print reporters rushed to push past one another to file their stories. After exchanging hugs with one another and the client, and accepting the congratulations of DeBruhl and Sparkman, Marc and Rob pushed the client past reporters' microphones to the hallway, where he and his parents were turned over to sheriff's deputies who would escort him to the stadium. He could still make tonight's game.

In the hallway, Marc and Rob found themselves confronted by a television news crew headed by a network reporter who identified himself as Tom Harrison. He shoved a microphone in Marc's face that Marc couldn't avoid in the press around him.

"Mr. Washington," Harrison asked, "do you agree this ruling is a victory for diversity, equity, and inclusion?"

Marc sighed and said, "I suppose. But I'd rather call it a victory for fairness, for civil rights. Think about it. There were people – well-financed – people, who, motivated by jealousy, maybe prejudice, or whatever, who wanted to do away with our client's eligibility and even, even, if you believe their expert, his freedom, based on his ancestry. People who thought they had a free shot at him because of the color of his skin.

"You all need to understand that. It was a victory for civil rights in a battle that never should have been fought. I say that loud and clear in case there's some fool among you who wants to call it a victory for white supremacy or some such."

He noticed a young tow-headed reporter behind Harrison make a face. Yeah, that's exactly what the guy was planning on doing, Marc thought.

Harrison moved the microphone to Rob. "Do you have anything to add to that, Mr. Ashworth?"

"No," Rob grinned. "Marc said it all."

Chapter 40
AFTERMATH MARTINTOWN, NORTH CAROLINA, OCTOBER 2022

OUTSIDE THE WEST BRAINERD FIELDHOUSE

When Doug Martin left the locker room after the game Friday night, he found that the Brainerd County Sheriff's department had cordoned off a space around the doorway, and would escort him to his parents' car once they made it through the press of the crowd to get to him. Otherwise, he would have been mobbed by media. He was grateful for the Sheriff's courtesy. He did not want to answer reporters' questions tonight, although he supposed he'd have to do so eventually.

The game itself had been, as expected, a rout. Doug arrived after warm-ups but before kickoff. Coach Watkins made him warm up on the sidelines before going in the game, so he didn't play until two full series had elapsed. The team had practiced as though he might not play anyway.

As it was, Doug played only for a little more than two quarters, scoring two touchdowns and getting one sack when he blitzed on defense. Reserves played most of the second half. Doug was nonetheless tired. The day-long hearing, not knowing until the end what the result would be, had been draining.

As he stood waiting for his mom and dad, the chain of deputies let one other person through. It was Eva. She walked toward him, smiling, knowing all eyes would be on them and apparently enjoying it. He wondered if she would walk up to him, stand on tiptoe, and kiss him on the cheek as she usually did.

Instead, when she reached him, she stood on tip-toe, snaked her arms around his neck, pulled his head down, and kissed him on the lips, provoking cat-calls and cheers from the crowd. It was not a deep and probing kiss, but more than a quick brushing of lips. Doug's face felt hot. He knew he was blushing.

She drew back and whispered, "I'll call you tomorrow. Then I'll come by and sneak you out somewhere we can hide."

"Sounds good," he said, smiling down at her.

I don't know where we're going with this, he thought, but I'm going to enjoy the ride.

VERONICA CLAYTON'S HOTEL ROOM FRIDAY NIGHT

Veronica Clayton and Danny Jarvis sat at the table in Veronica's suite. (She had been forced to accept a suite because all of the regular-rate rooms had been taken by reporters on expense accounts.) After the hearing, Danny had found her just as Nicole Bradley was about to corner her for an interview, and he'd helped her explain that she could not answer yet because she had to confer with her lawyers. Then he rushed her out to his car, back to the hotel, and through a side door up to her suite.

Both were exhausted. They had risen early to get to the college in the hopes that Veronica could wrangle a seat in the hearing room. She had managed that by saying she was a "relative" of the Respondent. Thankfully, the harried security guard had accepted what she said without asking questions.

Veronica did not want to be alone tonight. She hadn't wanted it last night, either. Danny had stayed with her; and despite their jitters about the coming hearing, or maybe because of it, they had given into their mutual attraction before falling asleep. She didn't regret it. She had long since forgiven him for breaking the story that had led to where they were.

The hotel was full of reporters. She didn't want to risk going down to the restaurant, and suggested they order room service. They'd now called in their orders and were waiting. In the meantime, Veronica found wine in the wet bar, and Danny found Scotch. They sipped in silence while they waited.

"Danny, I'm still worried the government will sue me for breach of my non-disclosure agreement," she said at last. "I do all right, but I couldn't pay back what they spent on me fifteen years ago. Not all at once."

Jarvis sipped Scotch, considering. "I wouldn't worry about that, Veronica. You didn't give away anything that wasn't already out there, except your part in the kid's birth, and others had already figured that out.

"But the main reason nothing will happen is that after their press release today, it would be really, really bad public relations if the DOD took legal action against you. Oh…you'll need to reach out to your contact there to ask what it's all right to say about it. But I think you're all right."

"Are you sure?" she asked, suddenly hopeful.

"Pretty sure," he said.

But she couldn't keep the parade of horribles out of her mind. "What about my business. All this will ruin it," she fretted.

"I don't think that's likely, either," Danny said. "You'll be a celebrity. Everyone will want the 'celebrity realtor.' I'd bet on it."

She felt better, but still had concerns. "I'm afraid my ex-husband will want a change of custody."

"I doubt it," Danny said. "Didn't you tell me he's re-married and has kids by the second wife? I thought so. He won't want more. And he wouldn't win anyhow, I don't think. Look, if he tries it, you can talk with your lawyers. But I don't think he will."

"Okay, maybe you're right," Veronica said. "But how do I handle all these reporters?"

Jarvis went to the wet bar for more Scotch. When he returned to the table, he said, "You don't tell them anything until you've talked to your guy at the DOD," he said. "After that? You'll need a press agent. And someone to help you write your book."

Veronica had been about to sip wine, but lowered her glass, and said, "Write a book? I can't write a book. I don't know how."

"Once you know what you're cleared to say, you really need to. It would be a best-seller. Probably made into a movie. So you need a co-writer." He smiled across the table. "I know someone who wants the job."

"Can I have it?"

Veronica's smile managed to be coy and grateful at the same time.

"Maybe," she said.

MARTINTOWN, NORTH CAROLINA, OCTOBER 2022
THE GILBERT HOME
SATURDAY MORNING

Monica Gilbert leaned against the counter in her kitchen, a steaming cup of coffee in one hand, and her secure phone against her ear. Dennis Springfield had just called her.

She really didn't want to talk with Springfield right now. She'd been about to place a call to her new love interest, the assistant professor at Carolina with the six-pack abs and the cleft chin, when Dennis had called. Yesterday's hearing had not bothered her too much. She didn't like it that "McCaffrey's bunch" had got their way again, but the whole deal had been Springfield's play, not hers.

But Springfield was not happy.

"Look," he was saying, "I don't blame you. You did your part. But I can tell you the Deputy Director won't be happy if the original leak is traced to us; and if he's unhappy, the Director himself won't be happy. And I have to put in the 'special assets' budget request in next week."

"Do you really think they can trace it to you?" she asked. She said "you" rather than us to emphasize he had orchestrated the leak himself. She'd just followed orders.

Monica waited patiently for him to answer. He was doubtless thinking her question over.

"No," he said. "I don't think so. I don't even think anyone will push it. That asshole Hutton suspects, I'm sure; but he doesn't have much motivation to pursue anything. He and his whole unit at DIA are coming out of this smelling like a rose. That grinds my ass!"

Monica wasn't sympathetic. But what he'd said reminded her of something.

"You know," she said, "I dropped a pretty good chunk of change on the Committee for Fairness in Athletics. I assume I'll be reimbursed soon."

She had to wait for an answer again, and that was irritating. He shouldn't have to think about it. He had promised.

"Monica," he said, his voice uncharacteristically hoarse. "I can't. The Committee will have to file a public list of contributors. If our records, or even one of our shell companies, sends you funds in the same amount, or even close, somebody will notice. At least someone in the Bureau."

"So, my hands are tied right now. Later, maybe I can do something. Maybe."

Monica's coffee suddenly tasted bad and burned her stomach.

"Maybe?" she asked, and repeated, "Maybe? *MAYBE*?"

"Monica, be reasonable…" Springfield began.

"I am reasonable," she said, her voice flat. "I reasonably expect you to keep your promises. Good-bye, Dennis."

She disconnected, and didn't pick up when he called back.

Springfield can't be trusted, she thought. And…he's not so smart after all. He can be replaced.

She had met the Deputy Director. She had Talents to offer. She had her own connections, at least one of them scary. It was time she had a little talk with Dennis' boss.

She was smiling as she poured out the cooling coffee and poured a fresh cup.

WINSTON-SALEM, NORTH CAROLINA, DECEMBER 2022
GROVES STADIUM ON THE CAMPUS OF WAKE FOREST UNIVERSITY

Darren and Laura Martin sat close to the aisle right about the fifty-yard line, about halfway up from the sideline. Veronica Clayton sat next to Lara, and her son Tommy, the 12-year old, sat next to her. (Sarah Ellen, the eight-year-old, was back in Brentwood with a baby-sitter.) Danny Jarvis sat next to Tommy. He had rehabilitated himself, somewhat, with the Martins, but not enough to place him beside them.

Beyond Danny sat Mitch and Diana McCaffrey, Ben and Alyssa Callahan, Marc and Tiffany Washington, and Rob and Samantha Ashworth, the latter two couples, despite the cold, basking in the partnerships their triumph in the Martin case had earned them. Everyone was bundled against the November chill.

There was time-out on the field, while both coaches argued with the officials about how much time remained on the clock. The West Brainerd Redwings were in the Class AAA championship game against a bigger school from down on the coast, and right now, things did not look good.

There was under a minute left to play, and West Brainerd was on its own thirty yard-line, trailing 25-30.

Still, Darren reflected, we can't complain even if we lose. After a few days of headline news nationally, and a few more after that in the state, Doug's case had largely given way to the news of election returns and the latest celebrity scandals in the public eye. He was almost, if not quite, just another outstanding player again.

Doug had confided to Darren and Lara that he had pretty much decided to sign a letter-of-intent with Carolina. He wanted to do Air Force ROTC as well as football, and the coaches said that would be okay. Darren really would have preferred that Doug try for an academy appointment, which he was sure Doug could have gotten. But at least, Darren consoled himself, he's going Air Force.

On the field, Coach Watkins had summoned the team to the sideline while the officials debated the time remaining among themselves. There was not enough time remaining to run the ball, they all realized, and probably not enough to use short passes. To no one's surprise, Coach called for the first play to be a long pass. Doug would remain in the backfield to block and every other eligible receiver would take off downfield.

That would put pressure on Harry Simpson, the right tackle, with help from Doug, to fend off the opposing left defensive end, Brady Atkins. Atkins was probably the best pass rusher the Redwings had faced since Markus Watson in the opener. Atkins was not as big at Watson, but he did weigh in at 260, and he was fast. Of course, the other side of the line would have to hold up, too.

The officials put two seconds on the clock, bringing the time remaining to forty seconds. The teams returned to the field, and the head linesman wound the clock. At the snap, Les Bronson dropped back and Doug set to block. Sure enough, Atkins was coming hard. Harry slowed him, but not enough.

Doug sensed that Atkins would try to push off him, and use his speed to get around him to the quarterback. He moved to the right, set his feet, and caught the big defensive end, hands flat and barely extended, shoulders hunched, squarely on the chest. He kept his feet moving. Atkins tried to spin around him. That move had worked earlier in the game, but Doug was prepared this time. He kept his feet moving and stayed with the pass rusher.

THE HEREDITY OF MAGIC

Intent on Atkins, Doug couldn't see Les step away from a blitzing linebacker and launch a spiral down the field. By the time he could turn to see what was happening, the play was almost over.

The ball made it to around the five yard line, where there was a crowd of russet and white uniforms, the entire opposing secondary, and all of the West Brainerd receivers, all reaching and jumping for the ball. Somebody tipped it, then another. Somehow Freddie was able to touch it and tip it backwards.

Javon Shade, only 5'-6" had hung back, unable to out-jump anyone. He dove, touched the ball, then gathered it and dove forward. When the official signaled it was a catch, the ball was on the four yard line. The clock stopped to move the chains. There were 27 seconds remaining.

The Redwings huddled hurriedly. Tommy Mason entered the lineup for Henry Warren.

"Coach says give it to Stump until we're in the end zone," he said.

Three plays later, with no time remaining, the Redwings were state Class AAA Champions.

The End

AFTERWORD AND ACKNOWLEDGMENTS

I suppose I should start with some disclaimers. First, while there has been much speculation about the possibility of cloning using DNA from fossils, including fossilized human remains, I know of no test case sponsored by any department of the United States government (or anyone else) such as the one depicted in this novel. Whether anyone will ever attempt such a test, or when, remains sheer speculation.

Secondly, while there is a North Carolina High School Athletics Association, and the Association has a Commissioner, who in turn has deputies, the Commissioner and Deputy Commissioners depicted in this novel are creatures of my imagination. Any resemblance they may have to those who now hold, or have in the past held, such positions is sheer coincidence. Likewise, I've no idea if the Association has held, or ever would hold, a hearing such as the one described in this novel. Frankly, I needed a hearing to permit my lawyer characters to do their thing.

My readers know that my novels are designed primarily to entertain. At the same time, I try to inject a serious point or two in each of them. I hope this novel illustrates the dangers of the current obsession over race, which some seek to inject into every issue, however unlikely. We all need to pay attention to Dr. King's admonition that people should be judged by "the content of their character," and Dr. Carson's observation that what makes us human individuals is internal, not external. We are all more than our genetic content.

I would like to thank Professor William N. (Bill) Duncan, chair of the Department of Anthropology at East Tennessee State University for his input and resource materials on Neanderthals. Rest assured, any errors concerning Neanderthals in this novel are mine, and not his. Also rest assured that the ETSU professor in the novel is imaginary, and not Professor Duncan or based on Professor Duncan.

As always, I want to thank my group of Beta readers, whom I find to be essential. These, as usual, include my sister Margaret Studenc and her husband, Bill (who is also a copy-editor), Anita Hughes (another copy editor), Lisa Fuller, Mary and Rod O'Mara, Roseanna Rigdon (who reminds me that not everyone knows legal acronyms), and Sam B. Miller II, whose own novels are quite good.

I join most of my fellow novelists in requesting of my readers online reviews. They need not be lengthy. But they are valuable and drive sales.

I'm sure I will return to the Haunted Law Firm. But my next project, I think, will be something different. I expect to have fun writing it.

Robert L. Arrington
February, 2023

ABOUT THE AUTHOR

ROBERT L. ARRINGTON practices law with the Kingsport, Tennessee firm of WILSON WORLEY, P.C. He holds A.B. and J.D. Degrees from the University of North Carolina, where he was admitted to Phi Beta Kappa. He is a member of the Tennessee Academy of Arbitrators and Mediators.

But his first love has always been writing.

He and his wife Deborah live with their two cats, Miss Katie, and BJ. You can find him on Facebook and LinkedIn.

The Heredity of Magic is his fifth book.

Made in the USA
Middletown, DE
23 June 2023

33302527R00187